Stolen

Susan Lewis is the bestselling author of twenty-six novels. She is also the author of *Just One More Day*, a moving memoir of her childhood in Bristol. She lives in Gloucestershire. Her website address is www.susanlewis.com

Susan is also a supporter of the childhood bereavement charity, Winston's Wish: www.winstonswish.org.uk and of the breast cancer charity, BUST: www.bustbristol.co.uk

Praise for Susan Lewis

'Utterly compelling' *Sun*

'Deliciously dramatic and positively oozing with tension, this is another wonderfully absorbing novel from the *Sunday Times* bestseller Susan Lewis . . . Expertly written to brew an atmosphere of foreboding, this story is an irresistible blend of intrigue and passion, and the consequences of secrets and betrayal' *Woman*

'A tear-jerker, and a perfect blend of passion, heartache and intrigue' *News of the World*

'Spellbinding! . . . you just keep turning the pages, with the atmosphere growing more and more intense as the story leads to its dramatic climax' *Daily Mail*

'A multi-faceted tear jerker' *heat*

'One of the best around' *Independent on Sunday*

'Sad, happy, sensual and intriguing' *Woman's Own*

Also by Susan Lewis

A Class Apart
Dance While You Can
Stolen Beginnings
Darkest Longings
Obsession
Vengeance
Summer Madness
Last Resort
Wildfire
Chasing Dreams
Taking Chances
Cruel Venus
Strange Allure
Silent Truths
Wicked Beauty
Intimate Strangers
The Hornbeam Tree
The Mill House
A French Affair
Missing
Out of the Shadows
Lost Innocence
The Choice
Forgotten

Just One More Day, A Memoir

Susan Lewis

Stolen

arrow books

Published by Arrow Books 2011

2 4 6 8 10 9 7 5 3

First published in Great Britain in 2011 by
Arrow Books
Random House, 20 Vauxhall Bridge Road,
London SW1V 2SA

www.randomhouse.co.uk

Addresses for companies within The Random House Group Limited
can be found at: www.randomhouse.co.uk/offices.htm

The Random House Group Limited Reg. No. 954009

ISBN 9780099550679

A CIP catalogue record for this book
is available from the British Library

The Random House Group Limited supports The Forest
Stewardship Council (FSC®), the leading international forest
certification organisation. Our books carrying the FSC label are
printed on FSC® certified paper. FSC is the only forest certification
scheme endorsed by the leading environmental organisations,
including Greenpeace. Our paper procurement policy can be found
at www.randomhouse.co.uk/environment

Typeset in Palatino by Palimpsest Book Production Limited,
Falkirk, Stirlingshire
Printed and bound by CPI Group (UK) Ltd, Croydon, CR0 4YY

Stolen

The sun was shining, the birds were singing and every-thing was so right with Rose's world that her smile was turning heads as she walked. Attracting almost as much attention was not-quite-three-year-old Alexandra, skipping along beside her mother, one hand clinging to the pushchair, the other carrying Snugs, her favourite bear. Inside the pushchair the twins, Simon and Becky – one fair like his father, the other dark, like her mother – were fast asleep. Tomorrow they'd be eighteen months old, so Alexandra had been helping her grandmother bake a cake this afternoon, which was now safely stored at the bottom of the pushchair ready for Alex to ice when they got home.

'Becky can't help, can she?' Alex asked for the tenth time.

'No, darling, she's too small.'

'She'll spoil it, won't she?'

'Maybe, but not intentionally. She's just little and can't do things as well as you can yet.'

'Simon doesn't want to make cakes.'

'No he'd rather eat them.'

Alex giggled and carried on skipping, careful never to let go of the pushchair, until they arrived at the station when she hopped up on to the footboard for the ride down the escalator.

1

'Good girl,' Rose praised, as they successfully disembarked at the bottom. 'Now, stay close while we wait for the train.'

'It's called a Tube really, isn't it?' Alex asked.

'That's right.'

'Why is it called a Tube?'

'Well, I suppose because the underground tunnels look like tubes.'

Alex peered wide-eyed into the darkness. 'Do monsters live in there?' she whispered, taking care not to wake them.

'No, only trains.'

Alex's earnest eyes turned to her mother. 'Daddy fights monsters and chops them up into little bits.'

Imagining his smile Rose felt her heart flood with love, and scooping Alex up she blew a raspberry kiss on her cheek.

Had anyone told her on her twenty-first birthday that by the time she was twenty-five she'd be married to the most wonderful man in the world with three beautiful children, she'd never have believed it. This was because she hadn't yet met the man destined to sweep her off her feet, but when she did, a month after the big celebration, she'd known, virtually at hello, that this was who she wanted to spend the rest of her life with. Amazingly, exhilaratingly, he'd felt the same way, so breezing past all the cautions and disapproval of family and friends, not to mention suspicions that she must be pregnant (which she wasn't), they'd headed up the aisle a mere ten months after their first date.

And not a day had gone by since when she hadn't felt their love deepening, nor had she ever experienced a moment's doubt about becoming a mother. True, they hadn't expected it to happen quite so

2

soon, nor so prolifically, and it certainly wasn't always easy – having twins, after the trouble-free ride Alex had given them, had come as a brutal awakening to just how challenging parenthood could be. However, they were all happy and healthy – and coping, even if there were times when she felt like screaming or taking herself off somewhere quiet for a very long lie-down.

'OK, darling, the train's coming, so stand back.'

Obediently Alex stepped in behind her mother and hid her face as the loud, nasty monster rattled into the station.

'Right, up we go,' Rose said as the doors opened.

Alex hopped up and followed her in giant steps to a bench seat.

The only other passenger was a man, half-hidden behind a paper, but then Rose had deliberately chosen to travel home from her mother's in the middle of the afternoon to avoid the rush-hour crush. Trying to manage three children amongst a bruising, impatient horde of commuters wouldn't have been wise, in fact it could be downright reckless.

Moments after the doors closed one of the twins started to wake up. Watching her eyes blink open and her tiny mouth widen in a yawn, Rose waited expectantly, and sure enough, the instant Becky spotted her, her precious little face broke into the sunniest of smiles.

'Hello you,' Rose murmured.

Becky burped and Alex gave a shriek of laughter.

'Say pardon me,' Alex told her.

Becky looked at her sister and frowned.

'Can I run down to the door at the end?' Alex demanded, already starting to go.

'No, sweetheart,' Rose told her.

3

'I want to.'

'I said no.'

'But I want to.'

'Mummy, up, up.' Becky was already half out of the pushchair, while Simon, in his usual fashion, simply carried on sleeping.

'You'll have to go back in when it's time to get off the train,' Rose warned as she lifted Becky on to her lap. Becky burped again and started wriggling in an effort to get down.

'Look at me, Mummy,' Alex called.

Gasping to see her at the other end of the carriage, Rose scowled at her meaningfully. 'I told you it wasn't allowed.'

'I want to run,' Alex pouted.

Rose glanced at the man seated opposite. 'You're being a nuisance,' she told Alex.

'Oh, please don't mind me,' the man said, and Rose noticed that his eyes seemed gentle, yet somehow sad, as he watched Alex darting past.

'Run, run,' Becky cried.

'You're too small,' Rose laughed, pulling her back as she tried to launch herself off.

'Let Becky run too,' Alex implored. 'I'll hold her hand.'

Rose looked at the other passenger again, and when he smiled she set Becky down on her wobbly legs and felt her heart fill with pride as Becky toddled off with Alex, so thrilled that she was gurgling with glee.

Though Rose knew she loved them all equally, she'd have to admit, if pushed, that she'd always felt there was something special about Alex, probably because she was their firstborn, or perhaps because she was so engaging. People always wanted to stop

4

and talk to her, and being the sociable little chatterbox she was she usually had plenty to say. Her daddy was completely smitten, to the point that he'd sit and watch her sleeping at night, listening to her breathing and marvelling at what a wonderful little miracle she was. He did the same with the twins, but Rose was aware of a special bond developing between him and Alex that she loved every bit as much as she loved them.

'Look at us, Mummy!' Alex shouted as she and Becky charged back through the carriage.

'Ssh,' Rose cautioned, looking at the man again.

Though he was smiling as he watched them, Rose was struck again by how melancholy he seemed, and being as soft-hearted as she was, she wanted to ask if he was all right. Of course she couldn't, and nor would she, but when he glanced her way she treated him to one of her warmest smiles. He seemed embarrassed, but pleased, and chuckled aloud as Alex and Becky stormed past again.

Since no one else got on the train as they passed through the next few stations she allowed the girls to carry on wearing themselves out, until eventually they were approaching Southfields and she called out for them to come back. Alex looked mutinous, but then Becky began squealing as she raced towards her mother, and not wanting to be last Alex sprinted after her. It was as Becky reached the pushchair that Alex caught up and pushed her. Becky fell, hitting her mouth on the wheel, and let out a terrible scream.

'Alex, you naughty girl,' Rose snapped angrily as she scooped Becky up. Blood was pouring from Becky's lip, and having found her voice she was belting it out. Then Simon was awake and crying too, while Alex gazed on in fear.

'You're in big trouble,' Rose told her over the din, 'now hold on to my coat while we get off.'

The train came to a stop as they reached the doors, and still trying to shush Becky, Rose bumped the pushchair on to the platform.

'I hurt, I hurt,' Becky sobbed.

'It's all right,' Rose soothed, afraid she might have lost a tooth. 'We'll make it better.'

'No, no,' Becky squealed, tightening her legs round Rose's waist as Rose tried to put her in the pushchair.

Becoming frazzled, Rose turned round to make sure Alex was behind her, and her heart skipped a beat when she realised she wasn't.

'Alex!' she shouted in panic. Then she saw her, still on the train, rooted to the spot.

'Alex, get off! *Get off!*' Rose yelled as the doors started to close.

Alex's eyes were huge as she stared at her mother.

'No, no, no,' Rose cried, thrusting Becky on top of Simon and dashing back to the train. 'STOP!' she screamed, as the doors slammed shut. 'Please, stop the train!'

There was a look of terror in Alex's eyes now.

'HELP!' Rose yelled as the train started to move. 'Help!' She was banging the doors, trying to wrench them apart. 'My baby, my baby.'

The man was out of his seat and standing beside Alex with a hand on her shoulder. 'Next station,' he mouthed through the window.

Rose's terror was blinding. She was shaking so hard she barely knew what she was doing. *Next station*, was what he'd said. Next station. He'd keep Alex safe and wait with her until Rose and the twins arrived on the next train.

Chapter One

Now everything was going her way, Lucy Winters wasn't at all sure this was what she actually wanted. Except it was, of course it was, she just couldn't help worrying about being careful of what she wished for, and all that . . . This wasn't going to backfire on her, was it?

Since it really didn't seem likely, she resolved to hold firm and hang on to the courage of her convictions, while Joe, damn him, didn't seem to be in the least bit fazed by what he was doing. If anything, he seemed to be rather enjoying himself, which might have been annoying if she hadn't known it was a front.

Joe was good at those – when he wanted to be.

As she stood in the bedroom doorway watching him, Lucy's deep brown eyes kept flicking to the mirror that was propped up against the opposite wall. They'd had this mirror for nine years now and Joe still hadn't got round to putting it up, so good job Lucy hadn't been holding her breath. Without her in it, the mirror would show a busy landscape of wild-flower wallpaper, a faux-leather headboard, one nightstand with a recycled Tiffany lamp and a pile of sports mags (on Joe's side), while hers had a matching lamp and various books about running a business and understanding antiques. With her in it, the mirror became a kind of portrait frame around a tall, gangly woman of thirty-seven with long, shiny dark hair that flopped loosely around her shoulders and a delicate heart-shaped face that became radiant when she smiled.

Not much radiance going on at the moment.

In fact, Lucy was wondering how she was managing to show no emotion at all when she was watching the start of her life as she knew it coming to an end. There was plenty going on inside, a whole party of dread, excitement, hope, anticipation, romance (of the strictly non-sexual variety), and *sooo* much she wanted to say that she simply couldn't understand how she was managing to stay zipped up.

Probably because what she was feeling hadn't yet formed itself into words that she felt safe enough to speak.

Hearing a door slam downstairs, she tensed and listened. It was either Ben, their son, returning from his friend's who lived over the newsagent's at the end of the road, or Hanna, their daughter, leaving home. She hoped it was Ben, not only because of how much steadier she felt when both children were in the house – as if each of their forays into the outside world was going to end in disaster, and plenty did around their neck of the woods, but don't let her get started on that – but because Ben, at eighteen, was so much better at handling his fifteen-going-on-twenty-five-year-old sister these days than Lucy was.

So, they were either both downstairs now, or no one was. Given the silence she had to accept it was the latter, which meant that Hanna had stormed off.

8

This caused a mixture of relief and worry to start battling for territory in Lucy's conscience, and she knew already that the latter would win.

Joe had always been great with their daughter, or that was what he liked to think, and it was true, they were close, but parenting skills had never really been his forte. However, should the need arise, Lucy was willing to believe that he'd dash into a burning building to rescue one of his offspring, as her own father had once done for her. This would be out of love, of course, and because Joe liked to consider himself a hero. She used to think of him as such during the first years of their marriage, but a lot had changed since then. For a start Hanna had grown up, and, in Lucy's opinion, it was because Joe had never yet grasped the concept of saying no to his darling daughter that they were now having such problems with her. Since she'd been old enough to understand, or manipulate, Hanna had always turned to her father for whatever she wanted, which made Joe, in her eyes, God, Santa Claus and Merlin the Magician all rolled into one. He could make any wish come true, or so it seemed to Hanna, and Joe was nothing if not gifted at glossing the myth. This meant that over the years most of the discipline had been left to the snarling old dragon called Mummy, who, Hanna had lately come to realise, needed to get over herself and get a life.

Well, Hanna was right about that.

According to Hanna everything that was happening now was Lucy's fault, and in this instance Lucy had to admit that Hanna had a case, since it had most definitely been Lucy's decision to get out of the rut they were in. Actually rut was far too mild a description as far as Lucy was concerned, because to her it felt like their very own pothole with endless passageways and no exit, and for someone who'd never have dreamed of taking up such a bizarre hobby she'd long ago reached a point where she needed to get out. Unfortunately Joe, youngest of the infamous East End Winters brothers, didn't think they were in a rut at all.

To Joe, this hallowed turf (his words, not hers) was the only place he'd ever wanted to live, or ever would, and his chosen career was the only one he intended to pursue, or ever would. In the case of his brothers a career meant either flogging from the back of a lorry at market (Charlie), or driving a taxi (Vince). In Joe's case it meant acting, mainly because once, way back when, he'd been cast in a soap opera that had run for several years and turned him into a household name. However, these days even the lowliest walk-on parts were proving almost impossible to come by, since reality TV had jammed a finger in the dyke of drama (Joe's choice of phrase, not hers). So, now, in between auditions and the odd commercial or voice-over, he was most often to be found in one of 'the lanes' (Petticoat, Brick, Leather), working the markets with Charlie; or driving Vince's minicab when Vince was too hung-over to crawl out of bed. The rest of the time he pumped iron at a gym owned by one of his uncles, or just as often he might be found at the Feathers catching up with a couple of his fellow thesps who, like him, weren't only role-less, but ageing and agentless.

Coming from such a different world herself – the only child of a modest and somewhat nomadic couple, thanks to her father's job setting up new offices for a multinational insurance company – when Lucy had first met Joe she'd been totally captivated by his fame and family and the whole nine yards of what it meant to belong to the same community for generations, dubious though some of the connections might be. It was everything she'd ever dreamed of: being part of a neighbourhood where everyone knew each other, the children played together, the men all supported West Ham, and the women exchanged recipes and beauty tips. To quote Joe, their part of London was as tight as a boxer's fist, and don't let anyone try to mess with them or they'd be sorry.

They'd met when Lucy was only seventeen and Joe was twenty-eight and starring in the soap as an East End bad boy. The nation had loved him back then, and so had she from the minute she'd started her work experience as a runner on the set of his show. She'd been in her first year of sixth-form college at the time, but once they'd realised how they felt about each other – or, perhaps more accurately, once they'd found out she was pregnant – all thoughts of further education and dazzling careers were banished from her mind. Joe Winters was so madly in love with her that he wanted to marry her and have at least five kids with her. She was going to be *the wife of Joe Winters*, who half the nation's women were swooning over! It was no wonder it turned her teenage head, especially after all the years she'd spent on the outside, always the new girl in class, the one who was teased and ostracised and made to feel worthless and ashamed. How she'd longed to see the faces of her tormentors when her photograph appeared in the papers with Joe Winters! And her dear, gentle parents, poked fun at by everyone for being so old, had been as won over by the roguish Billy Crowther, aka Joe Winters, as she was, so had simply shared her joy and barely even mentioned her age, or lost opportunities.

What a curse a little bit of fame could be, she often thought now. Had Joe simply been the bloke next door, with dodgy prospects and an equally dodgy reputation, would her parents have been so lenient, or welcoming, then? Come to think of it, would she have been as smitten? The answer was probably yes, because he'd been so heart-stoppingly good-looking and full of charm that it was hard to imagine how any starry-eyed girl of her age could have managed to resist him, fame or not.

It wasn't so hard now she was in her mid-thirties, and the sense of belonging she'd always craved had dwindled in the first few years. It was odd how having two children of her own, two brothers- and sisters-in-law, four nieces, three nephews, a father-in-law and dozens of extended family still hadn't managed to make her feel as though she fitted in. She wished she could understand what was wrong with her, why nothing, apart from her children, ever seemed to feel right, but the only answer either she, or her mother, could come up with was that she'd never got over being an only child with no aunts or uncles or cousins to help fill her world, since her parents had been only children too. The sense of isolation, and of feeling so apart from everyone else, particularly when she'd changed schools so often, must be so deeply imbedded in her that maybe it would never go away.

Perversely, she could only be glad now that she did still feel like an outsider, because leaving would have been so much harder if she were trying to disentangle emotional ties. Not that it was going to be easy saying goodbye to all the tradespeople she'd come to know and respect, and it wasn't as if she didn't care for Joe's family at all, because she did. However, she had to move Hanna away from here before things got any worse than they already were.

'You're a bloody snob, that's what you are,' Hanna had raged when Lucy had first told her they were leaving. 'Everyone says it about you. You think you're better, just because you speak with a stupid stuck-up accent and you started up an effing book club. But you only do the same job as Auntie Sandra down the call centre, and at the end of the day your shit smells too.'

Recalling the coarseness, Lucy winced. Hanna might be extremely pretty, with Joe's blond hair and blue eyes, and she might have a TDF – to die for – figure, but being lovely on the outside was no guarantee of being the same within. OK, she was a teenager so being headstrong and challenging was only to be expected, but the way Hanna was carrying on went far beyond what Lucy was prepared to tolerate. Just thank God she hadn't fallen pregnant yet, but two of her friends were already mothers and at least three had had terminations. Thankfully, Hanna had asked to go on the pill when she was fourteen, but even so Lucy detested the idea that she was having sex so young, especially with the kind of boys to whom she seemed attracted. Even Joe, who usually let Hanna get away with just about anything, had started to take a dim view of the crowd she was hanging out with. Not that he'd spoken to her about it, he didn't see that as his role, but he was prepared to agree with Lucy that Hanna needed a firmer hand. He especially didn't like to think of her rolling around drunk with her friends, mouthing off at the police and staggering into gutters, where her brother had found her on one memorable occasion. Thank God Ben had brought her home before anything worse could happen, and while Joe had dutifully sat next to her bed to make sure she didn't choke on her own vomit Ben had talked seriously to his mother.

'You've got to do something about it,' he'd told her. 'She's putting herself in real danger getting smashed like that.'

'I know, and I am doing something,' Lucy had assured him. 'I haven't told her yet, but when she breaks up for the summer we're leaving this house and we won't be coming back.'

The way Ben's sleepy blue eyes widened with interest had made her heart sing with love. Unlike Hanna, nothing ever seemed to faze him.

'You know how Granny and Grandpa have always wanted me to take over the business one day?' she'd continued. 'Well, I've had a long chat with them and it's going to happen sooner rather than later.'

Ben was clearly impressed. 'Cool,' he responded. 'Are you pleased? Sure you are, you've been dying to do it.'

Lucy wanted to hug him. He was the only person in her world who seemed to understand her need to make more of her life, and moreover he never took it personally, or tried to make it about him, the way Joe and Hanna did. 'I'd always intended to wait till Hanna went to uni,' she reminded him, 'but with the way things are I'm not even sure uni's still on her agenda. If I could see her doing what you did at her age, working to save up for a gap year, studying for your exams, I wouldn't dream of making her change schools now. I went through that too often myself to want to inflict it on her, but there's no doubt in my mind that I have to get her out of where she is.'

14

'You're doing the right thing,' Ben assured her. 'They're a real waste of space, the kids she's hooked up with. A couple of them even carry knives.'

Though Lucy had guessed this, hearing Ben confirm it had made her more anxious than ever to get the move under way.

'So what's going to happen? Will you live with Granny and Grandpa?' he asked.

'Only when we first get there. Once we're settled they're going to move to the cottage on Exmoor. Grandpa's not getting any younger, and Granny's quite keen for him to retire, so the summer holidays seemed like the perfect time for them to hand over to me. That way Hanna will have a few weeks to acclimatise before she starts her new school – and you'll already be off on your travels so I won't have to worry about you.'

Ben's grin was mischievous.

'All right,' Lucy conceded, 'of course I'll worry, we both know that, but at least I won't be interrupting your education or taking you away from a home you don't want to leave.'

Seeming to approve of the logic, Ben said, 'So where does Dad fit into all this? Don't tell me he's going to give up living round here.'

'No, he isn't, but he accepts that it would be best for Hanna to continue her education at a private school near Granny and Grandpa's. We'll have the money to pay for it once they've signed everything over to me, which is happening even as we speak.'

'Wicked,' Ben murmured. 'So you're going to be rich?'

'Not exactly, but we'll have a house that belongs to us and a thriving business to help keep things going.'

15

'And Dad's going to do what?'

With a guilty sigh Lucy said, 'He's decided to move in with Uncle Charlie and Auntie Kell for the time being. Their house is much bigger than ours and we're not sure he can keep up the rent on this place on his own.' He wouldn't have been able to pay a mortgage either, if they had one, but since the dark days, back in the mid-nineties when they'd had their home repossessed, they'd never managed to get on the property ladder again. Of course her parents had offered to help, but having learned the hard way how unreliable, even irresponsible, Joe was when it came to money, Lucy had flatly refused to let them take the risk. 'But he'll be coming to see us at weekends,' she told Ben brightly, while not adding that she actually wished he wouldn't, because more than anything she'd have liked to make this a trial separation between them. However, Hanna was going to find it hard enough being uprooted as it was: if she thought she was hardly ever going to see her precious daddy, Lucy was afraid of what she might do.

'So when are you going to tell Hanna?'

Lucy swallowed. 'Soon, and I know it won't be pretty.'

How right she'd been about that, because it really hadn't been. In fact it was so ugly at first that even Joe had ended up raising his voice to the girl, which had the happy result of making her run away. For two days and two nights they searched the neighbourhood, interrogated her friends, enlisted the help of the school and eventually the police. When she'd finally turned up looking a total wreck and sobbing her heart out, the reek of booze and relief that she was safe had finally convinced Joe that his hallowed turf was no longer the right place for his little angel to be. Until then Lucy had been half afraid that when the time came Hanna would manage to cajole him into letting her stay with him in London, and faced with that she really wouldn't have known what to do.

Fortunately that was no longer an issue. There were plenty of others still to be dealt with, however, not least of which was how much she was hurting Joe by leaving.

'Personally, I think you're off your head letting him go,' Stephie, one of his cousins, had told her. Stephie had no idea what Joe was really like, because she wasn't married to him. In fact, she wasn't married to anyone, but would give almost anything to be a wife. 'You don't want to know what it's like out here,' she cried passionately. 'The chances of meeting anyone else, or anyone sane, with hair and teeth and a decent job are next to zero, especially at your age.' Since Stephie, who was thirty, was a serial dater thanks to Match.com and various other Internet sites, Lucy was willing to accept that she had superior knowledge when it came to the foreign land of Sad and Single.

However, Lucy didn't want to meet anyone else. That wasn't what this was about at all. Now she was standing here watching Joe sorting his belongings into one of the holdalls they'd taken on honeymoon, so many happy memories were drifting in from forgotten lanes that she found herself wondering what he'd say if she told him she'd changed her mind. Not about going to Gloucestershire, it was far too late for that, and besides she could hardly wait to get there, but did she really want to view this as a trial separation? After all the agonised discussions, tears, fighting, persuading and even the occasional threat, would Joe be willing to carry on now as though she'd never even suggested such a thing? Knowing him as well as she did, she guessed he'd open his arms and smile in the way that always used to melt her heart, and tell her that all he ever wanted was to make her happy. He genuinely believed that was the truth, because he'd managed long ago to convince himself that she came first, when in actual fact no one ever mattered more to Joe than Joe himself. Which made him sound selfish and egotistical, inconsiderate and disrespectful, and he was indeed all of those things, but there was a lot more to him besides, such as his generosity and love of fun, willingness to help old people across the street and kindness to animals.

Why hadn't her marriage been a success, she wondered. Was it her fault? It couldn't have been all his, so what was wrong with her?

Why did nothing ever feel right? Even when things were going her way and she had every reason to be happy, all too often the shadows of unease and doubt would start looming in a way that made her feel out of kilter with her world and even sometimes estranged from those she loved. Well, perhaps not from her parents and children, but certainly from Joe, and the craziest part of it was that the longer they stayed together the more distanced from him she seemed to feel.

Why was that happening? Should she try to discuss it with him? She knew she should, yet at the same time she knew she wouldn't. All she did was continue watching him pack and wonder how far she would let him go before she suddenly blurted out something she'd very likely end up regretting.

'You keeping an eye on me in case I steal your jewels?' he teased, as he stuffed a pile of unpressed boxers into the holdall. She could have ironed them for him, she thought with a pang of guilt. She always used to. She'd forgotten now when she'd stopped. Had it been to punish him for being more like a child than a man, dependent, stubborn, always wanting his own way unless her needs happened to chime with his own, when he could put on such a convincing act of being the most big-hearted husband in town that even she was taken in?

She didn't have any jewels.

Remembering a time when they used to say what's mine is yours and had never even imagined dividing their assets, she said, 'We're doing the right thing.'

His arresting blue eyes came to hers in a way that made it hard for her to meet them. 'Yes, we are,' he agreed, 'so don't go upsetting yourself now. It's a brave decision you've taken and hard as it is now, for both of us, I don't have any doubts that everything will turn out for the best.'

This could only mean that he was happy for her to go, because if he weren't he'd be stomping about and throwing a Hanna-style tantrum, making her feel even worse about breaking up their home than she already did. And if he was happy for her to go it had to be because he already had something, or someone else, waiting to take her place. 'What do you think is the best?' she asked hoarsely. 'That we get back together, or end up going our separate ways for good?'

Coming to stand in front of her, he cupped a hand round her face and gazed into her eyes. 'What's best,' he said, 'is that you do whatever needs to be done to become the woman you think you might have been, if I hadn't turned you into a wife and mother when you were still not much more than a baby yourself.'

Her laugh was mangled by a sob. 'I was a willing party,' she reminded him, 'and I wouldn't change a thing.'

The irony that tilted his smile crushed her with yet more guilt, because they both knew that given half a chance she'd probably change everything.

'I know I made you a lot of promises that I haven't been able to keep,' he said, going back to his packing, 'so I'm hoping this will turn out to be a good opportunity for me to try and sort myself out too.'

Why was she feeling so bad about not asking him to come, when she knew very well that he wouldn't even if she did? He'd always been adamant about that, and she definitely didn't want him ruining her plans, which he almost certainly would given his enthusiasm for bending and stretching laws, plus his complete aversion to paying taxes or bills if he could get away with it. They'd have been in trouble by the end of the year and possibly in prison by the end of the next. His reckless generosity with other people's money, including hers, was why they still didn't own a house, or a car that could manage more than a dozen journeys without breaking down, or many of the trappings that most average families could boast these days.

Glancing at his mobile as it started to ring, she left him to answer the call and went off to the bathroom to start sorting his shaving gear and toothbrush into a spare toiletry bag. When she picked up his cologne the smell seemed to wrap around her like an embrace. She reached for the towel he'd used that morning and held it to her face. It was as though he'd already gone and she was trying to conjure him out of the essences he'd left behind.

By this time next week they'd all be gone. This

shabby terraced house where they'd lived for the past sixteen years, a stone's throw from the high street, would be a partly furnished shell with no voices or music, or love, or laughter bringing it to life. It would stand silently waiting for the next tenants to come and revive it with a whole new set of characters and a story that Lucy guessed she'd probably never know. Whoever they were, she hoped they'd be as happy here as she had often been, and didn't suffer anything like the same heartaches and frustrations.

'No one's life is perfect,' Joe had reminded her on more occasions than she cared to recall. 'It's only you who seems to think it's possible.'

But it wasn't perfection she was after, it was something else that she couldn't quite define, but it had to do with stability and feeling as though everything was worthwhile, and for some reason she hadn't been able to find it here. Maybe in Gloucestershire, with a home and business of her own, she would finally feel settled and stop this restless searching for she knew not what.

In the bedroom Joe was finishing his call. '. . . sure, yeah. No rush, whenever you can get here.'

Guessing it was Carlos, one of his actor chums, who'd offered to come and help him move over to Charlie's while Charlie and Kell were in Tenerife, Lucy continued the dispiriting task of removing her husband's toiletries from the forest of those left behind. It was kind of Carlos to help out, but since he only had a car because Joe had sold him their old one for less than half its worth, as that was all Carlos could afford, in Lucy's opinion Carlos jolly well should be chauffeuring his mate around.

They had another car now, a twelve-year-old Peugeot Estate which they'd have entered into the scrappage scheme had they been able to afford to change it, but they hadn't. Lucy was keeping it for the time being to get herself, Hanna and their belongings to Gloucestershire, then she might be in a position to buy something newer and more reliable.

Would that cheer Hanna up, to go shopping for a new car? It would take a lot more than that, but please God the country air and new friends would start to free her gentle and loving daughter from the shell of aggression and hostility that currently imprisoned her.

'Carlos'll be here in ten minutes,' Joe told her as she returned to the bedroom.

Tucking the toiletry bag into a front pocket of the holdall, she said, 'I'd have given you a lift.'

He flashed her one of his disarmingly ironic smiles that seemed to say 'I know, but I've decided to go my way, thanks.'

Though she was annoyed, she wasn't going to allow herself to start rowing with him now, or her guilt would no doubt force her into saying plenty she'd end up regretting. Besides, it had all been said before, and though she really did detest herself for calling him a loser, as she had on more than one occasion, the fact that he went on so few auditions these days and was so rarely cast never seemed to suggest to him that it was time to start rethinking his career. He just kept plugging away at it, staying as upbeat as if his phone never stopped ringing, talking up his fifteen minutes a storm to anyone who'd listen, while suffering more let-downs and rejections than even a thick-skinned Jehovah's Witness could surely have borne.

Joe never seemed to mind about being broke, probably, Lucy realised, because he could always come to her for what he needed, and scrape up the odd few days of work with his brothers. This was how he financed his club and gym memberships, shelled out for more than his fair share of rounds at the pub and took her somewhere for dinner a couple of times a month. Everything else was left to her, such as claiming their tax credits and child allowance – which had promptly halved on Ben's sixteenth birthday – putting food on the table, clothes on their backs, paying bills, handing out pocket money . . . It never seemed to bother him that she was the main provider, and maybe it wouldn't bother her so much if her job had allowed her the time to pick up a few qualifications along the way. As it was, in order to make ends meet, she had to grab as many hours as she could at the call centre where she'd been promoted to shift supervisor about eighteen months ago. Hardly the career dreams were made of, at least not hers, but the money wasn't bad and someone had to keep a regular income flowing their way or they'd starve.

She'd worked her notice now and had sunk a few glasses with the girls last Friday night to celebrate her 'great escape', and the start of a brand-new life running her parents' small auction house in Gloucestershire. Everyone had promised to stay in touch and even to be her best customers, but she knew it wouldn't happen. Still, the sentiment and encouragement had been uplifting at the time, and she was definitely going to miss the female camaraderie that had sustained her through many a crisis during the years she'd been with them.

Hearing her mobile ringing in the kitchen, she left Joe to his packing and ran downstairs. By the time she got there the call had already bumped through to voicemail, so allowing a few minutes for Stephie to leave her message, she opened the back door to let in some air. Not quite the heady elixir that would soon be wafting her way from the countryside around Cromstone Edge, but the tantalising aroma of Indian cooking drifting down from the Taj Palace wasn't entirely displeasing. In fact, she was probably going to miss it.

With a sigh she surveyed the mess in the backyard: old bikes, a broken lawnmower (and they didn't even have a lawn), terracotta pots too chipped or cracked to bother taking with her, a rotary washing line with sagging wires and various other items of junk that needed to be dumped. Deciding to tackle it tomorrow, she turned back to the cluttered galley of a kitchen where, unsurprisingly, Hanna had failed to wash up as requested before leaving, and a pile of dirty laundry was slumped in front of the washing machine as though it had struggled to make it this far and now needed help over the finishing line. Since most of it was Ben's she couldn't blame Hanna, which had been her first inclination, but nor would she pick it up the way she usually did. It was high time both children learned that she wasn't their skivvy, and Hanna at least was soon going to find out that when they arrived in their new home she intended to run a very different ship.

Good luck with that, she was thinking to herself as she reached for her phone, and not bothering to listen to Stephie's message, she clicked to return the call and got straight through.

'Hey,' Stephie said warmly. 'Can you talk? How's it going?'

Glancing down the hall to where piles of shoes and bags were bunched up under the overloaded coat rack, Lucy said, 'He's still upstairs packing.'

'You're kidding! He's actually going?'

'He doesn't have a choice, we've given our notice on this place.'

'Oh my God. How are you feeling?'

'Strange. Like I'm not really myself.'

'I bet he's feeling pretty weird too. I don't know how you can do it, but at the same time I suppose I get where you're coming from. Have you told your parents yet that he's not coming with you?'

'I spoke to Mum last night. She sounded a bit distracted, so I'm not sure she really took it in. Anyway, you know what she's like, she usually finds a way to support my decisions rather than get into a fight, even if it means her darling son-in-law is being cut out of the loop.'

With a smile in her voice Stephie said, 'She's such a sweetie, your ma. I always hated having older parents myself, they were so stuck in the mud and out of touch with everything. By comparison yours are a dream.'

'Believe me, you wouldn't think so if you'd had to suffer growing up with them. It used to drive me nuts never being able to have a good row. Still, I suppose I'm making up for it now with Hanna.' And Joe, she didn't add.

'Is she there?'

'No, but hers could be the key I can hear, so brace yourself.'

Stephie chuckled as Lucy watched the front door open. Seeing the sour expression on her daughter's young face, transforming her in one scowl from beauty to beast, she felt her insides contract with a mix of guilt and annoyance. 'Are you OK?' she said. 'Where have you been?'

Throwing a viciously daggered look her mother's way, Hanna tossed her hair extensions over one shoulder and flounced off up the stairs, no doubt to go and sympathise with her father – or to try again to persuade him to rescue her from the wicked witch who was threatening to turn her into 'an ugly little country bumpkin'. Hanna was nothing if not melodramatic.

With a sigh Lucy returned to her call. 'If only she was still the sweet little thing we used to know and love, she might be looking forward to this as much as I am. It could be a great adventure for us if she'd just enter into the spirit of it.'

'She'll be all right once you get there – or at least once she's made some new friends.'

Trying not to wince at Hanna's probable opinion of that, Lucy said, 'I wonder what's keeping Ben. He said he'd be back by four thirty and it's almost a quarter to six. Maybe I ought to give him a call.'

'Teenage boys are notoriously bad timekeepers which you know very well, having one of the worst culprits living under your roof. Where did he go?'

'To Ali's to sort out some last-minute travel plans. Ah, this must be him,' and with a quick unravelling of relief she watched her handsome young son lope in through the door, all mussy dark hair and his father's deep blue eyes.

'Hey Mum,' he called down the hall. 'Where's Dad? Is he still here?'

'He's upstairs,' Lucy answered.

After propping his guitar against the wall, he took the stairs two at a time, shouting to let his father know that the rock god was coming his way.

Smiling and feeling terrible, Lucy said to Stephie, 'I suppose I ought to go and join them. Are you doing anything later?'

'Would you believe, the security guard called again,

so I'm seeing him tonight. I know I should have played harder to get, but hey, life's short and I'm desperate, so why waste time with games? They never work anyway, or not for me.'

'I thought you said he was boring and smelled of must.'

'It's a Saturday night and the sun's shining,' Stephie wailed, 'anything's better than staying at home on my own. You know, I've been thinking about getting a sperm donor, but we can discuss that another time. Maybe when I come to stay for a weekend. I'll call later, or tomorrow to find out how everything went. Good luck, and I still say you're mad, but hey, what do I know?'

Aware how unlikely it was that Stephie would ever visit for a weekend, Lucy tried to stop herself feeling bad for not minding too much, and gathered up a linen basket full of clean sheets. As she started to climb the stairs she was wondering if she should embark on the next family scene by asking Ben to bring the last two suitcases down from the attic. Or should she try to avoid it altogether and go and lock herself in the shed?

Chapter Two

'Aha, here she is! The light of our lives.'

Joe was grinning boyishly as he sat astride the old dining chair they used as a dressing-table stool, elbows propped on the spindle back and heels hooked on to the bottom rungs. Ben, like an ad from Calvin Klein, was stretched out on the bed, hands locked behind his head, hairy midriff on show, while Hanna, all teary eyes and pinched rosebud lips, was glaring at her mother through smudged circles of Revlon's Fantasy Lash.

This was her family, the people who meant more to her than anything else in the world, who gave purpose to her existence – or certainly the children did – and yet she was breaking up their home. Lucy's heart churned with still more misgivings.

'I was just explaining,' Joe told her, 'that all this is like a temporary thing. Once you've got a handle on what's what down there, and I've got my act together here, we'll all be together again. Right?'

In spite of knowing he'd never get his act together, and even if he did she'd never return here, nor would he decamp to the country, Lucy said, 'Of course.'

'And you'll be going to visit them in Glos, won't you?' Ben chipped in.

'Yeah, but it's hardly going to be the same as having

him with us all the time,' Hanna protested belligerently, 'and how many more times do I have to tell you? I don't want to go to effing Gloucestershire. I hate it there and I don't see why I can't stay here with Dad.'

'Language,' Lucy warned.

Hanna's eyes flashed. 'I said effing, for God's sake. It's a letter of the alphabet with ing on the end.'

'I told you, sweetheart,' Joe broke in gently, 'that you'll be more than welcome to stay with me whenever you come to London, once I've found myself somewhere to live, that is.'

Hanna almost exploded. 'We've got somewhere to live,' she shouted. 'We're in it, now, so why do we have to leave just because *she's* decided we have to? There are four of us in this family, so how come she gets to make all the decisions? What happened to democracy, that's what I want to know?'

'You're always saying this place is a dump,' Lucy reminded her. 'I thought you'd be glad to get out of it.'

'Yes, to somewhere bigger and smarter and *round here* where all my friends and family are. Not to the back of sodding beyond with a bunch of cows and stinking fields.'

'You always enjoy Cromstone when we go to see Granny and Grandpa . . .'

'Oh, do me a favour. It's hardly the same as living there, is it?'

'Just think of that lovely big farmhouse,' Joe came in loyally. 'You've already got a bedroom and *bathroom* there all to yourself, and there's Sky Plus and a *dishwasher* . . .'

'I couldn't give a fuck about all that. Everyone I know is here and so are you.'

'I won't be,' Ben reminded her, with one of his more devilish grins.

'So?'

He appeared mystified. 'How could you not want to be wherever I am?'

'Well that's not exactly an option, is it?' she snarled.

'But it's going to be my home when I come back.'

'Yeah, till you go off to uni. Oh shut up,' she snapped. 'I don't get you going along with all this when you love it round here as much as I do, and all the girls are fat down there with buck teeth and spots. Which is what you're going to turn me into,' she shouted furiously at her mother.

'Don't be ridiculous,' Lucy told her. 'Living in the country is hardly going to change the way you look, apart from putting a bit of natural colour in your cheeks, which'll be a nice change from all that cheap blusher.' She was sounding like her own mother now, which was a bit scary. 'Anyway, you've always got along very well with Juliette who lives at the pub, and she certainly doesn't fit that description. In fact she's a very pretty girl and I already happen to know that you're going to be in the same class when you start the new school, which I'm told she's really looking forward to.'

Stuck for a suitably biting retort, Hanna slammed her eyes and turned away.

'I reckon,' Joe declared, 'that by the time I come to see you you'll already have a dozen new friends and at least as many boys chasing after you.'

No boys, Lucy was thinking with a shudder.

'Yeah, like that's really going to happen now she's signed me up for an all-girls school,' Hanna snorted. 'And that's another thing, I don't want to go to a new bloody school. I was getting on perfectly all right where I am until *she* decided to absolutely totally and completely ruin my life.'

Lucy looked at Joe.

'She *is*,' Hanna insisted when her father shook his head in dismay. 'That's absolutely what she's doing. In fact I might just as well commit suicide now, at least it'll be quicker than dying of boredom.'

Before Lucy could respond, a loud knocking reverberated through the house.

'Can only be Carlos,' Joe said, starting to get up.

'Noooo!' Hanna wailed, running to him. 'I'm not going to let you go. You can't. It's not fair. You belong here with us. It's only her who wants things to change. We want everything to stay the same so make it, Dad. Please.'

'Ssh, sweetheart,' he soothed, holding her close and kissing the top of her head. 'Don't get yourself into a state now. Everything's going to be fine, you just wait and see.'

'How can it be when she's chucking you out and forcing us to go and live somewhere we don't want to? It's all her fault. Make her go, Dad, and we can stay here.'

Joe's eyes flicked to Lucy's. 'Don't be daft,' he said, his expression seeming to remind her that she'd brought this on herself, and actually Hanna might have a plan. 'We've given notice on the house now, you know that,' he told his daughter, 'and you don't want to stay here, really. Think how cold it is in winter, the way the wind whistles in through the windows and Jack Frost creeps in under the doors.'

'But it's not winter, it's summer and I've arranged

to do loads of stuff with my friends these holidays. I was even going to Spain with Beth and her family, until *she* said I couldn't go.'

Feeling every bit as wretched as she was supposed to, though relieved since she had no great liking for Beth or her family, Lucy said, 'I'll go and answer the door before Carlos knocks it down.'

'No, wait,' Joe interrupted. 'You go, son, and take your sister with you.'

'No way! I'm staying here with you,' Hanna protested.

'I want to talk to Mum,' Joe said gently, 'so go and wait downstairs, there's a good girl. I'm not going to leave without saying cheerio, so don't worry about that.'

It was still all too much for Hanna. 'Please don't go, Dad, please,' she wailed, tightening her arms around him.

'Ssh, sssh, I told you, it's all going to be fine,' he murmured, stroking her hair. His eyes suddenly rounded and came to Lucy's in confusion as he lifted a hand – he was clutching a fistful of ponytail.

Ben gave a choke of laughter. 'Oh boy, are you in trouble now,' he warned.

'What?' Hanna snorted, turning round.

Joe was trying not to laugh, so was Lucy.

Seeing what had happened Hanna snatched the hairpiece back, saying, 'Well, I'm glad you think it's funny,' and shrugging her father off she stormed furiously out of the room.

'Carlos,' Ben said, performing an acrobatic-style leap off the bed as though Carlos's second rapping had somehow motored him.

Once he'd gone Joe stood looking at the open door for a moment, the humour fading from his eyes as the strain of what was happening began to crack his cheery mask.

Lucy took a breath. 'Before you say anything . . .'

'Listen,' he interrupted, putting up a hand. 'This is a big gamble you're taking with all our lives, but I understand why you're doing it, and for Hanna's sake I'm on your side. I just want you to know that I love you all and what's happening here is breaking my heart.'

Though she might have buckled under that sort of pressure once, she'd learned over the years how convincingly he could turn it on when he wanted to, and more often than not it would be in an attempt to make her feel even worse than she already did.

Unfortunately he was close to succeeding.

'If you decide you want to come with us,' she heard herself saying, 'well, that's fine by me.' *No it wasn't, it was the last thing she wanted. Why did she always have to be so damned weak?*

He cocked a sceptical eyebrow. 'Really?' he challenged.

Was she going to lie now and risk him accepting? Or was she going to tell him what in his heart he must surely already know, that she wasn't in love with him any more, and that she owed it to herself to stop the pretending so she could get on with her life? The trouble was, she still cared about him enough to hate hurting him, especially when he was looking at her the way he was now. So in the end she said, 'You know how hard Mum and Dad have worked to make the auctions what they are, so it's a measure of how much they trust us to be handing it all over like this.'

'Us?' he echoed.

As another stab of guilt deflated her, she said,

'You know they meant it for us both, but you haven't forgotten what happened last year when you came to help me run things while they were on holiday. Fortunately, no real damage was done, but it ended up costing us half of what we earned that week.' Feeling awful for reminding him of how close he'd come to causing an incident that would have mortified her parents had they ever found out about it, she tried to remove the sting by saying, 'You're a wonderful man in many ways, Joe, but you've said it yourself, you have no head for business. I'm not even sure I have,' she went on quickly, 'but at least I know I won't be talked into giving things away that aren't mine to give.'

'The way I saw it,' he reminded her, 'I was like a neighbourhood Robin Hood. The people in the big house didn't want their old wardrobe . . .'

'So they chose to put it up for auction,' she interrupted. 'It wasn't yours to give to the Barrett family who . . .'

'. . . happened to be in dire need of food, never mind furniture. And paying for the damn thing out of your own pocket was madness, but since you did the Bancrofts could at least have had the decency to donate it to charity.'

'Joe, what people do with their furniture or belongings isn't up to you. Anyway, we can't keep having this argument, what matters now is that I make a go of things, and having your support, even if it's only moral, is important.'

'It's OK, I've got the message. I just want to know what you're going to do about the Crumptons, because no way are they going to be happy about you taking over.'

Knowing how right he was about that, Lucy

sighed as she said, 'Mum's going to have a chat with them. I think she might offer Maureen a directorship, because even with all the temporary backup staff I won't be able to manage without her and Godfrey.'

'What about him? Doesn't he get a directorship too?'

Trying to put aside her dislike of the saleroom manager, as Godfrey Crumpton so grandly called himself, when he was actually more of a storekeeper-cum-driver, Lucy said, 'I don't know what she's decided about him,' *but if he shows any signs whatsoever of going anywhere near Hanna,* she was thinking to herself, *he'll be toast quicker than he can wink either of those disgustingly leery eyes.*

'They see themselves as the natural inheritors of the place, you know that, don't you?' Joe said tartly. 'They want full control.'

'What they want and what's going to happen are two different things. They can't just assume rights because they've helped Mum and Dad to build up the business. I'm their daughter, for heaven's sake, and they've never made a secret of the fact that they want me to take over. It was part of the reason they bought the place, so they'd have something to hand on – and to satisfy Mum's love of antiques, of course.'

Joe's smile wasn't pleasant. 'Antiques?' he repeated.

'All right, call it junk if you have to, the point is still the same. And I don't know why we're standing here discussing the bloody Crumptons when we've surely got better things to do right now.'

Sighing wearily, he dropped his hostility and came to wrap her in his arms. 'Whatever happens, I'm sure you'll do your parents proud,' he told her.

Touched by the kindness, she said, 'Thank you. I'm certainly going to try.'

He smiled wryly. 'So you'll be down there rattling around all on your own in that big old farmhouse, while I'm back here shacking up in Charlie's spare room . . .'

Knowing his tricks of old, Lucy pulled away. 'The farmhouse isn't that big,' she reminded him, 'and Hanna will be there, hopefully with lots of friends in and out all the time, and well, I suppose you'll be coming to stay.' Why had she said that? Because she had to, was the answer.

'In the same room as you?'

Though she froze inside, she heard herself say, 'Yes, of course . . . I mean . . .' She didn't want to get into how difficult she found it to make love with him these days, so she tried switching the subject by saying, 'I'm sure Hanna's going to end up loving it there. I'd have given anything to live in a place like that when I was growing up, all that space and a lovely village full of friendly people getting involved in all sorts of groups and activities.'

Cupping her face between his hands, he said, 'You know what, I reckon things are already on the up for us, because I'm seeing this agent on Tuesday. Apparently she's new to . . . Lucy, listen,' he said as she started to shake her head.

'Not now,' she broke in sadly. She'd lost count of how many new agents he'd seen over the years and how many dreams had turned to dust, and she really didn't want to hear it again. 'Carlos is downstairs,' she said, 'and even if he weren't, we can't go on talking ourselves round in circles . . .'

'All right, then tell me this, are you breaking us up so you can replace me with a younger or wealthier model? Is that what this is really all about? If it is, I'll probably have to kill him.'

'You know very well it isn't about that.'

He was gazing fiercely into her eyes, as though trying to force out the answers he wasn't hearing. 'And what do we do,' he demanded, 'if I meet someone who wants to comfort me in my loneliness?'

Though her heart tightened she knew that there was every chance he would, since he'd never seemed to think that the rules of fidelity applied to him. However, that really wasn't something she wanted to discuss right now, so all she said was, 'We should go down. Can I carry something for you?'

His eyes were still on her. 'It's OK, I can manage,' he said cuttingly.

She tried to make herself turn away, but it was hard when he was gripping her arms and she knew how much he was hurting beneath his tough veneer.

'You're going to take all the books and my record collection, right?' he asked.

'They'll be safe with me,' she assured him.

'Just don't go auctioning them off, or if you do make sure you get a good price.'

Her smile was weak. 'Come on,' she said, and pulling open the door she walked out on to the landing.

'Are you OK?' Ben asked, stopping halfway up the stairs. 'I was just coming to check on you.'

'We're fine,' Joe told him, hefting his bags out of the bedroom. 'I take it Carlos is still here?'

'Yes. He's on the phone.'

'Where's Hanna?' Lucy asked.

'In her room, I guess.'

Knocking on the door next to her own, Lucy said, 'Come on, sweetheart. Dad's going now.'

When there was no reply Joe said, 'Here, son, take these bags out to the car. I'll go and have a chat with my girl.'

'Just don't pull out any more of her hair,' Ben advised, 'she gets kind of weird about that.'

Slanting him a warning look, Joe handed over the holdalls and stood watching as Lucy followed Ben downstairs. At the bottom she turned to look up, but neither of them said anything. There really wasn't anything left to be said.

Ten minutes later Joe came into the cramped sitting room where Carlos, a small, wiry man in his early forties, was regaling Lucy with one of his theatrical anecdotes, which she'd heard at least a dozen times before. As always, she laughed politely at the punchline, then turned to Joe.

'Is she OK?' she asked.

He shook his head. 'Not really. She wants to know why I have to leave today when you're not going until the middle of the week.'

'So what did you tell her?'

He shrugged. 'It's the way things have panned out. I've promised to come back and help you pack, though, and I'll drive you down there on Wednesday if you like. Unless something works out with this new agent.'

'She's the business,' Carlos told Lucy. 'Everyone rates her.'

Lucy smiled. Theirs was such a bizarre and in many ways hopeless world, that she felt suddenly impatient to be free of it. 'I'll be fine to drive,' she assured Joe.

He nodded pensively, as though his mind had moved elsewhere. 'Right,' he said suddenly, 'I don't suppose there's any point in dragging this out. As of now I am no longer resident at number fifteen . . .' He broke off as Hanna banged noisily in through the door.

'I thought you might like to know,' she spat at Lucy, her creamy cheeks blotched red with anger, 'that I've already worked out how to kill myself, because frankly I'd rather die than go to Gloucestershire with you.'

'Hanna, Hanna,' Joe chided as Lucy paled, 'stop talking nonsense now. You know very well your mother has your best interests at heart, and . . .'

'No way is she thinking about me!' Hanna raged. 'She doesn't give a damn about anyone else . . .'

'Stop it, Hanna,' Lucy cut in sharply. 'If the only reason you've come down here is to make a scene then go back upstairs . . .'

'You can't order me around . . .'

'Any more cheek and you'll be grounded for the rest of the weekend.'

'Didn't you hear what I said? I'm going to kill myself, so who cares about being grounded.'

'Hanna, stop with the crap,' Ben interjected. 'No one's finding this easy, and you're just making everything worse.'

Clearly stricken at being told off by her brother, Hanna spun on her heel and stormed back up the stairs.

'I'll go after her,' Ben said. Then, hugging his father, 'It'll be all right, Dad. Everything'll work out, you'll see.'

'I know it will, son,' Joe assured him.

'Of course it will,' Carlos added. Apparently realising he might be surplus to requirements, he followed Ben out of the room and took himself off to the car.

Attempting a cheerful smile as he turned to Lucy, Joe said, 'Well, I suppose this is it then.'

Lucy's throat was too tight for her to do anything more than nod.

'You take it steady now,' he told her, 'and I meant what I said about coming to help with the packing.'

'I'm sure we'll be fine, but if we're not . . .'

He put a hand to his ear, mimicking a phone.

She nodded.

'I love you, Lucy Winters,' he whispered softly, and after pressing a kiss to her mouth, he stroked her face as he gazed into her eyes.

Moments later he was gone, and Lucy was standing at the window watching him getting into the car, wondering how, given her dread of goodbyes, she was allowing this to happen. She was waiting, bracing herself for the screaming to begin deep down inside, the terrible distant cries that made her want to hold on, no matter what. However, they didn't come, which surely must mean she was doing the right thing.

When the car reached the end of the street Joe didn't turn back, so he didn't see her wave. She guessed he probably hadn't noticed either how it had started to cloud over, nor would he know how long she continued to stand in the window staring at the emptiness he'd left behind, as though nothing in the world could ever fill it again.

Chapter Three

Sarah Bancroft was sitting at her father's desk in the bay window of their old manor house, gazing absently out across the village green and duck ponds towards the quaintly crooked high street of Cromstone Edge. With its several arty shops and cafes, old Norman church and straggling cobbled lanes that meandered out to the surrounding fields, the village had become a popular destination for tourists over the years, though mercifully only locals could drive through now. Even the two hundred or more residents of the new estate at the bottom of the hill had to be ferried up and down by a free bus. When the new traffic rules had first come into force the traders had been afraid of a negative effect on their businesses, but there had been no need to worry, since most of the villagers still bought their bread at Bob's Bakery and fruit and veg at Colin's in spite of a giant Morrisons being nearby. The tea shops were rarely empty either, even in winter, and the Drop Inn with its sloping gardens and views of the flowing hillsides continued to thrive. It was all helped, immeasurably, by the monthly auctions held at Cromstone Edge Barn, part of the farmhouse complex at the top end of the village, about a hundred yards along from the manor, across the road from the green.

The manor itself was a three-storey Georgian-fronted house with tall sash windows – apart from the two bays either side of the colonnaded porch that had been added by Sarah's grandfather in the fifties – and used to sit somewhat grandly over the village. Today it was a sadder, even shyer version of its former self, with bricks missing like broken teeth from the steps leading up to the porch, paint cracking and peeling from the window frames and a riot of brambles, ivy and some hardy roses struggling up over the walls. However, even in its neglected state it remained the only place where Sarah felt safe, and after the events of recent years she needed, above all, to feel safe.

Though she was an attractive woman of thirty-one, with large green eyes and soft fair hair that she generally clipped at the back of her neck, the haunted look in her eyes, combined with the dark shadows around them and the tightness of her pretty mouth, did little to enhance her looks. Since she'd given up vanity a while ago, she suspected her appearance was of more interest to others than it was to her; however, no one was ever unkind enough to say she was letting herself go. Once or twice, though, the vicar, or a passing tourist, had commented on what a shame it was to see the house falling into disrepair. In truth, she couldn't help but agree with them, especially as she knew better than anyone, having grown up here, what a dignified and welcoming place it used to be. And probably still would be were it not for the tragedy that had struck five years ago. After that the place had stood forlornly at the top of the hill with none of the family visiting at all, not even for Christmas or to check on mail that might have found its way in through the firmly locked door.

Then, fifteen months ago, needing refuge from a world that had turned on her again, Sarah had come to prise open the doors and peel away the cobwebs hanging from every cornice and lampshade. From the start she'd felt the house drawing her in, as though returning her to its heart where she'd always belonged, closing around her like a shell to protect her from any more of life's blows. It was only in recent months that she'd started to wonder if she'd done the right thing in coming, if it wouldn't have been more sensible, not to mention courageous, to have tried braving things out in Paris. However, the mere thought of even setting foot in the city now was enough to make her want to fold back in on herself and carry on hiding for ever.

The fact that she was still in love with her cheating b— of a husband after what he'd done was as depressing a truth as several others in her life, but self-pity had never been a state she cared to wallow in. Fury and vengeance were much more to her liking, and after a couple of glasses of vino she had no trouble mustering them, but as uplifting as devising her revenge could sometimes be, she didn't much fancy spending the next twenty-five years in a high-security wing. So, alas, her cunning little plots of disfigurement, dismemberment or something equally grim had to remain fantasy-bound. And as for her dreams of a reconciliation, well, she'd have had to be seriously delusional if she'd ever believed they'd come true. What a travesty that her heart should have an agenda totally unconnected to anything resembling good sense. Were it controlled by her quick, intelligent mind it wouldn't waste another twist of pain or lurch of longing on the philandering pig who'd impregnated another woman while still married to the woman he'd always claimed was the big love of his life.

Sarah supposed that his new wife, Margot, was now the incumbent of that dubious post. (With such a name the woman ought at least to have the decency to be fat and frumpy with a wart or two, but no, not this Margot. This one was all willowy gorgeousness and throaty French accent, with eyes that should be licensed, they were so brazenly seductive. Sarah liked to pronounce the t at the end of her name to make it rhyme with harlot.) Apparently she hadn't even bloated up much while pregnant, and now, according to friends in Paris, Marvellous Margot, design fashionista and supermum, was exquisitely back in shape, and back at work.

It was the baby that Sarah still found the hardest to bear. Not that she had anything against the little mite itself, how could she have when it was hardly his fault that he was the result of such a devastating betrayal? It was her suspicion that the pregnancy had been planned that really tore her apart. Kelvin had denied it, but there was no getting away from the fact that it had provided him with the perfect escape from a marriage that he'd claimed, at the end, he'd only stayed in out of pity and guilt. How insensitive, even cruel, he'd been during that time, not the man she'd known and loved at all. He'd turned into a stranger – a monster, even. How could he have treated her that way when he not only knew what she'd been through, but had been through it too?

She'd read since that many marriages broke up after the kind of tragedy she and Kelvin had suffered, but such cold information had brought no comfort all. She knew now that nothing ever would, not even time, because there was no understanding or accepting the reasons why Death would use such a sudden and violent hand to snatch their three-year-old son, Jack.

The same horrific car crash had taken her beloved father too, and Sarah sometimes wondered if it was the fact that her loss had been greater than Kelvin's that had turned him against her, as though there was some kind of competition that he could never win. Or maybe her inconsolable grief was too brutal and constant a reminder of the son he'd never see grow up. Perhaps on some level he even blamed her, since it was *her* father – not his – who'd been at the wheel of the car when it was crushed by a speeding lorry.

Since that terrible time, from which she now knew she would never completely recover – you didn't get over these things, you just learned to live with them – her mother, Rose, had shut up the house and gone to live quietly with her sister, Sheila, in France. Having always been emotionally fragile, for Rose to lose her husband and grandson in such a senseless and shocking way had proved too much for her to cope with. Though she spoke to Sarah on the phone every day, she almost never came back to England now. Her children, Simon, Becky and Sarah, had to travel to Provence to see her, which Simon and Sarah did quite regularly, while Becky made it as often as she could from New York.

With a sigh Sarah tried returning to her emails, but her concentration was poor again today, and feeling as edgy as she did she decided she might as well give up. Simon was the only one who'd worry if he didn't get a reply to his message right away, but she'd already let him know that she was still alive and kicking this morning, so she wasn't likely to receive a phone call in the next few minutes demanding to know what was wrong with her fingers that she couldn't type. Of all the people left in her world it was to Simon that Sarah felt the closest, possibly because they'd both been living in Paris for most of the past few years, so had seen a lot of each other. In any case, they'd always had a good relationship growing up, in spite of the five years between them, and him and Becky being twins. These days Simon, though a qualified lawyer, was running the European arm of an American multi-media company, which meant he was forever jetting back and forth across the Atlantic, allowing him far less time with his live-in partner, Giselle, than he'd have liked, and even less to visit Cromstone Edge. He'd promised to come soon, though, and Sarah knew that once he'd set the dates he wouldn't let her down, because Simon almost never did.

It was to Simon that she'd turned when Kelvin had told her about Margot and the baby, and typically of her brother he'd dropped everything to come and pick her up. By the following morning Becky was on a flight from New York and her mother was on her way up from Provence. Sarah still had no idea how she'd have made it through those first few weeks without her family to support her; she still wasn't entirely sure how she was managing without them now, yet somehow she seemed to be.

Closing her laptop she sat back in her chair and continued to gaze down at the village, where a few locals and half a dozen or so tourists were going about their day. A few minutes ago she'd spotted the couple who'd rented the Old Lodge on Greengables Lane going into the baker's. According to Milly Jameson, who owned the Quirky Shoppe, their name was Mckenzie and they'd taken the place for the full six months that Tom and Felicity Mercer were intending to spend in Canada with their eldest son and new grandchild. Though Sarah hadn't actually met the newcomers yet, she'd heard from Milly that they came from Scotland and spoke with a very charming burr. Apparently they'd retired about a year ago and had decided to test the southerly slopes of the Cotswolds to find out if it was an area that might suit them in their twilight years. Unusually for Milly she hadn't yet found out why Mrs Mckenzie wore a patch over her left eye, but Sarah didn't imagine it would be long before the redoubtable ex-postmistress managed to plug all the gaps.

What a very different sort of existence she was leading now to the one she'd been used to in Paris, with all its exotic soirées and dinners, fashion shows, movie premieres and the impossible deadlines of a job that had made her feel so alive. Who could say, she might even have made editor of the magazine had she stayed, but the blow of finding out that Kelvin had made another woman pregnant only three years after they'd lost Jack, then being told that the baby was a boy, had been so devastating that she'd had to get as far away from the betrayal as she possibly could. The awful irony of it was that she and Kelvin had moved to Paris in order to try and put their lives back together after the bereavement. They'd even been talking about trying for another baby when Kelvin had broken the news that he was going to have one with somebody else.

Spotting Mrs Fisher coming out of Bob's Bakery, Sarah jumped to her feet and ran outside. Since Mrs Fisher was heading her way she took the footpath across the green to wait for her to come up the hill, allowing the pleasure of sleepy birdsong and the glorious warmth of the day to wash over her. Why did even the beautiful things hurt, she thought sadly.

Feeling herself starting to knot up with angst about her mission, she wondered if this sudden impulse to consult Mrs Fisher should be put back on hold until she'd given it more consideration. That was laughable, since she and her mother had talked about little else during the last couple of weeks, and whether Sarah liked what she was about to do or not, she knew very well that she had to go through with it.

'Do you have a minute?' Sarah called out as Mrs Fisher turned towards the farmhouse. 'There's something I'd like to ask you.'

Though the diminutive owner of Cromstone Auctions with her loose linen clothes and blunt-cut hair was by nature quite shy, she was absolutely never rude, so it startled Sarah no end to be told in a brisker tone than she'd ever heard Mrs Fisher use before, 'I can't stop now.'

Thrown, Sarah watched her march on with her head down and one arm pounding the pace while the other flitted about like a broken wing. What on earth could have happened to upset her, Sarah wondered. Though she couldn't claim to know Mrs Fisher well, since she and her husband hadn't moved to the village until just after the manor had been shut up, she liked the woman and so felt tempted to go after her to find out if there was anything she could do. Moreover, having her impulse quashed so unexpectedly was suddenly making her doubly eager to go through with her plans.

To her surprise Mrs Fisher suddenly turned back. 'I'm very sorry if I was abrupt, dear,' she said, looking so agitated that Sarah could only wonder why she'd stopped. 'Is there something I can help you with?'

Sarah wasn't sure what to say, since now clearly wasn't a good time. 'Uh, it's OK,' she managed. 'We can talk another . . . Are you all right? You look a little . . .'

'I'm fine, dear, thank you.' She attempted a smile.

48

When she made no move to walk on Sarah peered a little more closely into her face. 'Would you like a cup of tea or something?' she offered. 'I was about to make one, or we could go down to the deli.'

Mrs Fisher shook her head. 'No, no. No. No thank you,' she said.

Sarah smiled. 'I guess that was a no.'

Mrs Fisher looked at her blankly. Then evidently realising she should respond with some humour she made another attempt at a smile, and seemed undecided about whether or not to walk on.

Bewildered, but sensing it wouldn't be right simply to back away, Sarah tried another tack, saying, 'What news on Lucy? Is she still coming this week?'

Mrs Fisher's head jerked up. 'Yes,' she said. 'Yes, she's coming tomorrow, with Hanna.'

Sarah said, 'That's good. I've been looking forward to seeing her. I mean, I don't know her very well, but . . . I expect she's quite excited about taking over, isn't she?'

Mrs Fisher seemed lost for words.

'Maybe,' Sarah said awkwardly, 'I should give her a few days to settle in, then come and have a chat with her about some things I'd like to sell.' She might even try talking to Lucy about a part-time job, anything to help get her out of the house, but she'd decide that at the time.

'Yes, of course. My dear, I'm sorry, but I do need to get home.'

'Of course. Is everything OK with Mr Fisher? I haven't seen him for a few days and . . .'

'Yes, he's . . . We've been very busy. Lucy's coming tomorrow with Hanna, so we're . . .' She frowned. 'I think I already told you that, didn't I?'

Sarah nodded. 'Is Joe coming too?'

'No, he's staying in London. His work keeps him there, you know.'

'Of course.' Sarah's tone was warm and understanding. She wouldn't want Mrs Fisher to know what she really thought of Joe Winters – that he drank too much, and wasn't anywhere near good enough for someone as lovely as Lucy, especially after the fling he'd had with Annie the mobile hairdresser when he and Lucy had come to provide holiday relief for her parents last year. This crime, in Sarah's book, damned him straight to hell, and the fact that he'd taken it upon himself to make a gift of her Victorian ash wardrobe to a well-known benefit-fraud family in Dursley, instead of putting it into the auction, had done nothing at all to redeem him.

'It's good to see you, dear,' Mrs Fisher said, grabbing Sarah's hand and patting it. 'Thank you. Very kind of you,' and leaving Sarah wondering what on earth there was to thank her for, she carried on up the path towards the five-bar gate that opened into the farmhouse drive.

Down at the Old Lodge, at the lower end of the village, John and Philippa Mckenzie were in the spacious pale green kitchen of their rented house unpacking the purchases they'd made in the local shops. A large bottle of Tuscan olive oil and tasty slab of Reggiano Parmesan from the Cheese and Olive deli; a freshly baked wholemeal loaf from Bob's Bakery together with a couple of scrumptious-looking flapjacks to enjoy with a cup of Earl Grey tea; and a colourful selection of salad veg from Colin's locally grown produce. Philippa had also picked up some scented candles and assorted aromatherapy oils from Milly's

Quirky Shoppe, while John had treated himself to one of Milly's prized hand-carved walking sticks in preparation for the Cotswold rambles they had planned for while they were there. A stop at the second-hand bookshop had produced an Ordnance Survey map of the area, along with several leaflets promoting the summer fete at the end of August and various other local events not to be missed.

'Did you realise that the woman we met at the baker's runs the local auction room?' Philippa remarked, as she inhaled the fresh scent of ocean spray from one of the candles.

John's distracted murmur showed that he was far more interested in the brochure they'd picked up from the gun store than he was in their new neighbour. 'You surely can't just walk into that shop and buy a rifle,' he commented darkly as he flicked over the pages. 'You must need a licence.'

'Of course you do,' Philippa replied, adjusting the crinkled mauve patch covering the space that used to contain her left eye. 'And if you're harbouring thoughts of equipping yourself with any sort of firearm at all then you can put them out of your head right now. We don't go in for blood sports in this family, as you well know.'

John's answering smile was sardonic. A tall, good-looking man with an unruly mop of snow-white hair that contrasted starkly with his olive complexion and cobalt-blue eyes, he had a natural magnetism about him that made many people warm to him on sight. Apparently not the woman at the baker's. 'What did she say her name was?' he asked.

'Something Fisher. Daphne, I think. I wonder if we said something to make her rush off like that? She didn't even buy any bread.'

'If she takes flight at "pleased to meet you" then I'd say she's got a problem,' he replied, tossing the brochure on the table. 'But her phone rang, didn't it? That'll be what made her abandon her mission. Anyway, everyone else seems friendly enough around here. Are you glad we came?'

As Philippa looked up from the candles, her good eye was showing a warning. Catching her gaze he gave her a playful wink and carried on with what he was doing.

With a small sigh of almost motherly despair Philippa went to take two mugs from a rack in the windowsill. From this point in the kitchen there was a pleasing view across the sloping back lawn to the hedgerows beyond, where the previous owners had installed a fence to provide added protection for their dog from the road outside. Ever since their retirement John had been all for getting a dog too, a Labrador or a Border collie seemed to be his favourites, whereas Philippa would have preferred a rescue dog. Knowing him as well as she did, she suspected she'd end up getting her way, and she didn't have to worry about the fact that she might not be around for much longer to take care of it, because whichever dog they decided on, she knew without a shadow of doubt that John would love it.

However, they needed to settle into their temporary home first, and with so many boxes still to unpack and a full orientation of their surroundings to be undertaken, she didn't imagine the pet hunt would rise to the top of the priority list for a good few weeks yet.

'It was a pity Mrs Fisher had to run off,' Philippa chatted on as she dug out some plates for the flapjacks. 'We could have talked to her about the furniture the Mercers left in the garage for her to pick up. Never mind, we'll pop up there later in the week. I'll be interested to see what sort of things they have for sale.'

Chapter Four

'Mum? *Mum!* What are you doing? Why are the curtains pulled?'

As Hanna snapped on the light Lucy quickly wiped away her tears and swung her legs over the edge of the bed. 'I've just got a bit of a headache,' she replied.

'Oh my God, you've been crying,' Hanna accused. 'And now you're going to blame me . . .'

'Sssh, I'm fine,' Lucy murmured as Hanna sank angrily on to the bed.

'I didn't mean what I said, OK?' Hanna told her hotly. 'You don't have to take everything so seriously all the time. I was just angry and you know how I get when you don't listen to me.'

Lucy's eyebrows arched. 'My darling, you're far too loud not to be listened to,' she teased her.

Though Hanna was known to have had a good sense of humour, today it was nowhere in evidence as tears started in her eyes.

'Come here,' Lucy said, reaching for her.

'You don't want to go either, really, do you?' Hanna sobbed into her shoulder.

Feeling for her despair, Lucy said softly, 'Yes I do . . .'

'Then why are you crying? I mean, I know I said

some horrible things just now, but I always do and they've never made you cry before.'

'Maybe not, but don't think they're not hurtful and you should . . .'

'So it *is* my fault . . .'

'No, no!' Lucy insisted, catching her back in her arms. 'This might come as a surprise to you, but not everything's about you, Hanna Winters.'

Hanna's voice was muffled by Lucy's collar as she said, 'That can't be true.'

Laughing, Lucy pressed a kiss to her forehead and pulled her in closer.

This was their last day in London, and though Lucy's resolve hadn't faltered, the strain of Hanna's outbursts, combined with the anxiety about all she was taking on, not to mention the sheer physical effort of packing, shopping, cooking and generally keeping their lives on track as they prepared for the move, had got the better of her just now. Maybe it wouldn't have reduced her to tears if Joe had kept his promise and shown up to lend a hand, but he hadn't and with no one to help deal with Hanna, or the relentless ebb and flow of his family and friends, she'd come upstairs for a quiet moment's respite to prevent herself doing the unthinkable – leaning on Ben. He was under enough pressure with his own imminent departure, and if she were a better mother she'd be in his room now helping him to pack his bags, instead of lying here dreading the prospect of him leaving almost as much as she was afraid of failing on all fronts – i.e., mother, daughter, businesswoman, and, she supposed she probably shouldn't forget, wife.

In spite of her moments of weakness, she knew she'd never let her parents down now. Apart from the pleasure it was giving them to be able to pass on the business, everything was already too far down the road to start turning back. All their regular customers and suppliers, not to mention the staff, accountants, lawyer, tax office, bank, local authority, even the *Cromstone Parish News*, had been informed that Brian and Daphne Fisher's daughter would be taking over the auctions from the beginning of August. The Fishers had already moved half their possessions down to their beloved old cottage on Exmoor where Lucy had spent so many wretchedly lonely holidays as a child. (She'd never told them that because it would hurt their feelings terribly, but if she never had to go there again she wouldn't mind one bit.)

Her parents had given her so much and worked so hard over the years that they deserved to start taking things easy now, particularly with her father well into his seventies. He was tired, Lucy could tell, and he didn't always seem as alert as he used to be, which was even more worrying with them going to live so remotely. Still, she'd have to shelve the problem of their location for now, because it was definitely the right time for him, and her mother, to start letting go of the reins. And it wasn't as if she'd never run the place before, so she at least had some idea of what she was doing, though she couldn't deny she'd never be able to manage without the Crumptons. So please God her mother had spoken to them by now, and they were happy about the way things were going to proceed. With a horrible sinking feeling she realised that if she believed that then she'd believe Joe was really going to get the part he was now auditioning for in Scotland.

'But we're leaving tomorrow,' she'd protested when

he'd called last night, from the airport, euphoric that his new agent already had him booked on a flight to Glasgow.

'I'm sorry, sweetheart,' he groaned, 'but I have to go for this. They've got a real buzzy scene going on up there, so it could easily lead on to something big.'

'Joe, your son's flying halfway round the world in the morning and Hanna and I . . . I thought you were going to help with the last-minute packing.'

'I swear to God I want to be there, but I can't let this agent down now, she's only just agreed to take me on.'

'How long are you going to be there?'

'No more than a couple of nights. I have to hang around in case I get a call back. I'll be there longer, obviously, if I get the part.'

'So where are you going to stay?'

'Not a problem. Oscar's offered to put me up at his place.'

'Who's Oscar?'

'A good mate. I worked with him a few years ago, last time I was in Glasgow as a matter of fact. Anyway, you know how much you hate goodbyes, so this way you can get in the car and motor off to Gloucestershire without having to think of me standing on the side of the road feeling abandoned.'

Lucy's hackles rose. To try turning her little phobia into a positive reason for why he shouldn't be here now, when his son was about to leave for six months, and when she could really do with his support, physically if nothing else, was taking artifice to a degree she didn't like one bit. However, that was Joe all over, never lost for a slippery route out of a guilty conscience, so what was the point in arguing, especially when he was already on his way north?

'I know he's my cousin and everything,' Stephie had stated when she'd dropped in later to find Lucy in a foul mood, 'but sometimes I have to wonder if you might not be better off without him.'

Though she didn't disagree, all Lucy said was, 'It's OK, I've had a vent now, so let's not start tearing him apart.'

Undeterred, Stephie said, 'What about the trial separation? Is it still a part of the deal?' Her hungry eyes were showing how torn she was between wanting Lucy to find out what it was like to be single, and hoping that her cousin's marriage would find its way back on track.

'As far as I'm concerned it is,' Lucy replied, 'but it's not easy to tell how Joe's viewing it from in the sand, which is where his head is stuck. Your mother was here earlier and apparently he told her that we just need a bit of time to figure out how we're going to make things work, with me being in the Cotswolds and him in London.'

Though Stephie had looked tactlessly doubtful about the chances of that working out, to Lucy's relief she'd promptly dropped the subject and launched into the intimate details of her second date with the security guard, who'd ended up staying the night, but then he hadn't called again since so did Lucy think she should call him?

No, Lucy didn't, but it wasn't what Stephie wanted to hear, so she'd had to sit through all the reasons why Stephie felt she should pick up the phone, or send a text, or maybe even a card to say thanks for a great evening.

Coming back to the present as Hanna entwined

their fingers, Lucy rested her head on her daughter's as Hanna said, 'I know why you were crying. It's because of Ben, isn't it?' Her voice began to quiver with tears. 'I don't want him to go either,' she said. 'Everything's changing and it's all horrible and Dad's not here which is the worst. Why does Ben have to go now?'

Why now? Why ever? Lucy was asking herself. 'You know he's had this trip planned for a long time . . .'

'Yeah, but it can be dangerous in Thailand with all those Red Shirts . . .'

'Please don't remind me of that.'

'You should stop him from going.'

'At eighteen he gets to make his own decisions,' Lucy reminded her.

'You're going to seriously regret it if something happens to him.'

Lucy said, more sharply than she'd intended, 'Nothing's going to happen to him. He'll be fine. He knows how to take care of himself and he's not reckless or stupid.'

'It doesn't have to be him who does something stupid. Someone might attack him, or steal all his stuff, or plant drugs on him . . .'

'Hanna, please don't do this. I'm working very hard to convince myself that he's going to be safe, and you're really not helping.'

'I'm just saying, that's all. God, you always have to have a go at me. I know he's your favourite and I just get on your nerves . . .'

Gathering her up tightly as she started to cry again, Lucy said, 'That is utter nonsense and you know it. I love you equally . . .'

'No, you don't.'

'Yes, I do. OK, we have our ups and downs, you

and me, but that's normal between a mother and daughter, especially when girls get to your age. I know I used to give Granny a pretty hard time when I was fifteen, so I guess I'm getting a taste of my own medicine now.'

Hanna looked interested. 'Were you really bad?' she said hopefully.

Lucy grimaced, though she wasn't prepared to concoct something awful in case it gave Hanna ideas. 'I sometimes wonder how poor Granny ever managed to put up with me,' she fudged, 'especially when she's so sweet and mild-tempered and never says anything to hurt anyone. It must have been pretty difficult for her when I was going through adolescence, but we've both survived. And you and I will too.'

Hanna was still locked into the idea of her mother as a rebel. 'Were you worse than me?' she asked.

Lucy tilted her head as she gave it some thought. 'No, no one's that bad,' she decided.

Realising she was being teased, Hanna smiled. 'I'm quite a lot like you, really, aren't I?' she said, seeming, to Lucy's surprise, not wholly appalled by the idea. 'We both have fiery tempers and end up saying things we shouldn't. Well, I do, anyway, especially to you. Ben's more like Dad. And like Granny, because he's all cool and laid-back, nothing ever seems to get to him. I wish he wasn't going, Mum,' she said, starting to cry again. 'I really, really love him and it's going to be horrible not having him or Dad around. Or my friends, or anyone who matters.'

'I know, sweetheart, but you won't let Granny or Grandpa hear you say that, will you, because I think they'd like to feel that they matter.'

'Of course they do, and so do you, but they're

going to be in Exmoor soon, and anyway, you know what I'm saying.'

Smiling, and pulling her into a deeper cuddle, Lucy sat gazing at the wall, tracing the cracks she'd come to know so well, while trying to stop her mind conjuring all the disasters and perils Ben might meet on his travels. She had to give this up, or getting through each day was going to become as difficult as trying to deal with the nightmares by night. It was yet another reason, and perhaps the most important, why she was glad to have the challenge of taking over the auctions. With any luck she'd be too busy to keep falling victim to her demons, particularly those where her children were concerned.

'What time's Ben coming back?' Hanna asked.

Surprised, Lucy said, 'I didn't know he'd gone out. Did he say where he was going?'

'He was just taking some stuff over to Ali's so it would be there in the morning.'

'Of course,' Lucy murmured, and feeling endlessly thankful that Ben's travelling partner was from such a respectable family, she almost relaxed. She wondered how Mr and Mrs Patel were feeling today, along the road in their newspaper shop. Probably as fearful as she was, particularly with Ali being their only child. She'd no doubt find out later when they all got together for the boys' farewell dinner.

'Do you think Dad'll ring tonight?' Hanna yawned.

'I'm sure he will.'

'Aren't you worried that he might forget about us, if we're not here any more? I know I would be, if I were you.'

'Oh Hanna, Hanna, Hanna . . .'

'Don't do that,' Hanna protested angrily. 'I hate

my name anyway and when you say it like that it really bugs me.'

Closing her eyes, Lucy said, 'It's a very pretty name.'

'Ugh! It's revolting. I don't know why you had to give me it. I bet it was you, wasn't it?'

'Actually, it was Dad's choice,' Lucy told her. 'If I'd had my way you'd be Rebecca.'

Hanna looked horrified. 'That's even worse,' she declared.

Lucy smiled. 'Well, I like it. Actually, according to Granny I used to have an imaginary friend called Rebecca.'

Hanna's horror was compounded. 'You are so weird,' she informed her.

Lucy's eyebrows arched.

Hanna's eyes narrowed suspiciously. 'So, what, like you used to pretend someone was there when they weren't?' she said. 'Did you talk to them and everything?'

'I suppose so. I don't really remember.'

'It's because you were an only child, isn't it?'

'Possibly, except that wouldn't explain why you had one too.'

Hanna's eyes nearly popped out. 'No way am I a raving loony,' she declared with certainty.

'I'm trying to think what you called her,' Lucy continued. 'Penny! That's it. She had to come every-where with us. We even had to feed her and buy her clothes. Dad used to give her rides on his back and I'd help you to wash her hair and tuck her up in bed.'

Hanna's expression was incredulous. 'You're winding me up,' she accused.

Lucy shook her head. 'You wouldn't be parted

62

from her for ages, then one day she suddenly wasn't there any more.'

Hanna nodded. 'That must have been the day I got a life.'

Laughing, Lucy started to get up from the bed.

'You were kidding, weren't you?' Hanna insisted.

'If you say so,' Lucy replied, pulling a brush through her hair. 'Is Sadie coming with us tonight?' When there was no reply she turned back to find Hanna's eyes full of tears again.

'She's my best friend,' Hanna wailed, 'and she's dreading me going nearly as much as I am. I think it's really mean of you to take me away. I so don't deserve it.'

'I'm not doing it to punish you,' Lucy reminded her, though in truth she could hardly wait to get Hanna away from the girl whose parents were known to be on drugs, and who had already earned herself a seriously unpleasant reputation. 'What time did you tell her to come over?'

'Six o'clock. We're going to hang out in my bedroom before we go.'

Probably texting boys or plotting how to shoplift from New Look, Lucy suspected with growing apprehension.

After Hanna had gone to run a bath Lucy began pulling out drawers and opening cupboards to make sure nothing was left inside. Since she'd performed this task half an hour ago she wasn't quite sure why she was doing it again. It wasn't as if something might have magically appeared in the last few minutes, or worked its way out of the cracks. Still, there was no harm in double-checking, or in feeling thankful for the first time in her married life that she and Joe had no furniture of any particular worth.

All those years of poring through magazines and browsing shops imagining how wonderful it would be to own a sumptuous Italian three-piece, or a huge wrought-iron bedstead, or some exquisite Eastern chests, or a dining table with no scratches and matching chairs . . . Dreams that had never come true, nor would they now, at least not here, but the good part was that it meant she didn't have to worry about moving any of what they did have to Cromstone – or getting rid of it at the dump, because the landlord had given them a hundred pounds to leave it in place. So, all she had to do now was load up the car with their personal belongings, hand back the keys and go.

As easy as that.

Except it wouldn't be, of course, because nothing ever was. For a start there wasn't enough room in the car for a couple of backpacks and two teenage boys, so she couldn't take Ben and Ali to the airport tomorrow. Charlie had offered, but then had taken off for Tenerife, and Vince would have done it if his minicab wasn't in the shop. So Ali's uncle was going to drive them. She and Hanna couldn't even go to the airport to say goodbye, since it would have meant leaving the car with all their worldly goods in a parking lot that had notices all over it warning people not to leave valuables in their vehicles. So she'd have to say goodbye to her son tonight, and the mere thought of it was already stirring up such an awful panic inside her that she was finding it hard to breathe.

'Shall I get that?' Hanna offered as she came back into the bedroom.

Realising the phone was ringing Lucy waved her on, and plonked down on a suitcase in an effort to squash it shut.

'Hello?' Hanna said. 'Oh, hey Granny. How are you?'

Pleased by the angelic front Hanna usually put on for her grandparents, and loving her for considering them worthy of it, Lucy bounced on the lid again and only became aware of how baffled Hanna was sounding when she heard her say, 'So when was the last time you saw him?'

'Saw who?' Lucy asked, using the bedpost to pull herself up.

'Grandpa,' Hanna mouthed. Then into the phone, 'Did he say where he was going?'

'Let me speak to her,' Lucy said, coming to take the phone as a new wave of foreboding washed over her. 'Mum? Is everything OK?'

'I think so,' her mother replied. 'I was just wondering if Dad had called you at all today, but Hanna says he hasn't.'

'No, but why are you asking?'

'Oh, no reason. Well, he went out in the car earlier and he hasn't come back yet.'

'What time did he leave?'

'About ten thirty this morning.'

Lucy reeled. 'Mum, that's over six hours ago. You have to call the police and local hospitals to make sure nothing's happened to him.'

'But if it had someone's sure to have been in touch with me by now.'

'You don't know that for certain. Would you like me to make the calls?'

'No, no. You've got enough on your plate, and I'm sure he'll walk in the door any minute. I just wanted to find out if he'd been in touch with you. I'll ring again as soon as I have some news.'

Before she could hang up, Lucy said, 'Mum, I know

you don't like talking about this, but we both know he's become quite forgetful lately . . .'

'Just a moment, dear, my mobile's ringing, it might be him.' A few minutes later her mother came back on the line sounding years younger with relief as she said, 'Yes it was and everything's fine. Silly me, getting all worked up. There's . . .'

'So where is he?'

'. . . nothing to worry about. I'd better ring off now. I'm sorry to have bothered you.'

'It's OK, but Mum, you have to start facing the fact that he might need some tests.'

With a sigh her mother said, 'One thing at a time, Lucy. Let's get him home first, then we can start discussing what, if anything, needs to be done.'

By the time they all left Frankie and Benny's that night Lucy seemed to have lost contact with what she was saying, or even thinking. She was merely aware, as they started towards home in a straggling group, of being thankful that her brothers- and sisters-in-law weren't suggesting coming back for another couple of bottles, the way they usually did when Joe was around – and that her father-in-law had managed not to upset any of the waiters with one of his choicer racist remarks. At least, she hoped he hadn't, but since she hadn't heard it if he had, she was happy to tell herself that for once he'd kept his revolting BNP views to himself. The only awkward moment she could recall was when Hanna had accused her of not engaging with her own family because she already considered herself too good for them. The silence that followed had made her realise that all the rough diamonds and hearts of gold sitting around the table were thinking the same way, and though they were wrong, she knew she wasn't as sorry to be saying goodbye to them as she probably ought to have been.

Ben had been unusually quiet during the meal too, and knowing him so well Lucy guessed it wasn't only nerves about his upcoming trip that were bothering him, he'd be worried about her too. He wouldn't have had to be told how hard she was finding it to face their imminent parting, he was perfectly aware of her phobia, so he was no doubt dreading the kind of scene she might create when it came time to let go. Hopefully, it wouldn't be anywhere near as mortifying as the day she'd sent him off on his first camping trip, aged eight, when she'd started banging frantically on the bus doors as they closed, begging the driver to open them again. Even she had been aware of the overreaction, but there had been nothing she could do to stop herself because she simply couldn't bear the thought of him being transported away.

In the end Joe had managed to prise her away so the bus could set off, but the next thing they knew she was running down the road after it shouting to the teachers to bring her little boy back.

How much teasing Ben had suffered as a result of her hysteria she still didn't know because he wouldn't talk about it when he came home, and Joe's only comment was that he'd always known she was off her head so this just went to prove it.

'Why do you think I get like it?' she'd asked her mother after it happened again when Hanna, aged seven, went for her first sleepover with a friend in Gidea Park. It hadn't been quite so bad on that occasion since she'd known exactly where Hanna was going and what time she'd be back in the morning, but even so, the terrible panic that came over her as Hanna waved from the back seat of her friend's mother's car had set off the silent screaming deep down inside her. She hadn't been able to sleep at all that night, or leave the window until Hanna came home. 'Did something happen in the past that I've blanked out now?' she ventured. 'I mean, it's not normal, is it, to get the way I do?'

Daphne had taken her hands between her own and held them tightly. 'Nothing bad's ever happened to you, Lucy,' she replied earnestly. 'You know Dad and I would never let it.'

But it had, because her father had once rescued her from a fire when a faulty main had leaked gas into their house and exploded. It was a miracle, she'd often been told, that she had survived the fire at all, never mind with so few burns, but that was all thanks to her father's quick thinking in wrapping her in a huge duvet to carry her out. Anyway, it hardly seemed to have a connection to her dread of goodbyes, so there hadn't been any point in bringing it up while trying to dig some sort of forgotten trauma from her mother's mind.

'But I did get lost once, in John Lewis,' she pointed out. 'I was about six, I think, and I remember how scared you were – and cross with me that I'd wandered off. Do you think it might stem from that?'

'I suppose it's possible,' Daphne concurred with a frown. 'There's never any knowing how a child's brain might process events, but you were only missing for a few minutes ... Anyway, what's important is that you try not to frighten the children with this dread of yours, or they'll become afraid to do things without you.'

Her mother was right, of course, and since the

last thing Lucy wanted was her children to feel tied to her out of fear, from then on whenever a school trip, or any kind of stay away from home came up, she let Joe take them to the bus, or the train, or the car outside, while she stood in the kitchen trying desperately to overcome the panic.

Now, after a protracted parting from the in-laws, who were clearly taking Ben's departure in their stride, they turned the corner to walk towards Ali's parents' shop where Ben was spending the night in the flat upstairs, ready for their early morning start. Lucy could sense his tension growing and was trying hard to come up with a way to put his mind at rest, but with no Joe there to help her she was becoming more enmeshed in her irrational fear than ever.

'Mum,' Ben said, taking her arm and letting the others walk on.

As she turned to look at him she tried to smile away the concern in his eyes.

'It's going to be all right,' he told her softly.

'I know, I know,' she replied, the words barely making it past the tightness in her throat. 'I'm – I'm not going to do anything stupid, I promise.'

He crooked a smile and chucked her under the chin. 'Dad should be here,' he said quietly, keeping his eyes on hers.

Though it was rare for him to criticise his father, and she certainly never encouraged it, he was right, Joe really ought to be with them tonight.

'Oh no, you're shaking,' Ben said miserably.

Lucy produced a rough sort of laugh. 'I'll be fine once it's over,' she assured him. 'Promise.'

'You have to be strong for Hanna,' he reminded her.

'Of course.'

Still looking anxious, he tightened his hand on her arm and started to walk on. 'One hug when we get there, OK?' he said. 'Then you have to go.'

Lucy's nod was more a jerk of her head. She'd stopped envisaging a plane crash now, or a fatal plunge into a canyon, or a murdering beggar with a dagger. She wasn't imagining anything at all, and yet she was still perspiring profusely and shaking hard enough to make herself sick.

'You didn't get like this when Dad went on Saturday,' Ben pointed out.

Taking a breath she said, 'I know, but he's a grown-up, he can take care of himself.'

'So can I, now.'

'You can,' she agreed, trying to mean it, 'but I'm your mother, so it's my job to worry.' How was she managing to sound calm when inside she was in such turmoil? *Please God keep him safe. Don't let anything bad happen to him.* They were almost outside the shop now. She wanted to stop the world and beg Ben to change his mind. Why couldn't he stay here where she knew he was safe and could take care of things if anything went wrong? What if he got lost in some godforsaken part of the planet and she never found him again? She could feel the fear burning like flames inside her and she couldn't bear it.

'You can do this,' he murmured in her ear as they reached the gate to the shop's backyard. 'You're going to be fine.'

She took a gulp of air and closed her eyes. 'Of course I am,' she assured him, and turned into his arms as he wrapped them around her.

'Oh God, please don't let her start going off on

70

one,' Hanna muttered. 'She is sooo embarrassing when she does.'

'You wait till you're a mother,' Lucy gasped, still clinging to Ben.

'I promise, I'll be nothing like you,' Hanna told her.

Lucy felt Ben starting to laugh, and somehow managed to find a smile of her own. 'I'll call when I get home to say goodnight,' she whispered.

'If you must,' he whispered back.

'Mum, your phone's ringing,' Hanna informed her, and digging into the back pocket of Lucy's jeans she produced the mobile. 'It's Dad.'

'Great timing,' Ben murmured.

Aware of how badly her hands were still shaking, Lucy let Hanna click on the line, then took the phone saying, 'Hi. How did you know to ring now?'

'A little birdie told me,' he replied.

Lucy's eyes went to Hanna. She must have texted him as they left the restaurant.

'She thought you could do with a bit of moral support,' Joe said, 'and I expect she's right. How are you doing? It's not too bad is it?'

'It's not great.'

'Where are you now?'

'Outside Ali's. They're about to go in.'

'Then put him on and let me have the last word for now while you get yourself off home.'

'You have to be joking! I need to say a proper goodbye . . .'

'Lucy, you don't know how to do such a thing where your children are concerned, so off you trot, there's a good girl.'

Lucy looked at Ben and felt as though she was moving on to some distant, other plain where she

71

could no longer reach him. She was so afraid, she didn't know what to do. She could hear the woman who screamed in her nightmares starting to scream again. It was her mother, she was sure of it, or perhaps it was her. She was banging on doors that refused to open, the world was moving so fast it was becoming a blur and she was being left behind.

'Mum, come on,' Hanna urged, slipping an arm around her. 'You can't show Ben up in front of our friends. I won't let you.'

In her ear, Joe said, 'Lucy, go with Hanna.'

Lucy was still looking at Ben. She wanted to put her hands around his face and never let go. If she could she'd push him right back inside her womb. *Please God don't let this be the last time I see him,* she was begging inside. *Don't take him away from me. I won't be able to go on without him.*

'Let me speak to Dad,' Ben said, and taking the phone he turned towards the gate.

'Let's go now,' Hanna whispered, tightening her arm round Lucy. 'I'll come back later for the phone.'

Lucy's mind was still spinning. She could hear the roar of an engine, the slamming of doors, a voice shouting, but she couldn't make any sense of it.

'What?' Hanna asked.

Lucy looked at her and shook her head. Then, registering what Hanna had just said, she told her, 'You can't go out on your own at night.'

'Duh,' Hanna said, rolling her eyes.

'I'll wait here till you turn the corner,' Ben told her, handing back the phone.

Taking it, Lucy looked into his handsome young face. Wave after wave of dread was coming over her.

'Come on,' Hanna said.

'Go,' Ben whispered.

Lucy wanted to, but she couldn't.

'Mum!' Hanna cried.

Mummy! Mummy! A child's voice was echoing through her head. She clapped her hands over her face.

The next thing she knew Ben had an arm around her and was walking her down the street. 'I'm going to stay at home tonight,' he told her, 'and leave early in the morning.'

Lucy nodded. Though she guessed he was angry and embarrassed, she simply didn't have it in her to tell him to go back. Nor could she assure him that it would be any easier tomorrow, because she already knew that it wouldn't.

Chapter Five

'Simon, hi, it's me,' Sarah said into her brother's voicemail. 'Call me back when you can.'

After ringing off she checked the clock, and calculating that it was nine in the morning New York time she dialled her sister's number next. 'Hi Becks, please don't tell me I've got you up.'

'Are you kidding?' Becky laughed. 'I've already done the gym and now I'm about to head off to a meeting. Is everything OK?'

'Yes, yes, everything's cool.'

'Oh, hang on, let me get rid of whoever this is. Don't go away.'

Wondering exactly where her sister thought she might go, Sarah wandered over to the back door of the manor to gaze out across the cracked stone terracing with its jaunty weeds and crumbling walls, down over the billowing acres of gardens that rose and dipped in a mass of overgrown pathways, bedraggled flower beds and dried-up lawns. At the furthest point, where a dense hedgerow separated their land from Farmer Hardy's, was a rocky, meandering brook that had never been visible from the house, unlike the view of the magnificent bridges spanning the Severn Estuary, which flowed and glinted like a silvery ribbon out to the far horizon.

Even in its neglected state Sarah loved the garden, mainly for all the happy memories it evoked. Their old tyre swing was still hanging from the horse chestnut where their father had tied it over thirty years ago, and parts of the slide he'd built were nestled in amongst the undergrowth close to one of the rusting pergolas. It wasn't difficult to envisage him standing at the bottom, eyes twinkling, hands outstretched ready to catch them as they flew towards him, when he'd scoop them up and spin them round and round in gleeful triumph.

Would she ever stop missing him? Would the emptiness he and her son had left behind ever go away? Knowing what a special relationship they'd shared was sometimes a comfort, because she could think of them being together, but it didn't always work, because more than anything she wanted them back.

'OK, so to what do I owe this pleasure?' Becky demanded, coming back on the line. 'Where are you, by the way? And please don't tell me still in Cromstone.'

Sarah braced herself. 'I could lie,' she suggested.

'Oh Sarah . . .'

'Becky, don't.'

'Sweetie, you have to come out of hiding and start getting on with your life. You've been there for over a year now . . .'

'I know, I know,' Sarah cut in before the nag could gather steam. Of course Becky was right, in fact Becky was usually right about everything, but Becky wasn't as afraid of the world as Sarah had become. Nor did Becky work in the cut-throat world of journalism. 'I've sent a couple of emails to some old contacts,' Sarah told her, knowing it was what her high-energy, totally focused personal coach of a sister would want to hear, even though it wasn't true. 'I'm kind of out of the loop now though, so it won't be easy.'

'Nothing is, Sarah, but you know I'm here to help. As soon as you're ready to start launching your comeback we'll make sure you present yourself in a way that can't fail. Are you eating these days?'

Sarah rolled her eyes. 'Enough to keep me alive. Anyway . . .'

'So you haven't put on any weight? Sweetie, too skinny is ageing, and I have to tell you, the last time I saw you I had quite a shock. We could almost pass for the same age, and while that might be good for me at thirty-six, it definitely isn't for you at thirty-one.'

'I'm eating,' Sarah told her firmly, 'and I promise I'm trying to get myself together. Right now that's the best I can do. So, do you want to hear the reason for my call?'

'Of course, but is it going to be long? If so, I'll call you back on the mobile so we can talk while I walk. I can't be late for this . . .'

'It won't take long. I just want to know if you're still OK about me selling some more stuff from the house. Mum's fine with it, but . . .'

'Sarah, I want you to do whatever makes you happy, but if it's money you need . . .'

'Please don't offer me any.'

'Just a loan . . .'

'Please, Becky. The closest I want to come to a handout is your word that you really don't mind me selling our heirlooms.'

'Heirlooms?' Becky laughed. 'There's nothing of any value there.'

'I know, but whatever I can raise will go towards sprucing up the house and garden, not straight into my pocket. That way it still kind of goes to you and Simon.'

'Very admirable, sweetie, but I thought we'd agreed, you need to start living again, and focusing on tarting the old place up is going to keep you there.'

'But we can't just abandon it. It's where we grew up, and it meant everything to Dad . . .' Her voice faltered, forcing her to break off.

'I know it did,' Becky said softly, 'and I promise, I want to see it restored to its best too, but it's going to take a fortune to do it, and I'm worried about you disengaging from the world. You're still so young . . .'

'Please don't start sounding like Mum, one of you's enough. Anyway, I'm hoping to get a job in the village.'

There was a moment's charged silence before Becky said, 'This is not what I want to hear, Sarah. Working in a shop, or . . .'

'With the local auction room,' Sarah cut in sharply. 'I don't know if they need anyone yet, but they're about to go under new management and the woman who's taking over is . . .'

'Probably going to exploit you.'

'Oh, for heaven's sake, Becky, will you at least try to have some confidence in me? I'm not ready to leave here yet, OK? And my own money is running out so I have to sell some of our possessions. If, by some miracle, there does turn out to be anything of value then obviously I'll split the proceeds with you and Simon . . .'

'Oh puhleeze, like we're going to take it. All we

care about, Sarah, is that you're setting yourself on the road to recovery. Now tell me, when did you last speak to Mum?'

Trying not to bristle at the *tell me*, Sarah said, 'Last night. She sounded quite up.'

'Well, there's a relief. The medication's obviously still working. You know, I keep worrying that you've inherited her depressive gene, because it's looking . . .'

'Becky, you're starting to annoy me now.'

'I'm just saying . . .'

'If you'd lost your son as well as your father, and your husband had got another woman pregnant . . .'

'Darling, I'm not trying to diminish what you've been through, please don't ever think that, but like I said a moment ago, you've been there a long time now, mourning and hiding yourself away, just like Mum used to. For God's sake, some of us are still in therapy about the way she carried on.'

'You've never told her that, have you?'

'No, of course not, but maybe I should.'

'Please don't. She can't help her depressions . . .'

'Sweetie, I'm sorry to interrupt, but if we're going to continue this I really *have* to call you back on the mobile.'

'Don't worry, you've already answered my question.'

'That's good. I'll call you tomorrow, OK? Love you, and you can call me any time, you know that.'

As the line went dead Sarah dropped her head in her hands and tried with all her might to suppress the awful neediness rising up inside her. She hated being alone, yet she seemed stuck in her isolation and being nagged by her family wasn't helping. Still, at least

Becky hadn't asked, as she occasionally did, if she'd heard from Kelvin, in spite of knowing that the split had been clean and final. Kelvin had kept what was his, the apartment and everything in it, and she had kept what was hers: clothes, computer and all the books and CDs. He hadn't even bothered to try hanging on to the first-edition, leather-bound volume of poetry she'd given him on their wedding day. Nor had he staked a claim on any of the music that had been such a wonderfully romantic part of their marriage. What a slap in the face that had been – along with all the others – knowing that he had no desire to cherish anything they'd once shared.

Turning back into the large oak kitchen, where sunlight was gleaming off the dangling copper pans, and the juicy fat garlic strings – imports from her mother's local village – looked almost ready to explode with flavour, she walked on through to the shabby, but recently dusted, front parlour to sit at her father's desk. For some reason she still couldn't think of it as hers, even though she was the only one who used it now. Wouldn't it be marvellous if she'd inherited his talent for writing, not as a journalist – her former career – but as a novelist, or a biographer, like him. His gift for bringing the subjects of his research to life with his 'unique brand of wit and pathos', to quote one critic, was, to quote another, 'unparalleled'. The literary world had lost one of its giants the day he'd died, someone had written in one of his obituaries, which had seemed to her an odd thing to say when her father had been quite a slight man with, it had to be said, no great affection for the fame he had acquired. She might be biased, but, as far as she was concerned, he was the most wonderful man – and father – in the entire world, so it simply didn't seem possible that it was managing to carry on turning without him.

They were all better people for having had him in their lives. He'd had a way of bringing out the best in everyone, of making them believe in themselves and find courage to face life's challenges when they felt sure they had none. She needed him now in a way she never had before. The void he and Jack had left in her life was so vast, and it just seemed to get deeper and deeper.

'Oh Daddy,' she whispered brokenly. 'Won't you speak to me please, in any way you can? I need to know if you and Jack are together. Please don't let him be afraid. He needs you to take care of him.'

As the silence seemed to close in around her she looked at the vases and fruit bowls she'd freed from cobwebs when she'd arrived, and wished it was possible for inanimate objects to hear or feel or to project a message in some sort of way. Maybe they were in touch with him on a level she didn't understand. 'I need some guidance, Daddy,' she said shakily. 'Am I doing the right thing in staying here?'

The first answer that came to mind would be his, she told herself, and the answer was,

'You should rejoin the world, my angel. You'll love again, and you might even lose again, because we know that life will always present challenges, but you have the strength and courage to meet them. You're your mother's daughter, and if she can come through all that she's suffered in her life, then so can you.'

Actually, that wouldn't be what he'd have said, because no one, least of all her parents, ever discussed what her mother had been through. All she, Simon and Becky knew was that something awful had happened to her before she'd married their father, but they were never allowed to mention it, or to ask what it had been. So they'd been left to speculate and worry as layer upon layer of secrecy and silence continued to swathe the reasons her mother used to take to her bed, sometimes for days on end without coming downstairs at all. Yet she'd never banned them from going to lie with her, if anything she used to encourage it, saying it always made her feel better when they were near.

Families were frustratingly complex and confusing at times, she was thinking to herself as her mobile started to ring, rife with intrigue and ghosts, and sometimes every bit as damaging as they could be nourishing.

Running back to the kitchen, she grabbed the phone, and seeing it was Simon she felt her spirits lift.

'You rang,' he said when she answered.

'What took you so long?' she quipped.

He laughed in a way that made her laugh too. 'I have some good news,' he told her. 'I'm scheduled to be in London the week after next, and I don't see any reason why I can't tie in a trip to Glos that could possibly last as long as a week. Now, if you tell me that isn't good news, or you won't be there, it'll be followed up with a very big *why?*'

'It's the best news ever,' she cried happily, 'and I will be here. Oh, Si, this is fantastic. Will Giselle be coming with you?'

'Alas no. She's going to be in Rio, or is it Rome? It'll come back to me. So, now, how's today going down at the family pile? Are you letting the place out for raves yet?'

Sarah laughed. 'No, but don't rule them out once I've got the place in better shape, which brings me to the reason I rang. Are you absolutely sure you don't have any objection to me putting your collection of old cars and soldiers into the next auction?'

'Of course I don't. What the hell else am I going to do with them?'

'If they turn out to be valuable I'll . . .'

'They won't be,' he assured her, 'so don't start getting your hopes up.'

'I'm not, but surprises can happen and if we did have a secret fortune stashed away, think how much sooner we could get this house restored to its former glory. I feel awful that it's taken me so long to get round to it, it's just that I haven't been able to face anyone coming into the house.'

'Then it's great that you can now, and when I'm there I'll be able to help you sort out the best tradesmen and . . .'

'I won't have the money by then. The next auction isn't until the third week of August.'

'If you stay local. What about selling it on eBay?'

'I could, but then I'd have to get involved in taking payments and packaging and delivery and all that fiddly stuff that would drive me nuts. And it's good to support a local business, especially one that I'm hoping to get involved in.'

'You are? As what?'

'Well, they employ lots of locals at the time of the auction to help display the items, or handle the phone bids, or take payments. I guess there are a thousand things that need doing, so hopefully the new owner will find a use for me which will at least get me out of the house once in a while.'

'New owner? Does that mean the Fishers are selling?'

'No, they're handing over to their daughter who I

think might already be here, because I'm sure it was her car I saw pulling into the farmhouse drive about an hour ago. Did you ever meet her? Her name's Lucy.'

'If I did I don't remember, but wasn't it her husband who tried to pull the stunt with the wardrobe?'

'Yes, but apparently he's staying in London, and Lucy gave me the five hundred pounds her parents had listed it at, which was extremely generous considering we had no way of knowing what it might have fetched.'

'You're right, I'd forgotten that part of it, so she's on a reprieve. If he starts to get involved though, we might want to take our business elsewhere. Hang on a sec, Giselle's shouting something at me . . . OK, she's running out the door but she sends her love and says she's going to try to get over to England sometime in September so she can have the pleasure of seeing you.'

Sarah immediately felt cheered again. 'Fantastic,' she cried. 'Can I start organising the wedding now, because it's high time you married her, don't you think?'

With a groan he said, 'Sarah, this is me you're speaking to. You know I don't do commitment.'

'You've been with her for over ten years, if that's not commitment . . .'

'Let's not do this.'

'It's time to make an honest woman of her.'

'It's not what she wants.'

'Have you asked her?'

'I have an instinct for these things.'

Sarah rolled her eyes. 'You're hopeless,' she told him, while thinking how happy it would make her if she herself could spend the rest of her life with him.

No betrayals or complications, no fear of another woman, or of losing a child. Only friendship and loyalty and lasting brotherly love.

'I'm afraid I'm going to have to head out myself now,' he told her. 'But before I go, has Mum told you that Becky's ordered *her* to get married again?'

Sarah started to turn cold. She couldn't imagine her mother with anyone apart from her father, nor did she ever want to. 'Why, has Mum met someone?' she asked, already feeling shut out if her mother had confided in the others and not her.

'Not that I'm aware of, but you know Becky and her self-assertion guff. Personally, I think it's highly unlikely Mum will take the plunge again. She was too close to Dad and I can't see anyone ever filling his shoes, but that's probably because I don't want to.'

'She doesn't either,' Sarah said firmly. 'She's perfectly happy with her life the way it is. She's got a lot of friends down there now, and someone's always turning up for a visit.'

'Exactly what I told Becky. Anyway, I have to fly. Love you, Sarah Delicious. Speak to you later.'

'Love you too,' she whispered, as the name her father had always called her flooded her with the memory of his tenderness.

After ringing off, rather than torment herself with the fear that her mother was moving on in a way she felt incapable of herself, she decided to call and find out. Minutes later she'd been assured by her Aunt Sheila that her mother had not become involved with anyone in a romantic sense, or even in a friendly one. 'It's just Becky being Becky,' Sheila had sighed, 'but I'll get Mum to call when she's back, shall I? She's out doing a spot of shopping at the moment.'

Sarah was still imagining her mother meandering

around the market stalls that lined the picturesque medieval streets of their nearby town, a basket over one arm and a straw hat shading her still beautiful face from the fierce Mediterranean sun, when she noticed one of Cromstone's newest residents looking up at the house. Since it was quite usual for visitors to assess the place for its architectural merit, Sarah waited to catch her eye and raised an arm to wave. With a surprised and cheery smile Mrs Mckenzie waved back, then suddenly she was being propelled to a bench beside the duck pond where her husband wanted her to star in his next shot. Sarah warmed to the natural humour that seemed to exist between them, since it reminded her of how easy her parents had been with each other. Maybe she should go out there and welcome them to Cromstone, but by the time she'd decided she would they were already walking away.

Her eyes followed them as they trekked towards the farmhouse where Lucy's daughter – Sarah couldn't remember her name – was perched on one of the gate pillars, apparently talking into her mobile phone.

She'd give Lucy some time to start settling in, she told herself, then she'd go over to register her little collection of bric-a-brac for the next sale.

Having managed to carry most of her and Hanna's belongings into the house, Lucy was now wandering around the courtyard that separated the enormous auction barn across the way from the main farmhouse, while her mother oversaw a delivery from the removal company she used for house clearances. From the moment her parents had first brought her to see this place, Lucy had felt a kind of connection to it that she'd never felt with anywhere else they'd lived, and over the past few years it hadn't gone away. If anything, it had seemed to grow, and now she was here, ready to take it on herself, the heady mix of excitement and trepidation was starting to eclipse even the wrenching loss she'd felt when she'd got up that morning to discover that Ben had already crept out.

In spite of understanding that he'd done it to avoid a scene, she'd still had a terrible struggle forcing herself not to go running down to the shop to drag him back again. In fact, had Hanna not thrown such an awful tantrum the minute she got up, Lucy knew it was highly likely she'd have ended up disgracing herself again, because the dread that she'd already seen Ben for the last time had been even worse than she'd feared.

Fortunately she was calmer now, since she was only incapable of dealing rationally with the first minutes of the actual parting. Once that was over, she could, more or less, get on with her life. And the fact that he'd rung twice already, once on his way to the airport and then just before he boarded the plane, was, she hoped, a sign that he'd keep his promise to be in touch at least every other day.

Putting her head back now to absorb the countrified scents mingling in the air around her – dry earth and silage, freshly mown grass and all kinds of piquancy from the trees overhead – she set aside her concerns for Hanna who, last seen, was storming off down the drive with her mobile. Lucy wanted, just for these few quiet minutes, to immerse herself in the promise of her new home. This ramshackle courtyard was at the hub of it all with the auction barn forming the longest side, the cowsheds that had been converted into offices making up the other, and a smaller, unrenovated barn at the far end which was used mainly for storage. Behind her was a high drystone wall with an arch that joined it to the rambling old Cotswold stone farmhouse and allowed access through to the front drive, or into the kitchen. It was another world back here, Lucy always thought, with all kinds of treasures spilling out of the barn like booty waiting to be claimed: old bed frames and mirrors; garden tables, stacking chairs, plant pots, marble and plaster statues, iron gates and even a Victorian church pew.

What made it all so entrancing, to her mind, were the untold stories that lay behind each and every piece. Ever since she was old enough to remember, her mother had been bringing inanimate objects to life in a way that was so thrilling and romantic that Lucy could hardly look at anything now without imagining where it had come from and where it might be going. Her mother could take something as simple as a pebble and tell a whimsical tale of its journey to the beach they were on, the oceans it had travelled, the sea creatures it had met along the way, and end the story with a secret message the pebble had brought for a rapt young Lucy. An old cameo brooch was the image of a woman who'd been in love with its creator; it had been to balls and grand dinners, weddings and christenings, until eventually fashions changed and it was left to languish in a drawer. This was where a grandchild had found it, many years later, but by then the brooch was angry so it had stabbed the girl with its pin, which was why it was at the antique market where Lucy and her mother had just bought it. So they had to be kind to it now, make it feel appreciated again, before they sent it on its way.

Though her father had often teased them for seeming to believe a candelabra or mirror, inkstand or tea set had feelings, he'd never walked away when they were conjuring the stories; sometimes he'd even join in and make them laugh, or cry, or want to box his ears. So it was fitting, Lucy had always thought, that her parents should have ended up here, running a kind of staging post for objects with dashing or tragic histories which were on their way to new owners and adventures.

Hearing the slam of lorry doors at the other side of the barn, followed by the starting of an engine, Lucy guessed her mother would be on her way back, so after sending a silent message to all the treasures waiting in the courtyard, letting them know that she was going to do her best to find worthy buyers to take them on the next leg of their journeys, she returned to the farmhouse.

A few minutes later she was staring at her mother in mounting frustration, while Hanna perched on the kitchen table pouring her own frustration down the line to Sadie.

'But Mum, the last time we spoke you said Dad was on his way back,' Lucy cried.

'No, Lucy, what I said was that everything's fine, and it is.'

Resisting the urge to shake her mother, Lucy said, 'So where is he?'

'I'm not sure. I mean, yes, he's at the cottage . . . Well, he was last night, by now he's probably . . . He said he was going out to buy some shelves.'

'Mum! For heaven's sake! If Dad's gone walkabout . . .'

'He hasn't gone walkabout,' Daphne cut in. 'Really, Lucy, you do make mountains out of molehills at times. He wanted to do some work on the cottage and stupidly forgot to tell me he was going down there.'

Lucy gazed sternly into her mother's softly lined face with its large brown eyes and delicate bones, and wasn't surprised when she looked away, since she always did her best to avoid confrontation. 'Does he have his mobile with him?' she demanded.

'Of course he does,' Daphne replied, going to put the kettle on, 'but as you know we can't get reception at the cottage. When he called he was down the hill outside the Mason's Arms.'

Sighing, Lucy said, 'OK, so when's he coming back?'

'I'm not sure. He didn't . . . Well . . . Oh dear, look what I've done,' she sighed as a box of tea bags tumbled to the floor.

'Mum! I'm going to lose it in a minute,' Lucy warned, stooping to help pick them up. 'Dad disappears on you, now we can't get hold of him . . .'

'Will you two give it a rest,' Hanna shouted, her eyes still puffy and red from having cried so much during the journey from London. 'I'm on the phone here.'

'Sorry, dear,' her grandmother said softly.

'Don't apologise to her,' Lucy snapped. 'If you can't hear take it back outside,' she told Hanna.

'I am like so glad I came,' Hanna seethed, and storming towards the door she threw back over her shoulder, 'If this is how it's going to be I'm on the next train to London.'

As she swept off Lucy turned to her mother, who was looking decidedly troubled.

'Don't take any notice of that,' Lucy told her. 'It's her threat of the moment. Next week she'll probably be threatening to do away with me. Now we need to . . .'

'I don't want to argue any more,' Daphne interrupted, taking a key from the dresser. 'I'm going over to the office to . . .'

'So that's it!' Lucy cried. 'We don't know where Dad is, we can't get hold of him and now you're just going to carry on as if it doesn't matter.'

'Lucy, I'm sure he'll call later so you can take it up with him yourself.'

As she walked away, Lucy clasped her hands to her head. 'You are the most maddening person at times,' she shouted after her.

'And be sure you have your moments,' Daphne retorted.

'This is not the kind of welcome I expected,' Lucy cried angrily.

At that Daphne stopped, and when she turned round her expression was so contrite that Lucy wished she was better at biting her tongue. 'I'm sorry,' Daphne said, and holding out her arms she came to give Lucy a hug. 'Everything's a bit topsy-turvy at the moment with the move coming up, and I suppose I'm a little out of sorts.'

'And I'm sorry I'm so irritable,' Lucy responded, hugging her tight. 'It's not your fault that Ben crept out this morning without saying goodbye – and before you say it I know it was probably the wisest course, but I really wish he hadn't.'

'He's going to be fine,' her mother assured her. 'He's a sensible lad and before you know it he'll be home again, so full of his adventures we probably won't be able to shut him up.'

'Roll on the day,' Lucy mumbled, and going to remove the kettle from the Aga she began filling the teapot with hot water. 'We do need to talk about Dad, though, Mum. OK, not now if you don't want to, but if you two are going to live so remotely we have to get a better form of communication set up between us. Has BT put any lines in yet? Surely the other houses must have something by now.'

'As far as I know everyone's still using their mobiles, but we haven't seen anyone for a while so I can't be sure. Anyway, we know Vodaphone doesn't provide coverage up there, so I'll have to see about finding a company that does.'

Lucy turned to look at her again, and seeing how unsure she seemed of herself her heart twisted with the same sort of protective love she felt towards Hanna and Ben. 'What is it?' she asked gently. 'Are you having second thoughts about giving all this up? I'll understand if you are. It's meant a lot to you . . .'

'No, no, I'm not having second thoughts. It's just . . .' Daphne shook her head and turned away.

'Just what?'

'Nothing. I'm sure I'm worrying unnecessarily.'

'About what?'

'Please, let's drop it.'

Lucy went to take her by the shoulders. 'Is it to do with the Crumptons?' she asked. 'Are you worrying about how I'm going to get along with them?'

Daphne's eyes came briefly to hers. 'You're going to need them,' she reminded her.

'I know. So have you spoken to them? Do they accept that I'm going to be in charge from now on?'

'Yes, of course they do.'

'And you've made them directors and increased their salaries?'

Though Daphne nodded, to Lucy's confusion she didn't appear entirely certain.

'Mum? For heaven's sake, what are you not telling me? I know there's something, so come on, out with it.'

With a protracted sigh, Daphne shook her head. 'I'm . . . Well, I've been wondering if we made a mistake coming here.'

Lucy couldn't have been more stunned. 'A mistake?' she echoed. 'But you've loved being here. Working with antiques is a dream come true for you, and what you've done with the business is nothing short of amazing.'

Daphne put on a smile. 'Thank you,' she said, clearly pleased that Lucy thought so. 'And I know you'll make it even bigger and better. I have so much confidence in you, but . . .' She swallowed hard as her eyes drifted away. 'Do try to keep Maureen and Godfrey on your side, won't you? They have a great deal of experience and . . .' She broke off as the phone started to ring, and after glancing at it she looked at Lucy. 'Shall I answer, or will you? It's the business line.'

Lucy's heart tripped pleasurably. 'I guess I should,' she replied, and scooping up the receiver she felt a flutter of excitement as she said, 'Cromstone Auctions, can I help you?'

'Mm, now that doesn't sound like Maureen or Daphne,' a male voice remarked at the other end of the line.

'No, this is Daphne's daughter, Lucy,' she told him, looking at her mother.

'Ah, Lucy, you've arrived. Excellent. It's Michael Givens here. I'm sorry we haven't managed to meet yet. My fault entirely. I've been in Italy for the past month, but I believe congratulations are in order. My partner tells me everything's now been signed over to you.'

Remembering that Michael Givens was the head of the law firm that had overseen the transfer of ownership of the business and farmhouse, Lucy said, 'Oh yes, hello Michael. It's good to hear from you. As far as I'm aware there are a couple more things for me to sign. I've got the details in an email somewhere. I'll dig it out and call your office to make an appointment to come in and do it.'

'Very good. I'll try to be here when you come so we can at least say hello. Now, would your mother be around? I'd like a quick word if she is.'

'She's right here, I'll pass you over.'

As her mother took the phone Lucy became aware of other voices outside besides Hanna's, and went to the window to investigate. It turned out to be a couple of tourists, judging from the guidebook and camera, and she could only wonder what Hanna was saying since they both appeared highly entertained.

'. . . so we just arrived today,' Hanna was informing the Mckenzies, 'and now here I am stuck in the back of flipping beyond with no friends, nothing to do, nowhere to go . . . I'm sorry, but anyone who wants to live around here seriously needs their head read.'

John's eyes were twinkling merrily. 'I'm sure they do,' he agreed. 'And would you happen to know yet which school you'll be going to?'

Hanna heaved a dejected sigh and rolled her eyes. 'Maiden Bradley,' she replied sourly. 'Sounds such fun, doesn't it? Oh God, please don't tell me you're teachers.'

'We're not,' Philippa assured her.

Apparently relieved, Hanna said, 'You are *so* lucky you're not my age.'

'Must be hell,' John sympathised.

'But I'd have thought getting involved in the

auctions would be quite interesting,' Philippa ventured.

'Oh yeah, like riveting, provided you're into piles of junk, because that's what most of it is. My mother, of course, likes to refer to it all as antiques, but she's someone who really needs to get a life.'

John's eyebrows rose. 'That's quite a sales technique you've got going there,' he commented.

Hanna scowled, until realising she was being teased she started to smile. 'Actually, I'm still working on it,' she assured him, tossing her hair over one shoulder, 'but I'm glad you think it's coming along. So how long have you lived around here? I don't remember seeing you before.'

'As a matter of fact, we've just moved in,' Philippa told her. 'We've rented the Mercers' house at the bottom end of the village. The Old Lodge. Do you know it?'

Hanna tilted her head to one side. 'Is it the big one, just past where you turn off for the farm shop?'

'That's the one. So we're all newcomers, it seems, though obviously you've been a regular visitor up to now.'

'Yeah, ever since Granny and Grandpa bought the business, which was about five or six years ago. He was in insurance before, and they lived all over the country because he was in charge of setting up new offices. Mum used to hate it when she was growing up, because she never really got to make any friends. Granny didn't like it much either, but she'd never say so, because Granny never complains. It was Mum who told me that. Anyway, getting into antiques was something Granny always wanted to do, so when Grandpa retired he said it was her turn to choose where they lived and what they did, and this,' she fanned out her hands, 'is it.'

John and Philippa cast admiring glances over the sleepy-looking farmhouse with its grey slate roof and riot of climbing plants of all varieties and colours. To the right, sloping away to the woods below, was a lush sweep of lawn, while to the left a high stone wall with a gated arch appeared to front a small cluster of buildings.

'Is the saleroom around there?' Philippa asked.

'Yeah, that's it over there,' Hanna replied, pointing to the roof of the barn. 'To get to it you can either go further up this lane and take the next turning on the right, or you can go through the arch just there into Steptoe's yard at the back – that's what Dad calls it, anyway. Mum and Granny like to call it the quadrangle, or courtyard, because it sounds posher. Duh! The offices are out there too. They used to be cowsheds, would you believe, but luckily they don't stink any more, and there's another little barn at the far end that no one's ever bothered to convert, so it does stink. I've been thinking about moving in there and rotting away along with everything else. I might just as well for all the action I'm going to see around here.'

John chuckled at that, which brought a look of surprise to Hanna's eyes.

'No one ever laughs at my jokes,' she said. 'Apart from my dad, but he's my dad so he would. And I suppose Mum does too, sometimes. Ben, that's my brother, thinks I'm hilarious, or that's what he says and he thinks it's soooo funny when he does. Not! He flew off to Thailand this morning to start his gap year. I am so going to miss him. It wouldn't be half as bad here if he'd have come too, except he'd be bound to find a girlfriend and dump me.'

'But we've spotted plenty of young people around

the village,' Philippa told her. 'And there are quite a few famous people in these parts too, I believe, so I really don't think you'll be short of friends, or bored.'

Hanna was shaking her head in a way that asserted her superior knowledge. 'You see, there are young people, and then there are young people,' she explained, 'and believe me, the young people here aren't anything like the young people where I come from. I don't suppose you have any interesting children, or grandchildren, do you, by any chance?'

'I'm afraid not,' John answered. His eyes were moving past her now to the striking young woman with long dark hair and an exquisite heart-shaped face who was coming towards them.

'Hello,' Lucy said, holding out a hand to shake. 'I'm Lucy Winters. I see you've already met Hanna.'

Taking her hand John said, 'We have, but we didn't know her name until now. It's a pleasure to meet you, Lucy. I'm John Mckenzie.'

'And I'm Philippa,' Philippa said, shaking her hand too. 'We've just moved into the Old Lodge at the other end of the village.'

'Oh yes, I know it,' Lucy said. 'Isn't it the Mercers' house? I heard they were renting it out, did they change their minds and sell?'

'No, we just have it for six months,' Philippa told her. 'It's a lovely place with a beautiful garden. I think we're going to enjoy our time there very much.'

'I hope so,' Lucy smiled, thinking how uplifting it was to meet people like this on the doorstep rather than yobs and drunks.

'Hanna's just told us that you're taking over from your parents,' John remarked chattily.

Lucy grimaced. 'Fingers crossed I won't let them down. Is that why you're here, about the auctions?

Whether you're interested in selling or buying, our aim is always to please.'

Hanna looked at her as though she'd lost the plot. 'Is that it?' she demanded. 'That's your opening line?'

'Have you got a better one?'

'As a matter of fact, I've already been complimented on my sales technique.'

Lucy blinked.

'She completely won us over,' John informed her with mock seriousness. 'And we are indeed here about the auctions, because the Mercers would like you to come and take whatever you might want from their garage.'

Lucy was thrilled. 'My first commission!' she cried triumphantly. 'Would you like to come in? I've made some tea, which has probably gone cold by now, but Hanna can always make some fresh while we look at the diary to sort out the best time to come.'

Hanna was incredulous. 'Hello?' she cried. 'What did your last slave die of?'

'I promise it wasn't making tea,' Lucy smiled, patting her head.

Philippa's good eye was twinkling. 'That's very kind of you,' she said, 'but I fear we'll be intruding if you've only just arrived. Why don't we come back tomorrow? Or perhaps we could offer you some tea at our house once you know when you can fit us in.'

'That's a great idea,' Lucy agreed. 'I'll just go and grab a pen so I can jot down your details.'

'No probs,' Hanna piped up, 'I'll put them into my phone.'

Pleased by the unexpected helpfulness, not to mention apparent good humour, Lucy waited as Hanna tapped in the Mckenzies' number, then said, 'I'll call later to fix up a time, is that OK?'

'Marvellous,' Philippa said warmly. 'We shall look forward to it. And you'll come too?' she asked Hanna. 'I know John and I are old and decrepit, but we're in need of making some friends too, so perhaps we can find a way to help each other out.'

Lucy tensed, but to her relief all Hanna said was, 'Whatever.'

'So gracious,' Lucy murmured, rolling her eyes. Then, holding out a hand to shake again, 'It was lovely to meet you.'

Appearing just as pleased, the Mckenzies reciprocated with warm handshakes, and as they strolled on down the lane to circle around the back of the village, Lucy linked Hanna's arm to walk her back inside.

'They seemed really nice, didn't they?' she commented.

'I guess so,' Hanna retorted in her usual bored tone. 'Why do you reckon she's got that patch over her eye? It looks really weird, but kind of cool the way the pink matches her shirt.'

'I've no idea,' Lucy replied, glad to realise Hanna hadn't blurted out the question to the Mckenzies, or she wouldn't be asking her. 'So are you going to come with me when I go to see them?'

Hanna sighed as she pulled a face. 'If I must.'

Realising pride wouldn't allow her to exude anything as uncool as enthusiasm, Lucy left it there and ushered her inside.

'It's not usually so busy at this time of day,' Daphne said apologetically as they came into the kitchen. 'All these phone calls, but it's only because Godfrey and Maureen are both out this afternoon. If they were here the calls would be going through to the office and barn.'

'We just met the new neighbours,' Lucy told her, going to take a yoghurt from the fridge and plonking it in front of Hanna. 'What was their name again?'

'What's this?' Hanna protested, picking up the Mr Men yoghurt pot. 'I'm not six, in case you hadn't noticed.'

With a gurgle of laughter, Lucy removed it from her hand and replaced it with a bottle of Baby Bio. 'It'll help you grow.'

'Yeah, very funny,' Hanna commented, taking the yoghurt back. 'Mckenzie,' she added.

'Ah yes, that's right,' Lucy said. 'Have you met them yet, Mum?'

When her mother didn't answer she looked up to find out if she was listening, but Daphne's back was turned.

'Hello?' Lucy called out. 'Mum? Are you with us?'

'Yes, yes,' Daphne answered, starting to rummage in a drawer. 'I was just . . . Oh dear, where is that number? I'm just going to pop over to the office. Back in two ticks,' and she took off at some speed, leaving Lucy and Hanna to look at each other and shrug in confusion.

Further down the lane Philippa's arm was linked through John's as they ambled along, taking in the heady smells of summer while listening to the birds chattering and chirruping in the trees. Since leaving the farmhouse neither of them had spoken, but Philippa could guess what was going through John's mind.

In the end, in an effort to reassure him, she said, 'It's all right to invite Hanna if her mother comes too.'

His voice was gruff as he said, 'Of course.' Then, 'She's a bonnie wee lass.'

'She is that,' Philippa agreed.

They continued on in companionable silence after that, skirting the edge of a meadow full of butter-cups until they reached a stile behind the pub, and decided to stop off in the garden for a drink.

Chapter Six

Having popped down to the village a few minutes ago, Sarah now knew, thanks to Jan from the Drop Inn whom she'd bumped into at the greengrocers, that their new neighbours, the Mckenzies, had seen Lucy and apparently Lucy was already making appointments. So, not wanting to waste any more time, Sarah was now trying the alternative number she had for Cromstone Auctions, having found the first one busy. This time she was answered on the second ring and certain, from the lack of local accent, that it wasn't Maureen Crumpton, and knowing it wasn't Mrs Fisher, she said, a little hesitantly, 'Is that Lucy, by any chance?'

'Yes, it is,' Lucy replied warmly. 'Can I help you?'

'It's Sarah Bancroft here,' Sarah told her, taking heart from Lucy's tone, 'from the manor. I saw you arriving a couple of hours ago and thought I'd ring to welcome you to Cromstone.'

'That's so kind of you,' Lucy cried, clearly delighted. 'How are you?'

Starting to smile, Sarah said, 'I'm fine, thank you. And you?'

There was an anxious laugh in Lucy's voice as she said, 'I'm OK. A bit apprehensive about taking over, if the truth be told, but one step at a time and all that.'

'I'm sure you'll do brilliantly,' Sarah declared, meaning it. Was she overdoing her friendliness now? She hoped not. What should she say next? 'Is your mother OK?' she blurted. 'Only when I saw her yesterday she seemed a little, well, out of sorts, I suppose. I mean, it's none of my business, of course . . . I'm sorry, it really isn't any . . .'

In a long-suffering tone Lucy said, 'I expect she was worried about my dad. He went off to their cottage on Exmoor to start some decorating and managed to forget to tell her he was going.'

Relieved that she didn't seem to have trespassed too far on to personal territory, Sarah said, 'I see. Well as long as everything's all right . . .' She cleared her throat. 'Actually, I was wondering . . . I have a few things that I'd like to put in your next sale if I can. Perhaps I can bring them over when you've had time to settle in?'

'Of course,' Lucy responded eagerly. 'Do you need some help carrying them?'

'I'm sure I can manage. There's an old wheelbarrow in the shed I can use. Tell me when's a good time for you.'

'Actually, why don't I come to you? That way we'll have a better idea of what we need to transport and whether or not we need help. My diary's empty at the moment, but I probably ought to consult the official one, so I'll get back to you in an hour or so, is that OK?'

'Absolutely,' Sarah assured her, already looking forward to it. 'No rush. Whenever's convenient.'

After finishing the call Sarah felt her spirits lifting as she went off down the garden to drag out the wheelbarrow, certain it would need a clean if it was going to be their transport, and probably a drop of oil to help it on its way. However, it turned out to be in need of a great deal more than a quick fix, such as a wheel and a barrow minus a hole.

'Great,' she muttered, and shoving it back into the shed she closed the door quickly, before the mountain of rusting garden tools could come crashing out on top of her.

'Hello! Anyone at home?' an all-too familiar voice shouted from the drive that led up to the side of the house.

'Down here,' Sarah called back, and starting across the garden she braced herself for Annie the hairdresser's pointed scrutiny of her woefully neglected state.

'Ah, there you are,' Annie announced as she pushed open the rickety wooden gate to come on to the back terrace. 'I thought you must be at home, because the front door was open. Lucky we don't have too many burglars around here, isn't it, or you'd be in trouble.'

Sarah smiled past her discomfort. It wasn't that she disliked Annie, with her swinging blonde bob and sparkly fingernails, it was simply that she'd never felt particularly at ease with her. Come to think of it, she didn't feel especially at ease with anyone outside her family these days, but there was no doubt that Annie's eagerness to be friends always seemed to make her withdraw even further into her shell.

'I was just passing,' Annie declared in her airy way, 'and I thought, seeing as I've got a couple of hours free, you might like a nice cut and blow-dry. No charge, I'd be happy to do it, because if you don't mind me saying, your ends'll split right up to the roots if you leave them much longer.'

Trying not to resent her for pointing it out, while knowing she was right, Sarah said, 'That's really kind of you, Annie, but . . .'

'No buts,' Annie came in quickly. 'Like I said, it's gratuitous' (Sarah realised she probably meant *gratuit*), 'and unless you tell me you're on your way out somewhere . . .' She raised her eyebrows, letting the sentence hang and apparently challenging Sarah to fib.

Sarah wanted to, but she wasn't fast enough.

Annie beamed a smile. 'Come on then,' she said kindly, 'let's go and turn you back into the princess you really are. Then who knows, you might even feel ready to come and join us girls on one of our Friday nights out.'

Unable to imagine anything she'd like to do less, apart from run into Kelvin and Margot, or maybe have her teeth drilled without anaesthetic, Sarah gave up the fight and allowed herself to be steered back into the house.

'Oh, isn't it looking lovely in here,' Annie commented, her vivid green eyes drinking in every last detail of the worn old kitchen and as much as she could see of the dining room next door. 'You've been having a bit of a spring clean by the look of it.'

Though Sarah had, she wasn't about to admit it in case she found herself dragged into an area of conversation that would bewilder her utterly. 'Would you like a cold drink?' she offered. 'I've got some lemonade in the fridge, or filtered water.'

'Oh, definitely water for me,' Annie responded. 'Very good for the complexion, did you know that? Not that *you* have anything to worry about in that department. I only wish I'd been blessed with skin like yours. Not a line in sight, and after all you've been through! Wouldn't mind your figure either, come to that. I have such a struggle keeping my weight down, you know. What I wouldn't give to be a little rake like you.'

Since Sarah was certain that Annie was perfectly thrilled with her 38 double Ds and hips as curvy as a hippo's, she merely smiled politely while going to sort out some drinks.

'Ah, that's better,' Annie sighed after emptying her glass. 'It's pretty hot out there today, isn't it? Not that I'm complaining, mind you. We could do with a decent summer after the sorry excuses we've had over the past couple of years, don't you think? Now, I'll just pop out and get my things from the car while you go and wash your hair, OK? Or would you like me to wash it for you? I've got some lovely shampoos you can choose from . . .'

'I'm fine, thanks,' Sarah assured her, and accepting that it would be much simpler now to go with the flow, she went off upstairs to do as she was told.

Ten minutes later, with a nylon overall fastened around her neck and a portable mirror propped on the kitchen table in front of her, Sarah was watching Annie snip-snipping away at her ends and feeling almost envious of how much she seemed to enjoy her work. There was a time when Sarah had loved hers too, but the adrenalin rush of deadlines and the thrill of snaring exclusives all felt a long way away now. Would she ever work as a journalist again, she wondered. Was the cut-throat rivalry of fashion designers, cosmetic giants, publishing houses, not forgetting the weekly magazines themselves, all in the past, never to return? During those hectic years she wouldn't have been able to imagine

105

surviving without the incredible madness of it all, or the camaraderie. Now she felt daunted even to think of trying to find her way back into the game.

'You know, I've always said you've got beautiful hair,' Annie was telling her chattily. 'My mum remembers you as a youngster and she said it was always lovely then. And you really don't do anything to the colour?'

'No,' Sarah answered.

'There's not many people can boast they're natural blondes, you know, especially not with a shade like yours. Take me for instance, all out of a bottle, this is, and the time it takes touching up the roots . . . Your brother's the same as you, isn't he? Lovely thick blond hair. Got it from your dad's side, I expect, because he was fair too, wasn't he?'

'That's right,' Sarah replied. 'And a couple of our grandparents.'

Snip, snip, snippety snip. A pause to assess, then a casual, 'So how is your brother these days? We haven't seen him for a while.'

Remembering that Annie had a bit of a crush on Simon, Sarah said, 'Oh, busy as ever.'

More snips, more assessing. 'Still with the same woman, is he?'

'That's right.'

'Mm, French, isn't she?'

'She is.'

'Mm, very exotic. Of course you lived over there yourself, didn't you, when you was married. I suppose you speak the lingo fluently?'

Sarah was starting to tense. *Please, please don't let her be leading up to asking about Kelvin.* 'I do,' she confirmed.

'And your mum's still over there, is she?'

'Down in the south.'

'Lovely part. I went to Biarritz once, with my ex. Is that near your mum?'

'No, she's further over, in Provence.'

'Oh, that's right, I think you told me before. So, have you got any plans to go down there this summer?'

'I was thinking about flying over the week after next, but Simon's coming here now, so I'll probably go later.'

'Oh, Simon's coming here, is he?' Annie said, in a tone that was presumably meant to be casual, but actually reminded Sarah of the reputation she had of being a Venus mantrap. She wondered if Lucy was aware of the fling her husband had had with Annie – if she wasn't, Sarah certainly wouldn't be the one to tell her. 'That's nice,' Annie went on cheerily. 'And what about his lady friend? Is she coming too?'

'Oh yes,' Sarah lied.

Annie's disapproval almost sliced the air. 'So how short do you want me to go?' she demanded, standing back to take a look. 'Oh hang on, that's my phone,' and responding to what bizarrely sounded like the *Titanic* going down, she dug into her bag and clicked on saying, 'Hello, Annie speaking. Oh Kim, petal, I'm in the middle of . . . Oh, yeah, that's right. No! Did you? So what did you think? Mm, me too. Really sweet, aren't they? Oh, yeah, definitely give them my number. I'll be glad to cut their hair. Right, you do that. I'll call you back when I'm done.'

After ringing off she said, 'That was my mate, Kim. She works at the kennels, you know, over by Wotton? Apparently she just ran into the couple who've rented the Old Lodge from the Mercers and they're interested in going on my books. Isn't that nice? A really lovely pair, they are.'

'So I hear.'

'Oh, so you haven't met them yet? Actually, they was asking the vicar's wife earlier if your family still owned the manor, so I expect they're fans of your dad's, don't you, because we tend to get a lot of them coming round, especially in the summer. Anyway, apparently she told them the manor was still in the family, but that only you live here now.'

Not quite sure what to say to that, Sarah went back to watching her reflection in the mirror until her own phone rang and Annie scooped it off the countertop to pass it over.

'Sarah? It's Lucy. I've looked at the diary and if tomorrow at twelve works for you . . .'

'That's great,' Sarah assured her, 'but I'm afraid the wheelbarrow's out of action.'

Laughing, Lucy said, 'Don't worry, we'll work something out. Hanna and I are going for another viewing in the village at eleven, so we can call into the manor on the way back.'

'Thank you. I'll look forward to it,' and clicking off the line Sarah held the phone in her hands as she returned her gaze to the mirror. 'Tell you what,' she said to Annie, 'it's time I had a completely new look, so over to you.' *Turn me into a woman who's not afraid of the world any more*, she wanted to say, but never would to someone like Annie.

The following morning, at the far side of the village, close to the disused tabernacle with its slender towers that rose like stone candles into the crimson morning sky, the church clock was beginning to strike seven. In the street between the two buildings Harry Buck, the milkman, was making his final deliveries to the colourful almshouses, while down on the high street Bob Sherston was rolling up the shutters at the front of his bakery. As the delicious aroma of freshly baked loaves spilled out like a cloud over the cobbles, several more windows and doors started to rattle and open. Even at this early hour the temperature was rising into the twenties, and according to the forecast, it could go as high as thirty today.

Having risen with the larks, who were fluttering and chirruping around the rooftops, Lucy was already at her mother's computer in the cowshed, making an early start on the emails. It was a long, narrow room with windows all along the front, overlooking the courtyard, and with four more desks in front of each and two secure booths at the far end for taking payments. Along the back wall was a haphazard arrangement of shelves and cupboards packed full of books, magazines and a cornucopia of curios that either hadn't yet found their way to pastures new, or had somehow managed to take up permanent residence here.

With the next auction due to take place in just over three weeks, the barn was already starting to fill up and offers of more lots were coming in all the time. As were requests for catalogues, dates and inspections, and enquiries about how to present an item for sale. There was also the scheduling of pickups and deliveries to be slotted into a constantly changing agenda; the organising of valuations; the registering and ticketing of each piece as it came in, followed by its careful storing with like objects to make sure it was easily found during the viewings.

Though Lucy was already reasonably au fait with how the place ran, there were certain aspects that she'd only been fleetingly involved in before, such as assessing the worth of each item, or putting the lots under the hammer. However, the latter was always left to professionals who came in for the two-day sale, while the former was generally undertaken by her mother and Maureen, unless they felt a particular item was in need of an expert eye. The day-to-day finances was another area shared by Maureen and Daphne, and had always looked, to Lucy, to be about as penetrable as a Greek knitting pattern. However, she felt certain that the firm's accountant would be happy to devise a more user-friendly system that she could follow, if she requested it. Once the emails were dealt with, she began to try and transfer the contents of the company Outlook Calendar over to her new BlackBerry, but it wasn't long before she was ready to hurl the whole lot against the wall. No matter how closely she followed the instructions nothing would budge, so for the sake of her own sanity she decided to make it a project for Maeve, the part-time office assistant and computer genius, when she next came in. A few minutes later she was in the process of printing out a set of draft catalogue pages to take over to the barn when the phone made her jump.

Though she knew Ben would most likely call her mobile, given the hour her heart leapt with hope anyway, and grabbing the receiver she almost sang, 'Good morning, Cromstone Auctions, can I help you?'

A bored female voice came down the line. 'It's Bevan's Courier Service,' she informed Lucy. 'We've got your delivery scheduled for between ten and twelve this morning. Will someone be there to sign for it?'

'Yes, they will,' Lucy assured her.

'OK, thanks,' and the line went dead.

Going back to her computer Lucy decided to check her bank account, not because she needed to, but because she wanted to feel the thrill of seeing her finances looking so healthy since her parents had transferred such a generous sum to help get her started. There was going to be no difficulty meeting Hanna's school fees now, or any more struggles for the next couple of months trying to make ends meet. Of course, money problems would reappear if she didn't make a success of things, but she wasn't going to worry about that now, instead she was going to close up the screen and answer the phone.

This time it had to be Ben!

'Hello, is that you?' she cried eagerly.

'What?' a countrified male voice demanded gruffly.

'Oh, I'm sorry. I was expecting someone else. You've reached Cromstone Auctions, can I help you?'

'Is that Daphne Fisher?'

'No, it's her daughter. Is there . . . ?'

'I want to speak to Daphne or Brian Fisher.'

Careful to keep a matching belligerence out of her own tone, Lucy said, 'I'm afraid my dad's away at the moment, and it's still quite early so Mum's not in the office yet. Perhaps I can help.'

'Tell them Eric Beadle rang and they're going to be hearing from my solicitor.'

Lucy's eyes widened.

'They know they cheated me,' he growled, 'and

111

they're not going to get away with it. You tell them that from me,' and he hung up.

Replacing her own receiver Lucy looked at the name she'd written on the pad, then returning to the computer she carried out a quick search to see if it appeared anywhere in the files. She didn't have to delve far. Apparently the man had submitted a walnut commode into May's sale which had gone for one hundred and twenty pounds – thirty below the list price. After a further investigation she discovered that the buyer had come to collect the item a day after the sale, and Mr Beadle had been sent a cheque, minus the agreed commission, a week later.

'Lucy,' her mother said brightly as she came into the office. 'I thought you must be out here when I saw the coffee had been made. Couldn't sleep, or eager to get started?'

'Bit of both,' Lucy admitted, as Daphne came to stand behind her. 'Do you mind me sitting in your chair?'

'It's yours now,' Daphne reminded her. 'You know, I'm sure half these things can be thrown out,' she added, surveying the mountains of catalogues, photographs, trade papers and old files. 'I can't think why we've hung on to them this long.'

As she started a quick glance through it all, Lucy told her about the call from Eric Beadle. By the time she'd finished, although Daphne's back was turned she was shaking her head in dismay.

'He's always been a tricky customer,' she said with a sigh, 'and this time he's annoyed because the chap who bought the commode was a dealer who happened to sell it on a few weeks later for somewhere around a thousand pounds. Eric's now got it into his head that Dad and I were in cahoots with the dealer and we've cheated him out of what was rightfully his.'

Knowing that her parents' honesty could make even the squeakiest clean look smeary, Lucy said, 'Do you think he really has consulted a solicitor?'

Daphne reached up to take down a broken clock. 'Who knows? If he has he'll be wasting his money. Unfortunately these things happen once in a while; someone gets wind of their lot being sold on for a much better price and they take exception. You know, I think we ought to try and get this working again,' she said, opening the back of the clock. 'It would be a shame just to throw it away when it could be quite pretty if we cleaned it up a bit and found it a new hand.'

Knowing her mother was seeing it as some kind of orphan in need of adoption, or a patient on a waiting list for surgery, Lucy suppressed a smile as she said, 'So Mr Beadle doesn't have any grounds for his complaint?'

Daphne was still inspecting the clock. 'I'm sure he thinks he does,' she replied, 'but I'm afraid it's the chance you take when you put something up for auction, which is why you, my dear,' she turned to look at Lucy, 'must be sure that you always get the client to sign an agreement when you set the price. That way there can't be any comeback later.'

Though Lucy already knew that, she nodded to show that she was happy to hear the advice again. 'So what should we do about him?'

Daphne tucked the clock under one arm. 'There's nothing we can do, unless a solicitor's letter turns up, but I really don't think it will. And even then it's not going to change what happened, so let's hope he gets over his chagrin soon and finds something else to occupy his time. Now, I've come to offer you a spot of breakfast to get you into the day. Fancy some eggs and bacon?'

The rumble of Lucy's stomach answered for her, making them both laugh, and abandoning her familiarisation programme for the moment, she linked her mother's arm as they started back across the courtyard. 'Did you speak to Dad again last night?' she asked as her mother stopped to unhook an empty bird-feeder.

'Not for long,' Daphne replied. 'By the time he'd spoken to you and Hanna his battery was running low, so we probably won't hear from him again until he's charged up and back in range. Are you satisfied now that he's fine and there's nothing to worry about?'

'I admit he sounded on form,' Lucy conceded, 'but to have forgotten to tell you where he was going wasn't good, Mum. And you know it's not the only time it's happened, because . . .'

'All right, all right, don't let's start getting into that again. We all become forgetful as we grow older, but it doesn't mean we have to go rushing for the nearest Alzheimer clinic. Anyway, he's coming back tomorrow, so you'll see for yourself that he's in no danger of losing his marbles just yet. Now, you can fill this up with peanuts if you will while I get started on the eggs. Shall we wake up Hanna or leave her to sleep in?'

'Let's leave her for now. I'll take her into Moonkicks for a latte and muffin on our way to see the Mckenzies.'

'Ah, yes, about that,' Daphne said, taking a frying pan from a shelf and placing it on the Aga. 'I thought I'd go myself, if you don't mind. I ran into them the other day at the baker's, but it was a little awkward, so I'd like to say hello properly before Dad and I leave. Two eggs or three?'

'Two,' Lucy replied, impressed that her once shy mother would now go out of her way to welcome a couple of strangers when, before coming to Cromstone, she'd far rather have avoided it. 'And the same for bacon,' she added. 'Are you going to have toast?'

'I probably shouldn't, but I'll share a piece with you if you don't want a whole one.'

After cutting off a slice of wholemeal and popping it in the toaster, Lucy said, 'That's fine about the Mckenzies. When I called yesterday to set a time they said around eleven, if that's OK. Hanna may or may not go with you, I guess it depends what sort of mood she's in when she gets up.'

'Why on earth would she want to come?' Daphne asked, going to the fridge. 'I'd have thought she'd be much keener to try and hook up with some people her own age.'

'Hopefully she will when she gets over her superiority complex,' Lucy muttered. 'Anyway, they seemed a very nice couple as far as I could tell, and quite taken with Hanna . . . Oh my God, what's this?' she demanded, pulling a small handgun out of the cutlery drawer.

Daphne glanced over her shoulder. 'Oh, it's Dad's,' she replied dismissively. 'He found it ages ago in a box that came in with a lot of other stuff from someone over near Monmouth, I think it was.'

'So what's it doing here, in this drawer? Is it real?'

'I think so. I suppose Dad put it there.'

'But Mum, it's a *gun*. You're not allowed to own one without a licence, so you should be finding out who it belonged to and returning it.'

'You know, I think Dad did get in touch with the people, but they didn't want it back so he decided to hang on to it. You know how he likes to tinker about with things. Don't worry, it doesn't work, so he's not in danger of shooting himself.'

'That's not the point. What if it was used in some sort of crime? I think you should take it to the police.'

Daphne rolled her eyes. 'You're definitely my daughter,' she teased, 'finding a drama in everything, but OK, you can take it if you want to . . . Is that your mobile ringing?'

'Yes it is,' Lucy replied, and dropping the gun she quickly hiked the phone out of her back pocket. 'At last,' she cheered, seeing it was Ben. 'Are you there now?' she cried, clicking on. 'Are you OK?'

Laughing, he said, 'Hey Mum. Yeah, I'm here and everything's cool. Seriously hot, but cool. How are you? Missing me?'

'No, not a bit.'

'Yeah, right.'

Her heart was singing. 'How was the flight?'

'Long and cramped, but at least we made it. We've checked into this hostel not far from the airport which seems pretty decent. There are loads of students around, American, Australian, British . . . Anyway, I take it you're at Granny's now?'

'Yes, we arrived yesterday afternoon, and I still haven't forgiven you for sneaking out . . .'

'Cut me a break, Mum! I'd still be there if I hadn't. So how's my baby sister? Still kicking up?'

'Let's say she hasn't been quite as bad as I feared. She's going to miss you though. We all are, and remember if you want to come home . . .'

'Mu-um!'

'All right, all right.'

'How are Granny and Grandpa?'

'They're both well. Grandpa's down at the cottage and Granny's here making breakfast. Would you like to say hello?'

'Love to, Mum, but I can't afford to stay on the line. Just thought you'd like to hear my voice.'

'Find an Internet cafe and email me.'

'Will do.'

'I'll send Dad your love.'

'Tell him I'll text him. And Hanna.'

'Love you.'

'Yeah. Got it. Bye then,' and a moment later the invisible thread that had tied them so briefly was gone.

Daphne was smiling as she turned round to start serving the breakfast. 'Well, at least we know he's still in one piece,' she commented wryly. 'I wasn't sure we'd hear from him this soon.'

Lucy's eyes were flooding with tears.

'Oh, come on now,' her mother chided. 'He's a big boy. He can take care of himself and the last thing he's going to want is you getting upset every time he's in touch.'

'I know, I know, it's just the strangeness of not having him around. It's like everything's changing and I don't know why, because being here is absolutely what I want, but suddenly I'm feeling ridiculously insecure.'

Daphne started to look worried.

'But I'll get over it,' Lucy assured her hastily.

'Of course you will,' Daphne agreed. 'It might have been easier if Joe had come with you, but I know how much his work means to him.'

Wondering how her parents always managed to be so understanding about Joe's 'work', when she had such a struggle with it herself, Lucy decided it was best to change the subject now. Confiding any sort of doubts or innermost thoughts to her mother had never been wise, since Daphne always seemed to take everything to heart and would then fret about it in a way that seemed to make it all her fault.

How difficult would it be for her, Lucy wondered, if she were to confess that the nightmare that used to plague her as a child had staged an unexpected and unwelcome return last night. For years she hadn't even thought about it, but then, out of the blue, the woman had started screaming again, screaming and screaming . . . Instinctively she knew it was her mother, but she looked different and terrified and all the time she was screaming she kept slipping further and further away, as though she was being sucked into a long dark tunnel.

When Lucy was young the nightmare used to distress her so deeply that she'd been almost impossible to console. This morning, being so much older and less easily fazed by the subconscious, she was managing to shrug it off much like any other dream. However, as she'd discovered a moment ago, lurking beneath all the heady emotions of excitement, joy and anticipation, an odd sense of insecurity and even loneliness was trying to stake its claim.

Chapter Seven

Though Sarah barely knew Lucy Winters, this was the first time since she'd left Paris that she'd felt not only brave enough, but even eager to make a new friend. She wondered why Lucy, when there were so many other women in the area that she could have tried to connect with. There were even a few she'd known since childhood, but for some reason she'd remained buried in her shell until these past few days. Was it Lucy's newness to the village that was making her feel more sure of herself? Or had her instincts picked up on something about Lucy the first time they'd met that she'd only begun to recognise now? She had no clear idea, she only knew that she had a very good feeling about Lucy and wasn't even going to try to imagine them not getting along.

Annie had worked a miracle with her hair. Sarah had never worn it short before, and couldn't imagine why not now, when the cute, boyish cut emphasised her chocolate-brown eyes and shapely mouth in a way that made her look like a young Twiggy, Annie had declared. Sarah had even laughed with delight, a sound she hadn't heard emanating with such enthusiasm from her own lips for way too long. She'd tried to pay Annie, of course, but Annie wouldn't hear of it.

'It's worth it just to see you smiling like that,' Annie had clucked away happily. 'All you need now is a bit of make-up and some decent clobber and all the blokes will be after you.'

Though that was the last thing Sarah wanted, or needed, she hadn't been churlish enough to say so, instead she'd thanked Annie with all the warmth she could muster and had promised to call and make another appointment soon, which she absolutely insisted on paying for.

It was amazing how uplifting a new haircut and the possibility of a new friend was proving, she was thinking as she flitted about the kitchen putting biscuits on a plate and coffee into a pot. She hadn't dared to feel this optimistic since the day her world had been shattered by a speeding truck. She wouldn't think about that now though, she didn't want the pain to anchor her soaring spirits back to the loss at her core. She wanted to be the person she used to be, if only for the next hour or so, effervescent, energetic, even quite extrovert at times and definitely brave.

Twenty minutes later she was feeling wonderfully like that person, as she and Lucy sat on the hastily weeded terrace drinking coffee and absorbing the sun that was turning the spectacular view across the fields to the estuary into a fairy-tale vision. To Sarah's mind, at least, they seemed so comfortable with each other it was as though this was something they did every day.

'I'm starting to feel as if I've died and gone to heaven,' Lucy sighed, shading her eyes as she watched a bundle of sheep milling around the gate to the next field. 'It must have been lovely growing up here with your brother and sister and the village right on the doorstep.'

Sarah smiled. 'I suppose it was,' she agreed, 'but like most children, we took it rather for granted.'

'Has the house been in your family for long?'

'Mm, quite. As far back as my great-great-grandfather, anyway.'

Lucy looked impressed. 'Are any of your grandparents still alive?'

'No, the ones on my dad's side died before I was born, and the others have gone now too. How about yours, are they still around?'

Lucy shook her head. 'No, sadly. My grandmother on my dad's side died when I was about four, I think, so I don't have many memories of her. Everyone says I'm like her though, lanky, olive-skinned, too much to say for myself . . . We've always referred to her as racy Granny because she used to sing at the local pubs in Carlyle, and she actually got a *divorce*.'

Sarah covered her mouth in mock horror. 'And no brothers or sisters?' she smiled.

Lucy sighed. 'No. Mum was already getting on a bit when she finally managed to have me – she'd had about eight miscarriages before that – and my birth wasn't easy so the doctors advised her not to have any more. Before I was old enough to understand I used to beg her to make me a brother, so I'd have someone to stick up for me when the other children were mean.'

Sarah felt a pang of sympathy. 'Were you bullied?' she asked.

Lucy shrugged. 'I wouldn't go quite that far, but we moved around such a lot thanks to my dad's job that I was always the new girl in class, the awkward one who didn't fit in, and then by the time I did we were off again. The worst part of it was having parents who were so much older than everyone else's. I used to get really upset when the other kids called them names, and then, typically of a child, I would go home and take it out on them.'

'That's so sad,' Sarah commented, hating to think of any child being pushed around or spurned by the others, and knowing how hurt she'd have been if anyone had ever said cruel things about her mum and dad.

Lucy smiled. 'Enough about that,' she said. 'Tell me about your family. Are you close, all of you?'

Sarah felt herself warming. 'Yes, I guess you could say that,' she replied, 'even though we're all in different countries now. My brother and I get along particularly well. We both lived in Paris until quite recently – he's still there. To tell you the truth, I don't know what I'd have done without him over the last few years.' Her eyes went anxiously to Lucy. 'I don't know if anyone's told you about what happened . . .'

'Yes, Mum did,' Lucy interrupted softly, 'and I'm so sorry.'

Sarah swallowed. 'Thank you, but I only asked in case I . . . Well, I tried to hold it together, but after my marriage broke up there didn't seem to be anything to hold on to any more.'

'Apart from your family?'

Sarah nodded. 'Mummy's been wonderful about letting me stay here and not nagging me to get on with my life the way she'd probably like to, and probably ought. My sister doesn't hold back much, but I know she means well.'

Lucy's eyes were full of compassion as she said, 'Heartbreak doesn't generally recognise time.'

'It's true,' Sarah sighed, as she gazed blankly out

at the view. 'I keep telling myself I should be more like my sister: she's so much tougher than the rest of us, knows how to overcome all her problems, she even sets goals for where she should be with them and by when. What's more, she usually achieves it. Mum and I are nothing like that. We go to pieces and then struggle to put ourselves back together in any way we can, and heaven only knows how long it might take us.'

'Then you're like most of the rest of us,' Lucy said comfortingly.

Sarah smiled her gratitude. 'Simon's a typical man, of course,' she went on, 'keeping everything bottled up, and being strong for us all but we all knew how hard it hit him to lose Daddy. They were very close.' She gave a gentle laugh. 'Everyone used to say that I was Daddy's favourite, but Daddy wouldn't hear any of our nonsense, as he called it. He said he loved us all equally, and I suppose he did. We adored him. He was just that kind of man, you couldn't help it.'

Lucy was watching her profile and feeling the aura of sadness around her as though it were a cocoon. She couldn't imagine anything worse than losing a child, but to have lost such a beloved father at the same time, and then for her husband to go and make another woman pregnant . . . It was no wonder Sarah had buried herself away down here – she must be terrified of what the world might throw at her next.

Glancing at her, Sarah forced a smile. 'I thought your daughter might come with you today,' she said. 'Is she excited about getting involved in the business?'

Lucy rolled her eyes. 'I'm afraid the reverse would

be true,' she replied. 'She thinks we've come to the end of the world with no U-turn.'

Sarah chuckled. 'What about your son? Ben, is that right? Is he going to join you?'

Feeling a quick tightening of anxiety inside her, Lucy said, 'He's just started his gap year, so I'm having to deal with the fact that I've no idea when I might see him again.' Suddenly realising what she'd said, she felt herself starting to colour. 'I'm sorry, I . . .'

'No, don't apologise. I understand completely how you feel. I'd be the same in your shoes. How old is he now?'

'Eighteen.' She felt she should get off the subject of her children now, since it had to be unimaginably painful for Sarah knowing that she'd never see her son grow up.

'Your mother said Joe's not coming to help with the business,' Sarah commented.

Lucy's smile was wry. 'I know you won't have forgotten about the wardrobe incident,' she said, 'so I'm not entirely sure that help, as we know it, would have been on his agenda. I think we . . . Is that your phone ringing inside?'

Sarah glanced at her watch as she stood up. 'It'll be Mummy,' she said. 'She generally calls around this time. I'll just tell her you're here, and that I'll ring back later, then maybe we should make a start on working out whether or not my family bric-a-brac is of any interest to you.'

Getting up too, Lucy followed her inside and rinsed the cups as Sarah said to her mother, 'I don't want you to get overexcited, but I have company this morning.' She turned and gave Lucy a wink. 'You're right, it is Lucy from the auction. Yes, I'd

124

forgotten I told you last night . . . No I haven't been into the attic, or the cellar. You said yourself, there's enough stuff in the house that we ought to get rid of, without going rummaging around . . . Don't worry, it's there, ready to go, but God knows who'd want to buy it.' She laughed, then said, 'OK, I'll speak to you later. Love to Sheila, and to you.'

As she rang off Lucy finished drying the cups, and said, 'OK, so lead me to it.'

'It's all laid out in here,' Sarah told her, starting through to the dining room. 'There's everything from Grandma's false teeth – joke – to an old portrait of my mother that she simply detests. I'm sure if I don't sell it she'll pay me to burn it.'

Laughing, Lucy followed her into a large oak-panelled room where the dining table was covered in sheets to protect it from the collection of wares awaiting her inspection.

'You might have guessed that I'm doing this because I need the money,' Sarah confessed as Lucy took out her camera and laptop. 'I'm not completely broke, but I'd like to try and fix this place up a bit and I certainly don't have enough for that.' She wouldn't mention anything about a job just yet, it would be far too presumptuous.

'Then we'd better get you the best prices we can,' Lucy declared, and after opening up a fresh screen on her laptop ready to make a list she started to look everything over. 'Let me see, what's this?' she said, picking up a large china bowl with garlands of roses around the rim and a handle on the side. 'It's either a jumbo tea cup . . .'

Sarah gave a choke of laughter. '. . . or a chamber pot,' she finished.

Lucy gave her a wink. 'Do we have a date on it?

Or a manufacturer?' she asked, turning it over. 'No, it doesn't seem as though anyone's been brave enough to put their name to it, but I do believe we have a matching sponge dish and toilet pail to make up the set. Thirty quid the lot?'

'Done,' Sarah agreed.

Lucy typed in the details, allocated a number, then said, 'OK. Next?'

'And here we have,' Sarah said, raising the next item as though she were presenting the prizes on a game show, 'a shiny pair of candlesticks in silver plate with heavy base and historical residue of wax dating from *circa* 1992.'

Dutifully photographing them, then entering the details, Lucy gave them a more careful once-over and said, 'Starting price, twenty to thirty pounds the pair?'

'Done,' and putting them aside Sarah lifted a painting from the floor. 'This little *chef-d'oeuvre* is a portrait of the highly disreputable Bancroft family featuring Douglas Bancroft himself . . .'

'But you can't get rid of that,' Lucy protested.

'Believe me, we have dozens of family portraits, and this one was done by the same dreadful artist who did the one of my mother, which is around here somewhere. We only kept them because he was a distant cousin of sorts, but he's popped his clogs now so we can let them go. Fiver?'

Lucy looked dubious. 'Ten,' she decided, feeling sure that Sarah's father and his siblings didn't really have heads that were far too small for their bodies. 'Next?'

'Aha, here we have a China candle snuffer in the form of a nun holding a prayer book.'

Lucy blinked.

'Before you ask, no idea where it came from, and no we aren't Catholic, but Daddy received some pretty wild gifts in his time and this doesn't even begin to do it. What do you think? It's Royal Worcester, so it might fetch a decent price.'

Lucy treated it to her inexpert eye. 'Fifty quid, but I'd like to run a comparison before we commit.'

'You mean with similar items you've sold in the past?'

'Exactly. What's that?'

Sarah turned to look where she was pointing. 'Ah, now that,' she declared mysteriously, 'is not what you might think it is.'

Lucy was all intrigue. 'Not difficult, as I don't have the faintest idea.'

'Well, if you look closely you will see that it is a rather ghastly oversized weathervane with, my mother assures me, nineteenth-century figures of a lady and gentleman in eighteenth-century costume.'

'Fantastic. What lives they must have led. How much, do you think?'

Sarah looked lost. 'Tenner?'

Lucy wrinkled her nose.

'OK, five.'

'I was thinking forty,' Lucy said.

'You're kidding? It's vile.'

'Someone might love it, so let's put it at thirty and see what happens.'

'OK, whatever you say. Now, here I have a Clarice Cliff Bizarre jampot shaped like an apple with a nasturtium pattern painted around the side and leafy top in the form of a handle.'

Lucy was busily typing it into the computer.

'Mum tells me it's quite valuable,' Sarah continued, 'so maybe we should start at fifty?'

127

'I'll mark it at a hundred and if necessary we'll stand corrected on the day.'

Really getting into this now, Sarah went over to another piece of family history waiting to be launched on to the next leg of its journey. 'OK, what about this HMV gramophone cabinet in oak? There must be an enormous market for one of these.'

Lucy's expression was deadpan. 'They'll come flocking once they see it in the brochure. Sixty pounds, and I bet we get it up to a hundred and sixty.'

'If we do, champagne's on me. Ah, now here we have my mother's portrait in which she looks – according to her – like a devil woman. I admit, she does scrub up a bit better than this, even at the age she is now. However, if you're into females who look like they enjoy the dark arts or S&M . . . What do you think?'

Lucy was gazing at it in astonishment. 'I'd never have imagined this was your mother,' she declared, feeling strangely moved by the painting in spite of its grisliness.

'Believe me, that's the best compliment you could possibly pay her, because it's actually nothing like her. She's much softer around the eyes, and nowhere near as buxom – I think the artist had a bit of a thing about her and got carried away when he came to the cleavage. Anyway, her hair's a reasonable like-ness, if only because she always used to wear it in a plait; and being of Spanish descent, from way back when, she does have a slightly swarthier complexion than the rest of us, but nothing like as dark as this. Actually, between us, this looks a bit more like Becky than it does Mum, but please don't ever quote me on that, because I know Becky hates it too.'

Lucy's eyes went to her, then back to the painting. She wondered why she should be finding it so compelling when clearly no one else did. 'I'm getting the feeling you're not too bothered about letting it go,' she said, throwing some irony into her confusion.

'It'll be a wrench,' Sarah informed her, 'but if we can get a couple of thousand for it . . .'

Lucy's eyes widened.

Sarah threw out her hands, 'OK, a fiver.'

Laughing, Lucy said, 'Actually, it's not that bad a painting in itself, and as a buyer's not going to be concerned about the likeness I'd say we should start at a hundred.'

Sarah choked. 'I can feel a whole new lawnmower coming on, complete with grass-catcher and roller,' she declared, and enjoying herself immensely now, she set the portrait aside to light upon a red oak tantalus complete with crystal decanters, one of which was chipped, but hardly noticeably.

By the time they'd been through everything, including a Victorian marble barometer (apparently confused); an art deco brass lamp (in need of a switch); a miniature train set *circa* 1980 with working signals; an assortment of toy soldiers and Matchbox cars together with a collection of first-edition soccer books by Billy Wright, it was past one o'clock.

'I don't know about you, but I'm famished,' Lucy announced as she closed up her laptop. 'If you're free, would you fancy a bite to eat at the pub?'

Sarah was thrilled. 'That would be great.'

'I'll call Mum and Hanna to let them know where we are,' Lucy said, taking out her phone. 'Would you mind if they joined us?'

'Not at all,' Sarah assured her, more pleased than

ever to find herself so willing to go out and mix. 'Let's hope they do.'

Minutes later Lucy clicked off her mobile saying, 'Oh dear, apparently my number one fan's turned up at the office.'

Sarah's eyebrows rose.

'Maureen Crumpton,' Lucy muttered, 'but don't worry, she's not on the guest list for lunch. It'll be just you, me and Hanna, who's apparently already at the pub – and didn't Maureen just love telling me that. I'll give Mum's mobile a quick try now to find out where she is.'

Daphne was walking away from the Old Lodge, along the drive, out through the gates and turning up towards the village. Whether the Mckenzies were watching her leave she had no idea, nor did she turn around to find out. It would probably have seemed odd if she did, unless it was to give them a cheery wave, but it wasn't her way to be overly friendly. Polite, of course, she was always scrupulous about that, and helpful where she could be, but insinuating herself into other people's lives was as alien to her as indulging in idle gossip, or carousing about the pub garden on Saturday nights.

Having said that, there were some social occasions she enjoyed very much, such as church garden fetes and the vicar's twice-monthly Bible readings, and she almost never missed the barn dances that made the village hall throb with gaiety every six weeks or so. Brian particularly enjoyed those, when his rheumatism allowed, and he was a very keen member of the skittles and darts teams too, even travelling around the West Country to take part in the various tournaments.

However, all that was a long way from her mind as she began the climb up Edge Hill towards the high street. All she was able to think about, as she put one foot in front of the other and tried to stop her mind from going in directions she hardly dared to take, was the answer Philippa Mckenzie had given when Daphne had asked, with a pleasant smile, what in particular had decided them on Cromstone for their retirement.

Never, even with an entire lifetime to try, would Daphne have guessed at the reply she'd received. It was so far from what she'd expected that she could still hardly make herself believe that they'd confided such a painful and shocking part of their past to a virtual stranger, when they had no idea whom she might tell, or what she might end up doing with their extraordinary secret.

As her mobile started to ring she clicked on and put it to her ear.

'Mum? It's me. How did you get on with the Mckenzies?'

Daphne's throat was so dry she had to clear it before she could speak. 'Fine, yes, fine,' she answered.

'Is there much stuff?'

'A bit. Actually, it turns out the Mckenzies are brother and sister, not husband and wife.'

'Really?' Lucy sounded surprised. 'How sweet. Anyway, Sarah and I are going to the pub for some lunch. Hanna's joining us and I thought you might like to come too.'

Daphne stopped walking as a wave of dizziness came over her. 'I – uh, actually, I'm not feeling all that hungry, dear.'

'Oh, that's a shame. Are you OK?'

'Yes, yes, it's probably just the heat getting to me a bit. Where are you now?'

'We've just arrived at the pub. Where are you?'

'On my way home, but I won't stop off. I'll see you this afternoon when you get back. *Bon appétit*, all of you,' and clicking off the line, she put a hand to her head to try and stop it from throbbing any more than it already was.

By the time she reached the farmhouse sweat was pouring from her skin, and she felt as though she might be about to pass out.

'Ah, Daphne, you're back,' Maureen declared, coming out of the barn as Daphne crossed the courtyard heading for the office. Maureen was a tall, fleshy woman with a great liking for red lipstick and chunky jewellery that jangled a percussive accompaniment to her clipping kitten heels as she walked. 'Godfrey rang about ten minutes ago,' she informed Daphne, 'they've managed to get the Mortons' grand piano on the lorry, so they should be on their way back by now. I was just making sure . . .' Breaking off as she seemed to realise Daphne wasn't listening, she said, 'Daphs? Are you all right, my old love? You're looking a bit peaky, if you don't mind me saying so.'

'I'm fine,' Daphne said, breathlessly. 'Just the climb up the hill in this hot weather . . .'

'I'll fetch you a drink, that should sort you out. Go on in and sit down now, I won't be a tick.'

'No, please don't worry. I can get one myself. I – uh, that's good news about the piano. Very good. Do we . . . Actually, you know, I think I will get a drink. You carry on, I'll come to find you in a minute,' and turning back to the house, Daphne went in through the open stable door and closed the bottom part behind her.

'Brian,' she said, when she was diverted to her

husband's voicemail, 'I need to speak to you, dear. Please call me, but don't worry, because I'm fine. Maureen's here and she's being very kind. I'm not sure what to do, Brian, so please call as soon as you can.'

Chapter Eight

Much later that day, Lucy was in the office with Maureen Crumpton going over the list of items Sarah was submitting for sale. The terseness of Maureen's assessments was confirming Lucy's suspicion that in spite of whatever her mother might have said to her and Godfrey they were still considering themselves overlooked, and possibly even cheated. In some ways, Lucy could understand their disgruntlement, since they'd been involved with the business virtually from the day her parents took over, and no one would ever dispute how invaluable their input had been. However, they must surely have been aware that Daphne and Brian had always intended to keep things in the family, provided that was what Lucy wanted, and Lucy had never hidden the fact that when the time came she was extremely eager to take over.

So, for Maureen to be throwing her ample weight around the way she was now, tutting at Lucy's valuations and being as negative as she dared about the items themselves, was making it abundantly clear to Lucy that she was not going to avoid an uphill struggle where Mr and Mrs Crumpton were concerned.

'We don't tend to go in for all these flowery descriptions,' Maureen commented sourly as she scrolled down the page Lucy had sent over to her computer. 'We like to keep it nice and simple so that the bidders aren't misled in any way. And see here, item seventeen, you've got so carried away that I can't make head nor tail of what it's supposed to be.'

Lucy located the offending article and tried not to smile as she read: *A pair of Lovatt Langleys with individually stylised hand-painted decorations from the fascinatingly inventive art deco period.* OK, it was over the top, but she and Sarah had had fun concocting it and it wasn't as if it was inaccurate. 'They're vases,' she said mildly. 'Sorry, I missed that bit out, but it's quite a well-known brand . . .'

'I'm aware of that, but not everyone is, so it's important to be precise and concise. People like your mum seem to have a natural gift for it, but not everything runs in families, does it?'

Catching the barb, Lucy almost smiled again. 'No, I suppose not,' she replied evenly, keeping her eyes on the screen.

'Take mine, for example,' Maureen rattled on. 'I know for a fact that our Tina would be hopeless at all this, whereas I, as her mother, found myself taking to it like a duck to water.'

Knowing that Tina was no more than twelve, Lucy decided to breeze over the ludicrous comparison. Making a start on trying to win Maureen over, she said, 'I know I have a lot to learn and I'm extremely thankful that you and Godfrey are going to be around to guide me.'

Maureen's eyes narrowed as she flicked Lucy a sidelong glance. Clearly she wasn't entirely sure whether or not she was being mocked, and in all honesty Lucy wouldn't want to be called on it.

'We've worked hard building this place up with

your parents,' Maureen told her, as if she didn't already know. 'Its reputation and its fortunes mean a great deal to us.'

'Of course, and I hope they'll continue to matter every bit as much in the future.'

Maureen sniffed and returned to her perusal of Lucy's amateur efforts. 'I'm going to enter all this the way I think it should be done,' she said, 'then we can go through it together once everything's come in. That way you'll be able to get a better idea of what I'm talking about.'

Considering that to be a complete waste of time, since it would make far more sense to rewrite it once she'd seen the items, Lucy merely smiled acceptance and closing down her own copy of Sarah's file, she opened an Excel sheet containing the figures for the last auction.

'What are you doing?' Maureen asked, craning her neck to try and see Lucy's screen.

'I thought it would be interesting to make a study of the last few sales,' Lucy answered.

'Why?'

'Well, to give myself some idea of trends and comparisons . . .'

Maureen heaved a weary sigh. 'You don't want to be bothering with all that now,' she declared. 'That's advanced stuff. It would be like jumping in the deep end when you haven't even learned to swim. What you'd be better off doing is sorting out some of that filing over there.'

Lucy glanced at the untidy pile Maureen was indicating. 'Isn't Maeve coming in tomorrow?' she asked pleasantly.

Maureen's nostrils flared. 'Tomorrow's one of her days, yes.'

'Well, as filing's a skill I don't need any practice at, and I don't want to be accused of taking Maeve's job, I think I should stay focused on the complex systems around how the business is run. So,' she went on before Maureen could object, 'I'm interested in what you might know about someone called Eric Beadle.'

Maureen's frown darkened. 'What are you asking about him for?' she demanded.

Lucy explained about the phone call she'd taken that morning.

'Oh, you don't want to be taking any notice of the likes of that old skinflint,' Maureen snorted. 'He's a bloody troublemaker, is what he is. I told your mum she should never have anything to do with him, but she wouldn't listen. I'm telling you, she's too soft by half she is, and the likes of Eric Beadle would walk all over her if I wasn't around to send 'em on their way. Me and Godfrey, we can see those sharks coming a mile off, and they know it, which is why they don't mess with us. So, any more calls from Mr Beadle, you get him to ring back when I'm here, and I'll tell him exactly what he can do with his bloody solicitor's letters. That's if he'll speak to me, and I'll bet you a pound to a penny he won't.'

'I see,' Lucy said carefully. This was a side of the business she hadn't considered before today, that certain clients might require a particular sort of handling, and if Maureen and Godfrey were already practised at it, then who was she to go blundering in where angels, like her mother, clearly preferred not to tread? On the other hand, without wishing to seem like a control freak, she'd have rather had her hands more firmly on the reins so that she too could deal with problem punters when they cropped up. 'If it's all right with you,' she said to Maureen, 'I'd like to know, in the interests of learning, you understand, how you handle these people. I mean, I fully appreciate how protective you feel towards my parents, and I'm very glad you do, but I think it might be a good idea for the Eric Beadle types to know that someone at the top is ready to take them on too.'

Though she hadn't intended to outmanoeuvre Maureen, one look at the woman's face told her that she had accomplished precisely that – and written in the margins was the steaming resentment at being unable to come up with a suitable response. Fortunately she didn't have to, because at that very moment Lucy's mobile rang, and seeing it was Joe she clicked on right away.

'Hello,' she said in a tone designed to let Maureen know the call was personal.

'Hey,' he replied chirpily, 'not too busy to take my calls. That's a relief.'

Feeling suddenly irritated, she said, 'Never too busy for that. How are you?'

'I'm cool. Just hanging out with a few of the guys while we wait for the call back, and catching a couple of shows while we're here. You wouldn't believe how much is going on in this city. Outside London it's got to be . . .'

'Oh, Joe, hang on, sorry. The phone's ringing and Maureen's just gone out . . . I'd better take it. Can I call you back?'

'Sure, if you have time,' he said tightly.

'Don't do that,' she snapped, and cutting their connection she picked up the landline saying, 'Hello, Cromstone Auctions, can I help you?'

After dealing with three calls in quick succession, two about sale dates and one asking for a rough valuation on a set of pine drawers, she tried ringing Joe's number, only to find herself diverted to messages.

'Hey Mum. Seems you've really pissed off Dad.'

'Ah, there you are,' Lucy said, turning round to find Hanna coming in the door. 'Please don't swear like that.'

'Yeah-yeah, yeah-yeah.'

'Where did you get to after lunch? You were there one minute and gone the next.'

'This would be because I have a life beyond you.'

'Don't be clever. Where were you? Granny's not well and . . .'

'*Exactly*. Which is why I rushed back when Maureen called to tell us that, and left you gassing to Sarah. You were like so into each other, you two. I just told Dad I think you might be turning gay.'

'Well how very helpful of you, my darling. I expect it was exactly what he wanted to hear.'

Hanna shot her a look that could have choked a snake, and started to leave.

'Where are you going now?'

'I have things to do.'

'Oh really? In the land of no hope and let's-completely-forget-about-glory?'

Hanna grinned. 'Did I say that? It's pretty good, isn't it?'

Suppressing a sigh, Lucy said, 'Is Granny still lying down?'

'Yep. She was asleep when I left her. She reckons she's got summer flu.'

'I wouldn't be surprised. She works too hard,

that's her trouble. She's probably exhausted and doesn't even realise it. I'm going to call Grandpa and find out when he's coming back.'

'No need, he's on his way apparently. Should be here in time for tea.'

Lucy brightened. 'That's good. I suppose we ought to think about what we're going to eat, then we can pop over to the supermarket when I've finished here.'

'We?'

'Don't you want to come with me?'

'To Tesco? Hold me back.'

Lucy couldn't help but laugh. 'Go and look in Granny's Jamie book for something nice and easy to prepare. And if you'd like to invite Juliette . . .'

'Stop trying to find me friends.'

Lucy threw out her hands. 'Hanna, I found you at the pub, where Juliette lives, so I presume you went looking for her yourself.'

'Actually, I was there for a quick binge, but then you turned up and spoiled it all.'

'I know very well that Juliette's mother would not serve you an alcoholic drink, so now maybe you'd like to tell me about your new admirer.'

Hanna was turning crimson. 'What are you on?' she demanded.

'I saw the way that very dishy . . .'

'*Buff* is the word . . .'

'That very buff young chap was looking at you at lunchtime. Have you found out his name yet?'

Hanna raised her eyebrows. 'Might have,' she answered.

'So?'

'If you must know he's called Lucas Audley – and what's with you suddenly acting like it's OK for me to talk to boys? You used to go ballistic if I went anywhere near one in London.'

'It was the type of boys you were mixing with that concerned me there,' Lucy reminded her.

'Not to mention what I might be getting up to with them, like I'm supposed to be the only virgin left on the planet.'

'I wish you were, because you're far too young to be . . .'

'Oh stop going on all the time, and anyway, I might be for all you know.'

Lucy's eyes narrowed as she looked at her.

'See, there you go, doubting me again. And now I suppose you think I'm already shagging Lucas, just because he happened to be in the same pub as me.'

'I'm feeling fairly confident that you haven't got that far yet. So what do you know about him?'

Hanna shrugged. 'Apparently he's done time for knifing a bloke in the back . . . Not serious,' she cried as Lucy's face darkened. 'How am I supposed to know anything about him, when I hardly even spoke to him?'

Lucy waited.

Hanna's growl was lost in a laugh. 'OK, Mrs Snob, this should work for you, because apparently he lives in this great big mansion over near Tetbury and he's in the sixth form at Burton Abbots, but that's all I know.'

Lucy was impressed. 'So things are looking up,' she commented teasingly, 'a new friend and a buff bloke all in one day?'

'You so exaggerate at times. Anyway, I've decided I will come to Tesco with you, provided we try to find somewhere nearby that does eyelash extensions.'

'But you don't need them.'

'Oh Mum, you're so sad at times,' and turning round as Maureen manoeuvred herself and a large empty gilt frame in through the door, she said, 'Oh, look at you, you're a right picture. Just don't go hanging yourself, OK?'

With a throaty chuckle, Maureen said, 'How's your granny? Still in bed?'

'Yep, and Grandpa's on his way back. Now, I have a date with Jamie Oliver to sort out what we're having for tea. See ya,' and a moment later she was gone.

'A lovely girl,' Maureen muttered. 'A handful, I don't doubt, but there's no question her heart's in the right place.'

Taking the praise as an olive branch of sorts, Lucy said, 'She has her moments. So, can I help with that frame?'

'It's all right, I'm just going to put it here for a moment . . . Godfrey and Carl are back with the piano. Apparently she's a beauty. Should fetch a pretty good price. I daresay.'

'Have you valued it yet?'

'Oh no, we get experts in for something like that,' and picking up the phone she began prodding the keypad with her bejewelled banana-shaped fingers.

Deciding to go and take a look at the piano, Lucy wandered across the courtyard to the barn, batting away a few flies as she went, and flipping her hair up and down to try and cool the back of her neck. It was with no small relief that she stepped in through the back door of the barn, where it took a moment or two for her eyes to adjust. The interior was vast, with two large mezzanines suspended from the towering vaulted ceiling that overlooked the well of the building. Endless racks of ceramics, glassware, rolled-up carpets, toys, mirrors, pictures and every imaginable item of furniture were stacked up around the walls, while in the middle several crooked rows of upright chairs were set out in front of the podium, as if for an audience.

After making her way towards the enormous cart doors at the front of the barn, which were allowing copious amounts of sunlight to stream into the Aladdin's cave, she found Godfrey's small removal truck parked in the drive that curved down from the outside lane. She was about to call out to see if anyone was nearby, when the sound of footsteps coming out of the shadows made her jump and wheel round.

'Oh, Godfrey,' she gasped, pressing a hand to her throat. 'I didn't see you in there.'

'No, I didn't reckon you did,' he responded with a grin that made her want to take a step back. With his frizzled silver beard, roving eyes and fat, moist lips, he was as unattractive to her as the entire female species was apparently attractive to him.

'I've come to have a look at the piano,' she told him, trying not to recall the day he'd had the gall to make a pass at her. Though it was a couple of years ago now, it still filled her with revulsion to remember how he'd had the audacity to put his pudgy white hand on her hip, while leering into her face as though truly believing his advances would be welcome.

Her put-down had been swift and severe, with a bone-crushing stamp on his foot and a threat to go straight to her parents, and Joe, if he ever tried anything like it again. Fortunately he hadn't, but she'd never felt easy around him since.

'I'm afraid she's still under wraps in the back of the truck at the minute,' he told her, 'but Carl and me, we'll be undressing her later on today. Then we can have a gander at her in all her glory.'

Finding the innuendo almost as disgusting as the man himself, Lucy wondered how the heck she was going to work with him if he kept this up. 'Where is Carl?' she asked, starting around the truck in the hope of finding the young lad who helped with pickups and deliveries.

'He's just popped off home to change his shirt. It's a sweaty old business moving stuff around in this heat, you know.'

'I'm sure,' she muttered, and flipping out her phone she said, 'Excuse me, I have to call Joe,' and hoping the reminder that she had a husband had hit its mark she strode on up the drive into the leafy lane beyond, rather than risk returning to the office via the barn.

Finding herself diverted to Joe's voicemail again she said, 'I hope you're genuinely out of range, or busy, and not sulking because I couldn't speak earlier. Call me back when you can, and if I don't hear from you my fingers will be firmly crossed for you tomorrow.'

By the time she rang off she was at the farmhouse gates, where Hanna was perched on one of the pillars busily texting.

'Grandpa's back,' Hanna told her. 'He's just gone up to see Granny. Oh, and I found a recipe I think we'll all like. I've even written out a shopping list, so now I'm ready to leave when you are.'

Going to rest her elbows on Hanna's knees, Lucy said, 'Did I ever tell you how much I love you?'

Hanna's lip curled. 'You're not getting round me as easy as that. I still hate it here.'

'And I expect you love me too?'

'Don't take anything for granted. Oh my God,' she cried, her eyes opening wide as she looked at her mobile. 'He's only been asking about me.'

Guessing she was talking about the new buff boy on the block, Lucy said, 'So it's not actually so bad being here?'

Hanna's eyes narrowed.

'Tell you what,' Lucy said. 'As soon as I've seen Grandpa, we'll go to Tesco, then sort out some eyelashes to flutter the pants off Mr Buff.'

With a gurgle of laughter Hanna said, 'I don't think you really meant that, did you?'

'No, definitely not,' Lucy agreed. 'Better forget I said it.'

'I might,' and starting to send a text back to Juliette she said, 'I'll be here when you're ready to go.'

Lucy had just walked into the kitchen when her father came trudging down the stairs looking tired and worried, and then faintly surprised to see her.

'Lucy,' he beamed, opening his arms to hug her. 'And Hanna's here too. Lovely, lovely.'

'Dad, how are you?' Lucy said, embracing him. 'I couldn't believe it when I found out you'd gone off to Exmoor without telling Mum.'

'I'm sure I did tell her, but she probably wasn't listening,' he chuckled. 'So how are you, my love?'

Clutching his precious old face between her hands, Lucy said, 'I'm great, thanks, but what I want to know is, how are you? And don't you try palming me off with right as rain or fit as a fiddle or one of your other little platitudes if it isn't true.'

'Oh, there are plenty of tunes left in these old bones yet,' he assured her. 'But I have to confess I'm a bit worried about your mother. It's not like her to be struck down by a bug, and this is the third time in as many months . . .'

'You're kidding me,' Lucy cut in. 'How come this is the first I'm hearing of it?'

'Oh, we didn't want to worry you, and we still don't, but I think it might be a good idea for her to see a doctor.'

'Darned right it would. I'll drive her there myself . . .'

'No, you don't need to do that. I can take her. She'll feel happier to know that you're here getting yourself adjusted and making sure everything's ticking over with the auctions. Now, how about a nice cup of tea?'

'I'll put the kettle on for you,' she told him, going to fill it, 'but Hanna and I are about to pop over to the supermarket to pick up some things for tea. Is there anything you can think of that you need?'

He gave a roguish twinkle. 'Wouldn't mind a bottle of Guinness?' he whispered. 'But mind you don't tell your mother. She reckons it's not good for me, but I know it is.'

'It'll be our secret,' she smiled, and after setting the kettle on the Aga she reached for her bag. 'I won't be long,' she told him, 'and I've got my mobile in case you remember something else you want.'

She was already half out of the door when he said, 'Lucy?'

Turning back, she was about to throw out a casual yes, when she noticed the troubled look on his face. 'What is it?' she asked, feeling a stirring of unease.

'I hope you're going to like it here,' he said gruffly. 'It'll mean a lot to your mother if you do.'

'Of course I will,' she insisted. 'I've always loved coming here, you know that.'

He was nodding and smiling. 'I'm sorry we moved around a lot when you were young, but you know it couldn't be helped.'

Frowning, she said, 'Of course I do, but why are you bringing it up now?'

He shrugged. 'No reason. Well, I suppose I just want you to know that you mean the world to us, and everything we've done has always been because we love you.'

Puzzled by what might really be going on in his mind, she was about to try getting to the bottom of it when Hanna said from the door, 'Are we going, or what?'

Brian beamed. 'Ah, look at you, a sight for sore eyes, Hanna-Banana.'

'Grandpa,' Hanna complained. 'I'm fifteen now.'

Brian's rheumy eyes went to Lucy. 'Too old for nicknames?'

Lucy nodded. ''Fraid so, but she'll come round to it again when she's about thirty.' Then, realising there was a chance he might no longer be with them by then, she went back to give him another hug. 'Dad, you're the best human being on the entire planet,' she told him warmly. 'And the best father in the universe of universes.'

'Hang on, I've got one of those too,' Hanna piped up.

'Then you're an especially lucky girl,' Lucy told her, 'because you're descended from the two most wonderful men in the world.'

'So it's not surprising they produced perfection,

is it?' Hanna finished, with a flip of her hands and a curtsy. Then, ducking Lucy's playful slap, she headed back outside, leaving her grandfather still chuckling with delight as her mother rolled her eyes and followed.

Chapter Nine

Lucy and Sarah were strolling through the old market town of Chipping Sodbury, a quaintly characterful place that was several miles from Cromstone, but also tucked into the foothills of the Cotswolds. It was a while since either of them had last visited, but little had changed. The main high street – or Chepynge as it had been known in medieval times – was still a wide, welcoming thoroughfare lined with speciality shops such as bakeries, royally appointed butchers, trendy delicatessens and restaurants, with plenty of parking on the wide sweep of cobblestones either side of the road and a fascinating display of architecture from several centuries.

As they paused to browse the window of a cake-decoration shop, Lucy was laughing at Sarah's story of how she and Becky had once signed her father and Simon up for the Sodbury Slog. They'd had to run for miles through ditches, streams, quagmires and endless open fields, only to fall by the wayside long before the finish.

'I was here, in the town,' Sarah was saying as they walked on, 'with Mum and Becky, ready to cheer their victory, and it seemed like hours before they finally came limping over the brow of the hill like a pair of wastrels. We hardly recognised them, they were so mired in mud.'

Loving the image as much as the sense of fun they'd clearly shared as a family, Lucy said, 'Let's not tell Hanna this story, OK? I don't want to be giving her any ideas, because she might think it a fit punishment for me for bringing her here.'

'My lips are sealed,' Sarah promised with sparkling eyes. 'So what happened to her? I thought she was joining us today.'

With no little irony Lucy said, 'She was, but then she was torn because Juliette, her new best friend, texted to say that she could possibly get her together with this Lucas chap later, and she decided she didn't trust us to get her back to Cromstone in time.'

Sarah's eyes widened in mock astonishment. 'Do we look untrustworthy?' she demanded.

Laughing, Lucy said, 'Apparently we were so engrossed in whatever we were chatting about the other day that we forgot she was there, and she's afraid it'll happen again. She's fifteen, remember, so has to be the centre of the universe, particularly mine, but only when she requires it. The rest of the time, much like during lunch on Thursday, she's happy to pretend I don't exist while she gets on with eyeing up the local talent. Now, where's this gallery we're supposed to be looking for?' she said, checking the envelope she was carrying. 'It doesn't seem to be on the high street, from the address.'

Taking a look, Sarah said, 'I know exactly where that is, because Michael used to have an office there.'

Lucy's eyebrows rose. 'And Michael would be?'

'Michael Givens – my brother's best friend from school, and uni, come to that.'

'You're kidding me,' Lucy laughed. 'If we're talking about the same person, and I guess we probably are, he's our lawyer.'

'That's the Michael,' Sarah confirmed. 'I think his offices are in Stroud these days, unless he's still got the premises here too. It seems ages since I last saw him, probably because it is. Don't ever let on, but I had a bit of a crush on him when we were growing up. I was way too young for him of course, but he went out with Becky for a while when they were in their late teens. In fact, I think they were each other's first, but they broke up in the end; she said it was like going out with her brother, she knew him so well. Isn't it great that you know him too?'

'I've never actually met him,' Lucy confessed. 'I've been dealing with someone called Teresa who I guess is one of his partners. Do you know her?'

Sarah shook her head. 'Ah, here we are,' she declared, turning into a narrow cobbled street. 'And by the look of it he does still have offices here, because there's his name on the sign over that door. I'd be tempted to go in and say hello if the place was open, but it doesn't seem to be. Nor, unfortunately, does our gallery,' she added, as they came to a stop outside a squat, double-fronted shop with an odd assortment of paintings and lithographs in the windows, and a postman making a delivery through the shiny brass letter box.

'If you're looking for Margie she'll be back in half an hour,' he told them. 'That's what the note on her door says, anyway.' He glanced at his watch. 'She left it at eleven forty, so five minutes ago.'

'Thanks,' Lucy said with a smile. She turned to Sarah. 'So looks like we have some time to kill.'

Clearly delighted by the prospect, Sarah took Lucy's arm, saying, 'I know it's not noon yet, but what do you say we head for the champagne bar?'

Lucy threw out her hands in amazement. 'How come I didn't think of that?' she demanded. 'Lead me to it.'

Minutes later they were perched on high stools in the champagne bar at the front of Lésanne's high-end boutique, with Lesley, the owner, popping a cork and filling two colourful glasses with Moët et Chandon.

'I'll leave you to it if you don't mind,' Lesley whispered, as she delivered their drinks. 'There's half a dozen people back there and you never know, someone might buy the Basler fur cape.'

'In this heat?' Sarah cried incredulously.

'How much is it?' Lucy wanted to know.

'Only three thousand.'

Lucy's eyes boggled.

Lesley smiled apologetically and disappeared off into the designer emporium, where Lucy remembered once buying a pair of glittery tights for a Christmas party. Things were looking up now that her income was about to more than double; however, she felt fairly certain she still wouldn't be splashing out on a genuine fur cape any time soon.

'OK, here's to us,' Sarah declared, clinking her glass against Lucy's.

'To us indeed,' Lucy responded, 'and to a little fortune coming your way from the next Cromstone auction.'

'Hear, hear to that,' Sarah laughed, and clinking their glasses again they both took a generous sip.

'I'm guessing this'll be Hanna,' Lucy said, as her phone bleeped with a text. 'Yes, it is,' she confirmed.

'She wants to know if it's all right for her to borrow five pounds off her grandpa before she goes out, which apparently I have to pay back.'

Laughing and waving a hand as the bubbles fizzed up her nose, Sarah said, 'What news on the hot date?'

'She's not meeting him until two,' Lucy replied, texting back a quick yes.

Sarah wrinkled her nose. 'Is hot date the right terminology these days?' she wondered.

'I guess so – oh what the hell do I know? Anyway, here's her day so far: Grandpa – *Grandpa* – drove her into town first thing so she could Bambi herself up with some eyelash extensions, and now, would you believe, she's at the Mckenzies', helping them to set up their new Wii Fit.'

Sarah was clearly impressed. 'They have a Wii Fit? How very modern of them.'

'Exactly what I thought, but Mum, *Granny*, was of the opinion that it was quite ridiculous for people of their age to be messing about with teenage gadgets. Between us, I don't think she's entirely sure what one is. Anyway, for some reason she wasn't at all keen on Hanna going to help out, but Hanna had promised, so, wait for this, Granny's gone too.'

Sarah almost choked on her drink.

'Don't let's go there,' Lucy advised, taking another sip of champagne. 'The main thing, at least for me, is that Mum's up and about again after two days in bed, though she's still not completely over this bug. Her throat's red raw and she can hardly speak she's so bunged up. Dad wants to take her off to Exmoor so she can get some proper rest, but she's refusing to budge until she's sure I'm ready to step into her shoes.'

'Which will be when, do you think?' Sarah asked.

With a sigh Lucy said, 'If I had the full support of Maureen and Godfrey I'd side with Dad and get him to take her now, but I'm afraid they might try to sabotage me while I'm still green enough to let them.' She took another sip of her drink. 'I'd never tell Mum this, but if I could I'd let them go, because frankly he gives me the creeps and she's doing her level best to put me down at every turn. However, without them I'd be up the proverbial without a paddle.'

Would now be a good time to suggest helping out, Sarah was asking herself. It certainly seemed to be, but then she was hardly a suitable replacement for the Crumptons, so all she said was, 'Did you ever hear any more from the bloke who threatened a solicitor's letter?'

Lucy shook her head as she put her glass down. 'And Maureen's convinced we won't. Interestingly though, I did a bit of digging around after everyone had gone last night and I found a few more letters from people claiming that Cromstone have auctioned off their items to someone who then sold the piece on for five or six times as much.'

Sarah's eyebrows rose.

'I know what you're thinking,' Lucy said, 'and I agree it doesn't look good, but at the same time I don't disbelieve Maureen when she says that a provincial saleroom like ours is always going to suffer accusations of that sort.'

'Yet,' Sarah said deliberately, 'I always imagined your mum was scrupulous about valuations.'

'You're right, she is, but that's her, and I don't suppose everyone's like her. For instance, you could sell your grandma's chamber pot through us at Cromstone's for, say, fifty quid, then whoever buys it takes it to another auction and manages to get the price up to a hundred. I imagine if you found out about it you'd feel slightly aggrieved that you didn't make as much for Grandma's depository when, after all, she was your grandma, and maybe you were the one having to empty the pot.'

Sarah laughed as she screwed up her nose. 'Point taken,' she said, 'but what does your mum say about the complaints?'

'I've only talked to her about Eric Beadle's so far, but I intend to mention the others when she's feeling a bit better.' She glanced at her watch. 'Personally speaking I'd love to have another glass, but I guess we ought to go and get these forms signed or I'll be late picking Joe up from the station.'

Taking out her purse, Sarah said, 'How long's he staying?'

'This is on me,' Lucy insisted, fishing out hers. 'Until Monday, he says, but we'll see. I just hope he's in a better mood than when we spoke last night, because he was pretty down about not getting the part he went to Glasgow for – especially as they cast someone half his age.'

'Ouch,' Sarah murmured. 'He's in a tough business.'

'And it doesn't get any easier, but he's adamant he'll make it back to the top one of these days, and yours truly isn't going to be the one to burst his bubble.'

After paying the bill, Lucy led the way outside to where a troupe of morris dancers was romping vigorously around the war memorial, with a small band of spectators clapping them on.

'Your husband's lucky to have someone so supportive as you,' Sarah commented, as she fell in beside Lucy.

Lucy cast her a glance, then smiled. 'I know you two got off on the wrong foot,' she said, 'but I was hoping you might give him a second chance and come and join us for dinner tonight.'

Sarah barely hesitated. 'I'd love to,' she declared, 'and please don't think I hold a grudge, because I really don't.' She might even, she was thinking, be able to put aside Joe's infidelity if it meant becoming a part of Lucy's inner circle. After all, it was perfectly possible that Lucy already knew about Annie and if she did, and had moved on, then she, Sarah, ought to as well.

'I was thinking of inviting the Mckenzies too,' Lucy said, as they turned back into the cobbled lane, 'but a large party is probably too much for Mum while she's still not fully fit. Have you met them yet, by the way?'

'I think I'm the only one who hasn't, but everyone's speaking very highly of them so I can't imagine I won't be charmed by them too. Aha, looks like the gallery's open so the owner must be back.'

'Sarah? Is that you?' a voice called from behind them.

Turning round, Sarah clocked who it was and gave a gasp of joy. 'Michael,' she cried, quickly crossing the street to greet a tall, dark-haired man who appeared equally pleased to see her.

'How are you?' he demanded, taking a good look at her. 'It's been too long.'

'I'm fine thanks,' she laughed, and looking up into his finely chiselled face she felt her own flood with colour. 'And you're right,' she told him, 'it has been too long. So how are you?'

'You mean apart from guilty of not keeping up

156

with old friends? How's Simon these days? Is he still in Paris?'

'Yes, but he should be over soon so we must all get together.'

'Absolutely,' he agreed, his eyes moving to Lucy.

'Gosh, where are my manners?' Sarah exclaimed, turning around. 'Michael, this is Lucy Winters, who's taking over at Cromstone Auctions. Lucy, this is your lawyer.'

Amused, Lucy crossed over to shake his hand.

'It's a pleasure to meet you,' he told her, his intense blue eyes gazing directly into hers.

'Likewise,' she assured him. 'I've heard a great deal about you, mainly from Mum, who could be one of your biggest fans.'

With a laugh, he said, 'The feeling's mutual, and I've heard a lot about you too, so it's high time we met. Has everything gone through now? All t's crossed and i's dotted?'

Lucy grimaced. 'I still haven't been in to sign for the house, but everything's finalised with the business. I'll call Teresa on Monday to find out when's a good time for her.'

'If it's just a signature we need I'm sure we can courier something to you, or I can pop it in to you myself if I'm passing. Having a place here and in Stroud, it's not much of a detour to get to Cromstone. So now, what brings you two ladies to Chipping today?'

Lucy held up the envelope she was carrying. 'I'm chasing signatures myself,' she told him. 'Margie, in the art gallery, did some valuations for us and forgot to sign before sending them back, so we thought we'd ring the changes from Cromstone for a while and bring them over in person.'

Michael's eyes were still holding hers. 'Well, if you're not in a hurry,' he said, glancing at Sarah, 'how about joining me for some lunch?'

'We'd love to,' Sarah cried delightedly. Then, remembering Joe, she looked sheepishly at Lucy. 'Wouldn't we?' she said lamely.

Deciding that actually, yes, they would, Lucy took out her phone. 'I'll call Dad and ask him to collect Joe from the station,' she said, 'then I'll come to find you after I've sorted things out with Margie. Where will you be?'

Checking his watch, Michael said, 'It's still early, so we'll probably get a table at the Italian. Do you know where it is?'

'I spotted it just now at the end of the high street.'

'If I'm going on ahead with Michael,' Sarah said, 'shall I order you a glass of wine?'

Lucy grimaced. 'Better not as I'm driving, but don't let that stop you.'

Twenty minutes later, with her forms signed and her father on his way to the station, Lucy was sitting on the shady patio behind the restaurant, sipping a mineral water while listening to Michael and Sarah catching up on their news. She wasn't sure why she was surprised to learn that he was the father of three young boys, all under the age of ten, she simply was, though the fact that neither he, nor Sarah, mentioned the boys' mother was what she found most intriguing. Then the subject moved on to Simon and how he and Michael had travelled around the world together during their gap year, and she soon found herself talking about Ben. She'd received two emails to date, she told them, which she'd probably read a hundred times each, even though he was only saying he was fine and having a great time. No details of where he was, or what the place was like, which she accepted was typical of boys, but she wished he'd told her something about the local culture, having never been to Thailand herself.

Since Sarah and Michael both had, they were happy to regale her with their own experiences, while trying not to alarm her with accounts of the more dubious aspects of the country.

By the time their food arrived the subject had changed again, this time to Sarah's mother.

'Have you ever met Rose?' Michael asked Lucy.

Lucy shook her head as she rolled a few slivers of duck into a crêpe. 'No, I haven't,' she replied, while realising she'd like to.

'She's quite something,' he told her, with a playful glance towards Sarah. 'We boys were always mad about her when we were growing up, which used to drive poor Simon crazy. He thought we were only his friends because of her and his two gorgeous sisters, and if I'm honest he wasn't entirely wrong. Staying with the Bancrofts was always first on everyone's list when it came to summer holidays, because it was where we always had the best time. Do you remember how your father used to set us his famous challenges so we could show off to you girls how well we knew your favourite poets?' he asked Sarah.

'And you were hopeless,' she laughed. 'But worse was when he'd bring in local bands for you to perform with. Not one of you was a gifted musician, that's for sure.'

Michael's hurt expression made Lucy laugh. 'And all the time,' he said, 'Rose was there with her girls, watching and laughing and teasing us mercilessly.'

'But then,' Sarah went on, starting to sober, 'she'd

disappear to her room with one of her migraines, as we used to call them, and Dad was left doing his best to keep us entertained.'

'Which he always did, masterfully,' Michael assured her.

Sarah smiled. 'He did, didn't he? And it couldn't have been easy when he was always so worried about her.'

'So if it wasn't a migraine, what was it?' Lucy asked, curiously.

Sarah sighed and picked up her wine. 'Who knows?' she replied. 'It's not something we've ever discussed with her, we just grew up knowing that she was prone to these so-called headaches. Becky calls them depressions and I think she's probably right. Certainly it's what Mum takes medication for and it seems to be working, because I don't think she takes to her bed like that any more.'

Realising her phone was vibrating, Lucy turned it over, and seeing it was Joe she excused herself to wander to the edge of the patio. 'Hi, everything OK?' she asked him.

'It would be if you'd come to pick me up,' he told her, his slurred speech letting her know that he'd travelled down in the buffet car. 'What's the big deal that you couldn't make it?'

'Something came up,' she replied. 'I could go into detail, but I don't expect you're interested to know about valuations and lawyers and . . .'

'Don't patronise me,' he snapped. 'I've come all this way to see you . . .'

'To see Hanna,' she reminded him. 'Where is she?'

'She left as soon as I got here, so I'm stuck with your parents.'

'I hope you're being nice to them. Mum hasn't been well . . .'

'Yes, I've heard all about it, thanks, and when am I ever not nice to them?'

Having to concede that actually, in spite of how dull he found them, he was always kind, Lucy said, 'I'm sorry. I spoke out of turn, but I can tell you're in a grumpy mood so I was worried that you might be taking it out on them. Anyway, I'll be back soon. Have you eaten?'

'Your mother made me an omelette.'

'Good, that should keep you going till dinner. Sarah's going to join us tonight and . . .'

'Who's Sarah?'

'Sarah Bancroft, from the manor.'

'What the . . .'

'Joe, get over it, she has. Now will you please text Hanna to ask if she'd like to invite a friend too? By the way, she's been invited to a party down in the valley that starts about ten and I've said she can go, provided she's back by midnight. She'll no doubt try getting round you for an extension, but that's late enough at her age, OK?'

'If you say so,' he retorted sourly.

'I'll be home in about half an hour, so I'll see you then,' she said, and quickly ringing off she returned to the table to find Michael and Sarah talking about what had happened to Sarah during the last few years. Realising she couldn't possibly interrupt to say she was leaving, Lucy sat down quietly, and soon found herself wishing she knew how to take away Sarah's pain. Still, at least she seemed to be enjoying herself today, and seeing Michael had clearly done her a power of good.

'I'm going to call Simon as soon as I get home,'

Sarah was telling Michael when they finally called for the bill. 'He'll want to see you when he comes over, I know it.'

'Just let me know the dates and I'll make sure I'm around,' Michael assured her, taking out his wallet. Then, turning to Lucy, 'It's been a real pleasure to meet you, and if we do all get together when Simon's here, maybe you'd like to join us?'

Loving the idea, Lucy said, 'I'll make sure I'm free.'

Minutes later, as she and Sarah walked back to the car, Sarah said, 'It was so lovely to see him, wasn't it?'

With raised eyebrows, Lucy said, 'He seemed just as pleased to see you.' Then, remembering the boys, 'Do you know his wife?'

Sarah pulled a face. 'Oh yes, we all know Carlotta. Our entire family went to the wedding, which was a seriously big do, in Tuscany, at her parents' villa. You should see it, it's more like a palace.'

'And what's she like?'

'Absolutely stunning and unless she's changed, an absolute nightmare, but I guess he doesn't think so or he wouldn't have stayed with her. Anyway, it'll be great if we do all get together when Simon's here. In fact, I might do something really wild and throw a little cocktail party at the manor in honour of his and Michael's reunion. It's been a long time since the old place saw any visitors, never mind any fun.'

Liking the sound of it, in spite of not feeling particularly thrilled by the prospect of meeting the exotic Mrs Givens, Lucy said, 'Then you must let me know what you'd like me to do to help. For now though, I'd better put my foot down or Joe's going to start feeling even sorrier for himself than he's already managing.'

Half an hour later, with the car windows rolled down to let some air into the old Peugeot's stuffy interior, Lucy was driving them into Cromstone when she spotted Philippa Mckenzie coming out of the One Stop Shop. 'Hello,' she called out, pulling up alongside her. 'How's the Wii Fit?'

'Oh, marvellous,' Philippa chuckled as she stopped to talk to them. 'Hanna got us up and running – and I mean running – in no time at all, the dear girl. Such an incredible invention.' She lowered her voice to a conspiratorial whisper. 'I think your mother might be interested in getting one for herself, you know.'

Lucy was incredulous. 'Did she have a go on it?' she asked.

'Oh yes, and she was very good at the yoga, I have to say. Very supple for a woman her age. Put me to shame, she did.'

Laughing as she sat back in her seat, Lucy said, 'Sarah, this is Mrs Mckenzie. Actually, it's Miss, isn't it? Or are you Ms?'

'Just Philippa,' she replied, stooping so she could see Sarah.

'And this is Sarah Bancroft,' Lucy told her. 'She lives at the manor.'

'It's lovely to meet you, dear,' Philippa smiled.

Sarah said, 'Welcome to Cromstone, Philippa. I hope you're going to enjoy your time here.'

Philippa's good eye twinkled happily. 'Thank you,' she said. 'And I shall hope that we see a lot more of you. My brother and I are . . . Well, we're old friends of your parents', you know?'

Sarah looked surprised. 'Really?'

Philippa was still smiling kindly. 'It was a very long time ago,' she said, glancing down the street as someone began honking to get by. 'Oh dear, I'd better not hold you up any more. Perhaps you'll both come for a drink at the Lodge one evening next week?'

Lucy looked at Sarah, who seemed all for it. 'We'd love to,' Lucy told her. 'Any day that suits you will be fine for us, just let us know,' and slotting the car back into gear she drove on up the hill.

'Goodness, such a social whirl we're entering into,' Sarah commented wryly. 'Next thing we know we'll be reading about ourselves in the gossip columns,' and as Lucy laughed Sarah felt a heady warmth running all the way through her. How lonely she'd been until Lucy had come to Cromstone, and how wonderful it was to feel moments of happiness again.

John Mckenzie was tidying up a rose bush in the back garden when his sister brought a jug of lemonade and two glasses out of the kitchen. She set them down on the mosaic-topped table sheltered by a clematis- and jasmine-covered pergola. The scent of the flowers was sweetening the air, and the sound of birdsong made a soothing, nostalgic accompaniment to the gentle grating of crickets.

'Aah, just what I'm in need of,' he sighed as he came to join her. And, after downing half a glass in one go, 'So how was your walk?'

'Very pleasant, thank you,' she replied. 'I didn't go far, just up to the top of the village and back. I see you've given up on the Wii.'

Chuckling, he drained his glass, then picked up the jug to refill it. 'According to Hanna, my new personal trainer,' he said, 'I was in danger of over-doing it.'

Philippa gave a splutter of laughter. 'You haven't really called your Mii Hanna, have you?' she protested, still wildly tickled by all this modern technology.

He was all innocence. 'She insisted, so what was I to do? Anyway, her grandmother thought it was a smashing idea.'

Philippa rolled her eyes. 'She's a lovely young girl,' she commented. 'I know if she were my grand-daughter I'd be very proud of her.'

The light seemed to fade from John's eyes as he looked at her. 'You should have grandchildren,' he told her. 'What you've been through for me . . .'

'Oh, don't let's start all that nonsense again,' she interrupted bossily. 'If I had my time over I wouldn't do anything differently.'

'But I would, and then you'd have had the life you deserve. A husband, children . . .'

'Och, listen to you,' she chided. 'I might not have had any of that anyway. Remember I'm older than you and I wasn't married by the time it all happened, so who's to say how things might have turned out. Anyway, that's beside the point now. We can't turn back the clocks, or undo old wrongs, all we can do is be grateful for the success we've enjoyed . . .'

'I know all that,' he cut in gruffly, 'but with what's happening to you, Pippa . . . Knowing that you . . .'

'John, please let's not keep going over this. Now, I have something to tell you. I was just introduced to Sarah Bancroft.'

Though John's eyes didn't move from hers, they seemed to lose focus as this new information took his thoughts elsewhere.

'I told her,' Philippa went on, 'that we used to know Rose.'

At that his eyes sharpened again. 'Do you think that was wise?' he asked.

'I'm not sure.'

He shook his head. 'Is she like her mother?' he asked quietly.

'No, not very. Listen, John, I might be in remission, but we both know the cancer could come back at any time, and I don't want to leave this earth before I'm sure that at least some of the injustices you've suffered have been put right.'

For a moment he only looked at her, then, understanding that he really did owe her that, he reached for her hand and pulled her into a tender embrace. 'Whatever you say,' he whispered gently. 'I just don't want anyone to be hurt.'

Chapter Ten

'I don't know what's got into you,' Joe complained angrily. 'You've spent all afternoon in the office, like you're trying to get away from me, then you spend the whole time talking to Sarah over dinner so no one else can get a word in. And now you don't want me to touch you. I'm beginning to wonder if Hanna's right and you are turning gay.'

Swinging her legs off the bed, Lucy went to the window to let in some air. The night was hot and still, and she could feel his eyes on her back as she stood gazing into the darkness. The distant sound of electro beats was throbbing out of a party down in the valley. She hoped to God Hanna wasn't getting drunk, or drugged up, or engaging in underage sex. Recalling how Joe had given her permission to stay out till two, when Lucy had specifically said she should be back by midnight, fired her anger again, but there was no point continuing to argue about it now. Hanna was there, fortunately with Juliette, whom Lucy trusted far more than any of the crowd back in London, and with any luck, under Juliette's influence, she wouldn't be led astray by this Lucas chap. Or by the likes of Marietta Babbage, whose party it was, and who was reputed to be as free with her favours as her hairdresser mother.

Inhaling the pungent scents of surrounding farm-land and dying barbecues, she tried to collect her scattered thoughts, but every time she managed to focus on her family, or the business, or anything at all, it was like trying to hold on to air. There was only one direction her mind wanted to take, and the harder she tried to stop it, the more it kept going there.

'So what's the deal?' Joe demanded from the bed.

'There is no deal, as you put it,' she responded.

'I can tell you're pissed with me, so come on, out with it, what have I done wrong apart from let Hanna stay out till two?'

Stifling a sigh, along with a surge of guilt, she made herself turn around to look at him. He was lying naked on the bed, his lithe, toned body swathed in moonlight and still semi-aroused, in spite of the way she'd just rejected him. But what was she to do, let him make love to her when it was the last thing she wanted? OK, she'd done it plenty of times before, but never while thinking about another man. Not that she wanted Michael Givens to be in Joe's place, far from it, but she couldn't get away from the fact that Michael had made an impression on her today that was lingering and pleasing in a way that wasn't easy to let go. 'You haven't done anything wrong,' she told him, trying to infuse some fondness into her tone as she hiked the thin strap of her nightie back into place. 'It's just hot, and I'm tired, and . . .' Did she dare to say it? Was their trial separation really a subject she wanted to get into at one thirty in the morning?

'I'm getting the impression you wish I hadn't come,' he said gruffly.

'That's not true,' she lied, 'but maybe . . . Well, maybe we should be in different beds.'

His shock was almost palpable. 'Are you out of your mind?' he cried. 'Why the hell would we do that when we've always slept together? And this *separation*, as you like to call it, is only temporary, remember, until we sort out how to have two homes and make it work.'

The fact that they didn't have two homes, and only would when she was making enough to pay the rent on somewhere in London for him, wasn't something she needed to point out now. It would only emasculate him further, and she could tell he was already struggling with the way she was making him feel.

His voice was roughened by unease as he said, 'It is temporary, isn't it? I mean, if you're trying to tell me . . .'

'I'm not trying to tell you anything,' she interrupted. 'I'm just trying to work out how we go forward from here.'

Getting up from the bed he came towards her, but as he made to put his arms around her, she felt herself taking a step back.

'I'm sorry, I can't,' she whispered, and seeing the hurt that came into his eyes, she wanted to drop her head in her hands and howl with despair. What was the matter with her? If she was hating herself so much for rejecting him, why didn't she just stop?

'I'm going downstairs to get a drink,' she said hoarsely.

He turned with her, watching her as she went past him. When she reached the door he said, 'I'll leave in the morning, if that's what you want.'

Wondering if she'd ever felt more wretched, she turned around. 'No,' she said, 'it's not what I want.'

'Then tell me what I have to do.'

'You don't have to do anything.'

'Look, I know you deserve more than I can give you right now, but it'll change, you know that, don't you?'

She nodded, even though she knew very well that it wouldn't.

'OK, I didn't get this part, but it wasn't really me anyway. This new agent, she's good, but she hasn't quite got what I'm about yet. The point is, she's had some fantastic results for actors my age, and she's got me a meeting with Robert Gates, the director, for a week on Tuesday. Apparently he's really keen to meet me.'

'That's great,' she said dutifully.

His eyes were showing his confusion, possibly even a hint of desperation. 'What is it, Luce?' he said. 'Tell me. Did I do something wrong with Sarah tonight? I didn't let you down, did I?'

Feeling awful that he was thinking that, she said, 'From where I was sitting you seemed to make a very good impression.'

He seemed pleased, and managed a smile. 'She's not as stuck-up as I was expecting,' he said. 'She's pretty cool, actually.'

'Yes, she is.'

He nodded, and pushed a hand through his hair. Then, moving back to dangerous ground, he said, 'So, what do we do now? Would you rather I went to sleep in another room?'

Taking a breath, as though to suppress the yes, she said, 'No.'

'Do you mean that? Or are you just worried about what your parents will think?'

'I mean it.'

He still seemed uncertain. 'You're always so

protective of them,' he said. 'I guess that goes both ways, because they're the same with you.'

'They're talking about going to Exmoor as soon as next weekend,' she told him. 'Dad's worried about Mum and I have to admit, she does seem quite tired and edgy.'

'Can you cope if they go that soon?'

'I can try.'

'What if I come to help?'

'No, you don't have to do that.' The response was too quick. 'I know how much it means to you to be in London, and Charlie depends on you to help with the markets, so does Vince with his taxi.' She tried to smile. 'And the last thing we want is you missing out on the big chance by being this far away.'

He only looked at her, but she could read his mind as clearly as if he'd spoken the words that shamed her for such artifice. But how could she tell him what was really in her mind regarding the business, when it would only end up making him feel more excluded than ever?

'Sarah, hello darling. Are you awake?'

Struggling to sit up in bed, Sarah said, 'I am now. What time is it?'

'Ten thirty my end,' her mother replied, 'which makes it nine thirty with you.'

'No! How did I manage to sleep so late? I must have had more to drink than I realised last night.'

'Really? Where were you?'

'At Lucy's.'

'I see. It sounds as though you two are becoming good friends.'

Sarah smiled. 'Yes, I think we are,' she agreed.

'You know how it is when you just gel with someone? That's kind of what's happening with us, I think. We're on the same wavelength, as you would say.'

'Is that what I'd say? Seems you know me better than I know myself. Anyway, I picked up your message when Sheila and I got home last night. How lovely that you've seen Michael again. How is he?'

Flipping back the sheet, Sarah said, 'As gorgeous as ever, and apparently doing very well because he has two bases now, one in Chipping and the other in Stroud. He asked all about you, and to tell you the truth, I think he might still have a bit of a crush.'

Rose's voice was light with humour as she said, 'I feel very sorry for him if he has. Did he talk about Carlotta at all? How are the boys?'

'On great form apparently, and growing up too fast.'

'So he still sees them? I'm very pleased to hear that.'

Sarah frowned in confusion. 'What do you mean? Of course he sees them, they're his children.'

'I just thought that now he and Carlotta aren't together any more, and knowing how temperamental she is . . .'

'Are you serious? He didn't say anything about that. How come you know and I don't?'

'I've no idea. Simon told me about a year ago, but I suppose it wasn't a good time for him to be telling you about marriages breaking up.'

Sarah's mind had started to spin. 'You know, I'm not sure whether I'm sorry to hear it or not,' she said. 'It must be awful for the boys, obviously, but that ghastly woman . . .'

'Ssh,' Rose cautioned, 'we're not supposed to say those things.'

'No one can hear, and don't pretend you liked her.'

'Oh no, she was dreadful. Of course, Dad and Simon were besotted with her . . .'

'Because she oozed sex appeal like a great big fat cake oozes cheap cream. So why did they break up, do you know?'

'Apparently she was having an affair that he found out about. Does that surprise you?'

Sarah's distaste made her lip curl. 'Sadly, not a bit. I was never convinced she realised how lucky she was to have someone like him. It was all show with her, and what he needs is someone who can see past his looks and fortune to the fantastic person he really is.'

'You mean someone like you?'

Sarah's heart skipped a beat. 'No, I don't mean someone like me,' she retorted truthfully. 'I don't think of him that way.'

'But maybe you could.'

'Don't do this, Mum. I'm really not interested in getting involved with anyone.'

'Then you should be. You're still young, Sarah. You've . . .'

'You're doing a Becky on me now, and I think of Michael the same way she does. He's more like a brother.'

'But he's not your brother, and you can't let Kelvin go on having this sort of control over you.'

Sarah bristled as her heart turned over. 'How can you say that, when I never even speak to him?'

'You're where you are because you can't face seeing him.'

'I'm here because it's where I want to be. It no longer has anything to do with him.'

Rose gave a gentle sigh. 'You're selling things from the house to try and make ends meet, how long do you think that can continue?'

'Actually, I'm selling them to raise funds to fix the place up,' Sarah reminded her. 'I still have savings to cover my living expenses and anyway, I'm thinking about getting a job.'

'With Lucy?'

'Yes, with Lucy,' Sarah replied, realising her mother had been talking to Becky. 'I haven't spoken to her about it yet, but they always take on extra people for the auctions and I'm sure if I ask she'll put me on the list.'

When there was only silence at the other end, Sarah didn't know whether she wanted to scream or cry, because of course, her mother knew that a part-time job in an auction room wouldn't even come close to restoring her to the kind of position and salary she'd enjoyed before. But she didn't want to go back, and this way forward, simple as it might be, was at least a start.

'I'm afraid you're wasting away in that house,' Rose said softly. 'It was a happy place for us once, but maybe our time there has come to an end.'

'No!' Sarah cried in a panic. 'Even if you don't want it any more, this is our home, mine, Simon's and Becky's, and none of us want to sell. We'd rather do the repairs and keep it for when one of us has children. It'll be wonderful for them to spend time here . . .' Her voice was breaking along with her heart as she thought of Jack, and how much he'd loved coming to stay. He'd even taken his first baby steps out on the terrace, straight into the arms of her father.

'I'm not going to try and force you to do anything

you don't want to,' Rose told her gently. 'I just want you to be happy again.'

'I'm fine,' Sarah insisted, but she wasn't, because the longing for Jack was all over her again, pulling at her heart, her mind, her limbs, her very soul. It was like this every morning when the first thoughts of him came to her, and these reminders of him now were making it worse.

'Oh darling,' Rose murmured as Sarah started to sob. 'I'm sorry I've upset you.'

Sarah's hand was pressed to her head as she tried to force the pain back. 'It's not your fault,' she finally managed, 'and now I'm upsetting you. This is what life does to us. Tears us apart, and makes us hurt one another, as though we're just puppets in its monstrous game.'

There was more tenderness in Rose's voice than Sarah could bear as she said, 'I know we can't change what it's done, but we have to keep hoping that one day life will smile on us again, and I'm sure it will for you, my darling. I really am.'

Unable to believe it, Sarah said, 'And what about you?'

'To see you happy will be enough for me,' her mother assured her. 'Now, tell me what you're doing today. Are you seeing Lucy again?'

'I'm not sure. Her husband's here, but there was talk last night of transporting my sale goods over to the barn. He was offering to help, but I don't want to push myself on them, especially on a Sunday.'

'Do you have any plans to see Michael again?'

'Sort of. We're going to get together when Simon's here. Actually, I'm thinking about throwing a little party when he comes.'

Sounding pleased, Rose said, 'A very good idea. Now, Sheila and I are due to meet some friends in the village for a coffee, and then we're off to a *brocante* in Salon. I'll talk to you tomorrow, OK?'

'I'm sure you will. Love you.'

'I love you too.'

It wasn't until much later in the day that Sarah realised she'd forgotten to tell her mother about the Mckenzies. Still, it wasn't as though it couldn't wait, and by then she was too busy helping to ship her things over to the barn for the thought to stay in her head for long.

'Daphne! Brian!' Joe shouted.

Daphne and Brian spun round from the barbecue, startled, worried, then relaxing as they realised Joe was pointing a camera their way.

'Great!' he told them. Then, waving a hand for them to stand closer together, 'Now let's get one of you smiling.'

Obligingly, they stood with Daphne's arm linked through Brian's and their best Sunday smiles radiating out to the camera, as Joe pranced and ducked around them like a hyped-up professional.

Watching from where she was setting a table under a giant maple at the far end of the courtyard, Lucy felt a flood of affection for her parents, who were always willing to do anything to make someone happy. Never mind that they were in the middle of deciding which of the various marinated meats to cook first, or that they'd never enjoyed being photographed, if Joe wanted their attention then Joe would have it.

Seeing flames starting to leap from the barbecue, she felt her throat turn dry, and was about to shout a warning when Joe beat her to it.

'Hey, watch out,' he laughed. 'We don't want you on the menu today. Would you like a hand there?'

'That would be lovely,' Brian replied, quickly grabbing the charcoal bag to empty more on to the fire. It was amazing, Lucy thought, how unfazed he seemed by the flames in spite of how much damage they'd once caused to his hands. Still, it was a long time ago, and it was good that he was over it now, or certainly enough to handle a barbecue on his own. However, he was all for being inclusive where his family was concerned, so if Joe wanted to boss him around that was fine by him, and off he went, laughing good-naturedly at Joe's jokes while marvelling at his flamboyant pirouettes with serving plates and lethal-looking tongs.

Joe was nothing if not an entertainer, Lucy was thinking to herself as she wondered what all the statues, fountains, pillars and benches that were accumulating for the next sale were making of him. What parties had they seen in their time? Who had admired them, or sat on them, or cooled their feet in them? How many secrets had they heard whispered, what illicit liaisons had they watched unfold?

'Dreaming again?' Joe shouted, tossing a ball her way.

Catching it, and throwing it back, she went on with what she was doing, knowing that his high spirits came as much from relief that they'd finally made love last night, as from his normal ebullience.

'Hi! Am I too early?' Sarah called out as she came through the arched gate into the courtyard. 'I've brought wine and sausages – and the last two rump steaks from Donald's.'

'You didn't have to do that,' Lucy protested as she went to give her a hug. 'We've got plenty and it's great that you can bear to spend another evening with us, especially at such short notice.'

'Oh, the problem I had rearranging my diary,' Sarah told her, with an exaggerated roll of her eyes. 'You can't imagine all the people I had to let down.'

Laughing, Lucy slipped an arm around her shoulders. 'Come on in,' she said. 'Everyone's looking forward to seeing you.'

'I really can't let you keep feeding me . . .'

'Oh, just you watch us,' Daphne interrupted with a smile as she came to greet her. 'You're very welcome, my dear, very welcome indeed.'

'Thank you,' Sarah replied, giving her a hug. 'And how are you feeling today? Better now?'

'Mm, I think so. I'm sorry I flaked out on you all last night, but I slept well, which is one good thing.'

'Sarah!' Joe cried over his shoulder from the barbecue. 'Thank God you're here, perhaps someone will pop a cork or crack a can at last.'

Chuckling happily, Brian took the hint and after welcoming Sarah in his own friendly way, he went inside to raid the fridge for a couple of lagers and a bottle of white wine.

'No Hanna?' Sarah asked, going to set her offerings down on the shady stone ledge next to the rest of the feast.

'She should be back any time now,' Joe told her. 'Better brace yourself though, because she's bringing a couple of friends.'

'She is?' Lucy said, surprised.

'I got a text about ten minutes ago. I expect you did too, if you look.'

'It's great that she's mixing so well this soon,' Sarah commented. 'How did her party go last night?'

'She hasn't said much about it,' Lucy replied, 'but

at least she was back by two and I didn't detect any signs of a hangover this morning.'

'I wonder if one of the friends is going to be Lucas,' Sarah said wryly as she held out a couple of glasses for Brian to fill.

'I guess we'll find out soon enough,' Lucy replied. 'Mum, shall I go in and finish the salads?'

'If you wouldn't mind, dear. No, no wine for me yet.' Daphne declined Sarah's offer of a glass. 'I like to keep a clear head at least until we eat.'

Turning to Brian, Sarah said, 'And how about you? Are you indulging yet?'

'I'll have a beer,' he told her, popping open a can. 'Have we heard back from Maureen and Godfrey yet to find out if they're coming?' he asked Daphne.

Lucy's head came up. 'I didn't know you'd invited them,' she said, trying not to sound as though she minded.

Daphne looked uncomfortable. 'We always do when we light the barbecue,' she said apologetically. 'But I think they were going to Maureen's sister's today, which is probably why they haven't got back to us yet.'

Wishing she didn't feel quite so relieved, Lucy said, 'Well, if we have two empty places, why don't we give the Mckenzies a call? Maybe they'd like to join us.'

Daphne's face started to colour. 'Oh, no, I don't think we should. We hardly know them, and . . .'

'But you spent yesterday morning with them . . .'

'And that's probably enough for now. We don't want to seem pushy, do we?' She was looking at Brian, who loyally shook his head.

Worried that her mother might not be feeling as strong as she was trying to make out, Lucy let the subject drop and promptly winced as a sudden blast of music exploded through the courtyard. 'Joe! Does that have to be so loud?'

'Sorry,' he shouted back, quickly turning the radio down. 'Better?'

'Just a bit,' she said ironically. Then to Sarah, 'Do you want to come and give me a hand with the salads?'

'Right with you,' Sarah assured her, and scooping up two glasses of wine she followed Lucy inside.

A few minutes later they were busy chopping, mixing and sprinkling while out in the courtyard Daphne was clucking and laughing as Joe twirled her round the flagstones to 'Build Me Up Buttercup'.

'He has a great relationship with your parents, doesn't he?' Sarah commented. 'I don't imagine life is ever dull when he's around.'

Lucy's smile was wry. 'Not very,' she agreed. Then, feeling a sudden need to be truthful, she said, 'You might find this hard to believe, but we're supposed to be on a trial separation.'

Sarah's eyes rounded as she looked at her.

With a sigh, Lucy said, 'Over the last few years . . . Well, you don't want to hear about it all, but things aren't the same as they once were. He's changed, or I have . . . I don't know. I guess you could say we've grown apart.'

A thoughtful silence fell between them, broken only by the squish and tap of a knife going through onions, and the Irish drollery of Terry Wogan coming from the radio outside. Starting to wonder if she'd gone too far when Sarah was clearly still suffering from the break-up of her marriage, Lucy was about to apologise when Sarah said, 'Do you still love him?'

Lucy took a breath, still not sure, out of an

ingrained loyalty to Joe, if this was a conversation she should continue, but she wanted to be honest with Sarah, so she said, 'In a way, I suppose, but definitely not in the way he'd like me to.'

'Does he know that?'

'I think he might have an idea, but he's avoiding it – and to a certain extent I suppose I am too.'

Sarah began to grind black pepper over her salad. 'So how do you see the future for the two of you?' she asked quietly.

Lucy could feel her mind going blank rather than try to picture it. 'To be honest,' she said in the end, 'I try not to think about it.'

Sarah nodded understandingly. 'It seems as though we're kind of in the same place,' she said, 'not wanting to think about where we go from here, or what we're going to do . . . Except you have the auctions, of course, and it's always helpful to lose yourself in work.'

Picking up on this, Lucy cast her a quick glance. 'Actually, I'm glad you brought that up,' she said, 'because I've been wondering if you might . . . Well, I know it doesn't offer all the glamour and dash of Paris, and it wouldn't have to be permanent or anything, but if you're at all interested, I'd love it if you came to work with me for a while.'

Sarah blinked in astonishment. As her emotions got the better of her, her eyes started to flood with tears. 'Lucy, I'd love to,' she laughed. 'Oh, God, you can't imagine . . . I was actually going to ask if there was something I could do . . . I mean, I don't know anything about the business, but I'm a fast learner and I can come in whenever you like . . .'

'I'm talking about fairly full-time,' Lucy warned. 'If you're up for it, of course.'

'Definitely I am. But are you sure? What about your mother? Is it OK with her?'

'She'll be absolutely fine about it when I tell her. It'll probably be a relief to know that I've got some kind of foil between me and the Crumptons.'

Sarah pulled a face. 'Ah, yes, what about them?' she asked. 'If they're directors now, don't they have to be consulted?'

'Not unless I say so,' Lucy retorted.

Though Sarah's eyes were sparkling, she gave a grimace of unease. 'I think we might have to handle it a little more tactfully than that,' she suggested.

Laughing, Lucy agreed. 'So you'll be my right-hand person,' she declared, 'and over time, if you find it's to your liking and it all works out, maybe we could talk about making you a partner.'

Sarah could hardly have looked more thrilled. 'I really wasn't expecting this,' she said, trying not to gush, 'but I think you've just made me feel happier than I have in over five years.'

Lucy dropped her knife and swept her into an embrace. 'Then it's worth it just for that,' she told her. 'And personally, I think we'll make a fantastic partnership.'

'I couldn't agree more. Watch out Christie's and Sotheby's, Cromstone Auctions is a-coming.'

'What's all this noise in here?' Daphne clucked, coming in the door. 'I thought you were making salad, but it sounds to me as though you're celebrating something.'

Sarah glanced anxiously at Lucy.

'Actually, we are,' Lucy announced. 'Sarah has just agreed to come and work with me.'

Daphne's eyebrows shot up in surprise. 'Well, my goodness, that wasn't what I expected to hear,' she commented. 'Are you sure this is what you want?'

Since Sarah was looking at Lucy, she didn't realise at first that the question was directed at her. 'Oh, yes, yes,' she insisted. 'I've been building up to asking if there might be something I could do, so I honestly couldn't be happier.'

In spite of the way Sarah was frowning, Daphne started to smile.

'Are you all right, Mum?' Lucy asked.

'Just a bit of a headache again,' Daphne replied, and taking a hand of each of them, she said, 'I'm very pleased for you both.'

'Hang on, Mum,' Lucy said as Daphne began to turn away, 'don't let's mention anything to Dad or Joe for now, OK? I think we should just relax today and forget about the business.'

Daphne put a finger over her lips. 'Not a word from me,' she whispered. Then, turning around again, 'Now, what did I come in here for?' She looked blankly about the kitchen. 'Goodness, I'm nearly as bad as Dad,' she mumbled to herself. 'I shall have to retrace my steps, see if it jogs . . . Ah, bread rolls,' and with a wink at Sarah she whisked an overflowing basket of baps from the dresser to carry off to the courtyard.

'She is such a sweetheart,' Sarah remarked.

Lucy smiled. 'She has her moments,' she said fondly. 'Incidentally, she doesn't know that Joe and I are supposed to be trying a separation. She'd only get herself all upset if she did, and that's the last thing I want.'

'Don't worry, I know all about mothers fretting themselves silly over things they can't control. Mine's just as bad.'

'Have you spoken to her today?'

'Of course. She rings every morning.'

Lucy glanced up with a smile. 'Did you mention the Mckenzies?' she asked.

'Actually, I forgot, but I will. Would you believe, she only started trying to pair me off with Michael?'

Lucy's heart gave a jolt. 'But isn't he . . . ? I thought he was married.'

Sarah was busying herself with a lettuce. 'So did I,' she declared, 'until my mother enlightened me to the contrary. Apparently he and Carlotta broke up about a year ago.'

Aware of an odd light-headedness coming over her, Lucy turned to reach a serving bowl from an overhead cupboard. 'What about the boys?' she asked, wondering what to put in the bowl.

'It seems they're with their mother, in Italy. He must miss them like mad, because he was always very hands-on as a father. I wonder where he's living now?'

Lucy said, 'Do you think you'd be interested? He's obviously a great catch, and you've known each other for so long . . .'

'Oh, please don't start siding with my mother. Honestly, I'm so over men after Kelvin and I can't see that changing any time soon, even for someone as gorgeous as Michael. Besides,' she shot Lucy a playful look, 'I kind of got the impression he was interested in you.'

Lucy's insides gave a wrench. 'I think you were imagining things,' she told her firmly.

'No, I don't think so. I wouldn't have said anything if you hadn't told me about you and Joe – or if I'd thought he was still with Carlotta – but I saw the way he was looking at you yesterday, and unless I'm completely mistaken I think I detected a little frisson . . .'

'You were mistaken,' Lucy assured her.

'I see,' Sarah responded.

Neither of them spoke for a moment, then their eyes met and they both started to grin.

'OK,' Lucy said, 'I'll admit he's . . .'

'Gorgeous, rich, totally irresistible . . .'

'Will you stop,' Lucy laughed. 'Even if I did find him attractive, and I'm not saying I do . . .'

'Actually,' Sarah interrupted, putting her head to one side, 'you look a bit like him.'

Lucy almost choked on her drink.

'You know how that happens sometimes, the way people end up with someone who's just like them?'

'I don't know what you're on,' Lucy chided, 'but I only met the man for an hour yesterday and if Joe were ever to hear even a whisper of what we're saying . . . I dread to think . . .'

'Mum! Mum! Where are you?' Hanna cried, running into the courtyard, with Juliette and another girl hot on her heels. 'Where's Mum? Oh, Dad, it's just so brilliant! Where's Mum, I've got to tell her. Grandpa, you've got to be in on it too. And you, Granny. We all must. It'll be hilarious.'

'What will?' Lucy asked, carrying a giant bowl of potato salad out to the table.

Hanna spun round. 'Oh, there you are! There's only a summer fete going on right here in Cromstone the last weekend of the month,' she informed her excitedly.

Stunned by so much enthusiasm from such an unlikely quarter, Lucy said, 'There are posters all over the place, so yes, I did kind of work it out.'

'No, you don't get it. We've all got to take part in some way. Juliette, Gracie and I are going to put on a fashion show for Tess's shop and model all her clothes; Juliette's brother, Tom, and one of his mates are going to dress up as clowns for the kids, if we can find some costumes . . . But anyway, that's not it. What is, is that there's this contest where we all have to put in photographs of ourselves as babies, and then we have to set someone the challenge to go and find us. So you did bring our albums with us, didn't you? Please say you did . . .'

'I'd hardly have left them in London,' Lucy responded. 'How young do you have to be in the baby photo?'

'Two or under. Granny, have you got pictures of you and Grandpa? It would be so cool if you could put yours in too. Dad, you'll be here for it, won't you? We've got pictures of you . . . Oh my God, you should see him when he was a baby,' she said to her friends. 'He was so cute and fat . . .'

'I was not fat,' Joe protested.

'A real bruiser,' Lucy pronounced. 'Sarah, you have to be part of this too, and I'll try to guess which one's you.'

'I'm up for it,' Sarah replied. 'And I'll try to guess which one's you.'

'Oh, no, you can't,' Hanna groaned, suddenly deflating. 'Oh Mum, I'm sorry, I forgot.'

'It's OK,' Lucy told her.

Sarah and the girls were looking baffled.

'We don't have any photos of Mum when she was that young, do we?' Hanna said to Daphne. And before her grandmother could answer she was telling her friends how her grandparents' house had burned down when her mother was still a baby. 'They lost virtually everything,' she informed them gravely, 'and only just managed to rescue Mum, who was upstairs asleep in bed at the time. Isn't that right, Mum?'

Lucy nodded. 'But thanks to Dad, here I am to tell the tale.'

Sarah turned to Brian, realising now why his hands were so scarred.

'He wrapped Mum in a great big duvet and carried her through the flames,' Hanna went on. 'If he hadn't done that she'd probably have died, or been all charred up.'

'Such a delightful image,' Lucy muttered.

Looking at Lucy, Sarah said, 'How old were you when it happened?'

'She was eighteen months,' Daphne replied.

'And you don't remember anything about it?' Sarah asked.

Lucy shook her head. 'Not really,' she answered truthfully, though she felt sure that the woman who screamed in her nightmares was a part of the memory that she had so effectively suppressed. However, it wasn't a subject for now, especially as Hanna had more news which was making her wail with misery.

'Lucas is only going to Spain with his family for the rest of the month,' she told Lucy, 'and he's bound to meet someone while he's there and forget about me.'

'No, he won't,' Juliette protested loyally.

'Believe me, my darling,' Lucy said, pressing a kiss to Hanna's hair, 'no one could ever forget about you, because you never give us the chance.'

'Meet my mother the comedian,' Hanna said to her friends.

Lucy was about to reply when she spotted her own mother moving to sit in the shade. 'Are you all right?' she asked softly, going to join her. 'Would you rather go upstairs and lie down?'

'No, no, I'll be fine,' Daphne assured her. 'It was just getting a little hot standing there in the sun. No need to worry. No, no. No need to worry about anything.'

Chapter Eleven

Now that the auction was drawing ever closer, life was becoming more hectic by the day. A veritable mountain of new lots was piling up in the barn and around the courtyard like a troupe of eager debutantes, all waiting to be properly admired and displayed, while calls were coming in all the time requesting home visits to assess the value of some neglected old heirloom, or in some cases entire contents of a house or shop. With Sarah in charge of entering each item's list price, ownership and lot number on to the computer, Maureen (who'd yet to speak a civil word to the new recruit) was making it her business to oversee all valuations and descriptions, ready for the website and catalogue. Lucy, when not dealing with advertising, client networking and scheduling, was beetling around the countryside in her old Peugeot picking up smaller pieces from those who had no transport, or itemising the contents of an attic or cellar ready for Godfrey and his assistant, Carl, to collect and Maureen to assess.

It was while she was over at Waterley Bottom, peeling her way through the cobwebs of an old man's cluttered garage, that Michael dropped into the office with the forms for her to sign. Though she was sorry to have missed him, she couldn't help feeling relieved too, since an embarrassing infatuation with her lawyer was something she really didn't need right now. What would have been far more useful was several more hours in the day and less of a guilty conscience about Joe, who'd come again last weekend, but had ended up spending most of it down at the pub while she worked. Hanna, on the other hand, was, amazingly, morphing into a little angel, helping out where she could, often ably assisted by her co-angel Juliette, and had loudly joined in with Lucy to insist that her grandparents should postpone their departure for Exmoor until Daphne had the results of the blood tests Lucy had persuaded her to have done.

So now, with her second full week at the helm under way, Lucy could proudly claim that everything, for the moment at least, was going to schedule and the sale itself was showing signs of being the biggest Cromstone had held that year. Though the prospect of such a large affair was undeniably daunting, the mere thought of rising to the challenge was enough to kick-start her adrenalin and not even Maureen's petty attempts at sabotage, which fortunately never quite came off, were managing to bring her back to earth. There were a few occasions, however, when Daphne, clearly troubled by Maureen's umbrage, felt it her duty to step in and try to smooth the woman's ruffled feathers, which Lucy was quite happy for her to do, since she had no intention whatsoever of pandering to Maureen's ego herself. If anything, she felt more inclined to tell the sour old bat that if she didn't start getting over herself soon and dealing with the new reality, then she might want to think about taking her huffing and puffing, tutting and muttering to another environment. It was only knowing how much it would upset her mother if she did that stopped her – plus the fact that it would be a hell of a bad time to lose such a crucial member of the team.

It was on the Thursday morning of that second week that Daphne's doctor rang with the news that her tests had shown nothing sinister at all. In fact, he declared, she was in remarkably good health for a woman her age.

'So you see,' Daphne told Lucy, who'd joined her in the kitchen for elevenses, 'there's absolutely nothing to worry about. It was just a bug, like I said, and I'm completely over it now.'

Since her mother's face had regained none of its usual colour, and she still, in spite of her words, seemed anxious about something, Lucy said, 'Then it's either the tension between me and Maureen that's getting to you, or it's Dad. I told you how he put the tea bags in the kettle this morning ...'

'Yes, you did, so you don't have to tell me again.'

'You know he's worried about you too, and no matter what the doctor says I'm sure he's going to insist that you get some rest.'

'I have no doubt you're right since the pair of you are obviously in cahoots, so you'll be pleased to hear that we're going to leave for Exmoor on Saturday.'

Experiencing a jolt of anxiety at the sudden prospect of finding herself alone, Lucy quickly pushed it aside. She could and would cope without her mother's support, and the sooner she started the sooner everyone, particularly Maureen, would have to accept that she was in charge. 'Have you told Dad you're ready to go?' she asked.

Daphne passed her a cup of tea. 'No, but I will when he gets back from Stroud. By the way, he took the forms with him to give to Michael, so everything's in your name now, including the house.'

Lucy's disappointment at missing an opportunity to see Michael was quickly eclipsed by the exhilaration of becoming the owner of so much, when she'd never actually owned anything before. 'I know I've asked you this a hundred times already,' she said, 'but are you absolutely sure? I mean, I'd be just as happy to run things with you still . . .'

'Lucy, I'm more sure now than I ever was,' her mother interrupted. 'Seeing how committed you are and knowing what a great success you're going to make of it pleases me more than I can put into words.' Her eyes went down as she took a sip of her tea. 'There'll be problems along the way, of course,' she said, her gaze starting to drift almost as though she was foreseeing them, 'but I have great faith in you. I know you'll be able to cope, and with Sarah on board now . . .' Her voice faltered slightly, but she cleared her throat and continued. 'She's a dear girl, and it's wonderful to see how well you two are hitting it off. It's . . . Well, it seems very fitting. Very timely, I suppose. Just please don't forget how hard Maureen has worked for me, and please bear in mind that she has feelings like anyone else.'

'I promise to do my best,' Lucy replied, turning at the sound of footsteps running across the courtyard.

'Daphs, thank goodness, there you are,' Maureen gasped. 'I'm sorry, my old love, but I have to go. Godfrey's only gone and done his flipping ankle in, jumping out of the lorry.'

'Oh my goodness, where is he?' Daphne cried, starting forward. 'Is there something we can do?'

'He's not here, he's in Tormartin somewhere. Or

he was, the paramedics are taking him to the Royal United in Bath. They reckon it might be broken.'

'Oh dear,' Daphne murmured, clearly quite distressed. 'I'm so sorry. You must go, of course.'

'I'll give you a call as soon as there's some news,' Maureen told her, and without as much as a glance in Lucy's direction she hurried off again.

Lucy was watching her mother as she turned around, already knowing what she was going to say. 'No, Mum,' she told her gently, 'this doesn't mean you should stay. You can't drive the lorry, nor can Dad . . .'

'But I can help to fill in for Maureen . . .'

'You might not need to yet. Let's wait and see what she says when she calls.'

By the end of the day the worst was confirmed – Godfrey had not only broken his ankle, but two bones in his foot, and was going to be laid up for several months. Though Lucy wouldn't have wished the injury on anyone, not even him, she couldn't help feeling pleased to be rid of his lecherous looks and gruesome innuendoes, at least for a while. However, losing him as a driver at such a critical time was as devastating a blow as realising that Maureen was probably going to need time off to care for him. But she'd only just started to panic when the fates apparently decided to return to her side, because within minutes of learning about the disaster John Mckenzie was on the phone offering his services as driver, removal man, storekeeper and any other role she'd like him to play. Philippa too, he told her, was keen to help out. She was a wizard with figures, a champion organiser and could probably turn her hand to just about anything they cared to throw her way.

Fired by their enthusiasm Lucy didn't even hesitate, thinking what a treat it would be to work with them instead of the Crumptons. However, to her dismay, her mother was less than thrilled.

'Lucy, I really don't think we can put them to all that trouble,' she protested. 'It's not as if they have any experience . . .'

'Maybe not with auctions, but remember they ran their own business for years. In fact, if you think about it, they could be absolutely what we need.'

'But they're not young, dear, and with her being ill I really don't think we should impose.'

'What do you mean, ill? What's wrong with her?'

'She's had a nasty run-in with cancer. It's how she lost her eye.'

'Are you serious?' Lucy broke in, aghast. 'How do you know?'

'She told me herself when I went to look at the Mercers' furniture.'

'But she's OK now, isn't she? She doesn't look ill, apart from the patch.'

'Apparently she's in remission, but it could come back at any time, so you must understand that John has a lot on his plate taking care of her.'

'Except they're offering to help, and if he's not worried about her doing it I don't see why we should be.'

Daphne turned around to busy herself at the sink. 'OK, you're probably right,' she said shortly. 'Yes, I'm sure you are.'

Belatedly realising what must have been going through her mind, Lucy gave a groan of guilt as she said, 'Oh Mum, am I making you feel shut out? You want to stay, don't you?'

'No,' Daphne answered, shaking her head. 'No,

Dad and I will press on with our plans. If you need us we won't be far away.'

Going to stand behind her, Lucy wrapped her in a tender embrace. 'I wish this had happened after you'd gone,' she said, 'you wouldn't feel so bad about leaving me then, but I can cope, Mum. I promise.'

'I'm sure you can.' Wringing out a sponge, Daphne started to wipe down the worktops. 'When is Sarah's brother due to arrive?' she asked, changing the subject. 'Didn't she say it was at the weekend? It'll be nice for you to meet . . . Yes, well, it'll be nice.'

'I'm looking forward to it,' Lucy told her. Then, turning her around, 'Mum, what is it? I can tell you're holding something back, so . . .'

Daphne pulled herself free. 'Please don't try to force me to say things I'd rather keep to myself,' she snapped. 'Now, Dad'll be back from his bowls any minute so we ought to start thinking about what we're going to eat. And where's Hanna? I haven't seen her all morning.'

Accepting that she probably wasn't going to get any further right now, Lucy said, 'She and Juliette went off with the Mckenzies to help them choose a new puppy, so I expect she's still with them if they managed to find one. Otherwise, they'll probably be Facebooking on Juliette's computer down at the pub. I'll send her a text to find out if she's going to eat with us. It might be a good idea to find out what she's doing tonight at the same time.'

Daphne looked startled. 'Why, is something special happening?' she asked.

'I told you earlier,' Lucy said gently, 'Sarah and I are going to the Mckenzies for drinks this evening. They invited us a few days ago, but with everything that's happened today it'll be a good opportunity to have a chat about how they can help.'

Daphne nodded, and seemed to start searching for something to do. 'I'd better peel some potatoes,' she decided, opening up a cupboard to take out a saucepan. 'Sausage and mash. Dad always likes that. Yes, that's what we'll have, sausage and mash.'

'Honestly, there are times,' Lucy was saying to Sarah as they strolled down to the Mckenzies later, 'when I could happily strangle her, especially when she's acting all weird and secretive the way she is now.'

Sarah's tone was ironic as she said, 'If you want weird and secretive you should meet my mother. She's been holding something back from us for years, and we all know it, we're just never allowed to discuss it.'

Waving out to Milly, who was packing up her Quirky Shoppe, Lucy said, 'But you must have some idea what it is.'

Sarah shook her head. 'I've hazarded a thousand guesses, but even if any of them are right I still don't know which one it is.'

'What about Simon and Becky?'

'When we were younger Simon used to taunt us with the fact that he knew something we didn't, but Becky was always convinced he only said it to make himself seem important. I'm inclined to agree, because in later years he's claimed to be as much in the dark as we are.'

Lucy was thinking of all the rooms at the manor and the items Sarah had put up for sale and wondering which, if any, might have witnessed murder; or a nervous breakdown; an agonised decision to have an abortion; a rape . . . She didn't offer any suggestions, of course, it wasn't her place to do so, and besides she strongly doubted that she could come up with anything that Sarah hadn't already considered herself.

'So here we are,' she declared, as they came to a stop at a solid oak gate that was set deeply into an ivy-clad wall. 'Are you sure they said just to go in?'

'Absolutely,' Sarah replied, and twisting the handle she gave the gate a push.

'Oh, isn't it heavenly?' Lucy murmured as they stepped into a sanctuary of roses, hydrangeas, fuchsias and some magnificently tall gladioli. 'The Mercers will be pleased to know that their prized garden is being so well taken care of.'

'Ah, here you are,' Philippa called out, waving to them from across a freshly mown lawn. 'Come in, come in. I'm so glad you could make it. John's preparing us some sangria. I hope you like it.'

'Sounds bliss,' Sarah swooned.

'This garden is nothing short of idyllic,' Lucy commented, her eyes sweeping around a cluster of lobelia-covered rocks that tumbled into a small goldfish pond with an ornate footbridge across it.

'Yes, we like it very much,' Philippa replied. 'It's brave of the Mercers to trust us with it, but I hope they won't be disappointed.'

'Excellent, you're here already,' John declared as he came out of the house with a tray of glasses. 'Sangria's on its way, and something for us all to munch on. Make yourselves at home. How lovely it is to have visitors, eh Pippa? You're our first, for cocktails anyway, so maybe we should have cracked open the champagne.'

'Sangria's perfect,' Lucy assured him. 'We've brought truffles for you to share, so I . . .'

197

'Oh my goodness, I shall have to be stepping up my sessions on the Wii Fit now,' Philippa laughed. 'I'm really not terribly good you know – apparently I have the fitness level of an eighty-six-year-old – how shocking, and most depressing. John is faring much better, I'm glad to say, but he's still a little overweight for a man his age.'

'Och, telling all my secrets,' he chided. 'Now, are you ladies ready to meet the latest member of our family? I'm afraid her manners are still a work in progress, because she's very excitable, but I hope you'll agree that Hanna made a marvellous choice.'

'You let her actually choose the dog?' Lucy cried. 'That girl is so bossy.'

'Let's just say it was love at first sight all round.'

'She's an adorable little beast,' Philippa assured them as John went back inside. 'Heaven only knows what breed she is, or what the mix is made up of, I should say, but who cares? We already love her to bits and I think Hanna was quite right in her choice of name . . .'

'She chose the name too! What a pain she must have been . . .'

'No, not at all. We loved her being there, and Juliette, of course. Such delightful girls.'

'So what is she called?' Sarah wanted to know.

'Ladies!' John cried through the open kitchen window. 'Get ready to meet Rosalind Ophelia Mckenzie.' A moment later the door opened and a supercharged sandy-coloured mutt with huge brown eyes and a hyper-hover tail leapt on to the terrace, tugging John carelessly behind her.

'Oh, she's so cute,' Sarah gushed, as she and Lucy stooped to greet her. 'I want you.'

'You're welcome to join the ranks of honorary godmothers and visit any time,' Philippa told her.

'Count me in,' Lucy laughed, as her face was ferociously licked. 'Are you really calling her . . . What was it again?'

'Rosalind Ophelia,' John beamed.

'How the heck did she come up with that?'

'I believe Shakespeare had a hand in it,' he responded, 'and we're going to call her Rozzie for short, but she's such a special little creature that we thought she should have a lovely grand name. Now, perhaps you can hold her lead, Pippa, while I go back for the canapés.'

Thrilled – and amazed – to think that Hanna had gone for something classical rather than some ghastly fusion of Kylie and Brittany, or Mystic Falls and Hollyoaks, Lucy could only feel pleased by the influence that other great Shakespearean heroine, Juliette, was apparently having on her.

A few minutes later, with Rozzie panting happily at Pippa's feet, and everyone else seated at the table with large glasses of John's excellent concoction, John proposed a toast. 'To new friends and soon-to-be colleagues.'

'To new friends and soon-to-be colleagues,' Lucy and Sarah echoed.

Sensing Philippa watching her, Lucy turned to her and smiled. There was such warmth and gentility in the older lady's expression that she had to quell a sudden impulse to squeeze her hand. 'Before we get completely off the subject,' she said, 'thank you for giving Hanna such a lovely day. I only saw her briefly before I came out, but she's obviously completely mad about the dog, and the Wii games you're letting her and Juliette play, but if they get too much for you, you must tell them to scarper.'

'Don't you worry about that, we're very happy to have them here,' John declared with an avuncular twinkle. 'It keeps us young, having a couple of teenagers about the place. Stops us turning into a pair of old fuddy-duddies, which is what I suppose we are. So now, do you have a work schedule for me tomorrow? I shall be up at the crack of dawn, as usual, so no problem if there's an early start.'

Loving his enthusiasm, Lucy said, 'Well actually, there is an early pickup over at Chippenham – a three-piece suite, TV stand and two side tables. If you can manage that, then a stop at Old Sodbury on the way back . . .'

'You just give me the names and addresses and I'll put the satnav on it and be there. The lorry does have a satnav, I take it? No worries if it doesn't, I'll just pick one up . . .'

'There's one installed,' she assured him, 'and Carl knows the area pretty well, having grown up in Badminton, so he'll be a very able assistant.'

'And what will I be doing?' Philippa asked excitedly.

Wanting to do anything she could to make this lovely woman happy while she was in her blessed state of remission, Lucy said, 'Actually, I'm hoping you'll take charge of the telephone bids. There's quite a bit of setting up involved, and then on the day you'll be at the end of the line dealing with the clients and making sure they get sent what they bought.'

Philippa was beaming delightedly, and the look on John's face showed how thrilled he was that his sister was being included.

'We shall do everything we can to turn your first auction into a resounding triumph,' he promised. 'And it's not just driving and telephones we're good at, so you must make use of us in any way you can.'

Sarah said to Lucy with a touch of irony, 'Maybe we could ask John to visit Eric Beadle to try and make the old fool see sense.'

John's eyebrows rose.

With an exasperated sigh, Lucy said, 'There's an old guy in Dursley who thinks we've deliberately sold him short on a commode. Mum and Maureen were convinced he'd go away if we just ignored him, but unfortunately we received a letter from his solicitor this morning.'

John looked interested. 'Saying what?' he asked.

'Basically that if we don't pay the difference between our sale price and the one the dealer who bought it sold it on for, they'll be asking questions about other items that have gone the same route out of Cromstone's.'

'And are there other items?' Philippa asked, reaching for the jug to top up their drinks.

Lucy threw out her hands. 'There are bound to be, because that's more or less what auctions are all about, especially for dealers – they buy something cheaply, then turn it around for a handsome profit. The thing about Mr Beadle is that he seems to believe we deliberately cheated him, and now his lawyer's threatening to cut up rough.'

'What do your parents say about it?' Philippa wanted to know.

'To be honest, I haven't told them,' Lucy confessed. 'Mum's already stressed enough about leaving ... But I suppose I'll have to if it starts blowing up into something serious.'

'I'd say a lawyer's letter is already quite serious,' Philippa remarked gravely.

'So would I, but according to Maureen they turn up on a regular basis, and if we start getting involved with lawyers ourselves we'd soon run out of money.'

'John? What are you thinking?' Philippa prompted, noticing how deeply he was frowning.

Raising his head, he said, 'Actually, I was remembering something someone once told me . . . It might not be relevant, no, I'm sure it's not.'

'Well tell us anyway,' Philippa urged.

John's eyes went to Lucy. 'I'm sure I'm going right out on a limb here,' he said, 'but first tell me, how long have the Crumptons been working with your parents?'

Feeling a curious jolt of unease, Lucy replied, 'More or less since they came here.'

'And what were the Crumptons doing before?'

Lucy shrugged. 'I'm not sure. I know they've always lived round this way, but that's about all I can tell you. Why? Have you heard something?'

He shook his head. 'No, we haven't been here long enough to be party to gossip, but listening to you just now reminded me of a conversation I had once with a chap who knew a lot about your world. What he told me . . . Well, have you ever heard of something called the Ring?'

Lucy and Sarah looked at one another and shook their heads.

'Mm, I can't say I know much about it myself,' he admitted, 'but from what I can remember it's made up of a group of buyers, or dealers, who enter into an agreement to keep the price of something low – in other words only one of them will make a bid for an item they know to be quite valuable, and the others will stay out of the running. This means they might pick it up for as little as seventy quid when it's actual worth could be around seven hundred, or even seven thousand.'

Sarah was puzzled. 'So what happens after the bidder carts off his bargain? How do the others profit from that?'

'I believe the chap who bought it then holds a second, secret auction, maybe in the car park, or at the pub, where they all bid against one another for the same item. This way they manage to cheat the auction house out of its proper commission, while the original seller is cheated out of far more.'

Lucy wasn't liking the sound of this one bit. 'So do you think that's what's happening at Cromstone's?' she asked.

'I've no idea, but if it is, it's a criminal act that could end up shutting the place down.'

Lucy blanched.

'I'm probably overstating it,' John said quickly, 'but it might not be a bad idea to run it past your lawyer.'

'We're seeing Michael on Saturday,' Sarah reminded Lucy. 'We could talk to him about it then.' To the Mckenzies she said, 'My brother's arriving at the weekend. He and Michael are old friends, so I'm planning to throw a little party for their reunion. It would be lovely if you could make it too.'

Philippa turned to John as she said, 'I'm sure we'd love to.'

Still looking grave, John said, 'We don't know yet if we are talking about a ring, and we really might not be, but the important thing, as I see it, is that nothing scurrilous or underhand manages to attach itself to Cromstone's. So whether it's contacting a lawyer, or trying to solve the problem ourselves, we must do everything we can to make sure your good name remains intact.'

Touched by such ready support, Lucy was about to respond when the puppy made a sudden lunge towards him.

With a chuckle John ruffled her ears and treated her to a morsel of confit canapé.

'I think we're getting an idea who'll have to dish out the discipline around here, don't you?' Philippa demanded with a knowingly arched eyebrow.

'She's a tyrant,' John told the dog, 'but don't worry, I'll be here to save you.'

Beside herself with joy, the puppy tried jumping on to his lap, but the lead was too short and she was yanked back mid-air.

Laughing, he detached her smart new tartan collar and lifted her up. 'I think we're going to be best buddies, you and me,' he told her as she mopped his face with her frantic pink tongue.

Watching, Lucy felt a sense of sadness descending over her. Maybe the reason for getting a dog was so that he wouldn't be alone if his sister's cancer did come back. She glanced at Sarah and suspected her thoughts were running along similar lines.

'I was wondering,' Sarah said, as John put the puppy down and rested a calming hand on her head. 'Well, Philippa mentioned a few days ago that you're old friends of my parents . . .' She let the question hang, not quite sure how to frame the rest of it.

John's eyes moved to his sister. 'That's right,' he said quietly. 'We were . . . It was a very long time ago.'

Sarah glanced at Lucy.

'So, how did you know them?' Lucy ventured.

John reached for his drink, but didn't pick it up. 'I think it would be better if Sarah's mother told you that,' he said, and smiling as he held up the pitcher to signal it was empty, he went back inside to refill it.

Bemused, Sarah looked at Philippa.

'So,' Philippa said happily, 'what are you two ladies planning to do for the summer fete?'

Later that evening, after Lucy and Sarah had gone home, Philippa was sitting quietly on the terrace watching John playing with the puppy, whose euphoria and energy seemed to know no bounds. The past couple of hours had tired her far more than she'd ever have admitted, though she knew they hadn't been easy for him either. She'd have liked to ask Sarah what she knew of her mother's past, but it would have been wrong to do so when it was possible that she knew nothing at all. Certainly John's name seemed to have struck no chords with her, and Philippa was left to wonder, for now, if Sarah's brother would recognise it when he came.

How was John feeling, she was thinking, knowing that very soon now he was likely to come face to face with his son? Was he ready for it? Would he be able to cope if Simon had no idea who he was? For years they'd talked about the joy it would bring to them both to be a part of John's children's lives again, but there was never any guarantee that reality would play out the same benignly happy scenarios as those conjured by fantasy. Sarah wasn't John's, but Simon and Becky were – had Rose ever told them that? If she had, did they know what had happened to their father?

In coming here neither she nor John had sought

to cause harm or heartache to anyone, except perhaps to themselves, but now Philippa was unable to see how they could avoid drawing others into the pain and injustice that had been such a large part of their lives. She was deeply sorry to find herself thinking this way, and angry with herself for not realising sooner that opening up the past was likely to destroy as much as it would repair. For her, her brother would always come first, but that didn't mean she had no care for others, particularly those like Sarah, and her siblings, whose innocence was as precious to John as it would be to Rose.

Thinking of the woman whose young life had been shattered along with John's more than thirty years ago had never been easy for Philippa. She'd known and loved Rose well, and would have continued to had it been possible, but it hadn't. A cruel and malicious fate had struck at the very heart of their family in the worst imaginable way, and caused such devastation that Philippa was sure Rose's scars were still as deep as John's. Why had it happened? What purpose was there to inflicting such appalling damage on blameless lives? Would they ever find out the reasons? After so many years it was probably madness to think they would, yet she knew, deep down, that neither she nor John had ever quite given up the hope that one day they might recover what had once been stolen from them.

Chapter Twelve

'Sheila, it's me,' Sarah said down the line to her aunt. 'How are you – or should I say, *comment tu vas?*'

'*En pleine forme, merci,*' Sheila replied with a very strong English accent. 'And *comment vas-tu*, my darling?'

'Yes I'm great, thanks. Loving being involved with Lucy and the auction house – I expect Mum told you about it, did she?'

'She certainly did, and we're both thrilled to think of you getting out more – and being paid, as well. *Très bon*, indeed. You might not have to sell off quite so many of the family treasures now, not that anything's worth much, Mum tells me. Anyway, you've just missed her, I'm afraid. She went off to her yoga class almost as soon as she finished speaking to you.'

'Yes, she said she was going, and actually it's you I want to talk to. Is this a good time?'

'As good as any, I'm in no rush to get anywhere. What's the weather like with you? Still sunny?'

'A little overcast today, with rain forecast for later. I'm guessing it's completely gorgeous with you.'

'I have to admit it is, though our view of the Med is a little hazy this morning. We're thinking of driving down to the coast later for a spot of lunch.

A pity you can't join us. When do you think you'll be coming?'

'I'm not sure now I'm working with Lucy. Definitely not until after the auction. Anyway, the reason I'm calling is to find out if the name John Mckenzie means anything to you?'

When only silence followed, Sarah's heartbeat started to slow. Was Sheila trying to remember, or had she, Sarah, made the right decision not to blurt it out to her mother? Lucy had agreed that she should go in carefully, since John's reaction last night had told them that the situation was likely to be delicate.

'Sheila?'

'Yes, darling, I'm still here. How . . . What . . . ?' Then, in a stronger voice, 'Why are you asking?'

Disturbed by the answer that was actually a question, Sarah said, 'He's renting a house here, in Cromstone, with his sister, Philippa.'

'Oh my goodness,' Sheila muttered.

More alarmed than ever, Sarah went on, 'He says he's an old friend of Mum's.'

'Yes, I suppose you could say . . . Is that all he's told you?'

'So far, but there's obviously more. Sheila, what's the big mystery? Has it got . . .'

'The mystery,' Sheila interrupted, 'there is no mystery. He's . . . Oh dear, we're going back a very long way, Sarah, and I'm afraid it's not my place to tell you what happened. I take it you haven't mentioned anything to Mum yet? No, of course not, that's why you're talking to me. Do you have any idea why he's there? Has he said anything . . . ? How well do you know him?'

Hardly knowing which question to answer first,

Sarah said, 'He's helping out at the auction house. He seems a really nice man. His sister, Philippa, is lovely too. She's had cancer, and lost an eye because of it.'

'Pippa has cancer?' Sheila said faintly. 'She's lost an eye? Oh my goodness, the poor thing.'

'Sheila, please, how do you know them?'

'Darling, if I could tell you that I promise I would, but your mother . . . Please don't mention this to her, will you, not until I've had a chance to talk to her. It's going to upset her far more than you realise. Well, how can you, she's never told you . . . We thought we'd never see him again . . . Does he want to see her? Is that what he's saying?'

Tense with frustration, Sarah said, 'No, I don't think so. It's not what he said. Sheila, for heaven's sake, you have to tell me who he is.'

'I'm sorry, darling. As I said, it's not my place to, at least not without your mother's permission.'

Suddenly Sarah wanted to scream. 'Don't you think I've been through enough these last few years?' she cried. 'I'm trying hard to pull myself together, but discovering there are some deep, dark secrets in my family that for all I know are the reason my mother's half crazy really doesn't help.'

'No, of course not. I understand that, but there's nothing for you . . . You're stronger than your mother, darling. Really you are. And please, don't let's say she's crazy because we know it isn't true.'

'OK, I'm sorry, but if you were in my shoes, Sheila, you'd be feeling pretty uptight too.'

'I won't disagree with that, and I'm truly sorry I'm not giving you the answers you're looking for, but they really must come from her.'

'Or John Mckenzie? Maybe I should ask him what you're all hiding.'

'For your own sake, please don't do that, Sarah. Besides, I'm not sure he'd tell you.'

Guessing from the way he'd been last night that he probably wouldn't, Sarah said, 'You realise, don't you, that I'm thinking terrible things now?'

'Then try not to, darling, because no one's done anything wrong. Your mother, John, they were victims of the most dreadful . . . No, I'm saying too much already. Just please don't think badly of anyone, and try to be patient. Once I tell her he's in Cromstone . . . She'll want to know how he is, I'm sure, and if he ever married . . . You said he's there with Philippa?'

'Sheila, I can't ask him those questions. I don't know him well enough.'

'Of course not. I'm sorry, I'm just trying to think ahead to what Rose might ask once she's had time to get over the shock.'

'So when are you going to tell her?'

'I'm not sure. I'll have to pick my moment, but when I do I'll be sure to let you know that I have.'

After ringing off Sarah continued to stand in the kitchen doorway, staring out across the valley to the meandering river and Welsh hills beyond. In her mind's eye she was picturing her mother with her cloud of ebony hair and exquisite oval face, roaming Provençal markets in her battered straw hat, stretching her slender body into impossible yoga positions, running across this lawn with Simon and Becky; standing right here watching the sun going down. She'd always been an exquisitely beautiful woman, and still was, with mesmerising blue eyes and a smile that seemed to light up the world.

Yet always there was the sadness, the distance that seemed to lurk in the shadows waiting to swallow her up.

Loving her mother as much as she did, it could easily break her heart to think of her pain, which was why she rarely allowed herself to do so. For a long time as a child she'd thought she was to blame. She knew now that Simon and Becky used to feel the same way, until their father had patiently and lovingly made them understand that all they ever brought their mother was happiness.

'Even when I'm naughty?' Sarah remembered asking, and her father had laughed and hugged her.

'Especially then,' he'd told her.

For a while after that Sarah had been deliberately naughty, and when her mother had asked why, five-year-old Sarah had answered, 'To make you love me more.'

How moved and delighted her parents had seemed with that answer.

Feeling the loss of her father and son starting to overwhelm her, Sarah took a tremulous breath as though to stifle the grief with air. She'd wondered several times over the years, but especially since losing Jack, if maybe her parents had lost a child too and that was why her mother was often so sad. But if that had been the case, why on earth wouldn't anyone have told her, particularly since she'd lost a child herself?

To her mind there could be nothing worse than being a parent one day and not the next. The loss was a terrible, wrenching, physical pain; the panic and helplessness were like a fever, burning, consuming, relentless and cruel beyond compare. Her arms were heavy with emptiness; her heart was

211

crushed by despair. Nothing and no one would ever be able to replace him. No matter how many children she might one day have, he would always be her firstborn, the child she'd loved with all her heart, and whom she now yearned for with all her soul.

Where are you, Jack? she whispered silently. *Are you with him, Daddy? Please tell me you're with him.*

She couldn't imagine anything being worse than this endless silence and suffering, but maybe something was – and whatever it might be, maybe it had happened to her mother.

'Hello, Cromstone Auctions,' Lucy said cheerily, while tucking the phone under her chin to carry on replying to emails.

'Lucy? It's Michael Givens here.'

'Michael,' she responded, feeling a quick catch in her heart. 'How are you? Did you get my email about Eric Beadle?'

'I did, and someone should have contacted you by now to request a copy of the solicitor's letter.'

'They have, and it's sitting on the scanner ready for Maeve, our trusty assistant, to send when she comes in. So what do you think, in principle?'

'It's an interesting problem, but I'll hold fire until I've got all the information, if you don't mind. For now, I'm calling on behalf of Margie Brooks who has the gallery opposite . . . Well, you know where she is, it's where I ran into you and Sarah a couple of weeks ago.'

'Of course. Is everything OK?'

'Perfectly, but Margie's taken up a last-minute invitation to spend a couple of weeks in Venice, so she's asked me to follow up on some of her outstanding business. As Cromstone Auctions falls into this category, I'm ringing to update you on the extra valuations you requested.'

'You mean for the paintings Sarah sent over earlier in the week? And now you're calling to tell me that one of them's worth somewhere in the region of ten mil.'

Without missing a beat, he said, 'Actually, Margie's putting it at twice that, so I sense a celebration in the air.'

Glancing up as Maureen breezed into the office, closely followed by Sarah, Lucy turned away in case her cheeks were as flushed as they felt. 'If only,' she said to Michael. 'So, starting with the portrait . . . ?'

'OK, apparently, if you can get a hundred for it the owner should consider themselves lucky.'

Lucy grimaced. 'I think she was hoping for at least double that.'

'I'm sure, but for some bewildering reason pastel portraits of Margaret Thatcher, even those signed by the artist, aren't setting many collectors on fire these days. On the other hand, the watercolour you sent with it is apparently an early twentieth-century Noel Leaver, signed by the artist with an interesting label verso on headed paper which could fetch something in the region of five to six hundred.'

Lucy's eyebrows rose. 'Not bad. The owner put it at around fifty quid tops, so provided we find a buyer he could be in for a nice surprise.'

'Margie's left me the numbers of a couple of dealers she thinks'll be interested. I'll get my assistant to contact them if you like.'

'That would be great, and I'll post it on the website as soon as we've finished this call. I think I've photographed it – I'm sure I have. Anyway, this is very good news. Do you have the paintings? I hope she hasn't gone off and left them locked up in her gallery.'

'She has, but I have the keys.'

'Excellent. So we need to work out a convenient time for someone to come and collect them.'

'If you like, I can drop them off in about an hour. I have to go in to Bristol and Cromstone's kind of on the way.'

'It is?' she said drolly. 'Out of interest, which route do you take?'

Laughing, he said, 'The one that takes me where I want to go – and by the time I get there perhaps you and Sarah will be able to tell me if you can make a charity polo match at the end of next month.'

Lucy's eyes grew wide. She'd never been to anything as swanky as a polo match before, nor had it ever been on her list of must-dos. However, she was living a new life now, with a different sort of people, and if polo was their thing, then maybe it might be hers too. 'I'm sure Sarah and I would love to,' she told him, already hearing Joe accusing her of social climbing. 'A charity polo match at the end of September,' she informed Sarah.

Sarah blinked in amazement. 'Who are you talking to?' she asked.

Wishing Maureen weren't around to turn her eavesdropping into gossip, Lucy said, 'Your friend Michael Givens.'

'I hope yours too,' he said at the end of the phone.

'Of course. It's just that . . . Anyway, I think Sarah's definitely up for it.' She raised her eyebrows at Sarah, who nodded vigorously.

'Excellent,' Michael declared. 'Maybe we can get Simon to join us too.'

'We can but ask. Incidentally, has Sarah let you

know what you're doing for the Cromstone summer fete yet?'

She almost felt his double take. 'I'm doing something for the summer fete?' he echoed. Then, in a darker tone, 'Why am I starting to feel worried?'

With a girlish laugh, she said, 'I'm in no doubt you'll be very good at it. In fact, we'll probably film it for YouTube.'

'Oh no, I'm liking this less by the minute. Exactly what has she signed me up for?'

'Morris dancing.'

There was a moment's stunned silence, before he said, 'Please tell me I didn't hear right.'

Grinning widely, she replied, 'We feel that you'll probably have a natural flair for it, and Sarah's certain Simon will too, who's also signed up. We're making a rule that anyone who laughs at you will be fined a pound and all proceeds will go to charity.'

'Then I shall hope the charity of choice is the Chipping Sodbury refuge for wounded egos.'

'Perhaps not a worthy enough cause, but we'll bear it in mind. Anyway, we'll expect you in an hour?'

'More or less.'

After ringing off she turned to Maureen, trying not to wish her a few hundred miles away. 'I wasn't expecting to see you today,' she said as cheerfully as she could manage. 'How's Godfrey?'

Maureen was not a happy-looking woman. 'Being a pain in the proverbial,' she snorted sourly, 'but that's men all over when they've got something wrong with them.' Though her face was painted in its usual gaudy colours, even the make-up wasn't disguising the dark shadows under her eyes. 'I came in,' she said, 'because I know you're up to your eyes and we don't want to be messing up the valuations while we've got Eric Beadle's solicitor on our backs. Is your mum around?'

'She's gone to the mall with Dad. They're leaving for Exmoor tomorrow, did she tell you?'

Maureen's face was still as taut as the size-twelve top she was wearing. 'Does she know about this Beadle nonsense?' she asked, starting to flip through a pile of paperwork on her desk.

'Not yet,' Lucy replied, feeling unsettled by the fact that Maureen, all of a sudden, seemed to be worried. 'I'm hoping we can sort it out without having to bother her.' She took a breath, and decided just to go for it. 'Tell me, have you ever heard of something called the Ring?'

Maureen's head came up and her nostrils seemed to flare with disdain as she said, 'Of course I have. Everyone in our business has. Why are you asking? Is that what you think's happening?'

'I don't know, but we have to admit that it could be.'

Maureen's puffy eyes were boring into Lucy's. 'Someone needs to go through the records to check what this solicitor's on about,' she declared. 'I'll do it myself when I've finished the valuations. How are you getting on with the catalogue?'

'Quite well, I think. Sarah's taken charge of it . . .'

'Please tell me you didn't just say that. She doesn't have any experience in that area at all! At least you've been around the business for a while.'

Lucy glanced at Sarah who was standing close to the door, entering new information on to the whiteboard. Since her back was turned it wasn't possible to know how she was reacting to being spoken about as if she weren't there, but Lucy wasn't liking it too much. 'Actually, I'm working with her,' she told Maureen, 'and as far as I'm concerned she's doing a fantastic job. I think you'll agree when you take a look.' Her tone was telling her that she'd better agree, though she didn't imagine Maureen would be much swayed by subtext.

'It has to be ready for the printer by the end of the day,' Maureen reminded her.

'And I'm quite confident it will be.'

With a small huff of doubt Maureen spun round and barged past Sarah en route to the door.

'Excuse me,' Sarah said quietly.

Maureen turned back. 'Sorry?' she demanded, her eyes flashing a challenge.

'I said, excuse me. I was obviously in your way.'

Maureen's face started to quiver, but to Lucy's relief whatever cutting retort she was planning didn't materialise, either because she couldn't think of one, or because she didn't quite have the nerve to deliver it.

After she'd gone Lucy heaved a weary sigh and was about to apologise on Maureen's behalf when she realised Sarah was far more upset than she'd expected. 'Oh please don't let her get to you,' Lucy implored, going to give her a hug. 'She's a monster, I know, worse than that even, but we're a pair of human dynamos, you and me, between us we can handle her.'

'Of course,' Sarah said, desperately trying to swallow her tears. 'I'm sorry, it's not her really, she just caught me at a low ebb.'

'Come and sit down,' Lucy said gently, and pulling out a chair she eased Sarah into it and perched on the desk next to her. 'Did you speak to your aunt?' she asked. 'Is that what's upsetting you?'

Sarah nodded, and tried to make herself laugh. 'It's all such a nonsense,' she declared shakily. 'So many secrets, no one ever telling me anything, and now it turns out that my aunt's as bad as the rest of them. I don't think they realise how hurtful it is . . . It affected us deeply when we were growing up. I'm not sure my mother's ever completely understood that. Now it's happening again, they're pushing me out, closing doors, refusing to answer questions and I guess I'm still too raw after Dad and Jack to be able to handle it . . . Oh Lucy, I'm sorry, I shouldn't . . .'

'Please don't apologise,' Lucy interrupted. 'Just tell me what she said.'

'That's just it! She wouldn't tell me anything, except that I mustn't mention anything to my mother about John until she's had a chance to speak to her first.'

Lucy's eyes widened. 'Well there's an admission anyway,' she murmured. 'Clearly he was a part of your mother's life, and by the sound of it a pretty significant one.'

Sarah swallowed as she nodded. 'I just don't get why no one can tell me . . . John says it's my mother who should do it, my aunt agrees, but how am I supposed to make her now my aunt's warned me off speaking to her? For God's sake, what can be so bad that no one's prepared to talk about it?'

Wishing she had some answers, if only to suggest what they could do next, Lucy took both Sarah's hands and held them gently in her own. 'Maybe we have to speak to John again,' she said, 'or to Philippa.'

'But you heard what he said last night, and she obviously didn't want to discuss it either.'

Lucy nodded. 'I know, but . . . Well, we'll work something out, I promise, because it's not fair to keep you in the dark like this. You're a grown woman, for heaven's sake. And like you said, what on earth can be so terrible that they can't tell you?'

Clearly relieved to have someone who understood, Sarah said, 'I called Simon before coming here, but he must be in a meeting or on the Metro because I couldn't get through, so I left a message for him to call back.'

'What about Becky? Have you tried her?'

'Not yet, I'd rather speak to Simon first.' Taking a Kleenex from the box on Lucy's desk, she blew her nose. 'I'm sorry, I really am. I thought I had myself together before I came here, but Maureen barging into me like that . . . It's so stupid . . . What does she think . . . ?'

'Forget her, because you're right, she is stupid and ignorant and festering with resentment because she thinks her position has been usurped by a pair of nobodies. Well, it's time she learned that throwing her weight around, either literally or metaphorically, doesn't impress me one bit, and if she tries anything like it again she'll be downright sorry.'

'Oh, is that so?' Maureen snorted from the door. 'And exactly how are you going to make that happen, may I ask?'

Shocked at being overheard, it took Lucy a moment to recover. Then, in the coldest voice she could muster, she said, 'Actually, no, you may not ask, but you can take what I said as a warning that I won't tolerate bullying or insubordination.'

Maureen's pencilled eyebrows went skywards. 'Oh, listen to you, Miss High and Mighty,' she sneered. 'You can't run this place without my help, not yet anyway, so if you want to keep things on track and not watch it all go down the pan like a giant turd I think you should mind your manners a bit, don't you?'

Lucy was aghast. 'How dare you threaten me,' she seethed, her eyes flashing with fury. 'If you're going to hold your experience and expertise over my head like that, then maybe it would be best if you did go now.'

'Lucy, no,' Sarah protested.

'I don't need you to fight my battles,' Maureen snapped at her. 'I can handle the likes of her, and for your information, Miss Totally Up Yourself, I won't be going anywhere until I'm good and ready.'

Lucy was hardly able to believe her ears. 'Just because you've always helped Mum to run the place,' she said, attempting to sound in control, 'doesn't mean she'll tolerate the way you're behaving towards me.'

'I don't give a damn what she will or won't tolerate. She knows as well as I do that this place can't function without me, and if you get it into your head to try and prove me wrong then mark my words, you'll be the one who ends up sorry.'

Lucy's face was turning pale. 'What exactly is that supposed to mean?' she demanded.

'Take it however you like,' Maureen retorted. 'Just don't think you can mess with me, because I've been round the block way too many times to end up shafted by the likes of you.'

Being so unprepared for this confrontation, Lucy was floundering for the upper hand. 'I really think it would be best if you went now,' she heard herself saying.

Maureen snorted with disdain. 'Oh you do, do you?

Well, for your information I'm not going anywhere till I'm good and ready, and like it or not, there's no way you can make me.'

Stunned by so much aggression, Lucy said, 'But my mother can.'

Maureen's lip curled. 'Is that so? Why don't you try it?'

Starting to quake with rage and frustration, Lucy said, 'Why would you want to stay when you clearly find it so objectionable to be around me?'

Maureen only smirked.

Lucy glanced at Sarah, who appeared as shaken as she was.

Apparently deciding that now was the moment to savour her triumph, Maureen started to leave.

Before she could stop herself Lucy shouted, 'Tell me, Maureen, how long have you been engaged in illegal practices?'

As Sarah gasped Maureen spun round, her eyes blazing with shock.

Already wishing she could take the words back, Lucy forced herself to meet the glare.

'Would you care to explain that remark?' Maureen snarled.

In spite of knowing what shaky ground she was on, Lucy's pride wasn't allowing her to back down. 'Is there a ring operating here at Cromstone?' she blurted.

Maureen appeared astonished, then her eyes narrowed craftily as she said, 'And what exactly do you think a ring is, may I ask?'

Refusing to be thrown, Lucy replied, 'I think you know.'

Maureen's eyebrows arched. 'What I know is that

221

you could get yourself into a lot of trouble with accusations like that.'

Aware of how true that was, Lucy said, 'I'm still waiting for an answer.'

'Then this is it,' Maureen spat, pushing her face towards her. 'If you've got it in your head to try pinning anything on me, it's your mother who'll suffer,' and spinning on her heel she stormed off across the courtyard.

Too shaken to continue standing, Lucy sank into a chair and tried to collect her thoughts. 'Tell me that didn't just happen,' she groaned. 'What was I thinking? Why did I let her get the better of me like that?'

Clearly just as shocked, Sarah said, 'She goaded you into it.'

'Nevertheless, to accuse her of being involved in a ring when we don't even know if there is one . . .'

'Maybe not, but did you notice that she didn't deny it?'

Realising that was true, Lucy experienced a jolt of alarm. 'Oh my God, what kind of can of worms have I just opened?' she murmured. 'And what she said about Mum . . .' Her eyes went to Sarah.

'I'm sure she wouldn't really do anything to harm her.'

Lucy wasn't convinced. In fact, the deeper into this she went, the more afraid she was becoming. 'You realise, this could explain why Mum's been so on edge lately?' she said. 'She knows that there is a ring, but doesn't know how to handle it.'

Sarah was looking equally worried. 'Except I can't imagine her letting you take the business on if there were some legal issues. At the very least she'd be sure to warn you.'

Lucy couldn't disagree. 'But if Maureen's been putting the pressure on,' she said, 'my mother's not sophisticated, or tough enough to know how to deal with bullies or thugs. She's just a decent, honest, straightforward person who always believes the best about people.'

Sarah wasn't doubting it. 'Until they prove themselves to be one of the Maureens of the world.'

Lucy was shaking her head, still hardly able to credit what had just happened. 'We need to talk to Michael about this,' she said. 'Luckily he's on his way here. Meantime, how do you feel about talking to John about it, given everything else that's going on?'

Sarah didn't flinch. 'It makes sense, since he's the one who told us what a ring was in the first place.'

'And if Maureen comes back . . .' Lucy's eyes sharpened. 'Do you think she will?'

'She'd have a nerve if she did, but if she's got something to hide I suppose we shouldn't rule it out.'

Lucy covered her face with her hands. 'Just when I thought my new life was off to a dazzling start,' she muttered.

Half an hour later Michael was regarding them carefully as Lucy finished telling him about what had happened.

'Well, I can quite see why you're suspicious,' he said, putting down the tea Sarah had made him. 'The solicitors' letters are worrying, and Maureen's reluctance to leave the company doesn't work well in her favour, considering the antipathy between you.'

'Plus, she didn't deny there was a ring,' Sarah

reminded him. 'And she was really threatening, especially about Lucy's mother.'

'Certainly she seems to be incriminating herself,' he agreed, 'but all I can advise for the moment is that you investigate further to see if you can come up with some solid evidence.'

'Of course,' Lucy responded. 'I'm just not sure how to go about it, because we don't have any way of knowing where, when or how anything has sold on after it's left here.'

'No, but you will have a list of who's bought what from you, and if a certain dealer's name keeps cropping up and happens to tie in with Eric Beadle's letter, or any of the other letters, it could give us a start.'

'And if we find there is a ring, how do we protect my mother?'

Michael's eyes came to hers. 'I'm afraid I have to ask you this, even though I'm already sure of the answer, but do you think there's any possibility at all that she might know what's going on? If indeed something is.'

Though all Lucy's instincts shied away from it, she couldn't ignore the way her mother had been lately, so she said, 'Obviously we can't rule it out, but there's no way she'd ever agree to do anything illegal. At least, not knowingly or willingly.'

'I don't think she would either, and to be frank, I've come across Maureen Crumpton often enough to know what a powerful character she is, so your mother could have been forced to turn a blind eye. And if that is the case, in a legal sense that would make her an accomplice.'

Lucy's face turned ashen.

'Fortunately you haven't been at the helm long

enough for suspicion to fall on you too,' he continued, 'but you should be prepared to face some awkward questions, should the worst come to the worst and it ends up in the hands of the police.'

Lucy's eyes went to Sarah as Sarah said, 'Even if something is going on we'll have to do our best to keep it covered up. I don't see any other way of protecting Lucy's mother.'

'You need to speak to her,' Michael said to Lucy, 'and get her to tell you what she knows.'

Remembering the way her mother had told her to stop trying to force her to say things she'd rather keep to herself, Lucy's heart sank. 'Well, this isn't what we were expecting today,' she said, trying to make herself smile as she looked at Sarah.

'No, but we can deal with it,' Sarah declared positively, 'and I guess we're business as usual for now?' she said to Michael.

'I don't see why not,' he replied. 'The auction's next Wednesday and Thursday, you've got your viewings set up for Monday and Tuesday . . . Actually, I'm experiencing the usual midsummer lull at the moment, so if you like, I'll pop in and out as I'm passing to find out how things are going.'

'I'd be really grateful if you did,' Lucy told him, wondering if it was as much an excuse to see her as it was to be supportive – and hoping it was.

His eyes narrowed playfully. 'Grateful enough to get me off the morris dancing hook?'

Laughing through a sigh of relief, she said, 'Maybe.'

'Or maybe not,' Sarah told him. 'No, I'm sorry, I'm not depriving myself of the hilarity of watching you and my brother hopping, mincing and skipping around in a circle, clicking sticks and waving your tassels. It just has to happen.'

'But Simon's probably not even going to be here,' he protested.

'I'll make him fly back.'

'And if he isn't you'll have John Mckenzie, our new driver, for company,' Lucy assured him.

With a roll of his eyes Michael said, 'There went my dignity, but hey, what price pleasing a lady?'

'That's the spirit,' Sarah grinned, carefully avoiding Lucy's eyes since they hadn't actually signed anyone up for anything yet. However, it was starting to seem like a mighty good idea. 'You know, I reckon John's going to turn out to be a demon morris dancer,' she declared, 'so you'd best start practising.'

After looking at her in a way that was probably meant to make her back down, but had no effect at all, he said to Sarah, 'Do you happen to know which troupe is on? I'm sure you do.'

'Cromstone's own,' she told him, 'so don't worry, you'll be amongst friends. Now, back to this ring business, are we all agreed that we say no more to Maureen until we've had a chance to go through the records to see if we can find some sort of evidence?'

Lucy looked at Michael and nodded as he did. Then, realising how deeply his eyes seemed to be penetrating hers, she felt an embarrassing heat spreading over her cheeks.

'I should be going,' he said, glancing at his watch. 'The paintings are in the barn, the paperwork's here, on your desk, and unless something's changed I'll see you both at the manor tomorrow night for cocktails?'

'Don't be late,' Sarah told him as he came to embrace her. 'Oh, and we're definitely on for the polo at the end of September, just email us the details.'

'Great. What time are you expecting Simon?'

'His flight gets in at twelve fifty, so mid-afternoon I guess.'

'OK. Now, this is me loving you and leaving you. If anything comes up, you have my mobile number.'

After he'd gone Sarah turned to Lucy, who was still sitting in her chair. 'So we're carrying on as though nothing's happening?' she said.

Realising she could as easily be talking about Maureen as Michael, Lucy replied, 'I think we should,' and picking up the paperwork Michael had left, she went off to inspect the paintings.

John Mckenzie was motoring along happily in the Cromstone Auctions truck with Rosalind Ophelia – aka Rozzie – at his side, doggie-belted into the passenger seat and gazing joyfully out of the window. Following a brief downpour earlier, the sun had come out again, making the hedgerows and fields sparkle and gleam like a freshly painted landscape. He knew he'd never tire of nature's beauty, no matter what the weather. After the kind of darkness he'd known in his life, he'd learned how to appreciate many things that other people took for granted.

He'd dropped Carl, the company's young helper, at a pub on the Tetbury road about twenty minutes ago, leaving him to start his weekend downing a couple of pints with his mates. The dear soul had invited John to join them, but not only would John never have dreamed of drinking and driving, he was keen to get back to Cromstone in case there were any more errands to run.

As he wound on through the country lanes he began naming flowers and trees to himself, while taking extra care to stay below the speed limit. The last thing he wanted was a ticket, much less a run-in with the police. Not that there seemed to be many police around these parts, in fact he wasn't even sure where the nearest station was – nor was he particularly interested in finding out.

Coming to a stop at a junction with the Stroud road, he waited for the traffic to clear and was just pulling out to turn left when he spotted a couple of young girls at a bus stop on the opposite corner, waving to him. To his surprise and delight he realised it was Hanna and her friend Juliette, and completing his turn to clear the junction he drove on a little way before coming to a stop.

He could see them in the wing mirror, running happily and carelessly along the verge to catch him up.

'Rozzie!' Hanna cried, tearing open the passenger door. 'Oh, look at you,' she laughed as the puppy tried to leap on her. 'You've got your very own seat belt. How cute is that? Look, Juju, isn't it amazing? She's got her own seat belt.'

'She's so sweet,' Juliette gushed. 'I wish she was mine.'

'Hello over there,' John said teasingly.

'Oh John, sorry,' Hanna laughed. 'It's just so fab to see Rozzie. You too, of course,' she added, bouncing up and down. 'Are you going back to Cromstone? Can you give us a lift?'

'Yes, and yes,' he chuckled, 'but we'd best put Rozzie on the floor, or there won't be enough room for you all. Careful she doesn't escape when I undo her belt. That's right. Good girl, Rozzie, down you go and no jumping up.'

A few minutes later Hanna and Juliette were buckled into the long seat, with Rozzie flopped obediently at their feet while gazing adoringly up at John.

'So what are you two doing all the way out here?' he asked as he pulled back on to the road.

'We've been at Juliette's cousin's house practising for our fashion show,' Hanna told him. 'She's got loads of clothes and her mum used to be a model, so she was teaching us how to walk. It's going to be so cool. I can't wait for when it happens. Oh my God, Mum told me you're going to do some morris dancing.'

'No way!' Juliette cried, her pretty dark eyes sparkling with laughter. 'That is so bad. I bet you're going to be brilliant.'

John's eyebrows rose. 'Thanks for the vote of confidence,' he said drily. 'I shall certainly do my best. Philippa's already arranged my first lesson for tomorrow evening at six. She's trying to get me ahead of the game, because the other novices are half my age.'

'Oh, you'll be great,' Hanna assured him, as though he was great at everything.

Laughing, he said, 'I think we shall all have great fun. We just have to find something outrageous for your mother and Sarah to do.'

'Oh yes, we definitely have to do that,' Hanna agreed. 'Apparently Mum used to be really good at walking on her hands when she was little, so maybe we can sign her up for that and sponsor her five p a step.'

229

'Not a bad call,' he responded approvingly. 'And Sarah?'

Hanna shrugged. 'I'm not sure. What do you think, Juju?'

'No idea, but her brother's supposed to be coming this weekend, isn't he? He might give us some ideas, seeing as she's roped him in for the morris dancing.'

'We'll definitely ask him,' Hanna declared. 'Now what about Philippa? What's she going to do?'

'Oh, I think you'd better leave that to me,' John said gently. 'I'll manage to think of something. How's the baby-photo competition going?'

'Actually, not bad,' Juliette told him. 'Mum's got over fifty photographs now, and you should see some of them. They're so hilarious we can't stop laughing. Have you given her yours yet?'

'I believe Philippa was intending to drop them in today.'

'It's a shame Granny and Grandpa aren't going to be here for it,' Hanna sighed. 'They were really sweet when they were young, both of them, but you should see what they were wearing. It's sooooo Dickensian, or Victorian, or something like that. Anyway, you never know, they might come back for the weekend. I expect they will if we ask them to.'

'Do you know what time they're setting off tomorrow?' John asked.

'I think sometime in the morning. Mum's really dreading it, because she doesn't do goodbyes. Honestly, you should see her, she can be so embarrassing the state she gets herself into. Anyone would think she was never going to see us again. Thank God Dad's going to be here, is all I can say. He's usually quite good at calming her down.'

'I'm looking forward to meeting him,' John remarked. 'Will he be staying to help out with the auction next week?'

'I don't know, I expect it'll depend on whether he has to work, or if there's an audition or something he has to go to. He was really famous once, you know, before I was born. We've got all the videos though, so I've seen him. Actually, I'm thinking I'd quite like to be an actor myself when I've finished uni, but if I ever say that to Mum I know she'll go mental.'

'I suppose it isn't the most stable of professions,' John murmured. 'What about you, Juliette? Do you have your heart set on something in particular for the future?'

'Not really,' she shrugged. 'I'd kind of like to be a model, but I'm not sure I'm going to grow tall enough. I bet you do,' she said to Hanna. 'You've only got to look at your mum to see how tall you're likely to get.'

'Yeah, maybe, but then look at Granny and Grandpa. They're dead short, so she didn't take after them. Mum's like her granny apparently, who was only *six foot one*! Imagine – she must have been like a giant. How tall are you, John?'

'Six one, as it happens,' he answered. 'Or I used to be. They say you start to shrink as you get older, so maybe I'm kidding myself these days.'

'No, you're tall,' Juliette informed him knowingly. 'Have you been using the Wii much since we set it up?'

'Philippa has. She's quite into the yoga, and I believe she has a little go at the tennis. I'm afraid I haven't had much time since I started my new job.'

'You know, it is so cool having you doing the

driving,' Hanna confided. 'We really detested Godfrey, didn't we?' she said to Juliette. 'He's such a letch, and once, he only came up behind me and put his hand on my bum! Ugh! It was so disgusting.'

John's eyes remained on the road as his face darkened. 'I hope you told your mother,' he said quietly.

'I was going to, but then he broke his ankle, and so I thought what's the point, he's not going to be around any more, or not for a while. If he does it again, though, I'll tell my dad, he'll really sort him out.'

'Yes, well you be sure to do that,' John told her. 'Or come to me if your dad's not around, because that isn't something we can allow to happen again.'

Hanna started to grin. 'You know, you're so cool,' she stated happily.

'Och, now that's exactly what I want to be,' he said gladly.

Laughing, she said, 'Mum's really pleased that you're helping with the auctions. She says she doesn't know how she'd manage without you, in spite of Granny saying we shouldn't be putting on you.'

'Is that what Granny says? Well maybe I ought to put her mind at rest, because I don't feel put on at all. I expect you're going to miss her when she goes tomorrow.'

'Yeah, I will, but we've got such a lot happening at the moment. Juju and I are going to help out with the auction, you know. Mum's got us down to work with Philippa, showing stuff off like we're game-show hostesses. Should be really cool.'

Slowing down as they approached the high street in Cromstone, John said, 'So where would you like me to drop you?'

'Actually,' Hanna said, 'we were going to pop in to see Philippa, because she said we could have a go on the Wii whenever we like, and then we're going to practise showing off some of your stuff ready for next week.'

'I see,' he said, both amused and concerned. He didn't want Philippa overdoing things, and a couple of lively teenagers could easily wear her out if he wasn't around to keep an eye on proceedings. On the other hand, she'd always loved young people, and having been deprived of their company for so much of her life it wouldn't have been fair to deprive her any further.

'Just make sure she doesn't get too tired,' he whispered, as he came to a stop outside the Lodge. 'She's not as young as she used to be, but for heaven's sake don't tell her I said that.'

Grinning, Hanna and Juliette crossed their hearts and jumped down from the truck, closely followed by the boisterous Rozzie.

'Take her in too,' John told them. 'It's time for her dinner, and she's a bit too much of a whirlwind to have around the barn.'

After watching them setting off up the drive, all long legs and naive young hearts, he slipped the truck back into gear to drive on up the hill. He knew he was foolish to think that the secrets of his past would never come out, but this short time before anyone learned the truth was a blessed interlude that he intended to cherish for as long as he could. However, now that Philippa had told Sarah he'd once known her mother, he didn't imagine time was on his side any more. He couldn't help wondering if Sarah had already asked Rose about him, and if she had, what Rose had said.

Merely to think of Rose and how she'd been the last time he'd seen her caused a pang of longing to sear through his heart. Over all these years he'd never stopped loving her, and knew he never would. Was it possible she'd say the same about him? Douglas had loved her well, he knew that, and she'd loved Douglas too, but what he and Rose had shared, what had bound them together back then and still did as far as he was concerned, went even deeper than love. It defied words as surely as it defied understanding, because what had happened to them, between them and because of them had no rhyme or reason, nor, until they were no longer a part of this world, would it ever have an end. The love and longing, just like the nightmare, went on and on, as cruel and inescapable as the mistakes that had torn them apart and the decisions that turned out to be wrong. They knew life's injustices first-hand, they'd learned what it was to be punished with the kind of vengeance no merciful god would ever inflict.

Was he wrong to be in Cromstone now? What good could come of trying to recapture what had been lost, when the most precious thing of all could never be found? He was doing it for Pippa, and, in truth, for himself too, because he surely deserved to know his children before it was too late. Would Rose allow him that? Would God, or fate, or whatever governed the unpredictable journey of life, continue to stand in his way? Tomorrow evening he would come face to face with his son. Thinking of it made him as fearful as it made him euphoric, but he knew he wouldn't back away from it now. Sarah, the beautiful, tragic and wonderful girl who was so like her mother in some ways, but more like Douglas in others, didn't belong to him, but Simon and Becky did. He wondered if they knew that. Had Rose ever told them? It didn't seem that she'd told Sarah, and the pact they'd made between them over thirty years ago didn't allow her to tell Simon and Becky either. Had Rose kept to it? How difficult was it going to be for her when she discovered that he was breaking it himself?

Seeing Lucy coming up the lane from the barn as he drove the truck in, he came to a stop. 'I've just brought your daughter home,' he told her. 'She's with Pippa on the Wii.'

Smiling as she rolled her eyes, Lucy said, 'You spoil her, you two.'

He wished he could tell her why it meant so much to him to be able to, but if he did he'd probably scare her, and for all the world he wouldn't want to do that. 'I've two matching leather sofas in the back from Helen Granger,' he said. 'Is anyone around to help me unload?'

'Joe should be here any minute,' she answered. 'If you leave them where they are till he comes, I'll make you a nice cup of tea while you're waiting. It'll be a good opportunity for me to tell you what happened here while you were out.'

He looked intrigued.

'Let's put it this way,' she said, 'if you're still in touch with the man who told you about an insider ring, it could be very helpful.'

Swallowing, he said, 'No, I'm not, but maybe we could find him.'

'I'll go and put the kettle on.'

As she turned away he sat with his hands resting lightly on the wheel, his mind in bitter turmoil as he watched her go. Lucy Winters, he'd decided, was special in a way that could almost break his heart. She was fond of him too, he could tell, but she didn't know yet that he'd met the man she'd mentioned while sharing his prison cell. However, he guessed she'd find out sooner or later – he just hoped it wouldn't turn her against him.

Chapter Thirteen

'Are you completely out of your mind?' Joe cried in despair. 'Why the hell are you trusting total strangers with this?'

'Michael Givens is our *lawyer*,' Lucy shot back, going to close the office door, 'and John here is part of the team now. And will you please keep your voice down. Mum and Dad are in the kitchen. I don't want them hearing this.'

'They're the ones you should be talking to, for God's sake. And actually, your mother went over to the church about ten minutes ago, so she isn't there anyway.'

Since this was the third time in as many days that her mother had gone to pray in solitude Lucy felt her misgivings increasing, since she felt sure she must be seeking guidance over what to do about the problems in which Maureen had enmeshed them. 'I don't want to discuss this with them,' she told Joe, 'because I'm pretty sure it's what's stressing my mother out, so I'd rather she got herself as far away from it as possible, as soon as possible, so that I can deal with it.'

Joe glanced at John, who was perched on one of the desks looking as awkward as lot number forty-four, which was the warped mirror behind him.

'No offence,' Joe told him, 'but I hope you're taking my point. Lucy hasn't even known you a month and she's confiding in you like you're family, when for all she knows you could be in on it.'

'Oh for heaven's sake,' Lucy snapped furiously. 'Of course he's not in on it.'

'How do you *know* that?'

'She doesn't for certain,' John conceded, 'but I can assure you I'm not. Apart from being completely averse to illegal activities, particularly those that involve defrauding innocent people of what is rightfully theirs, I also happen to be comfortably enough off not to have to participate in them.'

Joe regarded him dubiously. 'That might be true,' he retorted, 'but I'm trying to look out for my wife's best interests here, because if there is some kind of insider ring operating, then you, Lucy – or more likely your parents – could end up taking the rap.'

'I'm fully aware of that, thank you very much,' she told him angrily, 'which is why I've enlisted the help of friends rather than the authorities for the moment, to see if we can track down who Maureen and Godfrey are working with.'

'And these *friends* would be of how long standing? What can you actually tell me about any of them that could convince me you're not being taken for a fool?'

Lucy's eyes flashed. 'I've just told you Michael's a lawyer.'

'Yeah, bloody crooks the lot of them.'

'Oh, I don't know why I'm bothering to waste my time. And I don't see why I have to convince you of anything. This is *my* business . . .'

'Oh, I was waiting for that. I suppose next you'll

be telling me that the children are yours, and this house, and everything else we own . . .'

'*We* don't own anything!'

'I think I should probably be going,' John interrupted, getting to his feet.

'No, please stay,' Lucy protested. 'I'm sorry we're going off at a tangent, so let's try to get it back on track. And Joe, please start trying to be helpful, instead of persuading yourself that I'm surrounded by a bunch of villains, when I left all that behind three weeks ago.'

Joe's face tightened. 'Oh, that's nice, that is. I suppose we're talking about my family now . . .'

'Let's try to forget I said that . . .'

'And what are Maureen and Godfrey, if they aren't a couple of fraudsters? Or that's what you're trying to tell me, so don't give me all your crap about being surrounded by the archangel and his harpists . . .'

'Enough!' Lucy cut in. 'I can see we're not going to get anywhere.'

'All right, all right. Just tell me, how well do you actually know this Givens chap?'

Wanting to scream, Lucy said, 'I've just told you, he's a lawyer, and if you ever listened to anything I said you'd know that he's been representing Mum and Dad since they moved here. His firm also oversaw the transfer of everything to my name.'

'And that's got to make me trust him?'

'Joe,' John said gently, 'if you don't mind me saying, I for one am happy to trust Lucy's judgement as far as the lawyer's concerned.'

Bristling, Joe said, 'That's great. You, a stranger, are happy to trust a lawyer I believe you don't even know.'

'Sarah has, for most of her life,' Lucy cut in.

'And you've known Sarah for how long?'

Lucy's face darkened. 'You've met her, you know what she's like, so you tell me, do you really believe she's the type to get involved in a fraud, or to deceive me like that?'

'I guess, on the face of it, no I don't,' he conceded, 'but you can't deny she's a part of the toff world which is a place the likes of you and me know nothing about, because it's all inbreeding, dodgy handshakes and secret societies that make it their business . . .'

'Joe, please stop,' she groaned. Then to John, 'I'm sorry my husband's behaving like a class bigot who apparently suffers from an inferiority complex . . .'

'Don't apologise for me.'

'Well someone has to, because if you could hear yourself . . .'

'All I'm trying to do is make you understand that you need to be more careful about where you put your trust, because you haven't been here more than five minutes and you're still a novice at all this. You've got no idea what kind of hornet's nest you might have landed in, and . . .'

'For what it's worth,' John interrupted, 'your wife's been doing a grand job of running this place so far, and I'm sure she's a very good judge of character.'

'Well, you would think so, given that you're one of the new chaps on the block . . .'

'Joe!'

'I'm joking,' he cried. 'Honest to God, why do you have to take everything so seriously?'

'Because this is serious. We're talking about a crime that could land Mum up in court, or worse, jail, and let's not forget that Maureen's already made threats to that end. So now we have to decide what needs to be done.'

For all his bluff and bluster, Joe found himself looking to John for guidance.

'For the moment I think Lucy's doing the right thing,' John told him. 'The auction's going ahead, as planned, and we're all going to be on the lookout for anything odd, or anyone who seems suspicious. Meanwhile Sarah's going through the books to see . . .'

'At the risk of repeating myself,' Joe expostulated, 'Lucy's handing over to strangers. Apart from you, they've all been in this neck for most of their lives, and she's only just turned up . . .'

'Don't talk about me as if I'm not here,' Lucy snapped. 'And if you're so worried about Sarah going through the archives, perhaps you'd like to do it. After all, you're family, so it stands to reason you'll be able to understand everything, and be trusted, and know what to do when you find what you're looking for.'

'Don't be cute.'

'Then come up with something a little more productive than simply criticising everything I'm doing.'

'That's just it, I'm no more an expert at any of this than you are.'

'So where, in your book, does that leave us?'

'In my book I think we should be talking to an independent lawyer.'

'OK, you do that. I'm happy with Michael, but if you want to draft in someone else, at your expense, you go right ahead.'

John glanced at his watch. 'I really ought to be going,' he said. 'Pippa'll be wondering where I am.'

'Yes, of course,' Lucy said, wishing he would stay, but understanding how embarrassed he must be by now. 'I'm sorry we kept you so long, I was hoping . . . Well, it doesn't matter now. If Hanna's still at your place will you let her know her father's here? I'm sure she'll want to see him before she races off to wherever she's going for the evening.'

'Will do,' John replied, and picking up the wonky mirror to take over to the barn on his way out, he added, 'I'm off to Cirencester for a set of garden furniture in the morning, so I should be back with it around eleven, if that suits. What time are your parents leaving? I don't want to be in the way.'

'I think around ten,' she answered, the familiar dread of parting closing around her like a trap. She seemed to be getting worse, because right at this moment she wasn't too keen on letting John go either, though she guessed that was because she wasn't much looking forward to being left alone with Joe.

As it turned out she managed to avoid it for a while, as seconds after John left Hanna came bouncing in through the door, throwing herself straight into her father's arms as though she hadn't seen him for a month.

'Grandpa said you were here,' she gushed. 'It's so cool, because now you can come out with us for their farewell dinner. You know, everyone round here remembers who you are, well most of them anyway, and it's so cool that you're a celebrity. Ow Dad, you're squeezing too hard.'

Laughing as he let her go, Joe cupped her lovely young face in his hands and planted a smackeroo on her forehead. 'You're looking gorgeous,' he told her,

242

'and there was me thinking you were wasting away down here.'

'Oh no, it's really cool most of the time. I mean, I still miss my friends in London, and I wish Ben was here, but he texts me most days, and you were right about me making loads of friends here, because I have, and they're not a bit like I was expecting.'

Lucy's eyebrows rose, since the prediction about new friends had been hers. However, she was happy for Joe to take the credit if it was going to make him feel more included – something, she realised now, that she really wasn't managing very well at all.

'So am I getting to meet them?' Joe was saying. 'What news on Lucas, by the way? Any texts yet?'

Hanna's cheeks turned pink. 'Actually, he's sent two, but I haven't replied because I don't want him to think I'm just hanging around waiting for him to come back.'

'That's my girl, treat 'em mean, keep 'em keen. You'll have him eating out of your hand, you wait and see.'

Glowing at the thought, Hanna glanced at her mother. 'Why are you looking at me like that?' she demanded.

'Like what?' Lucy replied, mystified.

Hanna shrugged. 'Like you want to bite my head off. Anyway, Dad, did you remember to bring a photo of you as a baby like I told you? We're going to get Juju's mum to see if she can pick you out. Or Annie, Marietta's mum . . . Actually, we could always ask Pippa. She's so cool, even though she's quite old. You should see her boxing on the Wii Fit, she's brilliant at it.'

'And Pippa would be?'

'John's sister,' Lucy told him.

'She wears this eyepatch,' Hanna ran on. 'You'd think it would make her look a bit weird, like a pirate or something, but actually it's dead funky. Yep, I definitely think we should get her to see if she can pick you out, and maybe you should try to spot her. Except that would be a bit obvious . . .' She gave a choke of laughter. 'Though I don't suppose she was wearing an eyepatch as a baby . . . Anyway, we'll work it out. So, have you got the photo, because if you have we can drop it into the pub on our way out.'

'I have indeed,' he informed her. 'It's in my bag, so . . .'

'Yay!' she cried, leaping up in the air. 'That means you'll definitely be coming for the fete. I knew you would. Ben kept saying you'd probably be working with Charlie or Vince, or going for an audition, so I shouldn't get my hopes up . . .'

'Well, I guess Ben's right up to a point, because if something does come up . . . but I don't expect it will,' he said hastily as her face started to drop.

'I think we should go inside now,' Lucy told her, dismayed by how hard she was finding it to share Hanna's enthusiasm for Joe's presence at the fete. She wasn't especially thrilled by how left out she was feeling, either, having had no idea that the children were in such regular contact with each other, and their father. Why hadn't she known that? Had Hanna told her and she'd failed to listen, or was it simply more important to keep in touch with Joe?

Berating herself for such ludicrous jealousy, she started to turn off the computers as Hanna, still chattering away, linked Joe's arm to walk back to the farmhouse.

'So, how's it going with the new agent?' she was

asking as they left. 'Don't tell me he cancelled again, that would be so out of order.'

He? Lucy was thinking. The last she'd heard the new agent was a she.

'I'm afraid he did,' Joe admitted, 'but he had to because something major cropped up. He's definitely going to see me on Monday though, and if he lets me down again, well, who cares, I've got someone else interested in seeing me on Wednesday who knows Kenneth Branagh's agent.'

Hearing Hanna's groan of dismay as she realised he wasn't going to be around for the auction, Lucy tried not to feel relieved, while wondering if she should have been feeling guilty for not paying attention when he'd told her about another new agent. In fact, she'd been so busy since she'd last seen Joe that she'd barely spoken to him, so perhaps it wasn't surprising that he'd gone on the attack almost as soon as he'd arrived. He must be feeling angry and not a little resentful that she'd barely said hello before loading him with the legal issues, which she'd clearly discussed with everyone else before even mentioning them to him.

Deciding to make more of an effort to take an interest in his world over the weekend, and to down-play her absorption with the upcoming auction, she quickly made sure everything was off before setting the alarm and locking up. John had warned her before Joe arrived to be extra vigilant from now on, since they didn't want any mysterious burglaries or acts of vandalism resulting in the loss of documents or computers that might have contained some damning information. So, after checking that the barn was fully alarmed too, she started over to the kitchen, clicking on her mobile as it rang.

'Hi, everything OK?' she asked.

'More than,' Sarah replied. 'Simon just rang and guess what? He's on his way down the M4 even as we speak.'

Lucy blinked with astonishment.

'It turns out he flew into London for a meeting this morning which finished about an hour ago, so he decided to come straight here rather than go all the way back to Paris for one day. I'm so thrilled I can hardly contain myself.'

Smiling, Lucy said, 'That's fantastic news. I can't wait to meet him.'

'Oh, you'll love him, I just know it. He's always great with women, I don't mean in a flirty, letchy sort of way, I mean he listens to what we say. How many men do you know do that?'

Having to concede not many, Lucy said, 'Have you told him about the party tomorrow night?'

'Yes, and he's really up for it. He's dead keen to see Michael. As far as he's concerned he's the brother he never had. Trouble is, Becky and I have claimed him too, so Simon doesn't get exclusivity.'

'I'm sure he can live with it.' Then, finding herself spurred by Joe's suspicions, she said, 'Tell me, how long has it been since you were last in touch with Michael?'

Sarah thought. 'Let me see, five, maybe even seven years on my part. I'm not sure about Simon. Why do you ask?'

Annoyed with herself already, Lucy said, 'No reason, except my dear husband has got it into his head . . . Actually, it doesn't matter, forget I said anything.'

'OK, if that's what you want. So, have you decided where you're all going this evening?'

'Mum and Dad love the Gumstool at Calcot Manor, so we're taking them there. I guess you won't be joining us now, but I hope you know you were very welcome.'

'And I really appreciate it, but even if Simon weren't on his way, this is your last night with your parents for a while, so I think you should keep it to family. Now, before I ring off, I don't suppose you've heard any more from the ghastly Maureen?'

'Not a word, but I'm bracing myself. If she's not in touch again before the auction, I think I'll let Michael make the next contact.'

'Good idea, by which time he, or I, might have dug up some kind of evidence – or at least a lead or two.'

Feeling herself connecting with the seriousness of it again, Lucy said, 'I swear, if they do anything to try and drag Mum's name through the mud, I'll find someone to go over there and break a lot more than their bloody ankles.'

'I want to be a part of the hit squad,' Sarah muttered. Then, after a moment of savouring the thought, 'I guess I'd better ring off. I'll be there around nine in the morning I should think, or definitely in time to wave au revoir to your folks.'

With more stirrings of dread creeping over her like old ghosts, Lucy mumbled a goodbye and ended the call. Moments later she was on the point of entering the kitchen when she almost collided with Joe.

'Ah, there you are,' he said, catching her by the shoulders, 'we were wondering what had happened to you. Is everything OK?'

'Seems to be,' she said airily. 'Have you showered already?'

247

His eyes narrowed seductively. 'I thought we might take one together,' he suggested.

Forcing herself not to pull away, she said, 'I'm not sure we have time for anything like that. The table's booked for eight.'

He glanced at his watch. 'Two in the shower is twice as fast as one,' he pointed out.

Affecting her own playful look, she said, 'Not the way we take showers,' and planting a quick kiss on his cheek she breezed on by, hoping beyond hope that he wouldn't try to press the issue once they were upstairs.

To her relief, he didn't. However, by the time they were ready to go downstairs to join the others she almost wished he had, because, obviously rattled by the rebuff, he'd spent the entire time either berating her for letting Hanna run wild – an accusation he surely ought to have handed up to the mirror – or replaying his stuck record of how foolish she was to put her trust in strangers.

It was extremely fortunate, she was thinking to herself, as he drove them to the restaurant in her car, that he had no way of knowing how furious she actually was with him. Having had so much practice at hiding it, she was simply calling on her old skills now, because getting into another argument would serve no purpose. All she really wanted to do was forget everything that was bothering her, from Maureen and Godfrey right through to her marriage, and start focusing on making this as special a dinner for her parents as they deserved.

'Yay!' Sarah cried, running off the terrace with her arms spread wide as Simon pulled his hire car into the back drive. 'You're here already. You must have driven like a loony.'

Laughing as he threw open the door, he scooped her into his arms and swung her round like a doll. 'God, it's good to see you like this,' he told her, holding her hard. 'You're transformed from the last time I saw you.'

'That's what having a job and a friend has done for me,' she laughed happily. 'It's made such a difference, having a reason to get up in the morning.'

Easing her back so he could get a really good look, he said, 'I love the hair. It suits you short, and no more dark circles round the eyes. Wow!' His expression and tone were infused with relief and affection as he said, 'You're almost the old you.'

'And you're definitely the old you,' she declared, clasping her hands round his face. His deep brown eyes and side-parted fair hair were virtually identical shades to hers, while his features, though heavier and more masculine, had clearly been produced from the same genes. It was his smile that always set him apart, though, because it was as captivating and radiant as their mother's.

'I've been so looking forward to you coming,' she told him, linking his arm as she walked him back to the terrace. 'And to think you're going to be staying for over a week! How honoured I am.'

'I'd make it longer if I could, but even though Paris might shut down for August nothing so civilised happens in the States, which means, I'm afraid, that I'm still on call. However, unless something goes disastrously wrong with some contract or deal we've got cooking, there's no reason why I can't work from here.'

'Fantastic. I'm going to be extremely busy myself

over the next few days with the auction coming up. Actually, I'm hoping you'll put in an appearance for a couple of hours, if only to see our stuff going under the hammer.'

With no little irony, he said, 'You never know, I might end up buying it back. Who's the auctioneer? Don't tell me it's you.'

With a choke of laughter she said, 'Not yet, but don't rule it out, because both Lucy and I intend to learn. On this occasion though, a couple of professional auctioneers will be running the show who've run it before, usually with Lucy's dad and *Godfrey*, who I've already told you about.'

'Ah, the infamous Maureen's other half, if I'm remembering correctly. And you think he's a part of this ring?'

'If there is one, and we're all pretty convinced now that there is, then without a doubt he's involved. Our aim is to shut their operations down before any real damage is done.'

'If it hasn't been already,' he said gravely. 'That's the trouble when you start digging, you never know what's going to turn up. Still, it's good that you're on to it. You said Michael was coming later?'

'He should be here in about half an hour, which means I get you to myself until then, and I have something I need to ask.'

'Something else?' he cried in mock exasperation. 'Please don't tell me you've managed to get yourself embroiled in any more mysterious rings or dubious shenanigans, because there's a limit to my brotherly powers of getting you out of scrapes, you know.'

'Rubbish, you're brilliant at everything and I always know I'm perfectly safe when you're around.'

'No pressure there then,' he said drily, and stretching out his arms he gazed down over the billowing sprawl of the unkempt garden to the magnificent sweep of countryside flowing out to the estuary. 'God, it's good to be here,' he sighed pleasurably. 'I only have to look out at all that and listen to the birds to feel memory lane trying to swallow me up.'

'I know what you mean,' she murmured, leaning into him as she gazed out at the view too. 'I'm never sure whether it ends up making me feel sad or glad that our childhoods are behind us.'

'We had a lot of fun in this garden,' he reminded her, 'and out in those fields. I often wonder how many rites of passage were played out in the buttercup bowl over by the copse.'

With twinkling eyes she said, 'I know yours were, and Becky's, with Michael. God, it seems a long time ago.'

'Because it was. Have you spoken to Becky lately?'

'About an hour ago, as a matter of fact. She was on her way to an aerobic workout before dashing up to Connecticut for some linguistics conference. She sends her love and says to give her a call about the real estate project.'

He frowned. 'Which project . . . ? Oh yes, the one in southern California. Could be interesting, but we need to do more research. So how is she apart from that?'

'Oh, you know Becky, madly busy and bursting at the seams with get up and go. It can make me feel exhausted just talking to her sometimes. You can probably imagine how thrilled she is that I'm working again, though she doesn't really approve of the job. She says I'm not utilising all my hard-earned

251

talents, which is nonsense, because I am for the most part, and I'm also learning more. Still, it's been tough on her trying to deal with me shut away here like a wounded angel, as she likes to call me, so it must be a great relief to know she doesn't have to worry so much any more.'

'We've all been worried,' he reminded her, 'but I'll be able to put her and Mum's minds at rest the next time I speak to them, because, Sarah Delicious, you're looking *great*.' After giving her another hug he said, 'Now I'm going to fetch my things from the car and take them upstairs while you, my darling, fix us one of your wickedest Martinis.'

Lighting up again, she said, 'I haven't made one in so long. I just hope I've got all the ingredients.'

It turned out that she had, and the vodka was even in the freezer, though she had no idea when she'd put it there. Still, there were doubtless many things she'd done over the last year or so in a haze of grief, so she wasn't going to start giving herself a hard time over memory lapses now.

'Mm, I've just hit the fast track to bliss,' he declared twenty minutes later as he took his first sip of one of her driest.

Feeling the alcohol burning through her own veins and all the way into her spirits, Sarah smiled dreamily and reached for his hand. 'Thanks for coming,' she whispered.

Clearly knowing how much it meant to her, he said, 'I'd be here more often if my schedule allowed.'

'I know.'

'Giselle sends her love.'

'Thanks. Where is she at the moment?'

He glanced at his watch. 'Today Milan, Frankfurt

252

tomorrow till Friday, otherwise she'd have come with me.'

'It's always lovely to see her, but I can't help being pleased at not having to share you for a while. Having said that, I can't wait to introduce you to Lucy.'

'I'm looking forward to it myself, as I've heard so much about her. So now, what was this something else you wanted to ask me?'

Taking another sip of her drink, she braced herself against the nerves that coasted in with the reminder and said, 'I was wondering if the name John Mckenzie might mean anything to you?'

Simon frowned. 'I don't think so,' he replied. 'Should it?'

Finding herself torn between disappointment and relief, she said, 'I'm not sure.' Though a part of her wanted answers desperately, another was afraid of what they might be.

'Who is he?' he asked. 'Something to do with this ring?'

'No, nothing like – at least I hope not. No, he definitely wouldn't be. He and his sister moved into the Lodge about a month ago. You know, the Mercers' house at the bottom . . .'

'I know it.'

'Of course. Well, apparently they're old friends of Mum's.'

'Really?' he said, sounding interested. 'How do they know her?'

'Well, that's the big mystery, because I'm not sure. No one will tell me.'

Puzzled, he turned to look at her.

'He says I should ask Mum, and Sheila says I shouldn't, at least not until she's spoken to her first.'

Simon's eyes darkened. 'I don't know if I like the sound of that,' he retorted. 'Are you saying you think they had an affair?'

'I'm not sure what to think, but I can't see her cheating on Dad, can you?'

Though Simon shook his head, he was looking more troubled than ever. 'What else did Sheila say?' he asked.

Sarah looked at him anxiously. 'That Mum and John were victims of the most dreadful – then she cut herself off and told me not to think badly of anyone. She seemed to think the Mckenzies might have come to Cromstone because of Mum.'

'But she's not here.'

'Maybe they didn't know that until they arrived.'

Apparently liking this less as it went on, Simon stood up and walked to the edge of the terrace.

Though Sarah wanted to ask him what he was thinking, sensing his anger, or perhaps confusion, she decided to say nothing for now.

He turned towards her. 'It sounds as though whatever went on between them was quite a big deal,' he commented in a tone clipped with resentment.

Sarah's insides were clenching with yet more trepidation as she said, 'Si, when we were younger you used to say that you knew something Becky and I didn't. Is that true, or were you just teasing us?'

Taking a deep breath, he came back for his drink and took a sip. 'I don't know any more than you do,' he told her, 'but we all know there's something she's not telling us.'

'And you don't have any idea what it might be?'

He shook his head slowly. 'Like you, I can only guess,' he replied, and his eyes moved off towards the end of the garden. 'The way Mum used to be, shutting herself away for days on end . . . It had quite an effect on me when we were growing up. I used to think it was something I'd done, and I never knew how to make it up to her.'

Feeling her heart tear with the same childhood memories, Sarah squeezed his hand as she said, 'This is what happens when people keep secrets, things are misunderstood and all kinds of problems start kicking in.'

He didn't argue, only turned to her with a flicker of his usual roguish smile. 'Actually, the worst part of it,' he declared, 'was having two flipping sisters. All those dolls and playing house or shop or hairdressers . . . I needed someone to do high-speed roars round the garden and climb trees and steal apples . . .'

'All of which we did,' she reminded him hotly.

He was laughing. 'You're right, you did, but I still say it was lucky I had Dad, and Michael, or my testosterone might never have had a chance to develop.'

Sarah laughed, and leaned over to kiss him, but as the smile faded from her lips she said, 'So we're none the wiser about John Mckenzie.'

Simon's eyes darkened again as he took a sip of his drink. 'Tell me, is all this building up to me having a chat with him while I'm here?' he asked dubiously.

Though she hadn't formed that exact thought, now he'd put it into words Sarah wasn't about to shy away. 'Maybe it is,' she said, 'provided you can find the right moment. I just want you to know that he seems like a really nice man . . .'

'Everyone does until their darker side starts to show,' he reminded her.

'OK, but try to remember that Sheila didn't say anything bad about him. I mean, she didn't warn me away, or say anything like, "Oh my God not that monster . . ."'

With the faintest glimmer of irony he said, 'Is this you worrying about me being civil to strangers?'

She couldn't deny it. 'Just try to keep an open mind when you meet him,' she said, 'because I know what you can be like.'

'Oh you do, do you?'

'Yes, Simon Bancroft, I do, and until we know the whole story we shouldn't lose sight of the fact that we're all capable of making mistakes, or misunderstanding situations, or turning into someone different. I'm thinking of Kelvin now – we never used to see him as someone who'd be disloyal, or cruel, or all the things he's been since we broke up . . .'

'All right, all right,' he interrupted, holding up a hand. 'I'll be sure to be on my best behaviour. Now tell me, have you mentioned any of this to Becky?'

'No, I wanted to talk to you about it first.' She turned round as someone knocked on the front door. 'It must be Michael,' she said, getting up. 'He's really looking forward to seeing you.'

To her relief, Simon's frown started to fade. 'The feeling's mutual,' he told her. 'If you let him in, I'll sort the drinks.'

Moments later Michael was in the kitchen, treating Simon to a boisterous back-slapping hug.

'It's been too long,' they said simultaneously.

Laughing, Simon said, 'You're looking great, my friend. Something's obviously agreeing with you.'

'I could say the same about you,' Michael countered. 'How's Giselle?'

'On good form. She'll want me to send her love, I know. How go hostilities with Carlotta these days?'

Michael grimaced. 'Still a minefield, I'm afraid, but so far I've managed to hang on to my limbs. However, she's still after an arm and a leg in settlements, and the proverbial on a plate as some sort of compensation.'

Sarah was aghast. 'For what, exactly? And her family's richer than royalty, so why's she after your money?'

'I guess because it gives her something to do,' he answered drily. 'Fortunately I don't have to see her too often, because her sister usually flies back and forth with the boys.'

'When are you seeing them again?'

Taking the glass Simon was handing him, he said, 'That's still in dispute at the moment, because they're on some yacht cruising the Greek islands with their mother and one of her "friends", and if she gets her way they'll stay there till the schools go back.'

'And if you get yours?'

'They'll be here next week till summer's over, but I'm not holding my breath. Anyway, if you don't mind I feel in sore need of this,' and after raising a toast to old times and great reunions he took his first sip. 'Wow,' he murmured with closed eyes, 'this is good.'

Grabbing the shaker, Sarah led the way out on to the terrace where they all sat down at the table and managed to release a protracted, satisfied sigh in unison.

Laughing, Michael gazed out at the first crimson smudges of sunset edging the clouds as he said, 'God, it's good to be here again. Sometimes I feel as though my whole childhood was spent in this house and garden.'

'Funny, because that's how I remember it too,' Simon told him.

'You two were always like brothers,' Sarah smiled.

Simon's expression was ironic as Michael's eyebrows rose.

'So let's hear about this ring,' Simon said. 'Do you think it's real?'

Michael grimaced. 'I certainly think we have to assume it is for now, given the dreaded Maureen's threats against Lucy's mother, and her failure actually to deny its existence. However, apart from a few letters from disgruntled clients, or their solicitors, we don't actually have anything to go on yet.'

'The biggest concern is protecting Lucy's mother,' Sarah added.

Simon nodded thoughtfully. 'And you're absolutely sure she's not involved?'

'No way,' Sarah cried.

'If she is,' Michael said, 'I'm pretty sure it'll be against her will.'

Puzzled, Simon said, 'So why don't you ask her?'

'Lucy doesn't want to,' Sarah told him. 'She thinks it's what's causing her mother's ill health at the moment, and she's afraid if she starts quizzing her and bringing it all out into the open, it'll make her mother worse.'

'So it's being swept under the carpet?'

'As far as her mother's concerned, yes, but we can't let it go on, because it could end up having a disastrous effect on the business.'

Simon looked at Michael. 'So how are you going to play it?' he asked.

'I've already got someone checking out the free-lance auctioneers,' Michael replied, 'and Sarah's going through the company records, but this is an incredibly tricky problem to pin down. Almost everything will happen by word of mouth, so there's not likely to be any documentation to help us, and once an item's sold that's where its connection to Cromstone's ends. No one follows its trail afterwards, because there's no reason to.'

'So how does anyone know they've been cheated?'

'Usually they don't, because detecting a ring is almost as impossible as breaking it, but occasionally when a scammed item goes to auction somewhere else in the country it'll fetch a ridiculous price, whereupon it's reported in the trade press. Then, should the likes of Mr Beadle, or one of his family, happen to pick up that particular paper or magazine . . . Well, you can see how random it is, and you'll understand why the Beadles of this world, if they do get to find out, are none too happy.'

'But they still don't know for sure that they were scammed,' Simon pointed out. 'It could just be a combination of bad timing and bad luck.'

'Of course, which is why it's all so hard to prove, and why I'm planning to enlist the help of another lawyer who's more familiar with this sort of thing than I am. You might remember him. Teddy Best?'

Simon frowned thoughtfully, but shook his head. 'I don't think I do,' he replied.

'Well, he's a good few years older than us, but he's not only a great chap, he also happens to be a knock-out morris dancer.'

Simon looked askance as Sarah bubbled with laughter. 'And that's supposed to recommend him because?' he said dubiously.

Michael's expression was wry. 'I take it your dear sister hasn't yet told you about our date with humility.'

Simon's eyes narrowed as he turned to Sarah. 'Maybe now would be a good time,' he suggested.

Sarah was grinning happily. 'You and Michael are going to join the morris dancers at the summer fete,' she informed him.

Simon's face dropped.

'I thought,' Sarah pressed on, 'that it was a great idea, now that I'm learning to laugh again. Watching you two hopping and slapping about could make up for at least the last two years.'

Simon turned to Michael.

Michael shrugged.

'I won't be here,' Simon decided. 'I'll be back in Paris . . .'

'I shall insist you fly over,' Sarah informed him.

'What I'd like to know,' Michael said, 'is what you and Lucy are planning to entertain us with.'

Simon immediately looked interested. 'I think we should insist on something of the burlesque variety,' he suggested. 'Or hang on, I haven't met Lucy yet. Good idea?' he asked Michael.

Michael's eyes shone with laughter as he nodded.

'This is a fete that includes children,' Sarah reminded them, 'so no room for old men's fantasies.'

'We'll think of something,' Michael warned her.

'We'll look forward to it,' she replied with a teasing smile. 'Meanwhile, I hope you can still make our drinks party tomorrow night.'

'Of course, wouldn't miss it.'

'Who else have you invited?' Simon wanted to know.

'Lucy, obviously, and the Mckenzies.'

Simon looked less than thrilled.

'You'll like them,' she assured him.

Appearing surprised, Michael asked, 'Is there some reason why you wouldn't?'

After bringing him up to speed on the Mckenzies' ambiguous connection to his family, Simon added, 'Not that a party's going to be a good time to ask the man how he fits into my mother's life. Have you met him?' he asked Michael.

'Only briefly,' Michael replied. 'He seems a nice enough bloke.'

Turning back to Sarah, Simon said, 'So who else? Or is that it?'

'I guess Joe, Lucy's husband, will come if he's still around,' she told him. 'You might remember him from that soap, *Costa del Crime*, that ran for a while. Years ago now. He was Alan something or other, I've forgotten the name, but the baddie heart-throb chap.'

'I do vaguely,' Simon responded. 'So what's he like?'

Sarah gave it some thought. 'Actually, he's not unlike the character he used to play, good-looking, full of cockney charm . . . I don't think he's worked much since that series, but you never know, he might get a call from Mr Spielberg or one of the Camerons – Mackintosh, James – and have to go zooming back to London, so we won't end up seeing him tomorrow night after all.'

Simon's eyes went to Michael. 'I have plenty of contacts in that world,' he reminded them drily, 'maybe I'll make a few calls, see what I can arrange.'

'Or maybe you won't,' Michael retorted, and raising his glass he winked at Sarah as he took a sip.

Chapter Fourteen

'Mum! Stop shouting at him,' Hanna cried angrily. 'He only did what he thought was best.'

'Keep out of this,' Lucy told her. 'They're *my* parents,' she raged at Joe. 'How dare you send them off without allowing me to see them?'

'Because we all know what a basket case you are with goodbyes,' he reminded her, 'so we decided ...'

'No, *you* decided ...'

'... that it would be easier on them, and you, if they went off quietly before you were up.'

'And you seriously believe it's what they wanted?'

'They went, didn't they?'

'Because you told them to. You know what they're like. They hardly ever put up a fight if they think it's going to upset someone ...'

'And waiting to say goodbye to you wouldn't be upsetting? Why put them through it when you don't have to? This way they've gone off without all the drama and nonsense, which, frankly, is something they can do without when they've got a long drive ahead of them. Or long for them, anyway.'

'So you get to give all the orders and the rest of us have to obey?'

'Lucy, you're being unreasonable, and you know it.'

'No, what I know is that you ordered them out of their own home . . .'

'He did no such thing,' Hanna protested furiously. 'I was there when everyone agreed . . .'

'No, not everyone agreed, because no one asked me and there's . . .'

'It's because of you and your bloody phobia, or paranoia, or whatever the hell you want to call it, that an agreement had to be made at all,' Joe told her irritably. 'It was done with your best interests at heart, whatever you like to think, and with theirs too.'

'And anyway, they've gone now,' Hanna added, 'so why don't you stop having a go at us and start feeling thankful that we . . .'

'I've had enough of this,' Lucy snapped, and grabbing her mobile and keys she stormed out of the kitchen and across the yard to the barn, where John was strolling round from the front to find out where everyone was.

'Good morning,' he greeted her cheerily. 'I've collected the garden furniture and Carl, so we're ready to unload as soon as the barn's unlocked.'

Not wanting to take her bad mood out on him, Lucy summoned a smile as she handed him the keys. 'You've got the alarm code?' she said, as her mobile started to ring.

Tapping the side of his head, showing it was stored safely inside, he gave the keys a quick toss and left her to her call.

'Sarah, hi,' Lucy said into her phone as she turned towards the office. 'How are you this morning?'

'I've had better starts,' Sarah replied groggily. 'One too many Martinis last night, but never fear, I shall be with you in about half an hour for the fond farewell.'

263

'I'm afraid you're already too late for that,' Lucy said tightly. 'Joe packed them off at the crack of dawn because *he* couldn't face how sad I'd be to see them go.'

'Oh,' Sarah responded carefully, 'and you're obviously not thrilled.'

'Far from it, but it's done now so I suppose I have to let it drop, which might be easier if I wasn't going to have to put up with him for the next two days. Anyway, let's change the subject. There's a lot to get through today . . . No, first tell me how it went with Simon and Michael last night – or is it all lost in a Martini haze?'

'Absolutely not. A great reunion, but we ended up talking about this ring for most of the evening. Michael's already on the case, but I expect you know that, and apparently he's consulting another lawyer who specialises in fraud. And who also . . . wait for this, happens to be a demon morris dancer. So how's that for killing two birds with one stone?'

Managing another smile, Lucy said, 'Sounds good to me. Hang on, I need to unlock the door,' and putting her mobile on the ledge, she quickly let herself into the office and grabbed the phone again. 'Back with you. Did you get a chance to ask Simon about John Mckenzie?'

'Yes, but he'd never heard of him. He definitely wasn't too thrilled by the possibility that Mummy might have had an affair at some point, though.'

'I guess it's the most obvious assumption. Does it bother *you* that that might have happened?'

'Yes, I suppose it does, but if it helps explain her depressions . . . Except it's awful to think of her pining away for another man when Daddy loved her so

264

much. It might turn me against John, if that were the case.'

Starting to switch on the computers, Lucy said, 'Let's not jump to conclusions, because the last thing we want is to start condemning him for something he might not have done.'

'Of course, and I promise I'm trying to keep an open mind. Anyway, Simon mentioned something last night about taking us both to lunch today, but I told him we're too busy.'

'I'm afraid we are.'

'But you're still on for tonight, I hope?'

'I certainly am,' Lucy responded, flipping through the paperwork she'd left on her desk ready for attention first thing, 'but I'll have to bring Joe,' and feeling annoyed with him all over again, simply for existing, she said, 'So who else are you inviting?'

'I think I'll keep it to just us six, seven,' Sarah corrected. 'Simon's really keen to meet you, by the way. Oh, I forgot to ask, how did your dinner go last night?'

'It was fine. Mum and Dad were in their element having us all there, and Ben rang when we got back as a surprise for them. I just wish I'd seen them before they left this morning. Anyway, no point harping on about it. I'll see you in half an hour, yes?'

'Complete with two coffees from Moonkicks.'

After ringing off, Lucy was about to make a start on her emails when Joe tapped gently on the door and waved a white hanky before asking if he could come in.

Annoyed, but amused, she said, 'If you must, but I'm really busy.'

'I know and I won't hold you up, I just wanted to say I'm sorry and that I hope we can be friends again.'

'We're friends,' she told him, keeping her eyes on the screen as she typed.

'That's good, because I'd like to take you to lunch, if you can spare the time.'

'I can't, I'm afraid, and I've already turned down one invitation today, so it wouldn't look good if I suddenly accepted another.' She wasn't entirely sure why she'd added that, since there had been no reason to, and the tone of his response proved that she should try to keep her mind on one thing at a time in future.

'So who was the other invitation from?' he asked sourly.

'Simon, Sarah's brother,' she replied, still typing. 'Which reminds me, they've invited us for drinks this evening.'

'Really? How nice.'

Several minutes passed with only the sound of her fingers on the keyboard, until finally he said, 'You're really getting into it down here, aren't you?'

Still not looking at him, she said, 'It would be a bit of a problem if I weren't.'

'Even Hanna seems to like it, which I wasn't expecting.'

'I hope you consider that to be a good thing.'

'I do, except I can feel you all slipping away and I'm not sure how to keep hold of you.'

Stilling her fingers, she quickly tried to think of the right thing to say, but no words were coming, at least none that he'd want to hear. Feeling him moving in to stand behind her, she swivelled in her chair to look up at him. 'This is quite a challenging time,' she told him, as gently as she could. 'Now that Mum and Dad have gone I really am in charge, and with this problem we have bubbling under, plus the auction coming up . . .'

266

'Don't worry, I get how busy you are, but I surely have a right to be concerned about what's happening between us.'

Did she have to remind him again that they were supposed be having a trial separation? Why wasn't he taking it in? 'Joe, it's a really bad time to be having this conversation.'

His face tightened. 'So when will be a good time?'

'Not this weekend, I'm afraid, and probably not next either with all the clearing up there'll be to do.'

'You've changed already,' he told her roughly. 'You never used to be this . . . cold.'

'All I am is wrapped up in what's happening here, which is how it has to be in order for me to make a success of it. No, Joe, listen please,' she interrupted as he started to speak, 'I need to get on with this now, but if there's a lull in the schedule later, or sometime tomorrow, I promise I'll come and find you.'

'Well, thank you for that. I'm happy to know that I *might* be squeezed in, while drinks with your new friends is a definite.'

'Joe, don't do this, please.'

He averted his head, looking strained and pale, and clearly not knowing what to do next.

'Where's Hanna?' she asked.

'Upstairs getting ready to go and meet her friend. I hear they're coming to help out in the barn today.'

Lucy only looked at him, not knowing what to say. 'You could too, if you felt like it,' she suggested.

'No, I know you don't want me there . . .'

'That's not true.'

He was looking at his watch. 'I promised to take Hanna for a coffee before she meets Juliette. Maybe I could bring you back a cappuccino?'

'That would be lovely, thanks, but Sarah's picking one up . . .'

'Of course she is.'

As he turned away Lucy got to her feet and reached for his hand. 'Things will start to settle down soon,' she assured him.

He didn't look convinced.

'The weekend of the summer fete . . . Why don't we make a point of doing something together, just the three of us, if you like?' she said tentatively.

'Actually, I'm not sure I can make that weekend.'

Surprised, she said, 'But you've already given Hanna your photograph . . .'

'I know, but there's a chance I'll be moving into my new place on the Saturday.'

Lucy pulled back to look at him. 'What new place is this?' she asked. 'Where is it? How did you find it?'

He shrugged. 'It's in East Ham. It belongs to a mate of Charlie's he knows from the markets. He's going away for six months so I've agreed to take care of things while he's gone.'

'I see.' She was unable to tell from his tone how he was viewing this, nor was she entirely sure how she was supposed to be responding. 'Are you having to pay rent?' she asked.

'Course I am, but it's only a few hundred quid a month, plus bills.' He glanced off to one side, avoiding her eyes. 'I was thinking, if Hanna wanted to come back . . .'

'Don't even go there,' she warned. 'She's staying here, with me, so any thoughts you might have . . . Please tell me you haven't already said anything to her.'

'No, I haven't, but if it's what she wants . . .'

'She's settling in here, Joe. You know that, so please don't start spoiling it for her.'

'If she's so happy, how's it going to spoil it if I give her other options? She just has to say no.'

'She'll see it as having to choose between us, and that wouldn't be fair. You can't look after her on your own, and you know it, and you said yourself, this place you're taking care of is only for six months. What's she supposed to do then?'

He shrugged and started to turn away, but then seemed to think better of it. 'I'm going to need a deposit,' he said. 'It's a security thing, you know how it is.'

Stifling a sigh, she said, 'How much?'

'Five hundred, plus moving expenses and, you know, the rest of it. How about a grand?'

'That's a lot of money, Joe, and I'm not taking a salary yet.'

'But you can, any time you like. Remember, you're the boss.'

'Yes, but we need to reinvest and make sure all the overheads are covered . . .'

'Forget it. I'm sorry I asked.'

Understanding what was going on now, she said, 'I can probably do it this once, provided you promise not to try and talk Hanna into going to live with you.'

He seemed neither pleased by the offer nor embarrassed by the way he'd managed to get it. 'I'll pay you back one day, you know that, don't you?' he said.

'Of course,' she replied, going along with the delusion the way she always did. 'I'll contact the bank to arrange a transfer. Are you OK for cash at the moment?'

He took out his wallet and appeared surprised to find a small wad of twenty-pound notes inside. 'Ah yes, I was intending to pay for dinner last night,' he recalled, 'but your father wouldn't let me. So, looks like I'm quids in for the moment.'

'That's good, and thanks for thinking of making it your treat.'

'Next time,' he promised.

After he'd gone Lucy returned to her computer, deliberately pushing all thoughts of him and what was happening between them out of her mind. She simply didn't have time to start berating herself for not being able to respond the way he wanted her to. It would have to wait until she was in a position to deal with it in a more patient and tender way than she was even close to managing right now.

'Coffee's up!' Sarah announced as she breezed in the door ten minutes later.

Lucy turned from her computer wearing an expression that wiped away Sarah's smile.

'What is it?' Sarah asked. 'What's happened?'

'Take a look at this email,' Lucy told her, and vacating her chair for Sarah to sit down, she waited quietly until Sarah had finished reading.

'Oh my God,' Sarah muttered. She glanced up at Lucy, her own face showing almost as much strain. Turning back to the email, she read it again.

It is with great regret that Godfrey and I find we cannot continue to work for Cromstone Auctions owing to certain practices the proprietors, Daphne and Brian Fisher, have been engaged in over a period of time. Both Godfrey and I recognise that we were wrong to turn a blind eye to what was going on and that we should have reported it sooner, or at least left the company before now. We understand that both Mr and Mrs Fisher will deny any involvement in the aforementioned practices, but they were at the centre of it. We had hoped that when the new management took over the situation would change, but as we have no reason to believe that it will we are left with no alternative but to tender our resignations. Yours faithfully, Maureen Crumpton.

'I suppose she thinks this is a smart move,' Sarah muttered.

'It is,' Lucy responded.

'Have you forwarded it to Michael?'

'I was just about to. What I've been trying to do ever since it turned up is speak to my mother, because I don't think I can avoid it any longer. The trouble is her phone's either switched off, or she's out of range so I can't get through.'

It was about half an hour later that Daphne rang to report the journey's progress.

'Mum, thank goodness,' Lucy cried when she heard her. 'Are you OK? Where are you?'

'We've stopped at a Little Chef for an early lunch,' Daphne replied. 'Dad's been here before and likes the way they cook the fish. How are you, dear? I'm sorry we didn't get to say cheerio this morning. It was probably for the best though, wasn't it?'

'I suppose so,' Lucy said grudgingly, knowing that if she didn't agree it would only make her parents feel worse than they undoubtedly already did. 'Tell me, did you remember to stop off in Bristol to change over from Vodaphone to O2?'

'Oh, blast, it went right out of my mind, but don't worry, we'll do it in Taunton or Minehead one day next week.'

'Then don't forget. How's the drive been so far? You must be almost there by now.'

'Only about fifteen miles to go, which is why I'm calling now, while I know I can get hold of you.'

'I'm glad you did,' Lucy told her, picking up the

small pile of letters Sarah had discovered in Maureen's desk a few minutes ago. 'Something's come up that I need to ask you about. It's to do with Maureen and Godfrey. First of all they've resigned . . .'

'Heavens above! Why have they done that? Oh Lucy, you didn't quarrel . . .'

'Mum, please listen. We've had letters from four different solicitors on behalf of people who . . .'

'But we've been over that,' Daphne cut in, 'they're nothing to worry about. It happens quite a lot, I'm afraid, when people aren't happy with the price we managed to get for them.'

'I know that's what Maureen's been telling you, but it goes deeper than that, Mum. Now what I need you to tell me is if you've ever heard of something called the Ring?'

There was a moment before Daphne said, 'I'm not sure what you're talking about.'

'OK, then tell me this, have Maureen and Godfrey been leaning on you, or threatening you in any way?'

Daphne didn't reply.

'Mum? Are you still there?'

Still nothing.

Realising they'd been disconnected, Lucy swore under her breath and quickly redialled. Even before the phone could ring she was being diverted to messages. 'Call me back as soon as you can,' she said crossly. 'I need to get to the bottom of this.'

Sarah was still watching her as she clicked off the line and dropped the phone on the desk.

'I know what you're thinking,' Lucy told her.

Sarah said nothing.

'You think she rang off deliberately, and for what it's worth, I think you could be right.'

'So where does that leave us?' Sarah asked quietly.

Lucy looked down at the letters she was holding. 'With four legal demands for enquiries or compensation,' she answered, 'a pair of blackmailers and fraudsters, and the very real possibility of bankruptcy looming, and who knows, maybe even jail.'

Chapter Fifteen

The furrow between Simon's brows was deepening by the minute as he listened to what Sarah was telling him. Since she'd already shown him the email Lucy had forwarded to Michael, he was aware of the Crumptons' crafty manoeuvre in resigning before they were fired. However, he was less concerned about that for the moment than he was about Daphne Fisher's failure to call Lucy back.

'So what do you think?' Sarah prompted when he continued to look worried.

'Well, it's not looking good, is it?' he replied, reaching for one of the pistachios she'd just tipped into a dish. 'Whether Lucy's parents were being pressured to keep quiet, or even if they had no idea it was happening, their position, as I see it, is even weaker today than it was yesterday.'

'Because of the email?'

He nodded. 'And because Lucy's mother hasn't tried to get in touch since she was conveniently cut off.'

Sarah's expression was pained. 'Maybe she's afraid.'

'I imagine she is.'

'They're not criminals, Si. If you'd met them, you'd

know it too. What I think has been happening, is that the Crumptons have been threatening them in much the same way as they've started to with Lucy. "Say anything and we'll say we were just following orders." Or something along those lines.'

'I have no problem buying into that,' he conceded, popping another nut. 'What bothers me, though, is how you're going to get the Crumptons back on the hook when they've just quite effectively managed to get themselves off it.'

'Maybe,' Sarah said, passing him a corkscrew to start opening the wine, 'we could get someone from this ring, if that's what it is, to admit they've been working with them.'

Simon looked at her askance.

'What?'

'I was just wondering how you might propose achieving that, because the chances of someone coughing by polite request are about as likely as one of our family artefacts fetching a fortune.'

Sarah's eyes twinkled. 'Don't rule it out,' she cautioned. 'After all, I haven't forgotten how fond you were of old Humpty, so I expect you'll be pretty keen to buy him back for a handsome sum.'

Simon's eyes widened with alarm. 'Please tell me you haven't put him in the sale?' he demanded. 'I've been saving the old chap for my son and heir.'

'Who'd very likely toss him straight out of the pram, the wretched thing's in such a sorry state, but don't worry, Sebastian, he's safe.'

'Sebastian?'

'Flyte, and his teddy bear. Never mind.' Her voice faltered slightly as she said, 'What I'm more interested in is the prospect of a son and heir. Is there something you haven't told me?'

Clearly realising his gaffe, Simon stopped what he was doing and came to give her a hug.

'It's all right,' she said, swallowing her emotions, 'you're allowed to want children, you know. And no one will be happier than me if you have them, well, apart from Mum, I suppose.'

'Giselle isn't pregnant,' he told her softly, 'but even if she were I want you to know that Jack will always be our first, and the most special . . .'

'Ssh, not now,' she said, pulling away. 'Our guests will start arriving any minute, and I don't want to be upstairs repairing my make-up when they come.'

'OK, sorry. So backing up, past Humpty, to the Fishers . . .'

'Actually, we should probably change the subject altogether,' she interrupted, 'because Lucy's last instruction to me before I left was that she didn't want this to dominate the evening.'

'I'd be surprised if she could think about anything else,' he commented, 'but I'm happy to oblige. Incidentally, have you spoken to Mum today?'

'Yes, she rang this morning while you were still asleep.'

'How was she?'

'Fine, as far as I could tell, so I guess we can assume that Sheila hasn't said anything yet.'

'In which case, how am I supposed to play things with this Mckenzie chap this evening? As if I know he knew her once, or that I don't know anything at all?'

'I'm sure he'll be expecting me to have told you, but please don't sound as defensive about everything as you're sounding to me. Remember, we don't actually know anything yet, and even if they did have an affair we have no idea whether it was before

276

she married Daddy, or even if Daddy himself was always faithful.'

Simon looked at her incredulously.

'All right, it doesn't seem possible to *us* that he'd ever have strayed, but try to imagine what it must have been like married to someone like her. No doubt bliss in the up times, but what about when she went down? We've got no idea what really went on between them, any more than I know what happens with you and Giselle, or you knew about me and Kelvin – and look where we ended up. So, please, try to bear in mind that Lucy and I have found John to be the loveliest and kindest of men so far, and until he shows himself to be anything other, let's at least try to give him the benefit of the doubt.'

Simon raised his hands. 'OK, if that's what you want. Now, you've got enough nibbles here to feed the entire village, so why don't you stop emptying bags into bowls and let me take this lot outside?'

By the time he'd set everything out on the table and returned to the kitchen, Michael was coming down the hall with a bottle of champagne and a bunch of bright yellow roses.

'Oh, how gorgeous,' Sarah cried, taking the flowers. 'That's so kind of you. We'll put them at the centre of the table so everyone can see them.'

After greeting them both and handing the champagne to Simon, Michael said, 'So come on, put me to work. What can I do?'

'You can load that tray with glasses,' Sarah told him, 'while Simon finds some napkins.'

Opening a cupboard to show Michael the way, Simon said, 'So, I take it you've seen the infamous email?'

Michael nodded. 'A cunning move on the Crumptons' part, so definitely time to bring Teddy Best in to bat. I spoke to him just before I left home, so he's already aware of the case – and you'll be happy to know he's up for teaching us a few basic steps tomorrow around noon.'

Sarah gave a cry of glee. 'Maybe Lucy and I could come to watch,' she suggested. 'It'll be a good opportunity for her and Teddy to meet.'

'Maybe you couldn't,' Michael responded, 'but we can always try to set up something after, like a spot of *Doris* dancing for you two.'

Sarah's eyes rounded. 'There's no such thing,' she said.

'Don't bet on it. Now, shall I take these out to the table?' he offered, picking up his swiftly assembled tray of glasses.

'Yes please,' she replied, turning at the sound of voices as someone came in through the open front door. 'Through here,' she called out.

'Are we too early?' Philippa enquired as she stepped down into the kitchen, looking very striking in a pale blue eyepatch that blended perfectly with the shades of her floaty summer dress. 'We can always go away and come back again.'

'No, no,' Sarah protested. 'It's lovely to see you,' and after kissing her on both cheeks, she grabbed John by the hand to pull him in further, saying, 'Let me introduce you to my brother, Simon. Si, this is Philippa and John Mckenzie.'

As the two men faced each other, their eyes equally wary, a sudden tension seemed to cut through the air. Knowing it came from Simon, Sarah quickly said, 'John's been our saviour at the auction house since Godfrey broke his ankle.'

Though John smiled his gratitude, his face was still strained as he held out a hand for Simon's.

Taking it, Simon said, 'It's good to meet you.' His tone was so chilly that Sarah want to shout at him to behave.

'It's good to meet you too,' John said stiffly.

Beside him, Philippa was hardly daring to breathe, as she watched her brother seeing and touching his son for the first time in over thirty years. How on earth must he be feeling? The magnitude of it was such that she could hardly begin to deal with it herself. This tall, handsome man, who bore such a striking resemblance to her own father, was the adorable little nephew she'd held in her arms so briefly. It was so overwhelming and her emotions were so close to the surface that she couldn't trust herself to speak.

'Sarah's told me a little about you,' John was saying quietly.

'I've heard plenty about you too,' Simon retorted tersely. 'I believe you're renting the Mercers' house.'

'Just for the next few months,' Philippa said, somehow steeling herself to step into the hostility and try and disperse it. 'Are you planning to be in Cromstone for long yourself?'

Simon's flintiness was less marked as he turned to her. 'Until next Sunday,' he replied.

Philippa glanced at John, whose eyes hadn't left Simon's face.

Sensing the dawning of an awful silence, Sarah quickly said, 'So, what would you like to drink? We have most things, vodka, gin, sherry, wine of course . . .'

'I'd like a glass of wine,' Philippa told her. 'And I'm sure John would too.'

'Yes, that would be lovely,' he agreed, a faint colour returning to his cheeks as he smiled at Sarah.

'Aha, if it isn't Mr Mckenzie, fearless rescuer of damsels in distress and revered driver of trucks,' Michael declared as he came in from the terrace. 'How are you?' he said, shaking John's hand.

'Very well, thank you,' John assured him. 'It's good to see you again. Michael, isn't it?'

'That's right, and I'm guessing this must be Philippa.'

As Philippa matched the warmth of his greeting, Sarah gave Simon a withering look. 'Wine,' she muttered under her breath.

'Hi, anyone at home?' Lucy cried, sailing in through the front door and down the hall. 'Joe's dropping Hanna and Juliette at another friend's house, but he should be here any minute.' Her eyes lit with pleasure as they found the only person in the room who could be Simon. He was exactly as she'd imagined, except perhaps a little taller and better-looking, and so like Sarah she wanted to hug him. 'If you're even half as magnificent as your sister claims,' she said, grasping his hands, 'then you must do weird things in telephone boxes and wear your pants on top of your trousers.'

Laughing delightedly, Simon pulled her in to kiss both cheeks. 'And you must be Lucy,' he declared, 'and if anyone round here's capable of amazing transformations, it has to be you with what you've done for my sister. She's a changed woman, and you're even more gorgeous than she said you were.'

Lucy turned to Sarah aghast. 'You surely haven't been downplaying me,' she scolded, making Sarah laugh. Then, spotting Michael, she went to embrace him. 'I was hoping you'd be here,' she said. 'I'm dying to hear what you think of the email, except we're not going to talk about it this evening. So, quick change of subject, how's the morris dancing going?'

'Actually, John's just come from his first lesson,' Philippa informed them as Lucy turned to kiss her hello.

'Oh bliss!' Sarah cried, clapping her hands. 'How did it go?'

John's expression was wry as he said, 'Let's just say I don't think I have a natural bent, but it only lasted half an hour and it was my first attempt. I think the poor fellow was glad to be rid of me.'

'So they've roped you into this nonsense too,' Simon stated, as he passed Philippa a glass.

'I'm afraid so,' John grimaced, 'but I find it's easier to go along with them than try to resist.'

'Tell me about it,' Michael groaned, passing John the wine Simon had just handed him. 'Simon and I are having our first lesson tomorrow. Maybe you should join us. It would make more sense if we learned together how to make complete chumps of ourselves.'

With an uncertain glance at Simon, John said, 'I'm not sure . . . Well, I guess I'm game if you are.'

'Of course he is,' Sarah leapt in. 'We'll get it worked out. Now, shall we go into the garden? There are plenty of snacks, and Michael's volunteered to go for pizzas later if anyone's still hungry.'

'I have?' he said. 'I have,' and returning her mischievous wink, he followed Lucy and the others out to the terrace.

'Not so fast,' Sarah hissed, yanking Simon back. 'You promised to be civil . . .'

'What have I done?' he protested.

'You know very well that you're making him uncomfortable, and I'm ashamed of you. He's a guest in our home and deserves to be treated . . .'

'All right, all right, enough with the lecture. I'll try harder, will that suit?'

'Only if you mean it. Now go and talk to Lucy. At least with her I can feel confident you'll behave.'

'Ah, there you are,' Philippa said cheerily, as Simon came to join them on the terrace. 'We were just admiring the garden, and this very splendid view.'

Simon smiled weakly as he followed her gaze. 'The garden's a bit of a mess these days,' he said, 'but it's always been a special place for us.'

'I can quite understand why. Perhaps you'll tell us something of what it was like growing up here,' she suggested.

'Oh, Pippa, I'm sure . . .'

Ignoring her brother, Philippa said, 'You have another sister, I believe. Becky?'

'We have indeed,' Simon replied, sitting down next to her while watching Lucy talking to Michael. 'She lives in New York these days.'

'And how often do you see her?'

'Not often enough, I'm sorry to say.'

'Does she ever come here?'

'She hasn't been for ages,' Sarah answered, coming out of the house. 'She's always crazy busy, and even when she is here she's forever on the phone bossing someone around on the other side of the pond.'

Philippa chuckled. 'She sounds quite a character.'

'Oh, she's that all right, but we love her to bits, don't we, Si?'

'Indeed we do. We've always been a close family.

Dad made sure of it, and I don't see it ever changing.'

Since his comment was so clearly directed at John, Sarah felt herself colouring as she said, 'Simon, why don't you take Lucy for a stroll down to the stream?'

Overhearing, Lucy turned around, and reading Sarah's expression perfectly, she said to Simon, 'I'd love it if you would, because actually there's something I'd like to ask you.'

Getting to his feet, Simon clapped Michael on the back as he passed, and falling in beside Lucy as she started down the steps, he said, 'I suppose I've just been banished while I learn some manners.'

'I think that's a fairly safe assumption,' Lucy replied.

Laughing, he said, 'I know Sarah's told you about Mckenzie's past with my mother . . .'

'Actually, I was there when Philippa told her that they were old friends, and as far as I'm aware that's all Sarah knows too. At least for certain.'

Sighing, he said, 'All right, point taken. I promise to try harder when we return.'

Casting him a mischievous smile, she took a sip of her drink and allowed him to go first along a pathway hidden by overgrown shrubs.

'This place really needs some work,' he commented. 'It's even worse than I realised.'

'But it has a kind of charm like this,' she decided. 'It's as though it's protecting its own ghosts and memories.'

In a tone that surprised her, he said, 'I can assure you that it is, and not all of them need digging up.'

Placing a foot carefully on to the stone he turned to indicate, she said, 'I've always got the impression from Sarah that you had happy childhoods.'

'We did,' he answered, stopping to hold back a bramble, 'but believe me, this wasn't always an easy family to be in. Everyone used to think we were blessed, we seemed to have so much, and we were, but something awful lies at the heart of us, something none of us can put into words because our parents would never tell us.'

Thrown by a resentment she'd never detected in Sarah, Lucy stepped into a clearing to join him, and said, 'I'm sure they had their reasons. I mean, I can't imagine they ever meant to hurt you, not from everything Sarah's told me about them.'

'I'm sure they didn't, but one way or another their reticence, or secrecy or whatever you want to call it, has taken its toll on us all. Sarah's a perfect example, the way she buried herself away down here after Kelvin left her. Would she have done that if our mother hadn't set the example by shutting herself away for days, sometimes weeks on end? And Becky. She never stands still long enough to think about what the issues might be, possibly because she doesn't want to face them, or more likely because she knows no one will ever tell her.'

As they reached the edge of the stream Lucy stole a quick look up at him. 'And you?' she said softly.

Sighing deeply, he stuffed a hand in his pocket as he gazed out towards the horizon. 'I guess it's given me a sense of loneliness that I can never quite shake off,' he admitted, almost angrily. 'It's as though something's missing all the time, and the something, obviously, is the truth.'

Lucy looked down at the meagre trickle of water finding its way round the stones and thought of the children who'd lived here, trying to cover and smother their parents with love. She got the sense that their father had rejoiced in them, loving them as completely and unconditionally as any parent would. She thought the same about Rose, but like this stream, maybe there were times when the ability to give of herself had started to run dry.

Hearing a whoop of laughter from the terrace, they turned around and Lucy saw, with a guilty tinge of regret, that Joe had arrived. 'Seems my husband's keeping everyone entertained,' she commented wryly.

Simon looked at her and waited for her eyes to come to his.

As she looked back Lucy felt a kind of connection stirring between them, in much the same way as she had when she'd first got to know Sarah. It was wonderful and yet strange to feel so at ease with people she hardly knew; they might always have been a part of one another's lives, even though they clearly hadn't.

'Thanks for what you've done for Sarah,' he said, holding her gaze.

She smiled. 'I feel she's done a lot more for me, but I'm happy to know that our new partnership is working well for her too.' Then, remembering what they were facing, she said, 'It's awful to think it might be about to fall apart.'

'Michael will make sure that doesn't happen,' he assured her. 'That's provided, of course, your parents really weren't involved.'

She shook her head as she looked away.

'I know it's hard to think the worst of them,' he said gently, 'but isn't it true to say that no matter how well you think you know someone, they can always do something to make you wonder if you ever really knew them at all?'

She almost wanted to laugh at the way he'd taken the words out of her mouth. 'Yes, it certainly is,' she agreed, 'but maybe that's why I'm having such a hard time with it, because I still can't make myself believe that they were involved. What I feel much more certain of is that Maureen and Godfrey were ruling them in a despicable way.'

'I won't argue with that,' he said, gesturing for her to go on ahead. They started back up through the garden. 'From everything I hear it's the more likely scenario,' he continued, when they were free of the tangle of old bushes and brambles. Then, with a sardonic smile, 'Parents! Who'd have 'em?'

Smiling too as she looked up at him, Lucy said, 'Definitely more trouble than they're worth.'

Clearly experiencing the same surge of warm feeling as she was, he took hold of her arm and tucked it through his. 'I think I like you, Lucy,' he declared as they strode up over the lawn.

'You only think,' she teased. 'I felt sure you'd be completely mad about me by now.'

Laughing delightedly, he made a gallant bow as he let her pass to mount the steps first, and was about to ask for an introduction to Joe when he heard John Mckenzie saying to Sarah, 'Actually I'd known your father for several years before I met your mother,' and before he even knew what his words were going to be he was saying, 'I'm not sure that's something to feel proud of, are you, John?'

As an awful silence fell Lucy turned to look at Simon, but before she could think what to say Sarah was on her feet, red with embarrassment and rage. 'Please accept my apologies for my brother's rudeness, John,' she said, glaring at Simon. 'Simon, if I could speak to you, inside.'

'Actually, we should probably be going,' John said to Philippa in a way that invited no discussion.

As they stood up Lucy noticed that Joe was staring furiously at Simon. Then, catching Michael's eye, she moved towards him as the Mckenzies started to leave. 'How do we rescue this?' she murmured.

'I'm not sure we can,' he replied.

Looking regretfully at John as he came to embrace her, she said, 'Will we see you tomorrow?'

'Of course.' Though he smiled, the sadness in his eyes betrayed how shaken he was.

'I'm sorry,' Joe suddenly shouted, 'we haven't met, Simon, but frankly I think an apology's in order before these people leave.'

'Joe, it's all right,' John told him.

'No it's not,' Joe argued. 'All you said . . .'

'Joe, this has nothing to do with you,' Lucy hissed.

'I'm afraid it has everything to do with me when a man flirts with my wife in front of my face, and then insults someone who's merely making polite conversation.'

'Joe, I appreciate what you're trying to do,' John murmured, 'but let it drop now, son. Come on, Pippa, time to get you home.'

Putting down his drink, Joe said, 'I'm leaving too,' and before Lucy could stop him he was following the Mckenzies back through the house to exit by the front door.

The others remained on the terrace. Sarah looked at Lucy, who in turn looked at Michael. Simon's back was turned as he stared silently into the twilight.

'Well, thank you for that, Simon,' Sarah said bitterly. 'Is there anyone else you'd like to offend while you're at it?'

Turning around, he said, 'I'm sorry if I upset your husband, Lucy. It wasn't my intention.'

Lucy shook her head sadly. 'I'm afraid that's not good enough, Simon,' she told him. 'It's John you really upset, and there was no need for it.'

Flushing slightly, Simon raised his glass and finished the contents in one gulp.

'If you'd allowed him to speak he might actually have told us something,' Sarah snapped.

'And you'd want to hear it with everyone else around?'

She threw out her hands in despair. 'You see, there you go again jumping to conclusions. You've no idea what he might have said, and for God's sake, we're amongst friends.'

Simon's eyes went to Michael. 'Did you think I was flirting with Lucy?' he asked gruffly.

'Simon, it's not the issue,' Michael told him.

'I'm just interested to know what you think. Was the accusation justified?'

Michael shrugged. 'You seemed to be getting along well.'

'We weren't flirting,' Lucy told them, 'and I should apologise for Joe before I leave.'

'Oh no, don't go,' Sarah implored. 'Please stay and have another drink.'

Lucy looked torn. Though she didn't want to abandon Sarah she knew Joe would take it badly if she didn't arrive home soon after him.

'Will it help if I apologise to John?' Simon offered.

Surprised, and pleased, Lucy glanced at Michael. 'Yes,' she said, looking at Simon, 'it would, provided you mean it.'

'You can do it now, tonight,' Michael suggested. 'I'm sure one of us has his number.'

Both Sarah and Lucy were ready to offer it.

Simon's eyes moved from Michael to Lucy and finally to Sarah. 'OK,' he said, seeming to accept that he couldn't back out. 'Give me another drink, then I'll get on the phone.'

John and Philippa were on their way in through the front door of the Old Lodge when the phone started to ring. Being the closest, Philippa picked it up.

'Hello?' she said, her heart aching with pity as she watched her brother walk into the kitchen.

A male voice came awkwardly down the line. 'Uh, it's Simon Bancroft here,' he said. 'I'm ringing to apologise. I shouldn't have said what I did.'

Still sobered by the incident, but pleased that he'd called, Philippa said, 'It's John you need to speak to. If you hang on I'll get him,' and placing the receiver on the table she went into the kitchen.

John was standing at the window gazing absently into the garden.

'He wants to apologise,' Philippa said softly.

John didn't move.

'I think you should let him.'

Turning around he looked into her eyes, his own tormented with sadness.

She stood aside, gesturing towards the phone.

As he passed she put a hand on his arm. 'It was never going to be easy,' she reminded him.

Still saying nothing, John went to pick up the receiver. For one awful minute Philippa thought he was going to hang up, but then he put it to his ear and said, brusquely, 'Simon? What can I do for you?'

'I guess I spoke out of turn just now,' Simon replied, sounding equally brusque, 'and I'd like to say sorry.'

'I see,' John responded.

A silence followed that was hard for John to bear. 'The important thing,' he said, 'is whether you're apologising because you mean it, or because Sarah's asked you to.'

'Not asked, told, but you realise, I hope, that if you were to tell us who you are, how you fit into my parents' lives, these . . . incidents wouldn't occur?'

Turning away from the mirror above the phone, John put a hand to his head. He didn't want to look at himself; the pain was hard enough without having to see it written all over his face. 'I understand what you're saying,' he replied, aware of Philippa watching him, 'but I gave my word to your mother, a long time ago, as she gave hers to me, that we would never discuss what happened, or our reasons for doing what we did.'

He could sense Simon biting down on his frustration. 'This isn't helping,' Simon growled.

'I'm sure it isn't, but I'm afraid it's the best I can do.'

'Then just tell me this, was it an affair?'

John swallowed the terrible grief blocking his throat. 'No, son,' he said, hoarsely, 'it wasn't an affair.'

Simon fell silent.

'Whatever you're thinking now,' John said, turning to look at Philippa, 'please remember this, you have no reason to think ill of your mother.'

Sounding insufferably bitter, Simon said, 'Well thank you for that.'

John's eyes closed.

'For Christ's sake,' Simon suddenly exploded. 'What the hell can be so awful that you can't tell us what it is?'

Knowing how impossible it would be for him to

summon the words, even if he had Rose's permission, John said nothing.

In the end Simon said, 'Am I able to tell Sarah you've forgiven me?' His tone made it clear that he couldn't care less for himself.

'Yes, of course,' John replied.

'Thank you. Goodnight,' and the sound of the line going dead buried itself deep into John's heart.

'Thank you for ringing,' he said, and putting the phone down he stood looking at his sister, his eyes glistening with unshed tears. 'He's a man a father can feel proud of,' he said shakily.

Chapter Sixteen

'Oh, so you decided to come home.'

Immediately irritated by Joe's antagonism, Lucy bit back a sharp retort, and put her bag on the table. 'Is there any more where that came from?' she asked, indicating his empty glass.

'It was Scotch. Not usually your drink of choice.'

Going to the fridge she took out a bottle of wine, and was about to hand it to him to open when she decided to break the habit and do it herself. 'It wasn't your place to make a stand like that,' she told him, taking a glass from an overhead cupboard.

'The man was totally out of order . . .'

'There are issues that you know nothing about.'

Sarcasm dripped from his tone as he said, 'Well, of course, you would defend him, wouldn't you?'

Lucy's eyes flashed. 'I know what you're insinuating,' she snapped, 'but you're wrong and . . .'

'I know what I saw.'

'Oh, for heaven's sake!'

'Tell me you weren't attracted to him.'

Still struggling to hang on to her temper, she said, 'I'm not going to tell you anything of the sort, because I don't have to defend myself to you, or to anyone else.'

'We're still married,' he shot back angrily. 'I get

that you wish we weren't, but we are, and as long as you're my wife arrogant bastards like that can keep their ruddy hands off you.'

'This isn't a soap opera.'

His colour deepened. 'That's a cheap shot.'

Since it was, she tried to calm things down by saying, probably too pedantically, 'Simon is Sarah's brother and, much like when I first got to know her, I happened to strike up a rapport with him. If you choose to read more into it than that I'm afraid it's your problem, not mine.'

He continued to stare at her, furious, but clearly not sure how to play this.

'Are there any messages?' she asked, turning to the machine. 'Did Mum call while we were out?'

'You wish I wasn't here, don't you?' he challenged. 'If I weren't I suppose you'd still be over there, flirting your little heart out, and now you're pissed off with me for cramping your style.'

'Oh Joe stop this, please. It's been a long day, I've got a lot on my mind and none of it's connected to Simon Bancroft – other than how he might help sort out this wretched business with the Crumptons.'

Joe's expression remained stony. 'And turning to me for advice would be out of the question?'

Her eyes widened incredulously. 'Simon and Michael are lawyers,' she told him brusquely, 'and Michael's putting us in touch with someone who is well placed to take this on. Now, if you don't mind, I'm going back to the office to . . .'

'As a matter of fact, I do mind. I'm here to spend time with you . . .'

'No, you're here because there are no auditions at weekends, and presumably Charlie's got no work for you at the market. If you were gainfully employed, or had a proper home instead of that cupboard of a room at Charlie's, I doubt we'd ever see you.'

He looked so stunned she might have slapped him. 'I'm here,' he said quietly, 'because of you and Hanna, so to suggest I only came because I don't like my current accommodation . . .' He shook his head disbelievingly. 'How can you think I'm just using you because I don't have anything better to do?'

Sighing, she reached for the bottle to refill her glass. 'I'm sorry,' she said, 'it wasn't what I meant. I just wish . . .' She broke off, not sure it was a good idea to go any further.

'What do you wish?' he prompted.

Her eyes went to his, then back down to her glass. 'Nothing,' she said. Unless she was prepared to tell him to stop coming, which she wasn't because she didn't have the heart to, there was no point reminding him *again* that they were supposed to be on a trial separation.

'Neither of us has eaten yet,' he pointed out, 'so why don't we take a stroll down to the pub?'

She wasn't hungry and she didn't want to go.

Apparently sensing the rejection he said, 'You can't work every hour God sends.'

'You know how hectic it is leading up to an auction. Mum was always in the office until late . . .'

'She used to eat.'

'Joe, why are you making this so difficult? I need to focus on what I'm doing and . . .'

He was on his feet. 'Don't worry, I'm out of here, and if you've got it in mind to go back over there to Simon Bancroft . . .'

'Just stop it!' she shouted. 'I've told you what I'm

doing, now for God's sake, go to the pub, and leave me alone.'

After he'd gone she sat where she was for a moment, waiting for her conscience to start berating her. Unusually, it seemed slow in coming to life, but she had no doubt it would turn up at some point, whereupon she'd no doubt find herself trudging down to the pub after him to try and make up, and he'd be thrilled and forgiving and want to shower her in drinks and make love to her when they got home as though everything was completely repaired and all they'd had was a silly lovers' tiff.

Feeling suddenly angry again, she got to her feet. The hell she was going to let herself do that. She didn't want to go to the pub, nor did she especially want to make up, and she certainly didn't want to have sex. So whatever her conscience might have planned for later, it could just forget it, because she was going over to the office to continue examining Maureen bloody Crumpton's desk and computer to see what other little treats might be lying in wait.

Unhooking the keys from their usual place, she grabbed an apple from the fruit bowl and had just started off across the courtyard when she heard the phone begin to ring. Deciding to take it in the office she hurried towards it, keys at the ready, but to her surprise as she went to unlock the door she found it was already open.

With a beat of alarm, she took a step back. There were no lights on inside, and the phone was still ringing, but just because no one was answering didn't mean no one was there. If someone was, it might not be a good idea to burst in and confront them. On the other hand if it was Maureen, come to spirit away whatever evidence she might have left behind, she had to be stopped.

Wishing now that Joe hadn't gone out, she stood very still as the phone stopped ringing, waiting for the sound of someone moving.

Silence.

Inching quietly back to the door she tried to listen, but apart from the thunderous thud of her heart there didn't seem to be any other noise. However, if someone *was* in there they might well have heard her coming and could even now be waiting behind the door . . .

Stepping back again, she looked around the courtyard. It was exactly as it always was, cluttered with objects that must have seen who'd unlocked the office, but could never tell. Oddly shaped shadows were spreading and stretching like conjuring tricks in the glow from the wall lamps, turning chairs into sofas and wardrobes into caves, while an eerie bank of trees loomed over the rooftops, black in the moonlight and watchful in their stare.

Praying she was doing the right thing, she put a hand to the door and eased it further open. The creak of the hinge was like an audible searing of fear in her heart. She waited, terrified that someone would come rushing at her. She should have gone back to the kitchen to find some sort of weapon. Her father's gun flashed through her mind, and was gone.

Nothing was happening.

Surely no one was in there.

She pushed the door wider and quickly snapped on the light.

'Well, it certainly doesn't look as though anything's missing,' Sarah commented as Michael and Simon joined her and Lucy in the office twenty minutes later, after scouring the rest of the grounds.

'Are you all right?' Michael said to Lucy.

She nodded, and pushed back her hair.

Simon was inspecting the lock. 'It hasn't been forced,' he told them, 'so either you forgot to do the necessary when you left . . .'

'I didn't,' Lucy assured him. 'And I set the alarm. I remember, because Joe made some remark about . . .' She broke off, not wanting to admit that he'd said no one would want to make off with a load of old junk. 'It just stuck in my mind,' she said lamely.

Seeming to sense her discomfort, Michael turned to the others, saying, 'In which case, it has to come down to those who have a key and who also know the code.'

'As far as I'm aware,' Lucy said, 'there's only me, John, Maureen and Hetty who comes to clean.'

Simon almost laughed. 'Well, I know who my money's on,' he declared.

Since no one was going to challenge him on that, Michael said, 'The next question is: what's missing, because something has to be.'

Lucy shook her head. 'Nothing that's evident, but what we don't know is what might have been done to the computers, or if something's been taken from any of the desks or files that we had no idea was there.'

Michael was nodding thoughtfully. 'What could have happened,' he said, 'is that whoever was here was frightened off when Joe came back early. I take it he did come back here?'

'Yes, he did.' Since no one asked where he was now, she didn't volunteer it.

Michael said, 'We should check the computers to see when they were last used.'

As Sarah went to turn them on, Simon said, 'Do you want to contact the police?'

Lucy shook her head. 'I don't see what good it would do when we can't even say that someone broke in, much less tell them what's missing.'

Since no one could argue with that, Michael finished checking the computers and said, 'The latest one to be used is this one, and that was at seventeen thirty-six, so as it's your machine, I'm guessing it was you.'

Lucy nodded. 'That was about the time I left.'

Before shutting them all down again, he said, 'I know this is a bit after the horse has bolted, but maybe now is a good time to install some passwords.'

'Yes, we should,' Lucy agreed. 'Sarah, you can do yours, and I ought to dig out the instructions for the alarm so I can reset the code.'

'I can probably help with that,' Michael told her. 'It's the same make as the one I have at the office.'

'If you give me a couple of passwords,' Simon said, 'I'll sort out the other two computers.'

'Um, let me see,' Lucy said, trying to force her mind past the obvious Ben and Hanna, 'you can set mine as . . . nightingale, and the other one as sparrows.'

After doing the honours, Simon turned off both machines, and followed the others outside as Lucy entered a new code into the alarm before locking up and joining them.

'I know I'm probably going to get my head bitten off for this,' Simon said, as they started back to the farmhouse, 'but we're all presuming it was Maureen or an accomplice who was here, but you said John has a key as well. So are we . . .'

'Simon, you're in danger of undoing your apology,' Sarah warned.

'It wouldn't have been him,' Lucy said, 'and anyway it couldn't have been because he was with us when it happened.'

Accepting that was true, Simon said, 'OK, I just wanted to be sure we weren't ruling him out because no one can bring themselves to think ill of him.'

'You're making up for us all,' Sarah informed him as Lucy led the way into the kitchen.

'Hey, Mum, there you are,' Hanna declared, glancing up from the raspberry smoothie she was pouring.

'Hey you,' Lucy said, going to drop a kiss on her head. 'You're back earlier than I expected.'

'Really? I'd have stayed longer if I'd known that. Hey, Sarah.' She started to frown as Simon and Michael crowded into the kitchen. 'Where's Dad?' she asked.

Turning to put on the kettle, Lucy said, 'He popped down to the pub for something to eat.'

'What, on his own?'

'I wasn't hungry. Would you like some cocoa?'

'No thanks, I've got this.' She was still gazing suspiciously at the men.

'This is my brother, Simon,' Sarah told her, 'and Michael you might already know through your granny.'

Hanna's expression didn't lighten much. 'Hey,' she muttered, her eyes travelling from one to the other. Then, putting down her smoothie, she said, 'I think I'll go and find Dad.'

Realising she wasn't happy about her mother being with men she didn't know, Lucy let her go, and began trying to think of a way to get everyone to leave without seeming rude or ungrateful, before

Hanna dragged her father in to break things up his way.

'So,' Simon said, stepping into the awkward silence, 'what are your feelings about contacting Maureen?'

Lucy glanced at Michael, then Sarah. 'I'm not sure I can see what's to be gained from it,' she replied. 'Can you?'

They were both looking pensive as they shook their heads.

'She'll obviously deny having anything to do with it,' Michael said, 'and I'm not sure whether it's a good or a bad thing to let her know that we know she's been here. If she thinks we're still in the dark she might attempt it again – I mean if she didn't get what she came for.'

'And how are we even going to know if she did?' Sarah added.

With a sigh Simon glanced at his watch. 'I hope this isn't going to offend you,' he said to Lucy, 'but in light of what happened earlier, it's probably not a great idea for me to be here when your husband gets back.'

'I'm not offended,' Lucy assured him, 'and again I'm sorry for the way he spoke to you.'

Simon smiled wryly. 'I don't suppose it would help if I told him I have no designs on his wife?'

Lucy smiled. 'He's in a tetchy mood at the moment, so I think it's best if we all try to forget this evening happened.'

Coming to give Lucy a hug, Sarah said, 'I can hardly wait to see what my next party's like.'

Laughing, Lucy said, 'I'll see you in the morning.'

'Eight thirty sharp. We've got a busy day while these two mess about morris dancing.'

'You've got my number,' Michael said, giving Lucy a peck on the cheek, 'call if you need anything, any time.'

'Thanks,' she whispered. 'I appreciate it.'

Minutes after she'd closed the door behind them Lucy was still standing in the kitchen, sipping the abandoned smoothie as she went over the events of the evening. She was so engrossed in her thoughts that when the kitchen door suddenly burst open she almost leapt out of her skin.

'Oh, Hanna!' she snapped, as Hanna stormed in. 'Do you have to be so heavy-handed?'

'I thought you said Dad was in the pub,' Hanna retorted crossly, as though Lucy had deliberately misled her.

'It's where he said he was going. I take it he wasn't there?'

'No, and Juliette's mum said she hasn't seen him all evening.'

Lucy shrugged. 'Well, obviously he went to another pub,' she said. 'I'm sure he'll be home any minute. Now, have you eaten? There's still some quiche . . .'

'You gave me tea before we went out,' Hanna reminded her, taking what was left of her smoothie. 'I'm going to watch telly.'

'OK, I'll join you in a minute. I just want to text Ben, then I think I'll try Granny again. Has she been in touch with you at all today?'

'Not since this morning. They must be in Exmoor by now.'

'Of course. They'll have arrived hours ago.'

As she found herself speaking to her mother's voicemail again she was imagining Maureen, or possibly some other members of the Ring, creeping about the office looking for only they knew what. Or perhaps they'd been planting something! As the thought occurred to her she felt a sudden over-whelming sense of protection towards her parents. How dare anyone terrorise them and push them out of their business and home? No one had the right to do this to two such innocent and kindly souls, but someone was definitely trying, and when she found out their identity they were going to be more than sorry they'd ever crossed her path.

Sarah was on her way out of the bathroom, swathed in towels, when the phone started to ring. Hurrying along the landing, she called out to Simon, 'Don't worry, I'll get it,' while guessing he probably hadn't heard it anyway. It wasn't yet eight o'clock on a Sunday morning and he was a notoriously heavy sleeper.

By the time she got to the phone in her parents' room, now hers, whoever it was had rung off, but given the time of day she guessed it had been her mother and quickly rang back.

To her surprise she didn't get an answer straight away, and was just wondering if she'd misdialled when a beep on the line signalled that her mother was trying again.

'Hello, early bird,' she said, switching over to take the call. 'Sorry I didn't get to you in time.'

There was a pause before her mother said, 'This is the first time I've rung, so it must have been someone else.'

'At this hour? Heavens! Oh, unless it was Lucy. Maybe I ought to call and find out. Can I ring you back?'

'Sarah, before you go,' her mother said quickly.

'Yes?' Sarah prompted when her mother didn't continue. Then, with a tremor of unease, 'Is everything all right?'

'Yes, I'm . . . Tell me, how are you?'

Though warmed by the sunlight streaming in through the windows, Sarah felt a chill passing over her heart. This was the first time in more than a year that her mother had sounded this low, and all she could think was that Sheila had told her about John. 'I'm fine,' Sarah said quietly.

'And Simon?'

'Yes, he's fine too.' She tried a note of irony as she added, 'You know him on Sunday mornings. It's against his religion to stir before nine o'clock.'

There was no hint of a fond smile in Rose's voice as she said, 'He's always been the same.'

Feeling old demons starting to stir, Sarah's eyes moved to the large photograph of her parents she kept on a chest between the windows. They were laughing wholeheartedly, as though they had not a care in the world. She was trying to hold on to that memory, to bypass all the bad times and draw strength from the good, but it was like trying to bury herself in thin air. 'Mummy, what is it?' she made herself say.

Rose took an audible breath. 'Sheila told me . . .' She cleared her throat. 'Is John . . . ? Is he still there, in Cromstone?'

John. No Mckenzie, no Mr, just his first name, confirming that she'd known him well. Sarah hadn't really doubted that, so why was it bothering her now? Her gaze stayed on the photo, but in spite of the joy it exuded all she could see was her mother's beautiful face fading into a ghostly, anxious replica of itself – a replica that Sarah had come to dread over the years. *Oh my God, what is it? What is it?* She started to panic.

'Tell me,' Rose said hoarsely, 'I'd like to know . . .'

Sarah waited, too tense to speak, not even knowing if she wanted her mother to continue.

Starting again, Rose said, 'Sheila told me about Pippa.'

Pippa. The same affectionate diminutive that John used for his sister.

'Sarah, I'd like you to give me their number,' Rose said.

Sarah started to speak without really knowing what she was going to say. 'I can do that,' she said, 'but I need to know . . .'

'Darling, please don't ask any questions. Not yet. I will tell you everything, I promise, but I must speak to John first.'

Sarah was finding it hard to think past that. She knew Simon wouldn't let their mother get away with it, that he'd insist on knowing something before handing over the number. But with a sixth sense warning her that an awful amount of suffering was involved in whatever lay between her mother and John, Sarah felt ready to delay knowing what it was for ever, rather than experience any more pain for those she loved.

'Sarah,' her mother said softly, 'there's nothing for you to worry about, my darling.'

'Then why . . .' She swallowed dryly. 'Why all the secrecy?'

'There are reasons . . . I'm not sure if they're good any more, but what I did, what happened . . .' Her voice choked with emotion. 'Darling, I can't tell you anything over the phone. I'll have to see you, but first I must speak to John.'

Deciding there was no point in arguing any more, Sarah went to her mobile which was next to the photograph on the chest, and scrolled to John's entry. After reading out the number she said, 'I'll have to tell Simon I've done this . . .'

'No, sweetheart, please try not to tell him anything for the time being. Has he met John? Does he know . . . ?'

'They met last night, and yes, he knows that you and John have a history and I have to tell you, Mum, he's struggling with it.'

'Oh no,' Rose whispered shakily. 'Dear Simon, I can't . . . What did John say to him?'

'He hardly had a chance to say anything, because Simon turned on him . . .'

'But why? He has no reason to . . .'

'He thinks you and John had an affair, and he's angry. You know how close he was to Dad. Mum, please, you can't keep shutting us out . . .'

'I know, and it won't be for much longer, I swear. Once I've talked to John . . . Tell me, darling, how is he? Does he seem well?'

Hearing the tenderness in her mother's voice, Sarah cried, 'Oh my God, you did have an affair, didn't you?' Tears for her father were burning her eyes.

'No, we didn't, it wasn't that . . . I swear, I never did anything to hurt Daddy. I was always completely faithful to him, always . . . Listen, I know this is hard for you, and I probably should have told you a long time ago – Daddy always said I should, but it's very difficult for me even to think about . . . When you know, I'm sure you'll understand . . .' She took a breath. 'I'm going to ring off now. Thank you for giving me the number, and thank you, my darling, for not mentioning anything to Simon or Becky about this call, or about anything until I can speak to you all myself.'

After putting the phone down Sarah stood beside the chest staring blindly out at the fields, where a lingering dew was glistening and winking in the sunlight and the trees seemed to droop under the weight of their leaves. She was trying to imagine what her mother might be doing now – was she still standing beside the phone too, gazing out at the Med as her secrets started to surface from their hidden depths, like ghosts returning from the dead? Or was she talking to Sheila, asking her advice, needing to know what she should do next? Maybe she'd already dialled John's number.

The landline suddenly rang beside her, making her jump. Remembering she'd meant to call Lucy, she quickly picked it up. 'Hello?' The sound of her own voice seemed hollow and strange.

'Sarah, it's John. I hope I'm not too early.'

Feeling her legs starting to weaken, she sank into the cushions of a window seat and pushed a hand through her hair. 'No, not at all,' she assured him. 'I was just . . . Are you already at work?'

'No, I'm still at home. I rang Lucy a few minutes ago to let her know that I probably won't be able to join you until after lunch today.'

Sarah's head was starting to spin. Why was he calling to tell her too? 'Is . . . Is everything all right?' she asked. There had been no time for her mother to speak to him, so it couldn't have been because of that.

'Yes and no,' he answered. 'Lucy just told me that you're both aware of Philippa's medical history, and I'm afraid she hasn't had a very good night. She's insisting she's fine, of course, but I'd rather not leave her this morning, or not until I can feel sure she's perked up a bit.'

Buoyed by the warmth of her feelings for Philippa, Sarah said, 'Of course you must stay with her, and you know, if there's anything I can do, you just have to say the word.'

'That's very kind of you, and Lucy said the same, God bless you both. I'm very sorry to let you down today, but Carl's going to do his best, and I'm sure Joe will help out. I was hoping we might prevail upon Simon . . .'

'Of course,' Sarah broke in. 'I'll get him up right away.'

With a slight catch in his voice John said, 'I'm afraid I might have to stand down from our morris dancing too, which is a pity, but . . .'

'It's not important,' she said. 'It was just a bit of fun. What matters is that you're there for Philippa.'

Sounding more like his sardonic self, he said, 'Knowing her, she'll be trying to throw me out within an hour, but I shall be putting my foot down.'

'Good for you, and if you're faced with a rebellion just let us know and we'll come and sort her out.'

Chuckling, he said, 'She must consider herself warned.'

With a smile, Sarah said, 'We'll call in a couple of hours to find out how she is, OK? Meantime, John, there's something . . . Well, I should probably . . .' The words were coming before she could think them through. Did he need to know that her mother was about to call? Should she stop her? 'I ought to let you know that I've just been speaking to Mum,' she said, 'and she asked for your number. I don't know

if you wanted me to give it to her, but I couldn't . . .'
She stopped, waiting for him to speak, hoping he'd
tell her she'd done the right thing.

The silence stretched into excruciating seconds
before he said, 'How is she?'

'I think . . . She's fine, is what she said, but . . . John,
I'm not sure when she's going to ring, but with
Philippa not being well, if you like I can ask her to
put it off – I mean, if she was intending to call today,
and I don't actually know that she was.' How much
longer was she going to ramble and stumble around
a situation she didn't understand?

'It's all right, Sarah, we'll let her ring when she's
ready, but thanks for telling me and for passing on
my number. Does . . . Does Simon know?'

'Not yet. She doesn't want me to tell him or Becky
anything until after she's spoken to you.'

'I see. Well, I think that's for the best. I should
probably go now. I'll be at the end of the phone if
you and Lucy need to ask me anything, and if I can
I'll pop up later in the day to see how you're getting
along.'

As the line went dead Sarah pressed the connec-
tors and dialled again. Whether John wanted her
to tell her mother about Philippa or not, she was
going to.

Leaving the shower running, Lucy slipped into her
robe and opened the bathroom door a crack, expecting
to find Joe sneaking in after being out all night. To
her surprise she saw Hanna tiptoeing around, putting
things into a holdall, and clearly completely oblivi-
ous to the fact that she was being watched.

Guessing what was going on, Lucy felt a surge of
fury engulf her. However, until she was certain, she

was going to hold her temper in check and wait to see what happened.

When Hanna had finished and was creeping back to the door, Lucy said, 'Just a minute, young lady, exactly where are you going with that?'

Hanna spun round so fast she almost fell over the bag. 'Don't *do* that!' she protested. 'You could give someone a heart attack.'

'Maybe, but it won't be you. Now, I repeat, where are you going with that?'

Hanna's expression turned mutinous.

Lucy folded her arms and leaned against the door frame.

'OK, it's Dad's, all right?' Hanna huffed belligerently.

'Yes, I can see that, and I'm still waiting for an answer.'

'He wants me to take it to him.'

Struggling again with her anger, Lucy said, 'Where is he?'

'I don't *know*.'

Lucy raised incredulous eyebrows.

With an impatient stamp of her foot, Hanna said, 'All right, he asked me to meet him at Moonkicks.'

'Wait there,' Lucy told her, 'and don't even think about making a run for it.'

After turning off the shower, she belted her robe more tightly and returned to the bedroom. 'Put the bag down,' she ordered, walking past Hanna to stand in front of the door, 'and pick up the phone.'

'What?'

'You heard.'

'I don't know what you're making all the fuss about,' Hanna grumbled. 'It's only a bloody bag for God's sake.'

'Call your father now,' Lucy snapped, 'and tell him to come for the bag or I will take it to Moonkicks myself. The choice is his, but either way *you* will not be taking it.'

Letting the bag go, Hanna stormed across the room. 'God, I hate it when you get all bossy and stroppy. He just rang and said could I . . .'

'It's OK, I get the picture. Now give him my message and then you can go to your room.'

Hanna's eyes widened in protest. 'No way! I haven't done anything wrong.'

'Do as you are told,' Lucy said through her teeth.

Grabbing the phone, Hanna prodded in her father's number and turned to glare at her mother.

When he didn't answer Lucy realised he must have seen the landline number come up, and assumed it was her. 'OK, let's go and get your mobile,' she said to Hanna.

Hanna scowled blackly. 'I don't know where it is . . .'

'Don't lie to me,' Lucy shouted, 'now get the damned phone.'

'It's here, all right?' Hanna snapped, whisking it out of her pocket, 'and you don't have to get your knickers in a twist with me . . .'

'Just shut up,' Lucy cut in furiously, and grabbing the mobile she dialled Joe's number.

He answered on the first ring. 'Hi sweetie,' he whispered. 'Everything OK?'

Wanting to hit him, Lucy said, 'I'm going to hold back on what I'd really like to say to you, because Hanna's here – our daughter, who you are using in the most despicable way.'

'Lucy, listen . . .'

'No, you listen! If you're too much of a coward to

come and face me yourself, then you can go back to London without your damned bag,' and before he could say another word she cut the call and tossed the phone on the bed. 'This,' she said, snatching up the bag, 'is coming with me, and you, young lady, are going to your room where you will stay until I have time to deal with you.'

'It's not my fault. I didn't ask . . .'

'Go!' Lucy roared, yanking open the door.

Treating her mother to the most venomous look she could muster, Hanna blazed past and slammed the door behind her.

Carrying the bag to the bathroom, Lucy dumped it in the bath, put in the plug and turned on the taps.

Ten minutes later she returned to the bedroom, dragged on an old pair of denim shorts and a T-shirt, loosely braided her hair and went downstairs to the kitchen. Her and Hanna's breakfast dishes were still on the draining board, and the radio was still blaring. Turning it down, she loaded the dishwasher, then went to unlock the door.

Joe was sitting on a rickety bench just inside the courtyard, with one arm stretched across the back of it and one ankle resting on the other knee. She could see right away that he was attempting to emulate the chirpy, debonair scoundrel he liked to consider himself. What he was actually managing was unshaven, crumpled and guilty as hell.

Since Hanna's bedroom looked out over the other side of the house, Lucy closed the door behind her and in a voice loaded with fury she said, 'Staying out all night would have been bad enough, but getting Hanna to aid and abet your pathetic escape sinks you beneath contempt. What the hell were you thinking?'

311

'OK, OK, it was a bad call,' he admitted, raising his hands, 'but I had to get my stuff somehow . . .'

'And being too damned cowardly to get it yourself . . .'

'You're right, it was cowardly, I'll hold my hands up to that too. I guess I wasn't thinking straight, but when she rang to find out if I was all right . . .'

'She rang to find out where the hell you were. She was worried when you didn't come home . . .'

'I know, and I told her I'm sorry. I'd had too much to drink . . .'

'But you weren't driving, and you have a phone. So what stopped you ringing to let us know you were still alive?'

He peered at her sheepishly. 'Does that mean you wanted me to be?' he asked.

Feeling another urge to slap him, she said, 'I might have, until I realised how you were using Hanna. She's fifteen years old, for God's sake. What kind of example are you setting, getting her to creep around the house like a damned thief, assisting you in your disgusting deception . . .'

'Look, I knew you were going to kick up and I thought it would probably be for the best, with you being so busy and everything, if you didn't have to deal with me today. So I asked her to bring my stuff so I could get a train back to London without having to bother you.'

'No! Without having to face the consequences of failing to come home all night. Does she know where you were?'

'No, of course not.'

Lucy's eyes bored into his. 'So you have something to hide?'

Colouring deeply, he said, 'All I did was call up

an old friend who doesn't live far from here, OK? We had a few too many so I stayed the night.'

Lucy had no idea who the friend might have been, but was in little doubt it was a woman. However, she really didn't want to get into it now. What she wanted was for this not to be happening at all so she could get on with her day.

Hearing a car passing and pulling into the lane leading to the barn, she guessed it was Michael or Carl arriving, and feeling suddenly angrier than ever she went over to Joe and grabbed him by the lapels. 'I don't know what her name is,' she hissed, 'nor do I care. All that matters to me is that Hanna doesn't get dragged into your tawdry little affairs . . .'

'Hey, hey,' he cut in angrily, 'who said anything about another woman? I told you it was an old friend . . .'

'Whoever it was, you've crossed the line, Joe, and it's not going to happen again. Now, I want you to leave and if you ever attempt to use my daughter like that again . . .'

'*Our* daughter,' he corrected, 'and the real problem we're having here is that you don't have time for her father, so quit trying to make me the villain of the piece . . .'

'And you quit trying to twist this round to make it my fault.' Letting him go, she turned back to the kitchen and pushed open the door. 'You'll find your bag upstairs, already packed,' she informed him. 'Hanna's in her room, but before you go in there I want you to think about what you're going to say, and whatever it is, please try not to diminish your-self in her eyes any more than you already have.'

'That was below the belt,' he retorted, 'and anyway, she didn't seem to mind helping her dad out of a hole.'

'She's your daughter, not your accomplice!' Lucy cried. 'For God's sake, when are you going to grow up and start taking some responsibility around here?'

At that his eyes sparked with anger. 'Well, seeing as I'm not very welcome around here, I don't suppose it'll be any time soon,' he shot back, and straightening his shirt he started along the hall towards the stairs.

Needing some time to collect herself, Lucy went to put on the kettle. She didn't want a drink, she only wanted to put the last half an hour behind her before going to face her team. Damn you, Joe, she muttered furiously to herself as tears suddenly stung her eyes. Why did he have to do this now when she was too busy even to know how she felt about it, never mind work out what to do? All night she'd been trying to persuade herself that she wouldn't have cared if he'd found someone else, she'd even decided that it might have been a good thing, at least then she'd stand a chance of making him face their separation. Yet here she was in the cold light of day feeling every bit as hurt and betrayed as she had after the other times she'd suspected him of being with another woman.

Hearing voices upstairs, she took a deep breath and let it go slowly. She must try to think about this rationally and not let it get out of perspective. What was making this occasion worse was the fact that he'd done it in Cromstone, where she was trying to earn people's respect, not ridicule, or pity.

'Oh, Christ, Lucy,' she heard him groan as she reached the bottom of the stairs.

Realising he must have found his bag, she wasn't sure whether she wanted to laugh or apologise – or tell him it was what he bloody well deserved.

'What is it, Dad?' she heard Hanna saying as she

went into the bedroom. 'Oh my God! Did Mum do that? Mum, you are so *fierce.*' She started to giggle, and when Lucy got to the bathroom she found Joe laughing too.

'Well, I'm glad you think it's funny,' she told them, unable to suppress her own smile.

'And there was me thinking you didn't care,' Joe grinned, coming to hug her.

'I don't,' she told him.

'No, right, I can tell.'

If they'd been alone she'd have asked if he'd been with a woman, but she couldn't with Hanna there, and perhaps it was a good thing, because she really didn't have time to deal with it now.

'I'll get it,' Hanna announced as the phone started to ring, 'I expect it's for me anyway,' and bouncing into the bedroom she grabbed the receiver. 'Hello, Cromstone Farmhouse. Oh, hey, Granny, how are you? We were wondering if you'd got there all right.' Her eyes came to her mother's as she listened to the reply. 'So where are you now? Oh, I see. Yes, she's right here, I'll pass you over.'

'Where is she?' Lucy asked as she took the phone.

'In the car somewhere. She drove till she got a reception.'

'Mum, at last,' Lucy said into the phone.

'I know, it's a blinking nuisance not having the right phone,' her mother grumbled, sounding exasperated at her predicament, cut off in the wilderness. 'We'll get it sorted out by the end of the week, so not to worry. Is everything all right there? Your messages sounded quite urgent.'

'Because they are,' Lucy told her. 'I thought you'd call back yesterday after we lost the connection – or did you hang up on me?'

315

'Hang up on you?' Daphne repeated incredulously. 'Why on earth would I do that?'

Signalling for Joe to take Hanna out of the room, Lucy waited for the door to close and said, 'Maybe because I was asking questions you didn't want to answer.'

'Questions about what? Really Lucy, you do say some odd things at times.'

'I was asking what you knew about a ring that's . . .'

'Ah yes, I remember now. Do you mean one we've sold, or is it . . . ?'

'No, Mum. I mean an insider ring where the dealers get together to keep the bids down on an item they've recognised to be valuable.'

There was a moment before Daphne said, 'Why would they do that?'

'To go on and sell it at a much higher price, meaning that our seller gets cheated out of what's rightfully theirs.'

'Oh, Lucy, for heaven's sake, what are you getting into?'

'It's not me getting into it, it's Maureen and Godfrey.'

'Oh no, they wouldn't . . .'

'Please Mum, listen. Someone let themselves into the office last night, because I found the door open when I went over there and I know I locked it when I left to go to Sarah's. I'm not sure what was taken, but the only people who have keys . . .'

'Stop, stop,' her mother interrupted. 'I was the person who let herself in, and it sounds as though Dad didn't lock up when I told him to.'

Lucy was so stunned she hardly knew what to say. 'You mean you drove all the way back here . . .'

'I know, it was a daft thing to do, but we left in such a hurry and when we realised we'd left a few things behind Dad said we ought to go back and collect them.'

'But what on earth is so important that it couldn't wait till the next time I see you? And why the heck didn't you let me know you were coming?'

'We didn't want to be a nuisance, or to put you through a goodbye after all, so we thought it would be best if we just came in quietly while you were at Sarah's, and left again.'

As concerned now as she was confused, Lucy sat down on the edge of the bed as she said, 'So what did you come back for?'

'Oh, just a few boxes of family papers. I thought we might need our passports or birth certificates . . .'

Lucy blinked. 'What on earth for?'

'Well, you never know what might come up, especially when you're moving house. Anyway, it doesn't matter, because I'm sure you're right, we won't be needing them.'

Hardly able to make any sense of this, Lucy said, 'So you didn't find them?'

'No, I'm afraid not. I can't think where I put them, which is most unlike me, so I'm afraid Dad might have had them last. Or maybe they'll turn out to be at the cottage after all, tucked into one of the bigger boxes.'

'Well, if they don't turn up, let me know and I'll try to find them for you.'

'Oh no, no, you've got far too much on your plate to be wasting time looking for things I've mislaid. They'll turn up sooner or later, and we'll just have to hope that we won't need anything that's in them in the meantime. Now tell me how you're getting on with everything.'

Though Lucy was afraid her mother had just implicated herself big time by coming back the way she had, since it made her look guilty even if she wasn't, she decided not to pursue it until she'd had more time to think. 'Everything's more or less on target here,' she told her. She wouldn't mention anything about Philippa, because it would only fuss her. 'How's Dad?'

'Happy to be here, the way he always is.'

Easily able to imagine him pottering about the garden and garage, Lucy said, 'I want you to promise me you won't let him drive that old Rover. If it breaks down in the middle of nowhere, which it's likely to . . .'

'Lucy, dear, it only has three wheels these days, so it isn't going anywhere. He only keeps it to tinker about with, you know that, and because you were always so attached to it.'

When I was eight, Lucy was thinking. *Time to let go.* However, it was true, she'd become almost hysterical when her father had tried to sell it, unable to bear thinking of it being taken away by strangers and becoming lonely without them. So he'd ended up keeping it, and still, all these years later, it was like a trusty old member of the family – for her too, if she was being honest with herself. 'Will you call again later?' she asked.

'Yes, of course. Will just after lunch be a good time?'

'I should think so.'

'Good. I'll let you get on now then. Dad sends his love, and says not to forget to water the busy Lizzies.'

After an oddly protracted goodbye, during which her mother seemed to be on the point of ringing off several times before suddenly launching into something else, Lucy tried to set her misgivings aside as she ran downstairs to open the barn. However, it wasn't easy when she felt so convinced that her mother wasn't being completely honest with her, since it made absolutely no sense to come all the way back here last night to collect things they really wouldn't need in the foreseeable future.

Chapter Seventeen

For the rest of the day, and throughout Monday and Tuesday, as dealers, collectors and the world at large descended in very encouraging numbers for the viewing, Lucy and the others were so run off their feet that they barely had time to eat, never mind discuss anything other than matters at hand. After helping to move the heavy stuff into place on Sunday while his clothes tumbled about the dryer, Joe had taken an evening train back to London – making himself scarce, Lucy suspected, before she had a chance to ask again where he'd spent Saturday night.

To her great relief John returned to work on Monday morning with the irrepressible Philippa at his side, looking her usual glamorously piratical self. The temporary staff were all on board now, and going so efficiently about their business that Lucy hardly dared to think how she'd have been managing without them. Though one or two asked where Maureen was, most understood that she was having to take time off to look after Godfrey.

Fortunately Monday passed without a squeak from either of the Crumptons, which Sarah declared a cause for celebration as they closed the barn doors and set the alarm. As soon as they were able to get away from the office, they joined John and Philippa at the pub for wine and food. Michael returned to his office in order to attend to his own business, dropping Simon at the station on his way so Simon could be in London ready for a breakfast meeting the next day.

Now that Teddy Best had been fully briefed on the possibility of a ring and was in possession of the letters Lucy and Sarah had found, he'd advised them to abandon a trawl through the archives in search of more dubious transactions, since trying to find worthwhile documentary evidence was going to be next to impossible.

'It's only when it sells at a later date for a much higher price,' he explained, 'that you might hear about it, but even then it's unlikely, especially if it goes abroad.'

'So there could be a whole slew of stuff out there that's been bought up for next to nothing from us,' Lucy said, feeling her world sinking towards a downward spiral of police inquiries, arrests, lawsuits and eventual bankruptcy followed by extinction.

'Not really,' Michael replied comfortingly. 'It won't be often that something valuable comes this way without being recognised by the owner, or another dealer who's *not* part of the ring.'

'Don't worry, we'll get to the bottom of it,' Teddy assured her, 'and when the culprits are marched off to jail we'll do a little morris dance outside the court-room to celebrate.'

Though Lucy had laughed with the others, fearing that one or even both of her parents might be inside the courtroom was starting to keep her awake at night.

'Listen,' Michael said gently when he realised how worried she was, 'I'm as convinced as you are that they know nothing about it . . .'

321

'Actually, I'm not so sure any more,' she blurted. 'When I last spoke to my mother . . .' Spotting Carl heading towards them, she quickly shook her head. 'Not now,' she murmured, and leaving Michael to carry on milling about the barn on the lookout for anything that might appear suspicious, she returned to the office to make sure the cashiers' secure stations were up and running.

They were, and filling up the entire end space of the office like a mini bank, complete with alarm buttons and bulletproof glass, in case anyone fancied their chances at making off with the cash. Sarah was at her computer emailing details of two more telephone bidders to Philippa, while at least five of the temporary staff were busily manning the phones, or sorting through registration cards and catalogues, or setting up the credit-card machines ready for action.

Lucy glanced at her watch. It was five thirty in the evening with the first big auction day on a very close horizon, and she couldn't remember when she'd last felt so stressed or exhilarated. Or so admiring of her parents. To think that they'd run all this, and at their age, and so successfully, made her feel so proud of them that she made a mental note to send a text to tell them exactly that before she went to bed. She wondered if they were thinking about her now, and felt sure they were, simply because she'd always been at the centre of their lives. They'd be thinking that tomorrow morning on the dot of nine the first lots would go under the hammer and, provided all went to plan, by the end of the day on Thursday she'd have completed her first sale and actually made some money.

Just please don't let it be the first and last, she prayed inwardly.

'Has anyone seen John?' she shouted over the din.

'He was outside directing traffic ten minutes ago,' Philippa answered, glancing up from the instruction sheet Sarah had just passed her.

'I'm here,' he called out, coming in through the door. 'The rain's not letting up at all, so the lads are shifting as much of the outdoor stuff as they can inside.'

'Thanks,' Lucy said, squeezing his arm. 'Did you manage to get permission to use the next field for parking?'

His eyes twinkled. 'Fifty quid did it.'

Laughing, she said, 'I'll make sure you're reimbursed.'

'Oh crikey, look at the time!' Sarah cried, springing to her feet. 'I'm supposed to pick Simon up at a quarter to. I'll have my mobile if anyone needs to get hold of me. Ah, Hanna, there you are, did Juliette find you? She popped in a few minutes ago. I sent her over to the barn.'

'I'll go find her,' Hanna said, lowering her hood. 'Mum, did you see Granny's text? She wants to make sure you booked the auctioneers.'

Lucy gave a choke of laughter. 'It's a bit late to be reminding me now,' she retorted. 'Text back and tell her Percy Beach and Frank Lowman are doing it. They were here just now, has anyone seen them?'

'They left as I was coming in,' John replied. 'And by the way, I thought I'd volunteer myself as security for the next two days, because someone ought to be in here with the girls while money's changing hands.'

'Fantastic, maybe you could work shifts with Simon, because Sarah's put him down for the same. Who's on the door over in the barn?'

Inwardly flinching at the prospect of running up against Simon again, John said, 'Right now, Michael and someone whose name I've forgotten. The large chap with the balding head who lives over Milly's shop.'

'That's Hector, her son. Great. It's time to start ushering the punters out now so we can shut up shop by six. Philippa, you're an angel,' she declared, as Philippa thrust a pizza menu into her hand. 'I'll have a ham and pineapple. How many are we for dinner?'

'Six at the last count,' Philippa told her. 'Apparently Hanna's eating at Tess's after they've finished their rehearsal for the fashion show. So I can ring the order in as soon as I have a complete list. I expect John will be happy to go and pick them up.'

Keeping her voice down, Lucy said, 'You've been here all day again, are you sure it isn't too much for you?'

'And I shall be here again tomorrow,' Philippa informed her hotly. 'I have a dozen or more people depending on me to handle their bids.'

Searching her face for signs of fatigue and finding none, Lucy gave her a hug. If she did have another seizure, which was apparently what had happened the other night, they would cope and she, Lucy, would join forces with John to make her see a doctor. 'You must promise me that the instant you feel tired, or just want to go home . . .'

'Och, it's not going to happen,' Philippa scoffed dismissively. 'Now, I should go and find Michael to get his order.'

'Actually, I'll do that, because I need to talk to him anyway. Would you mind answering that phone, then we probably ought to put the machine on or we'll never get out of here.'

After running through the rain Lucy dived into the back of the barn and weaved her way through to the front, where Michael was explaining something to an elderly German couple in their own language.

'Wow, they're coming from all over,' Lucy laughed, as they saluted him happily with their catalogues and went to find their car. 'Everything OK?' she asked as someone bumped past her.

'Seems that way. There's been a lot of interest so far, that's for sure.'

High on adrenalin, Lucy wanted to throw out her arms and dance. However, knowing that a hectic viewing was no guarantee of a monster sale, she managed to rein in her enthusiasm with a sobering reminder of the problem they were facing. 'Did you spot anyone that bothered you?' she asked.

He shook his head, and waved to someone who was leaving. 'As I said before, Maureen and Godfrey are bound to have put the word out that they've blown their own cover, so whoever they've been working with will almost certainly stay away. Now, you were mentioning something about your parents last night.'

Feeling her insides churn, Lucy said, 'I'm not sure what you're going to make of this, but my mother informed me on Sunday that she came back here on Saturday night with my father to pick up some "family papers" that they've apparently mislaid.'

Michael looked surprised. 'So it was them who left the office door open?'

Lucy nodded, and braced herself to go further. 'I'm afraid the excuse of "family papers" seems pretty thin to me,' she said, 'when they can hardly need them that urgently, so I can only assume that they came back to remove some sort of incriminating evidence.'

Michael frowned. 'Mm,' he responded thoughtfully, 'I guess that seems a logical conclusion, so I think when the auction's over we'll have to sit down and have a good long chat with them, to find out exactly what they do and don't know about this ring.'

'Definitely,' Lucy agreed, already dreading it, but relieved to know that he'd be with her. 'In the meantime, let's hope the main operators, whoever the heck they are, do decide to stay away, because we don't want them round here ruining our business.' She pulled a face. 'But if they do, that's not going to help us find out who they are, is it?'

'The best-case scenario is that they've already decided not to darken your doorstep again – that way you won't have to take anyone to task and risk dragging yourself and your parents into something that certainly won't be good for business. However, we're not thinking about that now, we're focusing on what a spectacular first sale you're going to have, and I predict it will be exactly that. Both auctioneers have checked out with flying colours, so no scandals there, and Percy remarked before he left on how well set out everything is.'

Lucy beamed. 'What do you think of our new art gallery?' she asked. 'Did you see it on the upper level?'

'I did, and it works very well up there. Personally, I'm not sure I'd want to own any of it . . .'

'Oh God no, it's awful, isn't it – apart from the one,' she drew quote marks, 'in the manner of Peter Kinley. I quite like the shadings and angles in that one, and . . .'

'Actually, you've just reminded me,' he cut in, 'I noticed that painting in the catalogue and then stupidly forgot about it. Am I right in thinking it's part of a house clearance from Malmesbury?'

Puzzled, Lucy said, 'I'm not sure, I'd have to check. Why?'

'If it is, then I'm representing the estate and I happen to know that they owned quite a good collection of originals by lesser-known artists. Some will have gained in value over the years, such as a Peter Kinley, but there's a good chance their grandson, who's inherited, has no idea of that, so he's just lumped everything in together and shipped it out ready to sell the house. I'm guessing that unless asked you don't get a valuation?'

'That's right, especially not on items that come in as part of a house clearance. There are too many, so we rely on the owners to put forward any special requests.' Not sure whether to be worried or excited now, she said, 'Do you think we should withdraw it from the sale until an expert's looked it over?'

'Mm, yes I do, just in case, because if it does turn out to be valuable . . .'

'Hang on, are you thinking it might be something Maureen has deliberately downplayed so that one of her cronies can pick it up for next to nothing?'

'It's possible, though I have to say I think the chances of us catching her out that easily are almost non-existent, but you never know, so let's take it down anyway. We can always put it in a later sale, once Margie's had the chance to look it over.'

Turning as John came to join them, Lucy told him about the painting while Michael ran upstairs to lift it from the wall. 'Have you ever heard of the artist?' she asked John.

327

'I can't say I have,' he replied, 'but I'm afraid I'm a bit of a philistine when it comes to art.'

'You and me both. I wonder how much it's worth, if it does turn out to be real.'

The answer to that question came an hour and a half later, after the barn and office had been secured for the night, and the pizzas were on order. The main players, as Lucy called her core team, were all in the kitchen farmhouse with the painting – out of its ersatz rococo frame – laid out on the table under the central light that Michael had lowered to enable a close inspection. In the bottom left-hand corner, now exposed where before it had been hidden by the frame, was the artist's signature and date.

Lucy's eyes were glittering as Michael straightened up, and seeing how bright his own were she almost let out a squeal of excitement.

'Obviously, I'm no expert,' he said, looking from her to Sarah and back again, 'but if Margie does confirm it's genuine, I'm guessing it could be worth somewhere in the region of twenty thousand.'

Lucy almost gasped.

Sarah did.

John said, 'And its list price in the catalogue is how much?'

'Between two and three hundred,' Michael told him. To Lucy he said, 'We have no way of knowing this for certain, but by listing it as "in the manner of Peter Kinley" there's a good chance that we are looking at something the ring had in their sights for tomorrow.'

Lucy's heart skipped a beat. Had her mother been the one to list it, knowing its value? Surely not. It must have been Maureen.

'Is there a way of finding out for certain if the

ring is targeting it?' Philippa wanted to know, speaking in unison with Simon who was asking the same thing.

'We'll only know that once we have an idea of its true value,' Michael replied, 'but it'll be interesting to see if anyone makes enquiries tomorrow as to why it's no longer in the sale.'

'One last question,' John said, 'if the painting's so valuable, where should we keep it until we know for certain what it's worth?'

Lucy turned back to Michael.

'Your insurance should cover it,' he told her.

'Yes, but if it does get stolen we won't have any idea how much to claim – apart from the list price.'

'There's a large unused strongbox at the Lodge,' Philippa said. 'I'm sure it'll fit in. It'll probably be safer than keeping it here.'

As Lucy nodded she tried not to notice the mistrustful look Simon was giving John, as though John had somehow contrived all this in order to make off with the piece.

'If it does turn out to be the real McCoy,' Michael was saying, 'you're going to have some fun marketing it when the time comes. I'd like to be around when it goes under the hammer.'

'If it actually fetched twenty thousand,' Sarah said, 'it would make us something in the region of . . . four hundred and fifty quid on just one item.'

'Great! We can all retire,' Lucy cried, clapping her hands.

'Don't mock,' Michael advised, 'because the publicity could turn out to be worth ten times that.'

'I should bring the owner up to speed,' Lucy said, going to answer a knock on the door. 'This'll be the pizzas.'

It was, and as they sat down to tuck in, with glasses of wine filled to the brim and the auspices looking so good for the next two days, Lucy felt so excited she was almost afraid.

'There's no way it's all going to fall apart,' John assured her, when she murmured her misgivings as he was leaving with the carefully packaged painting under his arm. 'You've worked damned hard to pull this together under difficult circumstances, and I, for one, feel very proud to be a part of it.'

Loving his kindness, Lucy gave him a hug. 'It's all thanks to you,' she said generously, 'because if you hadn't stepped in when you did I dread to think where we'd be now.'

'It's been a team effort and you're a pleasure to work for, lassie. Now, I should get the jolly pirate home before she sinks any more of that wine.'

'Oh look,' Philippa hiccuped as she came to join them, 'it's still raining. Always a good sign, I think.'

Lucy laughed. 'Thanks for everything, Pippa,' she said, the familiar name coming as naturally as if she'd always used it. 'I'm so glad you're going to be with us tomorrow.'

'And the next day,' Pippa reminded her. 'Now, let's be off, brother dearest, I need to decide on my wardrobe for the morning.'

Going back to the others, Lucy sat down next to Hanna who'd just returned from her fashion-show rehearsal.

'What gets me,' Simon said, 'is how ready you all are to trust that man. Off he goes with a painting that could be worth thousands, and none of you bats an eye.'

'We have no reason to,' Sarah replied, 'and if you're going to be like that I shall take you home.'

Picking up his glass, he took a large sip of wine and sank into a moody silence.

'You did a great job today,' Lucy told Hanna, giving her a hug.

'Am I going to get paid?' Hanna wanted to know.

'Of course. As will Juliette.' She tilted Hanna's face so she could see it more clearly. 'You look tired,' she told her. 'Why don't you go on up to bed? I can clear away here.'

'It's OK, I'll stay up with you.'

Realising she didn't want to leave her mother in what might appear to be a foursome, Lucy pressed a kiss to her head and said, 'Then why don't you text Granny to tell her we've had over three hundred people for the viewings?'

'Cool,' Hanna responded, reaching for her phone. 'I've already texted Dad and Ben, they were like, no way!'

Smiling, Lucy began stacking the plates while Sarah rinsed them and Michael and Simon poured themselves more wine.

'You don't *have* to be typical men,' Sarah informed them.

Michael laughed, and stretching out his legs he folded his hands behind his head as he said, 'I have to admit I'm looking forward to the next couple of days.'

Lucy glanced over at him. 'Are you going to be here the whole time?'

'That's my intention. I'll be at the end of the phone if anyone from the office needs me.'

'Speaking of mothers,' Lucy said, turning to Sarah, 'which I know we weren't, do you know if yours has . . .'

Sarah quickly shook her head.

Remembering Simon didn't know that Rose was going to call John, Lucy could have kicked herself. 'Uh, has she, um, asked to see a catalogue?' she quickly improvised. 'I thought she might want to see how we've listed some of her worldly goods.'

'She's been checking us out online,' Sarah answered, 'and so far she seems to approve.'

'Sorry,' Lucy mouthed when she was sure Simon wasn't looking.

'It's OK,' Sarah mouthed back, 'and no, she hasn't called him yet.'

John was still smiling as he walked away from the stairs, having stood guard at the bottom watching Pippa weaving her way up to bed.

'Good night,' she called out again.

'Good night,' he called back.

It had never taken much to make her tipsy, and though he couldn't help fearing that too much alcohol might bring on another seizure, surely the couple of glasses she'd downed wouldn't have done any harm. What really mattered was how happy she'd seemed since they'd come to Cromstone, because more than anything she deserved that. In fact, seeing her so buoyant was helping him deal with his own feelings about being here, which weren't always good, though he was careful to hide his misgivings. He wanted this time to be as special for Pippa as she hoped it would be, since no one in the world had ever meant as much to him as she did. That was with the exception of Rose and his children, of course, and the fact that they were strangers to him now would have easily broken his heart, had it not already been broken a long time ago.

If it weren't for Pippa he might well have put an end to it all during his time in prison. The closest he'd come was when he'd agreed to let Douglas adopt his children. Giving up all rights to them, knowing he'd probably never see them again, had been worse than death; it had been like entering a living hell, a dimension of cruelty and injustice that had no equal; an eternity of longing and loving with nothing in return. The father in him, the husband, the man who adored his family, had been buried that day, taking his belief in God, righteousness and redemption along with him. Now, because of Pippa, that man was being carefully resurrected. Like an avenging angel she wanted the wrongs put right and the healing to begin before she was no longer around to make it happen, and he couldn't deny her that even if he wanted to, which he didn't. Douglas had gone now, Becky and Simon were grown up, and the missing link, the link that had held them all together until it had been snatched from the heart of them, would never be found. That break to his heart would never be healed.

After locking the painting in the strongbox he went to pour himself a Scotch. Perhaps the nightcap would drive away the demons that kept him awake at night, or help him deal with his son's hostility. As he sat down heavily at the kitchen table, he was thinking with great tenderness of Sarah and Lucy, and how warmly they had welcomed him and Pippa into their lives. Since Rose, only Pippa had ever given him a sense of belonging, or a feeling of worth. Lucy and Sarah were doing it now. Sarah, Douglas's daughter. How Douglas must have loved her. There was no doubt in John's mind that Douglas had loved Becky and Simon too, because Douglas was that sort of man.

Raising his glass, he drank a silent toast to the friend who'd been like a brother, the loyal and trusted partner who'd so bravely stepped into his shoes. Then he looked at the phone and wondered, as he had so many times over the years, but especially these last few days, when, if, Rose would ever call. More than anyone he knew how hard this would be for her, and more than anything he wanted to lend her his strength. All he could do, however, was let her come to him in her own time, and on her own terms. When, if, that happened, he'd want her to know that all he regretted about the decision he'd made over thirty years ago was the fact that he'd ever had to make it at all.

This was the hour Lucy had been waiting for. Her mother had always come over to the barn very early on the first morning of the auction, and Lucy wanted to carry on the tradition, not only out of a sense of loyalty, but to absorb herself in the strange tranquillity of so much history before it passed on its way.

As she wandered along the outer aisles of the barn, passing walnut commodes and Georgian chests, French armoires, Victorian bureaux, Edwardian tables and Russian chairs, she could easily have been a traveller in time moving back and forth through the last four centuries. Virtually everything fascinated her, whether a chesterfield sofa that could once have belonged to a duke, a pair of carved elephants possibly created for a maharaja, an ornate lady's compact from a film star's handbag, or a three-baguette diamond ring thrown overboard after a broken engagement. Everything had a story, a past, a secret that made it as individual as if it were a living thing. She wondered who'd made the glass vase with its hand-painted orange flowers and foliage: what had inspired it, who'd been the first to buy it, how many shelves had it decorated since? Where might it end up after today? Had the Pendelfin rabbit figures brought joy to a child, or many children? What triumphs and sadness had the silver trophy seen? Where were the winners and losers now? How many pagodas had been lit by the Japanese lanterns, and where were the people who'd sat under them today? Who had been present at the dinner parties that had gathered around the brass candlesticks? Which directions had those diners taken since? Did they ever wonder what had happened to their old treasures? Did they care? Were they even still around to know?

Feeling as though a thousand or more ghosts were watching, breathlessly, invitingly, as she came to stand at the centre of the barn she put her head back to look up at the mezzanine. Carpets and rugs were draped like proud flags over the railings, and three dozen or more paintings hung on the walls. There were mirrors and panels too, tapestries and sketches. Everything had had a previous life, or lives, and was now en route to another. Cromstone Auctions was like a crossroads at the heart of twelve hundred journeys – the number of lots they were auctioning today and tomorrow. No matter where something had started, how many shores it might have crossed, or roads it had travelled, for the moment it was pausing here with her, waiting to find out which wall or floor or dressing table it might find itself on next. New environments, new owners, new families, none of whom would know about, or perhaps even think about, where it might have been before.

She walked on slowly. The still, dank air was alive with a hundred scents, lavender flirting with tobacco, must smothering pine, paraffin wafting around wax. She could almost hear the music of old-fashioned balls tinkling in the chandeliers and blending with the clatter of rolling dice; a cacophony of voices, some raised in anger, others in joy, or laughter, or grief. There were so many worlds here, more than she could name, and in a strange sort of way she felt a part of each one, as though she too was on a journey, bound by a secret she could never reveal. Her secret had no words, nor shapes, only an instinct gathered around a feeling that she'd done something wrong in her life and couldn't go back.

As she climbed to the upper level and strolled along her newly devised art gallery, past the jewellery cases and shelves of stacked glassware, she found herself imagining what all these orphaned objects might get up to at night when the doors were closed and no one was watching. She smiled to think of walking sticks fencing with garden hoes, while mirrors went in search of new reflections. How many china dolls gathered around the books who were telling stories of their creation, instead of those set out between their covers? Did the teapot sitting proudly on its silver platter, keeping its brood of teacups close by, ever tell how one had been lost? Did it mind? Was it like a family trying to get along without a missing loved one?

As the sun began finding its way in through the skylights, painting the Aladdin's cave of secrets in a crimson-honey glow, she wandered down the spiral staircase, passing a gramophone cabinet with a collection of LPs appearing a little forlorn in their tattered sleeves. There were boxes and boxes of trinkets and ornaments, old games and toys, match-stick people and clockwork cars.

When finally she stepped up to the auctioneer's podium she was feeling both weighted and exhilarated by the sense of something wonderful and sad that seemed to envelop her. It was only here that she ever experienced a sense of belonging, yet even as she tried to hold on to it, it seemed to slip away, leaving her feeling as she had as a child, when she'd arrive at a new school afraid of how long it might take to make a friend. She used to think she was different from everyone else, or that they all knew a secret that they'd never tell her. It was only in later years, when she'd confessed that early paranoia to one of Ben's teachers, that she'd learned how many children felt that way. So feeling as she did now, that she was with the wrong husband, the wrong children, the wrong parents, even in the wrong skin, meant nothing at all, particularly when she knew very well that her children were hers, and for all their faults and idiosyncrasies she'd never doubted how much her parents loved her. Joe too, in his way.

Looking up, she smiled to see a dream-catcher overhead. If she could dream now and have it come true, what would it be? Possibilities began drifting in and out of focus, until, feeling disloyal and vaguely unnerved by the direction her fancies were taking, she let them go and smiled warmly as John's familiar silhouette appeared in the open doorway.

'Ah, it's you,' he said, stepping into the shadow. She could see now that he was panting from his early-morning run and coated in sweat. 'I was passing and saw the doors open. Is everything all right?'

'Yes, everything's fine,' she told him, and stepping

down from the podium she went to join him outside. 'It's going to rain,' she said, looking up at the sky as a billowing mass of grey cloud drew a veil over the sun.

'The forecast's not good,' he agreed, almost apologetically.

Please don't let this be a bad omen, she was thinking. 'Let's keep our fingers crossed that it doesn't make everyone stay away,' she said, and linking his arm she walked him over to the farmhouse where Hanna was already up and making coffee.

Two hours later, at nine o'clock sharp, the bidding got off to a lively start, with over two dozen people seated in the well of the barn on chairs that would later go under the hammer themselves. Ceramics were first on the agenda, and it almost made Lucy's head spin to see how speedily the auctioneers handled each sale. By nine thirty almost fifty items had gone for more than the reserve price. Sarah was especially thrilled when one of her pieces – a plaque with a painted decoration of an Elizabethan woman – fetched the grand sum of forty-five pounds.

'Not bad when we had it listed at thirty,' she whispered in an aside to Simon.

During the next ten minutes the bids took a downward turn, with a few items receiving no interest at all and several more going for less than the list price. However, things suddenly picked up again when a glazed earthenware charger priced at £300–£400 caused a flurry of excitement by going to five hundred, six, *seven, eight,* and finally selling for the princely sum of nine hundred pounds.

'Someone recognised something there that we

didn't,' Lucy murmured to Michael, who'd come to join her up on the mezzanine.

'That's the beauty of what you do,' he reminded her. 'There's always room for pleasant surprises.'

Buoyed by the promising start, she reached for his hand and gave it a squeeze. Feeling his fingers curl around hers, she allowed herself to be turned towards him, and seeing the look in his eyes her breath caught on a powerful wave of longing.

'The paintings are up after the glassware,' she whispered, hardly aware of what she was saying, 'so around noon I'd say, at this rate. It's going to be interesting to see if anyone reacts when we announce that Lot 340 is no longer for sale.'

'Indeed it will,' he agreed. His eyes were still on hers, but this was neither the time nor the place, so releasing the pressure on her hand, he said, 'Have you been able to talk to your mother about it yet?'

As Lucy shook her head she felt as though part of her was unravelling. 'I thought she'd have been in touch by now,' she murmured.

'Maybe she's tried and couldn't get through. It's been pretty hectic from what I hear.'

'True, but she could at least have sent a text. Even Hanna hasn't had one and . . . Oh, look, there she is, holding up the *Red Maid*. Apparently Red Maids' is a school in Bristol, so I suppose if you're someone who went there . . . Oh my God, did that ghastly thing just sell for eighty pounds?'

Laughing, he said, 'Along with its partner from Colston Boys', I believe.'

Grinning widely, she rubbed her hands as she said, 'I'm beginning to enjoy this.' Then, noticing several more people arriving, she whispered, 'How's everything going out front?'

'Fine, as far as I can tell. Poor Hector's drenched to the skin going back and forth to the car park, but John thought we should make an effort with umbrellas or people might not bother to get out of their cars. Ah, there goes Simon, presumably to take over from John with the cashiers.'

Spotting Pippa on the opposite mezzanine, Lucy gave her a silent round of applause as she secured an art deco glass bowl for her telephone bidder. With a bow of thanks, Pippa put aside the phone and continued to work with Hanna and Juliette displaying objects as the auctioneers described them, until it was time to get her next client on the line.

It was just before midday that Lucy's eyes rounded with shock as Maureen, pumped up with attitude and dripping in paste jewels, stalked into the barn and plonked herself down in an aisle seat. By now Lucy was standing next to the auctioneer's podium, having just returned from the office where the cashiers were merrily running cards through their machines and stuffing notes in their tills, while Simon did his duty as security guard.

'I don't believe the nerve of her,' Sarah whispered, coming up beside her.

Though Lucy's heart was thudding with unease she was keeping her eyes fixed on Maureen, determined not to be the first to look away. 'Her timing's interesting, wouldn't you say?' she muttered.

'I certainly would.'

Since the paintings were already under the hammer, and the suspected Peter Kinley was due to come up about halfway through the section, they didn't have long to wait.

'I've been told,' Frank, the auctioneer, informed the gathering when the moment arrived, 'that Lot 340 is no longer available. So, moving on to Lot 341, a gouache and mixed media still life signed bottom right Ximenes and in a gilt frame. Am I offered forty pounds?'

Maureen's eyes were boring so hard into Lucy's that Lucy almost took a step back.

'Gotcha,' Sarah murmured.

Having got wind of the new arrival, Michael and John were also standing with Lucy by now, as she waited for Maureen to flounce out. However, Maureen remained rooted to her chair and didn't move until she'd made the only bid for a set of nineteenth-century engravings. Having secured them for the eighty pounds at which she'd listed them, she rose to her feet, delivered a superciliously smug look Lucy's way and went off to pay.

'Was that supposed to throw us off the scent?' Michael murmured in Lucy's ear. 'Or were they really what she came for?'

Lucy was still watching Maureen stalking up through the barn like a grande dame with a bad smell under her nose. 'I've no idea,' she replied, 'but I think I'll go and have a word.'

By the time Maureen had paid for the engravings Lucy was in the courtyard, under an umbrella, ready to block her exit. 'Before you go,' she said as Maureen tried to brush by, 'wouldn't you like to know what happened to Lot 340?'

Maureen's answering look was withering. 'I've got what I came for, thank you very much,' she retorted.

Lucy raised an eyebrow. 'Are you sure about that?'

'Perfectly. Now, if you don't mind . . .'

'We're watching you, Maureen.'

Maureen only smirked. 'Then you're looking the

wrong way,' she told her, and seemed about to move on until apparently she thought better of it. 'Who do you think sent me here for these?' she demanded, her eyes blazing the challenge.

Lucy glanced at the parcel of engravings.

'It was your mother,' Maureen hissed in her face.

Lucy blanched as she took a step back. 'I know you're lying,' she told her angrily.

'Am I? Then prove it,' and shooting open her own umbrella she marched triumphantly on her way.

'Of course your mother didn't send her,' Sarah cried indignantly.

'I'm sure you're right, but it's her word against my mother's,' Lucy pointed out, 'and actually, there's something I haven't told you . . . Last Saturday, when I found the office open and we assumed it was Maureen or someone working with her who'd let themselves in? Well, I'm afraid it was my parents.'

Sarah blinked with astonishment.

Lucy looked from Michael to John, who appeared equally thrown.

'Apparently they came back for some family papers,' Lucy told them, the flimsiness of the excuse dismaying her more deeply than ever.

No one voiced the incredulous question: *they did that drive twice in one day for family papers?* Or: *why didn't they lock up behind them, or let you know they were coming, or ask you to look for them?* Nevertheless, the words were hanging in the air.

'There's always a chance,' Michael said, 'that your mother was telling the truth and that is why they came back.'

'Thank you for that,' Lucy said, 'and I'd really like

to believe it, but the timing and coincidence...'
Dropping her head in her hands, she let out a growl of frustration. 'I don't know what to think,' she murmured angrily. 'Those solicitors' letters have to be answered, and if we start pointing the finger at Maureen we know exactly what she's going to do. She'll swivel it right back at my mother, and frankly whether Mum was actively involved, or being leaned on, or whatever the hell's been going on, she'd never be able to go through the stress of a police inquiry, much less a trial.'

'I'm sure it won't come to that,' Sarah said, glancing at Michael for backup.

'We've already agreed we need to talk to her,' Michael said, 'and we must do it face to face, because the only way you're going to know if she's telling the truth is if you can see her eyes.'

'Of course,' Lucy sighed, 'but I can't get down there this week with all that's going on, and next week's diary is already full. I'll have to try and persuade her to come here, which might be a damned sight easier if I could flaming well get hold of her.'

Chapter Eighteen

It was during the afternoon of the second day that the auction took a turn no one saw coming. With the bulk of the sale already complete, there were only a small number of punters left in the barn, and bidding for the remaining miscellaneous items had become lacklustre, to say the least. However, Percy was doing his best to keep it all going, mustering his usual jolly tones as he asked for twenty pounds to start the bids on a box Sarah had provided. It contained an old biscuit tin half full of sixpenny bits, an ironwork candlestick, a collection of cabinet keys, a large wooden chess piece and a brass and silver letter knife.

At first there was only a white-haired man in the fourth row who responded, and since there seemed to be no other interest Percy was about to declare the item sold when Philippa, on the phone up on the mezzanine, raised her hand.

'Twenty-five,' Percy announced. 'Do I have thirty?'

The man with the white hair nodded.

'Thirty-five?'

Philippa nodded.

'Forty?'

Again the white-haired man nodded.

When the bidding reached a hundred Lucy and Sarah exchanged glances across the barn, startled by what was happening. Even Percy was starting to look baffled as the bids continued to rise, reaching two, then three, then four hundred pounds, but that was nothing compared to Sarah's disbelief when the contest soared on to a thousand.

Stunned, she could only stand and watch as Percy declared, 'Two thousand pounds. I have two thousand. Any advance . . .'

Philippa's hand went up.

'Two five.'

The white-haired man raised his paddle.

'Three.'

Back to Philippa.

'Three five.'

To the white-haired man.

'Four.' Then, 'Four five. Five. Five five. Six.'

When the bidding reached ten thousand Lucy was at Sarah's side, and both were feeling the need to sit down. By the time it got to forty, word had spread to the office, bringing the rest of the team, minus cashiers, into the barn.

'Forty-five thousand,' Percy announced. 'Do I have fifty?'

The white-haired man nodded again.

Percy looked up at Philippa, and after a beat her entire body seemed to slump as her client apparently decided to withdraw from the race.

Percy's hammer hit the desk. 'Sold for fifty thousand pounds,' he declared with an astonished grin.

There was a moment's stupefied silence before the spectators broke into a bewildered round of applause.

'What the hell was in that box?' Michael

murmured to Lucy, as the white-haired man smiled in their direction on his way out.

'You'll have to ask Sarah,' she replied, laughing at the blank amazement on Sarah's face. Then, catching a glimpse of Philippa fanning herself on the mezzanine, she sprinted up the stairs to make sure she was all right.

'What a trip,' Philippa chuckled as Lucy reached her. 'It's better than drugs.'

With a choke of laughter, Lucy said, 'And there was me thinking you were about to faint.'

'I think we all are. Did that really just happen? Fifty thousand pounds for a box of junk?'

'Come on, I think we should go over to the office to find out which part of it our chap with the white hair clearly didn't think was junk.'

'But I'm still on duty,' Philippa reminded her, 'and Percy's off again. I'll catch up with you at the end of the day.'

'No, no, the others can carry on without you now – unless you've got more phone calls.'

'No, that was my last one, and boy, what a finish!'

Arriving in the office moments later they found Sarah and Simon, both still in a state of shock, along with the rest of the team crowding around the white-haired man, whose name turned out to be Lionel Everett. He was an antiques dealer, he was telling them, specialising in oriental chess pieces.

'And this rather ordinary-looking chap,' he declared, plucking it from the box and holding it between his finger and thumb, 'is from an extremely rare sixteenth-century Tibetan set.'

Sarah's eyes were still round with disbelief.

'Awesome,' Hanna murmured.

'How do you know?' Simon asked, peering closely

at what to him looked like a lump of chipped wood that might, with some imagination, resemble a rook.

Lionel Everett smiled. 'It's my business to know,' he replied, 'and lucky for you there was more than one of us who spotted it, otherwise I might have picked this little fellow up for twenty quid.'

'Where did it come from?' Sarah asked Simon.

'You're the one who found it,' he reminded her. 'Can you remember where?'

She shook her head. 'How did you know it was here?' she asked Lionel.

'I didn't until I came for the viewing on Tuesday – and even that was pure chance, because I was on my way back to Lincoln after staying with my brother in Somerset when I saw one of your roadside signs. I wasn't in a hurry so I thought I'd drop in for a browse, and I can tell you it was an exciting moment when I realised what you had here. Of course, I hadn't anticipated someone else identifying it too.'

Hearing John chuckle, Sarah said, 'I'm sure this question isn't allowed, but I'm going to ask anyway, how much is the piece actually worth?'

Lionel's eyebrows performed an amusing little dance. 'Like anything, as much as someone's willing to pay for it. In my collector's case he'd instructed me to go considerably higher if I had to, so in his eyes he's probably just got himself a bargain.'

Sarah almost whimpered as she rocked back on her heels, and Lucy gently propped her up again.

Lionel glanced at his watch. 'Now, I think we should probably sort out a method of payment as I really do need to be on my way.'

'Absolutely,' Lucy agreed, starting towards the cashiers.

'But until the payment goes through,' Michael put in, 'perhaps the little fellow should stay with us?'

Surprised, then realising she should have thought of it herself, Lucy turned back to Lionel.

'I have no problem with that,' he told her. 'As soon as the funds have cleared I'll send one of my people to pick it up.'

By the time details had been taken and the chess piece was in the safe, the auction across the way was drawing to a close and the heavens were opening up again.

'Did that really just happen?' Sarah said to Lucy, as they returned to the barn to see the last punters out.

Still recovering herself, Lucy said, 'Unless we're in the same dream, I think it did.'

'But once I've paid the commission and VAT I'm going to have . . . Let me see . . . Well, somewhere in the region of forty thousand quid. Yay! Where's the champagne?'

With a splutter of laughter Lucy said, 'Very good question.'

'Count me in,' Hanna cried, bouncing up behind them. 'Mum, that was so amazing, wasn't it? I've already texted Ben and Dad. They're going to be so like, no way.'

'What about Granny and Grandpa? Did you text them too?'

'No, but I'll do it now.'

'Send them my love and tell them they should have been here,' Lucy instructed. 'And now,' she added to Sarah, 'what were you saying about champagne?'

'Do you know what's bothering me?' Simon asked, as much later that night he and Sarah strolled home from the pub where the team, plus half the village, had been celebrating the success of the auction.

Stifling a yawn, Sarah said, 'No, but I'm sure you're going to tell me.'

'Well, that chess piece was a pretty amazing turn-up, wouldn't you say? With a value of fifty grand or more, just lying there in a box of junk that we never knew anything about . . .'

'Makes you wonder where the other pieces might be,' she twinkled mischievously. 'Mum says we should start searching the attic.'

'Did she have any idea where it might have come from?'

'No. The only chess set she can remember is the one you and Dad used to play with . . .'

'Which I have now,' he finished. 'Anyway, what do you reckon the chances are of a specialised dealer dropping in out of nowhere like that to discover the piece? Correction, two dealers if we presume that's who Philippa was bidding for.'

Sarah frowned. 'What do you mean, presume? You surely don't think she was bidding herself?'

'It could have been a collector, but to be honest I'm not really sure what I think, except I'm not a great believer in coincidence and for something like this to happen on the first sale . . .' He broke off, still not quite sure what he was getting at.

'Come on, I'm sure you've got at least one theory cooking in that overactive brain of yours,' Sarah challenged as they crossed the green.

'Not a theory, exactly, but I do keep coming back to the fact that Philippa was the one on the phone. OK, I know it doesn't make any sense, but tell me this, where was she tonight? Why weren't she and her brother celebrating with the rest of us?'

Hardly able to imagine where this was going, Sarah said, 'She was exhausted after all the excitement, so John took her home. Honest to God, Simon, why can't you just accept that something fantastic happened this afternoon, without trying to find some sinister side to it?'

'I didn't say it was sinister, I'm just saying it strikes me as odd that a complete stranger turned up out of nowhere to pay a fortune for a single chess piece that we didn't even know we owned.'

'And because Pippa was acting for the other bidder – whose details will be registered, let me remind you, so we can easily find out who it was . . .'

'Then maybe we should.'

'No, maybe what *you* should do is come clean about the fact that you're dying to discredit the Mckenzies in some way, shape or form, though God only knows how you think you're going to do it with this.'

Simon's jaw tightened. 'I don't get why you always defend him,' he stated irritably. 'You're all taking him at face value, treating him like he's the answer to everything, when you don't actually know anything about him, apart from the fact that he's claiming to be an *old friend* of Mum's.'

Going into the house ahead of him, she said, 'I don't know what you want me to say. I like him, he's been great to me and Lucy . . .'

'I know all that, but *why*? That's what I want to know. What's in it for him when he's supposed to be rich enough not to need the money?'

'Not everything has to be about money, but if you're so interested why don't you ask him? No, no,' she cried when he started to answer, 'I don't want to discuss it any more, because you're becoming irrational and I'm way too tired to try figuring you out. So, moving on, what I want to know is why Michael left so early this evening.'

Reaching for two glasses from an overhead cupboard, he said, 'He had a call from Carlotta earlier. Apparently she's cut short her holiday in Greece so he wanted to go and try to get to the bottom of why.'

Sarah looked concerned. 'I hope everything's all right with the boys.'

'I'm sure it is, but you know what she's like, never one to miss an opportunity to make a crisis out of a drama.'

Remembering that only too well, Sarah stifled a yawn as she said, 'Well, it's been a hectic few days and tomorrow's not going to be any easier, so I have to get to my bed or I shall fall asleep standing up.'

Passing her a glass of water, he said, 'I'll make sure everything's locked up, then I'll be right behind you.'

Sarah had got as far as the door before a niggly little suspicion that had been hanging around for the past few days staged an unexpected comeback. 'Tell me,' she said, turning back. 'Am I misreading things or are you starting to develop a bit of a fondness for Lucy?'

Losing a yawn to a laugh, he said, 'Well, I admit I didn't see that one coming. What makes you say that?'

She shrugged. 'I'm not sure really. Am I right?'

Narrowing his eyes menacingly, he said, 'In case you'd forgotten, I already have someone in my life.'

'Who you're mad about, I know, it's just that you and Lucy seem . . . Well, quite suited, actually.'

Going to put his hands on her shoulders, he gazed affectionately into her eyes as he said, 'What interests me far more than your befuddled imagination is when you're going to start thinking about your own love life, because it's time, you know.'

Feeling her heart contract, she said, 'Even if that's true, and I'm not saying it is, the right man doesn't just turn up because you want him to – and even if he does, who's to say he's the right one anyway? I thought that once, and look how wrong I turned out to be.'

'OK, but if I said Jean-Marc's been asking about you . . .'

'Don't, Simon, please. There's no way I'm going back to Paris . . .'

'He could come here. As an artist he can work anywhere, and you know he's always been mad about you.'

'And I adore him too, but please, don't let's have this conversation. I'm happy doing what I'm doing for now, and the last thing I need is something or someone coming along who might disrupt or complicate things.'

'Joe? What time is it?' Lucy mumbled into her mobile phone.

'You don't need to know,' he answered softly. 'I just got Hanna's text about the chess piece and I wanted to say well done.'

Flapping a hand round for the light and finding it, Lucy squinted at the time. 'For heaven's sake, it's gone two o'clock!' she protested. 'Couldn't you have waited till morning?'

'I guess I could, but I felt pretty excited when I read the message . . . Fifty grand!' He gave an admiring whistle. 'Ay-mazing, as one of our children would say. How much of it do you get to keep?'

Wishing she'd brought some water to bed, she said, 'I don't know. Where have you been all evening?'

'There was a match on at the club so I had to turn off my phone, then a few of us went for a couple of jars after and I forgot to put it on again.'

Taking a moment to register that, she said, 'So where are you now?'

'At Charlie's, but wishing I was there. It's OK to come at the weekend, I take it? Hanna's dead keen for me to, and I've got to see this chess piece. You still have it, do you?'

'Only until the funds clear and someone comes to collect it.'

'So who is he?'

'A dealer. Joe, I really need to get some sleep.'

'Sure, sure. I just wanted to congratulate you, that's all. And Sarah, obviously.'

'Thanks. Now, if you don't mind . . .'

'It's OK, I'm gone. Love you, Mrs Winters, sweet dreams.'

After dropping the phone back on the nightstand and turning out the light, Lucy lay with her eyes closed wishing he hadn't called her that, since the proprietary attitude was grating. Even more annoying was the fact that he'd woken her, particularly when she didn't want to start connecting with her earlier misgivings at this hour of the night. It wasn't that she didn't believe in fate, or coincidence, or whatever anyone wanted to call it, nor was she at all inclined to believe in one of the cashier's rubbish about rooks being bad luck, but at some point during the evening a peculiar feeling had come over her that something wasn't quite right about the sale of the chess piece. She couldn't be sure exactly what was unsettling her, whether it was the timing, or the white-haired man, or the piece itself, she only knew that something about it wasn't feeling right.

Having already checked who Philippa had been bidding for, she knew that it was a dealer in Southampton who, when Googled, appeared perfectly genuine. As did Mr Lionel Everett of Lincolnshire. So why were her instincts so uneasy about it all? Or perhaps uneasy wasn't the right word, she might have meant intrigued, because she wasn't sensing anything underhand, or criminal, exactly, more something . . . Well, it had to be said . . . Something benevolent to get her off to a flying start, and if she was right about that then there were only two people in the world who'd want to do something so crazily generous, and who'd also have the money to do it.

So was that why her parents had been keeping such a low profile all week, trying to be careful not to appear too interested in the auction, while actually managing to appear not interested enough?

It was certainly one explanation, and was in fact the only one she could come up with, so rather than keep going over and over her suspicions she tried to push them from her mind and think of something else. It wasn't easy when Maureen's unexpected visit came swooping in from the wings, worrying her all over again. Had the woman been bested by the withdrawal of the painting, or had she managed to put one over on them with the engravings? Plus there were the concerns Lucy now had over how to deal with the trade and local press, who'd already been in touch about the sale of the chess piece. Since Lionel Everett had requested anonymity for his collector, adding an air of mystery to the story, it could mean some great publicity was heading their way. Which would be extremely welcome, if only this damned ring business would go away.

Probably because of the hour, and because she'd drunk too much wine, her thoughts soon became entangled in a bizarrely bad dream where Joe was trying to steal the chess piece, with Michael and Simon helping him, and Sarah shouting across a wide divide. Except it wasn't Sarah, it was her mother with her arms out begging her to come, but no matter how hard she tried she couldn't move.

By the time she woke up in the morning she felt more tired than she had before going to sleep. However, when her mobile rang and she saw it was Ben, her tensions quickly melted away as she clicked on the line to hear his voice for the first time in almost a week.

'Mum, you'll never guess what,' Hanna cried, bursting into the office with a look of outrage on her face and a stack of three box files in her arms. 'They're only talking about cancelling the fete if this rain keeps up. They can't do that, can they? We've been practising our catwalk stuff for ages, and it would be really mean if they end up saying we can't do it.'

'I think it's only the outdoor events that are under threat,' Lucy told her, barely glancing up from her computer screen. Now wasn't the time to tell Hanna that flood warnings were being issued on radio and TV. In truth, she was barely taking it in herself. 'You can do your show in the village hall,' she thought to add.

Hanna was still looking mutinous. 'Yeah well, we'd better, is all I can say. Anyway, where do you want these?'

'What are they?'

'No idea. One of the cleaners piled them on to me to bring over. She found them at the back of a shelf, she said, and they don't have a lot number so she didn't know what to do with them.'

Glancing around for an available space, Lucy was startled to see how cramped they'd become in only the last half an hour, with lots constantly being carted over from the barn ready to be packed up and shipped to their new addresses. The temporary team was back again this morning, printing out labels, stacking parcels and entering details into the computers, while Jessica and her assistant were at the cashier stations, preparing to hand over to the accountant when he came in later.

'OK, put them on the floor next to Sarah's desk,' she said. 'I'll take a look when I have a minute.' She was on the point of returning to her emails when a sudden surge of euphoria made her eyes start to shine. 'The figures are looking really good,' she confided in a whisper as Hanna plonked the boxes down. 'The turnover's massive, mainly thanks to the chess piece, but we didn't do badly with everything else.'

'That's brilliant,' Hanna whispered back. 'So is it looking like we really will be able to go and have a holiday with Ben, like Dad said?'

Lucy frowned. 'When did Dad say that?' she asked, instantly irked by the way Joe seemed to be viewing Cromstone's profits as hers – or even his.

Not that she didn't want to see Ben, she'd have liked that more than anything, but apart from still not being able to afford it, there was simply no way she could take any time off in the foreseeable future.

'This morning when he rang,' Hanna answered, taking out her mobile to see who was texting her. 'He's so chuffed about how well you've done. You should have heard him. He reckons we could probably all fly first class . . .'

'Hang on, hang on,' Lucy interrupted. 'To begin with . . .'

'Lucy!' Jessica called from her cashier point. 'That was the bank on the line, the funds have cleared.'

Lucy's heart tripped with excitement. 'You mean for the chess piece?'

'Absolutely. It's all there in the company account.'

As everyone cheered and clapped, Hanna cried, 'Yay! We're rich, we're rich! I have to text Ben to let him know we're coming.'

'No!' Lucy said sharply. 'Most of that money's Sarah's, and whatever we've made isn't for us to spend . . .'

'Oh Mu-um! Lighten up, will you? We *never* go on holiday, and it would be so cool to see Ben, wouldn't it?'

Becoming more irritable by the second, Lucy said, 'I can't talk about this now. I'm up to my eyes sorting out where everything has to go, and if you'd care to help you could always . . .'

'Sorry, got a rehearsal,' Hanna interrupted, already backing away. 'And you still haven't paid me yet for all the work I did during the auction.'

'If you need anything now take ten pounds from my purse, if you can find it.'

Moments after Hanna had dashed off into the

teeming rain Sarah came bundling in through the door, with rivers running from her umbrella and down over her mac. 'Thank God we're at the top of the hill,' she declared, poking her brolly into a stand and kicking off her wellies, 'you should see the way it's gushing down the high street. Someone said they might start evacuating the estate at the bottom if it keeps up any . . . Oh blimey, what's this?' she grunted, tripping over the boxes Hanna had dumped next to her desk.

'Sorry, sorry,' Lucy apologised. 'My fault. We're running out of space . . . I've no idea what's in them. If you could take a look we can decide what to do with them.'

Stooping to pick up the papers that had spilled from the top box, Sarah's eyebrows rose. 'Well, I do believe we've located the boxes your mother was looking for,' she said, holding up Daphne and Brian's birth certificates.

'Mm?' Lucy said distractedly. Then, registering, she looked up at Sarah. So her parents *had* come back for family papers. With a laugh of profound relief, she said, 'Put them by the door, I'll take them into the house when I go.'

'Why don't I pop them over now to make some room?' Sarah offered. 'Fancy a coffee while I'm there?'

'Yes please,' a chorus sang out from around the office.

Grinning, Lucy said, 'That'll make ten if you include the guys in the barn.'

'I always knew I'd missed my vocation,' Sarah quipped, and stuffing her feet back into the wellies and covering the boxes with a bin bag, she drew her brolly like a sword and surged back into the driving stair rods.

By the time she came back Michael had arrived with a selection of buns and cakes he'd picked up on the way through, making himself doubly welcome.

'The funds for the chess piece have cleared,' Lucy declared, throwing him a towel.

'Great news,' he replied, rubbing his hair while the others started to delve into his bakery boxes. 'Where's the piece now?'

'Still in the safe. I had an email from Mr Everett just now, letting me know that he's arranging for it to be couriered to him in Lincoln.' After checking that the others had returned to their desks, she kept her voice low as she said, 'I know we don't have any reason to be suspicious, but I still can't help thinking there's something we're not seeing . . .'

'Honestly, you're as bad as Simon,' Sarah broke in. 'He was even online researching antiquated chess pieces when I left this morning. Have you seen him yet today?' she asked Michael.

'I just called in.' He grinned. 'And I'm very sorry to tell you, ladies, but it looks as though the morris dancing's off tomorrow – not only because of the weather, but Teddy Best and his brother, who's also in the troupe, have had to zoom up to Cheshire where their ageing father's had a fall.'

Sarah's eyes narrowed. 'You didn't go up there and give him a push, did you?' she asked.

Laughing, he said, 'It's true we were prepared to go to many lengths, but I can't own up to that one. Anyway, we're not off the hook yet, because they're insisting we join them for the mop next month.'

Sarah gave a cheer. 'Perfect. Full-on public humiliation, because they come from all over for the mops. Mops are fairs,' she told Lucy, 'but of course you already know that. The great thing about the ones at Chipping Sodbury is that they're seriously huge.'

As Lucy and Michael exchanged glances, Sarah delved into one of the goody boxes and pounced on a flapjack. 'Diet starts next week,' she declared, biting into it.

'Like you need to,' Lucy commented, selecting a custard tart for herself.

'Oh, Michael,' Sarah said, swallowing quickly, 'Simon mentioned you had a call last night . . . Is everything OK with the boys?'

'They're great,' he assured her. 'Back in Italy earlier than expected, because I'm afraid their mother managed to fall out with her hosts. This is good news for me, as I stand a much better chance now of getting them here for the last week of the holidays.' He glanced at his watch. 'Anyway, I'm afraid I can't stay. I just dropped in to let you know that the letters to Eric Beadle's solicitor and others have all gone out now. My secretary will email copies later today. Basically, we're pointing out that Cromstone Auctions merely acts as a clearing house for objects people wish to dispose of, and though you do your best to facilitate valuations et cetera, your terms and conditions state very clearly that you cannot be held responsible for what happens to the object after it has left you.'

'Good for you!' Sarah applauded.

'Do you think that'll make them go away?' Lucy asked cautiously.

'It might, since it'll be a costly business to pursue things much further.'

'It has to go away,' Sarah insisted. 'I mean I'm sorry for those who've missed out on the true value of whatever they gave us, but they have to take some of the responsibility themselves – and after we've got off to such a great start, there would be no justice in the world if it all fell apart now.'

'Hear, hear,' Michael agreed, glancing at his watch. 'Now, I'm off. If there are any deliveries for my neck of the woods that are ready to go I'll be happy to take them.'

'You angel,' Sarah cried, jumping to it. 'John is so rushed off his feet it's a miracle he's still standing, and the removal company we use is just as snowed under. Come on, umbrellas at the ready, let's go and load you up.'

'Before you disappear,' Lucy said to Michael, 'if you're actually looking for a part-time job . . .'

Treating her to a playful wink he launched off into the rain with Sarah, leaving Lucy feeling ludicrous and embarrassed for having made such a stupid remark, simply because he'd dropped in a couple of times during the auction. Of course he wasn't looking for a part-time job, and she couldn't think now what had made her say that. Was it an attempt to be witty? If so, she should give it up, because it had just made her look foolish. Luckily she was too busy to dwell on it now, or she might have gone on cringing for the rest of the morning. As it was, she put him firmly out of her mind and returned to the mountain of work that needed to be conquered before the focused search, collection, registering and display of lots for the next auction came snowballing their way at the start of next week.

It was past seven o'clock that evening by the time Lucy ran through the torrential rain back to the farmhouse, her head still spinning with all they'd achieved and all that remained to be done. Having had enough of the office since the others had left a couple of hours ago, she was carrying a stack of work to go over in the comfort of the sitting room once she'd eaten and found out where Hanna was.

'I'm where I said in my text,' Hanna told her when she answered her mobile.

'And that would be?'

'At Juliette's, and I'm staying the night so we can go to Pippa's early in the morning to do some Wii Fit before we get ready for our fashion show.'

'Oh, so it's still happening.'

'If you'd read my text you'd know it's in the village hall and we're on at twelve, so don't be late. I also texted to say that Juliette's mum is taking us for a Chinese, so if you want to come we're leaving in about five minutes.'

Having already turned down Sarah and Simon's offer of dinner with some old friends of theirs at a pub near Stroud, Lucy said, 'There's still a lot to do here, so you go ahead and have a good time. Have you heard from Dad?'

'Ye-es, and I expect you have too if you check your phone. His train gets in about eleven tomorrow, he said, so he probably wants you to pick him up. That means he'll be here in time for the fashion show, which is brill. Anyway, have to go, Juliette's mum's already gone to get the car.'

'Hang on, hang on, any texts from Granny or Ben?'

'One from Ben and none from Granny – and don't worry, I haven't said anything to Ben about holidays. He's told you about his girlfriend, has he?'

With a strange feeling of nervousness, Lucy said, 'No, which girlfriend?'

'I forget her name, but he'll tell you. Right, I'm gone, see you tomorrow.'

'Love you,' Lucy said, but she was already talking to air.

After clicking off she pressed in her own mobile number, and hearing a muffled ringing not too far away she finally tracked the phone down to behind the boxes Sarah had brought over earlier in the day. Remembering what was in them, she tapped in a quick message to her mother letting her know that they'd been found. *Will bring with me on Sunday* she finished. *Coming there because seems only way I can get to speak to you. Love to you and Dad, must check our chess sets in case we have some hidden treasures! Xxxx*

After wolfing down some cheese on toast, while deliberately not thinking about Ben's new girlfriend, whoever she might be – Thai stripper; Vietnamese drug dealer; Russian trafficker – she carried her mother's boxes through to the sitting room and slumped down on one of the comfy sofas, intending to watch the news before getting started on yet more work. However, the cushions were so snug and she was so tired that it wasn't long before the rhythmic thunder of rain on the windows and feisty gusts flurrying down the chimney lulled her into a deep and dreamless sleep.

It was the clatter of something blowing over in the courtyard that woke her half an hour later, but she was too tired to be bothered to move. There was nothing breakable out there that she could recall, and if anything was damaged she'd rather pay for the repair than venture outside on such a dreadful night.

Yawning and stretching, she looked around for the remote control, and saw to her dismay that she'd have to get up to reach it. Her mother's boxes, however, were close enough to reach from where she was, so pulling them towards her she flipped open the lid of the top one and prepared herself for an amusing little trip down memory lane.

The first papers she pulled out were her parents' passports and birth certificates, which was only surprising in that they were so close to the top, when as far as she was aware they hadn't travelled out of the country for at least two years. However, they'd probably needed them when signing the house and business over to her, so setting them aside she fished in again and came up with a slim brown envelope. It was sealed closed and had a Cromstone Auctions stamp over the seal with the date handwritten across it. On the front were the words *Last Will and Testament (Original with Michael Givens).*

Finding such efficiency typical of her mother, she gave an affectionate roll of her eyes and laid the envelope on top of the passports. Next out of the box was a carefully dated and ordered pile of old cheque books and bank statements, followed by back copies of utility and telephone bills for the past year. Reaching in again she pulled out a large, battered envelope whose contents, once she realised what they were, made her smile with some very mixed emotions. She was looking at her old school reports and not a single term was missing, by the look of it, from the date she'd started infants, till the abrupt end to her studies during sixth form. There were even some of her old exercise books, bound by a pink elastic band, and tucked inside coloured files of their own were all the birthday and Christmas cards she'd made for her parents over the years. Then she found her junior swimmer badge in the same envelope as a gymnastics diploma, a show-jumping certificate, the pattern for a tea cosy she'd tried to knit, aged about eight, and several spectacularly untalented paintings she'd brought home at various times, some of which she could even remember being magnetised to the fridge. Whether the fridge had been in Hull or Coventry, Chichester or Norwich she had no idea now, she only knew that for two decades or more, possibly even until they'd moved here, her parents had always had the same one. This was something else they'd kept because she hadn't been able to stand the thought of letting it go in case it felt unwanted.

Starting to enjoy herself now, she decided to have a poke around in the next box and found a small bundle of letters, all addressed to her, from a long-forgotten pen pal in Durham. There was also a scrapbook she'd filled with pressed flowers, tickets to the zoo, a couple of flattened butterflies and several photographs of children she'd never known. Remembering how she used to cut those photographs out of newspapers and magazines, pretending they were her friends, or brothers and sisters, she felt her heart reach out to the lonely little girl who'd put it all together. Thank goodness she'd had two children, and that she and Joe had always lived in the same place – until now, of course, but this was Hanna's first disruption, and in spite of all her early resistance she seemed to be enjoying Cromstone well enough.

Going back to the box she pulled out a small blue book with *Secrets* embossed in gold on the front, and in a childish scrawl inside the cover was written: *This book belongs to Lucy Fisher, if you read it a spell will be put on you and you will turn into a frog forever and ever (kisses won't work).* Turning over the pages she started to read some of the entries she'd made: *I wish I could have a kitten; I poked my tongue out at a teacher today, but she didn't see; I hate Ruth Medlock, she smells and is always mean to me; I wish we had a great big house, like a castle, full of servants and children and no grownups. I want to be a popstar. I'm a better singer than Jacky March. When I leave school I'm going to own an orphanage. I had a dream about the lady who shouts at me again last night, but I don't know what she's saying, I think she's frightened and it frightens me. I think I'm really a princess and one day prince charming will come and find me.* Thinking of Joe, and how perfectly he'd seemed to fit that bill when she was seventeen, made her sigh and laugh and wonder where on earth their relationship might be heading now.

For a while, as she continued to browse through more letters and cards, prized home-made jewellery and virtually empty address books, all belonging to her, she could almost hear her own voice, and others, echoing down the years. There were the children who used to call her fishface because of her name, and other unpleasant jeers meant to hurt, which they had. Then the gentle sound of her mother singing her to sleep after she'd had a bad dream; and her father doing his best to make the move to another new home sound exciting. She smiled wistfully at her squeals of joy when she'd finally got a kitten; but then came the inconsolable grief when it went out one day and never came back. How long had they searched the neighbourhood for that dear little creature, going through everyone's gardens, sheds, dustbins? Her father had put notices on lamp posts offering a reward for its return, and if her memory was serving her correctly she'd even made him report it to the police. She'd never asked for a pet again after that, she was too afraid that it would go out and never come back.

Suspecting the last box contained similar memorabilia, though hopefully a little jollier, she hauled it towards her and found, to her surprise, that it was taped shut. It was also, she realised, quite a new box, though that didn't make it any different from the others, since they were in fairly good nick too, suggesting that her mother had probably quite recently transferred everything from its original containers because the old ones had worn thin. Making a note to seal them all when she'd finished, Lucy peeled off the tape feeling quite certain that she was about to come across her parents' own childhood memories, and possibly some handwritten versions of the stories her mother used to make up when she was small based around her toys, or curious objects they'd picked up from parks and beaches and all kinds of market stalls along the way.

The first thing she came across was her parents' wedding album, which she hadn't seen in years. The pages were yellowing now, and the leaves of tissue between each one were brittle and seemed like they might disintegrate at a touch. The photographs were still in place, however, held firm by little corner pouches with a neatly printed inscription beneath giving the names of the guests. To Lucy's amusement her mother had even written *Daphne and Brian* under the pictures of the bride and groom. Then there was Brian's mother – racy Granny – who everyone said Lucy resembled, and his father, George, who used to make rocking horses but alas, he'd died before he could carve one for his only

367

grandchild. The other guests were people Lucy had no recollection of ever meeting, but if the way they seemed to be enjoying themselves was anything to go by, they'd been good friends of her parents at one time. She wondered what had happened to them all, and if her parents were ever in touch with any of them now.

Underneath the album she found a long white envelope with two newspaper cuttings tucked inside. Expecting them to be wedding or birth announcements, it came as a surprise to see that the first one was a news story. Then, as the reality of what she was reading started to sink in, she felt her interest folding into bewilderment which soon gave way to a complete failure to understand.

The headline read: *Baby Dies in House Fire*.

Eighteen-month-old Lucy Fisher tragically lost her life in the fire that swept through the family home in the early hours of Saturday morning. Firemen rushed to the scene, but by the time they arrived thick smoke and flames made it impossible for them to enter the house. Lucy's parents, Brian and Daphne Fisher, managed to escape the inferno, but Mr Fisher was treated in hospital for third-degree burns to his upper body and hands after trying to get back inside to save his baby daughter.

Lucy's throat was turning dry. That was what her father had done, she knew that, so why was this report saying she'd died when she hadn't?

Reading on, she felt her tension increasing. *Lucy was the Fishers' only child and, according to neighbours, was 'the centre of their world'. Felicity Norman, who lives next door and who had to evacuate her home during the fire, said, 'Daphne and Brian had to wait a long time before Lucy came along. It would be hard to imagine a child who was more wanted, or parents who felt more blessed. It breaks my heart to think of what they must be going through now.'*

Experts from British Gas are at the scene. Police have ruled out any suspicion of foul play.

Feeling as though the world was tilting out of kilter, Lucy tried to take a breath and found she couldn't. Why was this saying she'd died in the fire, when everyone knew her father had rescued her? Then, realising the other cutting must be correcting the mistake, she tried to find it. It was in her hand a moment ago . . . Spotting it on the cushion beside her, she picked it up and turned it over, and as she read she started to turn cold to the core:

FISHER Lucy, a little angel who God has taken to be at his side, but you will always be in our hearts. Sleep peacefully my darling, all our love Mummy and Daddy.

FISHER Lucy, you were with us such a short time, but you lit up our world. It has gone dark again now, but we hold our memories like candles. God bless you and keep you safe till I join you, love Granny.

Feeling a blinding confusion descending over her, Lucy picked up the box, certain there must be more inside to explain the mistake, but there was nothing else there.

Chapter Nineteen

It was approaching midnight by now, and the rain was coming down so hard it might have been trying to break the roof. Nevertheless, Lucy had the top half of the kitchen door open, because after leaving a message for her mother she'd needed the air.

'Mum, I've seen the cutting about the fire,' she'd said into the voicemail, 'and the . . . the announcements . . . I don't understand. I need you to explain. Please call me.'

Though she wasn't expecting to hear tonight, when the sound of footsteps reached her, running down the drive, she thought for one disorienting moment that her parents had come.

It turned out to be John.

'Lucy!' he cried breathlessly as he appeared in the doorway, dripping from every inch of his waterproofs. 'Thank goodness you're up. Are you OK?'

'Yes, I'm fine,' she replied. What else could she say? Then, registering the hour and his sense of urgency, she rose quickly to unlatch the bottom door. 'What's happened? Is it Pippa?'

'No, no, she's fine,' he assured her, stamping his feet on the mat. 'They're evacuating everyone from below the pub, because of the floods. That means us,

370

and I was hoping you'd let Pippa and Rozzie stay here for the night. They're . . .'

'Yes, yes, of course. Where are they?'

'Outside in the car. We didn't want to seem presumptuous. I'll bring them in, then I must go to find out what needs to be done down on the estate. Will you be able to put anyone else up? The police are knocking on doors . . .'

'Just bring whoever needs shelter,' Lucy told him. 'We have five bedrooms here. I'll start making up the extra beds.' Grabbing her mobile as it rang, she saw it was Hanna and quickly clicked on. 'Darling, are you all right? Where are you?'

'At the pub,' Hanna cried. 'It's really scary. Everyone's pushing in through the doors and the police are trying to make them go back. I want to come home, Mum . . .'

'Of course, but don't go out on your own. I'll come and get you.'

'Hanna?' John said as Lucy rang off. 'Where is she?'

'At the pub.'

'OK, I'll fetch her. You stay here with Pippa and brace yourself for the influx.'

'Have you contacted Sarah?' Lucy asked quickly as he started to leave. 'She'll take people in . . .'

'She's already on it. Simon's with the others down in the valley, helping to bring out the children and old folk,' and dashing back through the rain he stopped at his car to tell Philippa to go inside, before running on down the hill to the centre of operations at the pub.

Within an hour the farmhouse kitchen was as crowded as a happy hour cocktail bar, and with much the same atmosphere, as everyone's adrenalin raced. It was like the war, someone shouted who wasn't old enough to have known, and though the bedrooms, sofas and even floors were ready to accommodate them all, no one was showing any signs yet of wanting to head in that direction. So Philippa and Hanna began handing out hot drinks, while Lucy and a couple of the women made sandwiches and toast.

As the chatter and laughter buzzed around her Lucy had no time to think of her own issues, and could only feel glad of it. All that mattered for the moment was that Hanna was safe, and that they did their best to make their neighbours feel that way too. She found herself noticing the prized possessions they'd brought with them, one little boy's brand-new bike that had cost 'a bloody fortune', his mother announced to anyone who was listening, so no way were they leaving it behind. The local computer expert had predictably brought his laptop and a box full of software, while Annie, the hairdresser, had stuffed a large pink vanity case with the tools of her trade. She was even offering free dos if anyone wanted one, with her daughter, Marietta, saying she'd do the shampoos, though Lucy hadn't noticed any takers yet. Most in evidence were bags, boxes, even suitcases full of photograph albums, a few of which were causing shrieks of hilarity as their owners browsed them for the first time in years. Lucy had once read somewhere that it was always the albums people rushed for first at times like this, and with a wrenching feeling inside she thought of the photographs her parents had lost to the fire.

What had really happened back then? How was she supposed to make any sense out of what she'd read?

Feeling her head starting to ache with confusion, she turned to find out who was tugging her shirt and discovered two adorable but worried brown eyes gazing up at her. 'Hello,' she said softly, stooping to the little boy's level, 'are you all right?'

'I want my dog,' he said brokenly, as Rozzie tried to push her nose into his hand. 'He's at our house. Can you get him please?'

'Oh dear,' Lucy murmured. 'Where's your mummy?'

'Just there, feeding my sister.'

Glancing over to where a very young, rotund woman was holding a small baby to her breast as she gossiped and laughed raucously with the others, Lucy said, 'And what about your daddy? Do you know where he is?'

The little boy shook his head.

Wanting to hug him, Lucy said, 'OK, I'll tell you what we'll do. We'll call one of my friends who's down by your house and ask him to go in and get your dog. Is that a good idea?'

The little boy nodded solemnly, then swung round as his mother shouted, 'Jase! Jase, look who's here!' His face lit up as a bedraggled but clearly ecstatic black and white mutt came bounding towards him.

'Aha, so that's who the little fellow belongs to,' John laughed, as the boy flung his arms round the dog and Rozzie tried to join in. 'You keep hold of him now, son. I'm sure Lucy won't mind if he stays here too.'

Lucy's eyes were dancing as she threw out her hands. Was she really going to say no when the beast, filthy and wet though he was, clearly meant so much to the boy?

It wasn't until she offered John a hot drink that

she realised the room had fallen silent. Baffled, she looked around to find out what was happening, and felt even more bewildered when she realised everyone was looking at John. Then, seeing the discomfort on his face, she was about to ask what was going on when he said in a whisper, 'I take it Pippa's already in bed, so I'll go back to the house,' and before she could insist that he stay he was gone.

Moments later the party-like atmosphere was back in full swing, leaving Lucy and Hanna to look at one another in blank confusion.

'No idea,' Lucy murmured, before Hanna could ask. 'We'll try to get to the bottom of it in the morning. Right now, we ought to start encouraging them to go to bed.'

By the time the diehards finally settled down for the night dawn was already starting to break on the horizon, and Lucy was light-headed with tiredness. Since Hanna had offered her room to Annie and Marietta, she was cosily snuggled up in Lucy's bed by the time Lucy slipped in next to her. After brushing a stray strand of hair from her flushed young cheek Lucy lay gazing at her, loving her with all her heart as she thought of the cuttings again and wondered what on earth they could mean.

The message was waiting on the answering machine when John returned from the evacuation. Given the lateness of the hour and the awful incident on the estate that Simon had witnessed, he almost ignored it, thinking that whoever it was it could wait till morning. Then, concerned in case it was Pippa, or perhaps Lucy to ask him to explain what had happened when he'd walked into her kitchen, he hit the replay button.

When the message started to play it was as though the world he was standing in started to slip slowly away.

He soon lost count of how many times he listened to it, losing himself in the smoky smoothness of her voice, and remembering, as though it were yesterday, how much they had meant to one another.

'John, it's Rose,' she said softly. 'You were always a night owl so I was . . . I was hoping to catch you.' She took a breath and he could picture her so clearly, the translucent glow of her skin, the mesmerising lavender-blue eyes. 'I've thought so often,' she continued, 'of what our first words might be if we were to . . . If something happened and we were able to see one another again. I was always afraid the time wouldn't come, but then I felt sure it would.' Another pause and he imagined her putting a hand to her mouth, the way she always did when something overcame her. 'Sarah told me about Pippa,' she said shakily. 'I'm so sorry, John. I know how close you two are, it must be very difficult for you.' He heard a tremor in her breath as she hesitated again. 'I guess I'm rambling now. I'd hoped to speak to you, but you're not there so I shall call again.'

As the machine clicked off he sat gazing at his memories as though they were playing out in front of him, while the resonance of her voice continued to steal all the way through him. It was like an elixir, making him feel young and strong again. He found himself smiling past the pain as he pictured the man he used to be, crazily in love with the most beautiful woman in the world. How happy they'd been, and devoted, and so certain that nothing would ever tear their perfect little family apart. Then the tragedy and cruelty of it all swept through him with such force that he lost his breath. Hearing her was bringing it all back, the horror, the fear, the sentencing and then the slam of the prison doors.

How could thirty-five years have passed so quickly and yet still feel like an eternity? Was she still his Rose? The tenderness in her voice told him that she was, and the ache of missing her and longing for her was oh so hard to bear.

'Rose,' he whispered, as though she could hear him, and the sound of her name, so sweet and full, was as beautiful to him and as restful as coming home after a very, very long time away. Could he dare to hope that fate would play them a kinder hand this time around and bring them back together before it was too late?

The billowing, windswept landscape of Exmoor was hazed by a lingering drizzle as Daphne drove to what she called her telephone spot in a layby not far from Landacre Bridge. During one of her stops she'd spotted several red deer grazing the brush, but this morning they were nowhere to be seen, only a small bevy of quails pecking about the sodden earth.

After turning off the engine she took out her mobile, knowing already that there were several texts, because she'd heard them chiming into the phone as she was driving. Much as she'd expected they were mostly from Lucy, the first letting her know that the funds for the chess piece had cleared. The next was a little snappy as Lucy demanded to know where the heck she was and why she hadn't called.

Knowing she'd been remiss, Daphne's eyes closed as she struggled with her conscience. Hurting or upsetting Lucy in any way was always very hard for her to bear.

Making herself scroll on to the next message, she read the few simple words and felt the chill of a bitter fate starting to close around her. *Found your boxes, will bring with me on Sunday.* Afraid to go any further she sat staring through the windscreen, her heart thudding wildly like the rain. Lucy had found the boxes . . . If she'd opened them . . .

Swallowing hard she reminded herself that it was just a small envelope, easily overlooked, and Lucy was so busy at the moment . . .

Inhaling deeply, she opened the last text. It was from Hanna, letting her know that half of Cromstone was being evacuated and some of the families from the estate were camping out at the farmhouse. Sensing the thrill Hanna was getting from that, Daphne almost smiled, but her nerves were too tight to allow more than a glimmer.

How desperately she wished there were no voice-mails, but there were, so going through to her messages, she keyed in 1 to play back. Hearing Lucy's tone as she said, 'Mum,' was enough to confirm that the nightmare had begun.

'I've seen the cutting about the fire,' Lucy said, 'and the . . . the announcements . . . I don't under-stand. I need you to explain. Please call me.'

Dropping the phone in her lap, Daphne covered her face with her hands. To say she'd always known this day would come wasn't the truth, because she'd never allowed herself to think it. Instead, she'd given thanks to the Good Lord every day of her life for the comfort He had brought to her anguish at a time when she'd never have believed any comfort could be had. He'd delivered Lucy in His own special way after so much longing and heartbreak, proving that He did exist and that He did care after all. How was she to know that so many years later He would lead her to Cromstone, where He would show her that what He could give He could also take away?

It was a long time later that she turned the car around and started back to the cottage. She barely saw the landscape she was passing, hardly even registered the road. Her mind was no longer here on Exmoor, on this day in this year. It was in another place, a very, very long way away in both distance and time.

On reaching the cottage with its grey stone walls covered in flowery trellises, she went inside to find Brian dozing in his chair next to an empty hearth.

'Ah, there you are,' he said, coming to as she closed the door. 'I thought you'd got lost. How's Lucy? Is everything all right?'

Bringing him the phone, Daphne connected it to voicemail and sat down at the table as he listened.

When his eyes came to hers his confusion fired her frustration, even as it seared through her heart.

'Brian,' she said gently, 'do you understand what the message means?'

He swallowed nervously and nodded.

'Are you sure?'

'Yes, I understand,' he assured her.

Though not convinced, she couldn't have borne to make him spell it out, so choosing to believe him she said, 'Then you know what has to happen now?'

His eyes came to hers again, almost childlike in their bemusement.

'Yes you do,' she insisted softly. 'We've talked about it and we agreed. We have to do it for Lucy.'

'Yes, of course, for Lucy,' he echoed, and his eyes

followed her as she went to take a writing pad and pen from a drawer.

Since everyone at the manor had bedded down much earlier than those at the farmhouse, Sarah had risen with the lark ready to prepare two dozen breakfasts for her impromptu guests. Mercifully, the rain had eased off, so she'd been able to get down to the baker's for bread and over to Hardy's farm for fresh milk and eggs. There still weren't many people about, but the general feeling of those she spoke to was that the lower reaches of Cromstone hadn't faired as badly as some of the other low-lying villages around.

For her guests' sakes, as well as her own, Sarah hoped they'd be able to return home today, since she knew she'd never find the heart to turf them out if they had nowhere else to go, but she really didn't relish the thought of trying to cope with them all once Simon had gone.

Fortunately he wasn't due to leave until tomorrow, so at least she'd have his backup for today – once he managed to drag himself out of bed. She wasn't exactly sure what time he'd come home this morning, but it must have been after three because she was still awake at that time, listening to the rain and planning how she was going to spend her unexpected windfall.

By mid-morning she'd served everyone scrambled eggs and toast, regaled her mother with tales of what had happened during the night, and stripped all the beds ready for the wash. Most of her guests had trudged off down the hill by now to inspect what damage, if any, had been done to their homes. Early reports back were mostly positive, with only a few garden sheds and a couple of fences appearing any the worse for the storm. Nevertheless, all residual plans for the fete were cancelled, setting up a howl of protest from Hanna and her friends, who'd been sent over to the manor by Lucy to find out if Sarah needed any help.

'Don't worry, we'll organise something especially for you,' Sarah assured them, glancing up as a bleary-eyed and unshaven Simon padded into the kitchen. 'If the weather improves we can hold it on the green at the front, and if it doesn't we'll find ourselves another time slot in the village hall.'

'I don't see what the problem is, now that everyone's house is all right,' Hanna grumbled, passing a basket of clean washing to Juliette who passed it on to Marietta who stood holding it, not sure what to do. 'I mean, it's not as if it's raining now, or anything.'

'No, but everyone's still a bit shaken up at being ordered out of their homes,' Sarah reminded them, opening the tumble dryer to give Marietta a clue, 'and no one got much sleep last night so they won't be up to much today. Si, are you just going to stand there or would you like to say good morning?'

Glancing briefly over his shoulder, Simon raised a hand to the girls.

'Hey,' they said in unison.

Sarah rolled her eyes. 'Playing hero has worn him out,' she explained. 'I expect he got his pants in a twist over the top of his tights.'

As the girls giggled Sarah waited for a response from her brother, but he was still gazing out of the window, apparently lost in a world of his own. 'Well, I guess I'd better see what I can give him to aid the resuscitation,' she said, going to fill up the kettle.

'How are things over at the farmhouse, Hanna? Don't tell me Mum's back at work already?'

'She's gone to get Dad from the station,' Hanna replied. 'Everyone's left now. Pippa went last because she wanted to stay and help, but Mum said she'd done enough already and then John came to get her anyway.'

'Is their house OK?'

'I think so. We're going down there later to do our Wii Gym.'

'I'm impressed that John was up and about so early,' Sarah commented, glancing at Simon again. 'I thought he was out as late as everyone else.'

'He was,' Hanna told her, 'and Pippa's saying he has to go back to bed, which is why we can't go down there till this afternoon. Anyway, if you don't need us to do anything else we'll go and find out what's happening at the village hall, like nothing.'

'I'm sure they'll be busy cleaning up after everyone who stayed there last night.'

Hanna's eyes widened with alarm. 'That is such a good point,' she said to her friends, 'so we should rethink where we go next or they'll rope us in. What about yours, Juju? Or no, let's go back to mine, because Dad'll be there any minute and he might have some great ideas what to do about our fashion show.'

'Your dad's so cool,' Marietta was sighing as Sarah waved them off. 'I wish mine was the same, not that I ever see him.'

Going back to the kitchen, and finding Simon still miles away, Sarah finished reloading the washing machine before turning to face him. 'What's up?' she asked, folding her arms to show she meant to get an answer.

After casting her a quick glance he went to start making some tea.

'Well that was very informative,' she commented, opening the fridge to pass the milk.

His eyes stayed on what he was doing as he said, 'Something happened down at the estate last night that was . . . Well, definitely not good.'

Her eyebrows rose. 'Floods generally aren't,' she reminded him.

'I'm not talking about that. I'm talking about an incident in one of the houses I went into to help a young mother with her two kids. John came in after me and the woman suddenly started going berserk, telling me not to let him put his hands on her children, and to get him out of there.'

Sarah blinked in astonishment.

'She called him a murdering bastard,' Simon continued, 'and told him to eff off out of Cromstone because they don't want the likes of him living anywhere near decent people.'

Sarah's face was turning pale. 'What on earth was she talking about?' she demanded. 'What did John say?'

Simon's expression remained grave as he said, 'He just apologised and backed out again.'

Sarah couldn't believe it. 'But she's got it wrong,' she declared firmly. 'She's obviously mixed him up with someone else.'

Simon's eyes came to hers. 'She said everyone's talking about it on the estate, how he murdered his own daughter.'

Sarah reeled.

'According to her he was released after serving fifteen years . . .'

'No!' she cried, slamming a hand on the table.

'They've got the wrong John Mckenzie. It's a common enough name so it would be an easy mistake to make.'

Simon didn't argue. 'She told me that a few of her neighbours are getting up a petition to try and drive him out of Cromstone, so they must be pretty sure of their facts if they're going that far,' he replied.

Suddenly furious, Sarah shouted, 'Well this is exactly what you wanted, isn't it? To find a way to damn him, so you're ready to believe someone who . . .'

'Sarah,' he broke in gently, 'when I got back this morning I went online to check.'

Sarah could only look at him.

'Her name was Alexandra Mckenzie,' he said. 'She wasn't quite three when . . .' He swallowed and dragged a hand across his face. 'When he committed the crime.'

Sarah's hands were pressed to her mouth as she stared at him with horrified eyes. She didn't want to believe it, she just didn't.

Coming to put his hands on her shoulders, he said, 'I'm sorry. I didn't want to be right about him like this . . .'

'Do you think Mummy knows?' she whispered shakily. 'Could she . . . Is that . . . ?' What was she trying to ask?

'I can't answer for Mum, but I do know that we should speak to Lucy. Hanna spends a lot of time in that house . . .'

Slapping his hands away, Sarah said, 'Please don't even start to suggest she's in danger. I just won't have it.'

'OK,' he conceded, 'but think about it, if it was

your daughter going down there all the time, wouldn't you want to be told?'

Philippa's good eye was shadowed with tiredness and anxiety as John told her what had happened at Katie Freeman's house during the night. Easily able to imagine her brother's hurt and humiliation, she sorely wished she was able to stomp down there and put the wretched woman right in a way she'd never forget. However, on hearing that Simon had witnessed it all, she felt her heart ache with so many heavy emotions that Katie Freeman was forgotten.

'What did he say?' she asked, reading the pain in John's eyes and feeling it as though it was hers.

'He didn't get the chance to say anything,' he replied. 'I thought it was best just to get out of there.'

'So he didn't try to defend you?'

'Why would he? He doesn't know who I am, or what happened back then.'

Unable to take any more, Philippa begged, 'John, stop, please. You can't let him think . . .'

'No, Pippa, you stop. It happened. I went to prison. People were always going to find out, because in the end they always do.'

'Listen to me,' she urged passionately. 'I am *not* going to my grave leaving things as they are . . .'

Realising she was close to tears, he reached for her hands across the table. 'It'll be all right,' he assured her.

'How?' she cried, pulling away. 'You have to speak to Rose, John, because if you don't I will and . . .'

'Pippa, she called, last night. She's been in touch.'

Seeing the joy and relief in her brother's eyes, Pippa could only groan with dismay even as she got to her feet to go and hold him tightly, hoping that it might squeeze some sense into him, though she knew the time had long passed for that. 'What did she say?' she asked hoarsely, already bracing herself for the answer. It had better be what she was hoping to hear, or she really would take matters into her own hands.

'It was a message on the machine,' he told her. 'She didn't leave a number, but I know she'll call again.' Gazing tenderly into her eyes, he said, 'It's still there. After all these years that special something we shared . . . It's never gone away.'

Smiling through her tears, Philippa put a hand to his cheek as she said, 'I never thought it had. I just wish it hadn't cost you so much.'

As Joe looked up from the cuttings Lucy had given him, he was frowning irritably. 'Well, obviously there's some sort of mistake,' he stated, as though it might in some way have been Lucy's fault. 'I mean, what else are you trying to say, because where I'm coming from that's the only explanation.'

'It is for me too, but until I speak to my mother I can't know anything for certain.'

'Except that you clearly didn't die in the fire, or you wouldn't be sitting here.'

Wondering if he was refusing to connect with what this might mean for her, or if he just didn't get it, she said, 'I've been online to check, and an eighteen-month-old girl called Lucy Fisher, daughter of Daphne and Brian, died in a fire in Hastings the day before that report was printed.'

Glancing down at the cuttings again, his whole body seemed to tighten as the confusion of it continued to confound him. In the end he said, 'Well, it stands to reason, you'll have to go down to Exmoor and speak to your mother. Or are you trying to tell me now that she's not your mother?'

Too afraid to put into words what she was really thinking, Lucy simply stared at the cuttings.

He jerked back in his chair. 'For God's sake . . .'

'Joe, listen, please. I've been going over and over this. You said yourself I obviously didn't die in the fire, but it says there that I did . . .'

'This is bollocks,' he growled. 'Total and utter bollocks.'

'And what about the death notices? They were printed over a week later, so clearly a child did die and if it wasn't me . . .' She tried to take a breath, and found she couldn't. 'You understand what I'm saying, don't you?' she pleaded.

He only looked at her, evidently not wanting to be the one to voice it.

'This could mean that Mum and Dad aren't my real parents.' Hearing the words spoken aloud tripped a terrible feeling in her heart.

'Then who the hell are they?' he demanded belligerently.

Her voice shook slightly as she said, 'That's not the right question, because we know who they are. What we possibly don't know is who . . . who I am.'

Shooting to his feet, he said, 'This is crazy, Lucy, and you know it.'

'No! All I know is what I've read,' she cried, feeling absurdly sorry for herself as he continued to fail to see this from her point of view, or even consider what a nightmarish position she was in, 'and you're not helping, taking this attitude when I could really do with your support right now.'

'OK, you have it, but not in jumping to the kind of conclusions . . .'

'Then give me a better explanation. Tell me how I died in a fire, when I'm sitting right in front of you. How can that happen? What makes . . .'

'I already told you, you have to speak to your mother.'

'You think I haven't tried?'

'Go down there, for God's sake.'

'I will, as soon as I can get away . . .'

'Sod what's going on here . . .'

'That's easy for you to say when it's not your company. If I don't clear up after the last auction it'll be chaos for the next. And, in case you'd forgotten, I have to think about Hanna. I can't just leave her here.'

'Then take her with you.'

Lucy looked at him in disbelief. 'You surely don't think I want her knowing about this?'

Flushing at his mistake, he said, 'OK, OK, let her come back with me for a few days. She can catch up with her old friends . . .'

'No, that's not the answer. Even if she went with you, I've just told you, I can't get away.'

Throwing out his hands, he demanded, 'Then what do you want me to say? I don't have the answers you're looking for . . .'

'No, but you *could* go down there for me.'

He gaped with astonishment.

'You can take the car,' she pressed on before he could protest. 'I'll cover all your expenses . . .'

'Lucy, it's not going to happen.'

'For God's sake, all I want you to do is take the cuttings and ask who the little girl is, and why they've kept them.'

'No way,' he told her, starting to back off. 'This has nothing to do with me. They're your parents, not mine. I can't go down there demanding answers like it's me they owe an explanation to.'

'Maybe they do,' she cried furiously, 'because if I'm not who we think I am, then we could end up with you married to a dead girl and your children as . . . bastards.'

As his face blanched, she pressed her hands to her head. 'I'm sorry, I didn't mean to blurt it out like that, but can't you see . . . ?'

'Ssh,' he broke in sharply, 'someone's coming.'

Turning from the door before it opened, Lucy quickly tried to pull herself together in case it was Hanna.

It turned out to be Sarah and Simon – and to Lucy's horror she heard Joe say, 'Sorry, friends, now's not a good time . . .'

'For God's sake,' Lucy snapped at him. 'Come in,' she told them. 'I'm sorry, we were just discussing . . . Can I get you a coffee? What a crazy night we've all had. Were you inundated over there?'

Clearly realising they'd walked into the middle of something, Sarah said, 'I'm sorry, we can come back . . .'

'No, no, it's fine,' Lucy assured her. 'I'm glad you're here, because we're already behind with the shipments, and since all our backup staff are cleaning up after last night . . .'

'Oh, what a shame that is,' Joe cut in scathingly.

Lucy turned to him in astonishment.

'Do excuse me if I'm getting in the way,' he said bitterly. 'I've only just realised that what I have to say counts for nothing now your friends have turned up, so maybe you'd like to discuss your *problems* with them.'

Before Lucy could explode with rage, Sarah said,

'Joe, I'm sorry if we interrupted. It's just that there's something we need to talk to Lucy about, and you too, actually . . .'

'Leave it,' Simon cut in, putting a hand on her arm. 'It can wait,' and easing her back to the door he threw a blistering look at Joe before saying to Lucy, 'Are you sure you're OK?'

Joe's face turned white with fury. 'What do you mean, is she OK?' he growled, advancing across the kitchen. 'Who the hell do you think you are . . .'

'Joe, stop this now!' Lucy shouted.

'. . . coming in here, asking *my* wife . . .'

'Joe! For God's sake!'

'This bastard's had it coming,' he seethed. 'Don't think I don't know what goes on when I'm not around, how he's always here, sniffing about, trying to get laid . . .'

'You're out of your mind,' Simon told him scathingly.

'Come on,' Sarah whispered, grabbing Simon's arm.

Simon's eyes were still blazing into Joe's. 'What, and leave her here with this madman?'

'Joe!' Lucy yelled as he slammed a punch into Simon's jaw.

'And there's more where that came from,' Joe snarled as Simon staggered back against the door.

Simon's hand moved so fast that no one saw it until he had Joe by the throat. 'It's only out of respect for Lucy that I'm not making you pay for that,' he seethed. Drawing Joe in even closer, he burned his eyes menacingly into his, before shoving him so hard into the wall that Joe grunted as his head hit the stone.

Seconds later Simon was marching along the

drive, barely seeing Hanna as she came towards him.

'Hey Si,' she sang breezily. 'Hey Sarah,' as Sarah followed him. 'Dad here yet?'

'Yes, he's here,' Sarah muttered, stopping as Simon stalked on. She was thinking fast to give Lucy some time. 'Tell me, have you been to John and Pippa's yet? If they're awake I thought I'd pop down there.'

'No idea, we're not expected till two.' Then, in a sympathetic whisper, 'Simon still in a bad mood?'

Going along with it, Sarah grimaced. 'He's had a challenging start to the day.' She quickly glanced back at the kitchen door. 'I'd better go and find out where he went, we don't want him upsetting the natives, do we?'

With a giggle, Hanna skipped on into the house. Blithely ignoring the way her father was glowering at her mother, she rushed into his arms. 'Hey, Dad, how's your world?'

'Oh just great,' he responded, his eyes still boring into Lucy. Then, in a softer tone as he smoothed her hair, 'Now I've found someone who's pleased to see me.'

Letting the barb hook into thin air, Lucy slipped the cuttings back into their envelope, and without uttering a word to anyone she took them upstairs for safe keeping.

Finding no sign of Simon back at the manor, Sarah seized the opportunity while alone to call her mother. Since there was no reply from either of her numbers, she left a message on her mobile saying, 'Mummy, something's come up about John Mckenzie. Maybe you don't know anything about

390

it, but I think . . . Well, maybe you do, so please get back to me as soon as you can.'

After ringing off she tried Simon's mobile, but he evidently hadn't taken it with him, because she could hear its familiar ringtone jingling in the kitchen. So, deciding she could spend a few minutes online before going back to start work with Lucy, she went to open her laptop.

Moments later she was staring in horror at the screen. Though the story contained no details of his crime, it told how, aged forty-four, John Mckenzie had been released from prison after serving fifteen years of a life sentence for murdering his tiny daughter, Alexandra.

Feeling oddly bludgeoned, Sarah sat back in her chair and tried to connect the man she knew with someone who could commit such a violent act on his own child. It just wasn't possible. It must have been an accident that had been blown into something more sinister. It happened all the time, especially where babies were concerned. Or maybe Alexandra had had a terminal illness, and her father had carried out a mercy killing. Would she, Sarah, have had the courage to do something like that if it happened to a child of hers? It wasn't possible to say without being in that situation, but she couldn't imagine standing by and doing nothing if someone she loved was suffering. She couldn't imagine John doing it, either.

Knowing the answers must be there somewhere, she started another search, this time using Alexandra's name. It took only moments for the screen to begin downloading the image of the sweetest little face, so happy and vibrant that Sarah felt her heart turn inside out. Surely to God no one could hurt her, least of all her own father.

Clicking on to a press story from that time, she

had only read the first few lines when the phone started to ring.

'Darling, it's Mummy, I just got your message. What's happened? Is everything OK?'

Closing down the screen almost guiltily, Sarah rose to her feet as she said, 'I'm not sure. I . . .'

'You said something had come up about John,' her mother interrupted, sounding worried.

'Yes, it has. Some of the neighbours have found out . . . Well, I just checked it online and it's saying that . . . that he killed his daughter, and . . .'

'No!' Rose shouted. Then, more violently still, 'No! Don't ever say that, do you hear me?'

Sarah's head started to spin.

'It's not true. You must never repeat it and you must never let anyone else,' her mother insisted.

'Mummy . . .'

'Listen to me, Sarah. Listen. John's a good man.'

'So why are they saying . . . ?'

'They've got it wrong. He never laid a finger on her. Oh God, where is he? Does he know people are turning against him? You mustn't let it happen. Sarah, you have to make it stop.'

'I'll try if I can, but if you're so certain he didn't . . .'

'He didn't!'

'But how do you know?'

'Because she was my daughter too,' Rose sobbed, 'and I *know* he didn't kill her.'

As shock hit her like a blow, Sarah reached for a chair to steady herself. 'Your daughter?' she whispered. 'Oh Mummy, what are you . . . You have to tell me . . .'

'I will, I promise, but I have to call John now. Does Simon know about any of this?'

'Yes, he's ...'

'Oh God, I'll ring you back,' and the line went dead.

John was staring at Simon, feeling the challenge in his eyes and the anger in his heart as though they were physical forces. He wished he knew how to reach him, but right now finding a way through the years of misunderstandings and mistakes to a place where it was safe and Simon was still his son was impossible.

'Don't you have anything to say for yourself?' Simon demanded curtly. 'I just told you, they're getting up a petition and ...'

'All I can tell you,' John interrupted quietly, 'is that I didn't kill my daughter. I loved her with all my heart. She was as special to me as ...'

'So what happened to her?' Simon cut in. 'I know you served a sentence ...'

'Yes, I did ...'

'John,' Philippa broke in.

John put up a hand to stop her. 'Maybe you could answer the phone,' he suggested in a tone that brooked no dispute.

After she'd gone he directed Simon to a chair, but Simon shook his head.

'Convicted criminals always claim to be innocent,' Simon stated gruffly, 'and I don't blame you for trying to cry off this one, God knows anyone would, but you were tried, John, twelve jurors found you ...'

'There was no jury. I pleaded guilty.'

Simon's face became more pinched than ever. 'Why? If you didn't do it?'

As John started to answer Philippa came back into the room.

'I think you should take this call,' she told him. Her eyes went briefly to Simon before returning to her brother. 'It's . . . I think you know.'

Almost closing his eyes at the powerful jolt in his heart, he said to Simon, 'Would you mind? It would . . .'

'Go ahead,' Simon told him. 'I'm done here anyway,' and ignoring John's protest he nodded curtly towards Philippa as he went past her and out of the door.

Taking the phone John allowed his eyes to connect briefly with Pippa's, then turning away he spoke very softly as he said, 'Hello, my love,' and there was so much feeling in the 'love' that no one could have ever been in any doubt of how deeply he meant it.

'Oh John,' Rose responded brokenly, 'just to hear you . . . Are you . . . ?'

'I'm fine,' he came in gently. 'How are you?'

'Yes, yes, I'm fine too, but Sarah told me what's happening there.'

'You don't need to worry yourself . . .'

'John, listen, please. I'm coming over, but Sheila has to sit her exams on Tuesday. She's been studying so hard to become a translator . . . and I promised . . .'

'Be there for her,' he said, reading what she was trying to say.

'There's a flight into Bristol on Wednesday. Will you pick me up from the airport?'

He turned back to Philippa, his eyes shining with happiness as he said to Rose, 'Yes, my love, I'll be there to pick you up from the airport.'

Chapter Twenty

'Mum, can I talk to you?' Hanna said, in a tone that was fairly muted for her.

Glancing up from her desk Lucy was about to say not now, when her heart jolted as she realised Hanna had been crying. 'What is it?' she asked, turning away from the computer. *Surely Joe hadn't told her about the cuttings. He wouldn't.*

Slumping down on the chair in front of Sarah's desk, Hanna said, 'I've just had a humungous row with Marietta. God, she is such a bitch. And a liar. I should have smashed her for saying what she did, because I know it's not true, she just makes things up . . .'

'What did she say?' Lucy cut in gently.

Hanna glanced at her then away again. 'She reckons . . . I *know* it's not true, but she's telling everyone that Dad's having an affair with her mum. She said it's where he was last Saturday night when he didn't come home. I went mental when she said that, because I know he wouldn't have an affair, but she just kept on and on, so I told her to eff off and walked away.'

Torn between fury, outrage and an overwhelming sense of protection towards her daughter, Lucy wheeled her chair closer and took Hanna's hands in her own. 'I'm sorry Marietta's saying those things,' she said softly.

'I know they're not true,' Hanna insisted.

Reaching up to stroke her hair, Lucy couldn't help wondering if it was time to stop protecting Hanna from some of the less welcome truths about her father. She didn't have to be brutal, or try to make Hanna choose sides, all she needed was to begin with at least a part of the reality. 'I don't want to lie to you,' she said quietly, 'because it would be the wrong thing to do . . .'

'Oh my God, please don't say he is,' Hanna panicked.

'I'm not sure if it's an affair, as such,' Lucy replied, holding more tightly to her hands, 'but we know he didn't come home that night, and . . .'

'But he was with an old friend. He told us that.'

Wishing she hadn't got into this now, for Hanna's sake much more than her own, Lucy found herself saying, 'That could be how he thinks of Annie.'

'Oh God, I can't stand it,' Hanna wailed, pressing her hands to her cheeks. 'You'll divorce him now and we won't ever see him . . .'

'Sssh. He's your father and whatever goes on between me and him won't ever change how much he loves you.'

'But you must hate him for cheating on you. I know I would.'

Realising that she didn't love Joe enough to hate him, Lucy said, 'Where is he now? Have you seen him this morning?'

Hanna shook her head. 'You know he never gets up early on a Sunday.' Her eyes came to Lucy's. 'Mum, if you weren't always working . . . I mean, look at you now, in here at the computer . . . You've never got any time for him when he comes so really, who can blame him for going off with somebody else?'

At any other time Lucy might have been amused by how swiftly it had become her fault, but today she simply wasn't in the right frame of mind to deal with it. 'I'm not going to get into defending myself, or him,' she said, more brusquely than she intended. 'We've both made mistakes, and it's not going to help if you start choosing sides.'

Hanna's eyes flashed. 'That's so typical of you,' she shouted. 'You always manage to turn everything round so you can have a go at me, well I'm fed up with it. It'll serve you bloody right if Dad does . . .'

'What's all the noise in here?' Joe broke in chirpily as he came through the door. 'You're not shouting at your mother again, are you, princess?'

'*Why does everyone always blame me?*' Hanna shrieked, and leaping to her feet she tried to shove past her father.

'Hey, not so fast,' he protested, catching hold of her.

'Let go of me,' she seethed, chopping at his hands. 'I don't want to speak to you ever again.'

As she dashed back to the farmhouse Joe turned to Lucy, blinking with confusion. 'What's got into her?' he demanded. 'Don't tell me you decided to load all that crap about your parents on her . . .'

'Actually,' Lucy cut in bitingly, 'the crap she's upset about is the crap you brought into our family by sleeping with the village bike. For God's sake, why did you have to choose Annie Babbage of all people? It was bound to get out, and I hope you feel proud of yourself now that it was your own daughter who came to tell me.'

397

Joe's face was sour with guilt.

'Go away,' Lucy said irritably.

Staying where he was, he said, 'I know what you're really pissed about. It's the fact that I won't go to see your parents.'

'This has *nothing* to do with them,' she yelled furiously. 'For once in your life will you start facing up to what you've done and stop trying to throw it all back on to me?'

'OK, right, so you're upset about Annie, but what do you expect when . . . ?'

'No, it's Hanna I'm upset about, and the fact that she's just had a bust-up with one of her friends over something you did, and now she's terrified we're going to break up over it . . .'

'So you told her we were? Great.'

'I did no such thing, but we've got to face the fact, Joe, that it's on the cards. We can't go on like this, or I can't, and after the way you behaved with Simon yesterday . . .'

'He had it coming, the supercilious bastard.'

'You see, you just don't get it, do you? He's a decent man who was showing some concern . . .'

'About my wife . . .'

'Stop, stop, stop,' she shouted, clapping her hands over her ears. 'All I want to hear you say now is that you're ready to go and apologise . . .'

'To him? No way is that going to happen.'

'Joe, please. They're my friends . . .'

'Anyway, I thought you said he was leaving today.'

Remembering that Simon had probably already gone, Lucy turned away. 'I've got too much to do here to go on with this,' she said shakily, 'and Sarah's over in the barn. I don't want her walking in on yet another row between us.'

'There wouldn't have to be a row if you . . .'

'Please go and talk to Hanna. I don't know what to say to her myself, and as you're the one who's betrayed her trust you should be the one to deal with it.'

As she tried to refocus on the letter she'd been writing when Hanna came in, she could feel him watching her from the door.

'Look, I can understand that finding that stuff about the kid dying in a fire and what have you has thrown you a curve ball,' he said, 'so it's no wonder you're getting everything out of proportion . . .'

Finding herself on the brink of exploding again, or asking him how the hell he'd feel if he were in her shoes, she quickly pulled herself back. She didn't want to discuss anything with him any more. They just kept going round and round in circles, and any conversation would only continue to come back to the same crushing reality: he was a cheating bastard who wasn't prepared to help her sort out something that meant so much to her.

'Oh right, it's the Coventry tactic now, is it?' he challenged.

'Actually, no, it's the I've-found-another-way-of-dealing-with-it tactic,' she told him bitterly. 'I've left a message on Michael Givens' machine asking if I can see him tomorrow, and after that I'm going to drive down to Exmoor.'

Having heard Lucy's and Joe's raised voices coming from the office, Sarah had discreetly taken herself back to the barn, not wanting to eavesdrop on what was appearing to be an ongoing battle between them. She had no idea what it was about, since apart from apologising on Joe's behalf for the way he'd punched

399

Simon, Lucy hadn't mentioned the altercation they'd stumbled into yesterday. It had struck Sarah that Lucy was being uncharacteristically withdrawn at the moment, which suggested that whatever the problem was between her and Joe she wanted to deal with it in her own way. Sarah completely understood that, which was why she'd decided not to burden Lucy with what the rest of the village now knew about John, or what else she'd found out from her mother. In fact, she hadn't even told Simon yet that their mother and John had once been married and had had three children together, because her mother had asked her not to until she was able to explain everything herself.

'I'm coming on Wednesday,' she'd promised when she'd rung Sarah back after speaking to John. 'John's going to pick me up, and as soon as we can get Simon and Becky to Cromstone we'll tell you everything about Alexandra, and what really happened to her.'

'Just answer me this,' Sarah had said before she could ring off, 'was Daddy my . . . is he . . . ?'

'Yes, he's your father,' Rose told her softly. 'But Simon and Becky are John's.'

Still stunned by it all, Sarah pushed a stray tear from her cheek as she thought of her father and how very much she'd loved him. He'd loved her the same way, she'd never been in any doubt about that, and she knew he'd loved Simon and Becky too, because he'd never done anything to betray the fact that she was his only child. So for now she was left to wonder how Simon and Becky had come to bear his name, and if either of them had any memory of John.

And if they did . . .

How were they going to feel when they discovered

that Douglas, whom they'd always adored, wasn't their real father? If it were her she knew she'd be devastated. How she wished he was here now. She wanted to put her arms around him and make sure he knew how wonderfully special he was, as special as he'd never failed to make every one of them feel.

Lucy was watching Michael's face as he absorbed the details of the two small cuttings she'd brought with her. When his eyes finally came up to hers she could see how baffled he was, and a horrible sort of shame started to come over her. She'd experienced it that morning while staring at the mirror. It was as though she had no right to be where she was – she was an intruder, or a ghost cut adrift in a world that wasn't hers.

What was Michael thinking? Was he wishing he could distance himself from her? Or was he, by some miracle, about to offer an explanation she hadn't thought of? Maybe her parents had confided in him, though why in him and not her made no more sense than anything else – apart from the fact that what they told him wouldn't strip him of his identity the way it was stripping her of hers.

'I can quite understand how difficult this must be for you,' he said, his eyes gazing intently into hers. 'And you say you haven't been able to get hold of your parents?'

Lucy shook her head. 'They're not answering any of my calls, or my texts.'

'But they know that you've found these?'

'I'm not sure. I left a message on Friday night, but I haven't had a response.'

He looked down at the articles again. 'I guess there's always a chance,' he said, 'that you're their second child, and after the tragedy they decided to name you Lucy too.'

Lucy swallowed. 'I thought of that, but look at the date – that Lucy would be thirty-seven now, the same age as me.'

He nodded thoughtfully. 'Except,' he said, 'if you aren't this Lucy we can't actually be sure of how old you are.'

Feeling herself falling apart inside, she tried to laugh as she said, 'Then let's hope I'm younger and not older.'

His eyes showed a welcome tenderness as he replied, 'Whichever way, you'll still be beautiful.'

Touched by the compliment, her voice caught on a breath as she said, 'Thank you.' Then, because he was being so understanding, she felt tears starting to well in her eyes. 'I'm sorry,' she said, searching for a tissue, 'self-pity's not a very good thing, is it?'

'I'm not going to pretend to know what you're going through,' he said honestly, 'but I do know that if I was facing something like this I'd be finding it pretty difficult too.'

Lucy's eyes went down. His kindness might be making her emotional, but at least it was reassuring her that she wasn't going mad after all.

'If it turns out that I'm not . . .' She swallowed as she gestured to the cuttings. 'Will there . . . Do you think it would be possible to find out who I really am?'

Sitting back in his chair, he kept his eyes on hers as he said, 'The obvious answer, of course, is to ask your parents.'

'But what if they won't tell me?'

He took a breath. 'I think we'll have to cross that bridge when, if, we come to it. What's important now is to confront them with this.'

Lucy's throat was too dry to form the thank-you for his use of 'we' – it made her feel less alone.

'We need to contact the records office,' he continued, 'to find out if a death fitting these dates was registered at that time. I'll get my assistant on to it right away. Hopefully it won't take long, but in the meantime I think we should take a trip down to Exmoor.'

Hearing the 'we' again, Lucy almost sobbed with relief. 'Does that mean you'll come with me?' she asked, needing to be sure.

'Of course, unless you'd rather I didn't.'

'No, no, please, I want you to.' She thought of Joe's response, and how different he was in every way from Michael. He was like a stranger now, someone who'd never really been right for her, while Michael was . . . He was everything she'd ever wanted, but she couldn't allow herself to think of that now because she was far too close to the edge as it was, and so in danger of blurting something she shouldn't. Then, suddenly not wanting to burden him further, she rose to her feet. 'I should be going,' she told him. 'Thanks for fitting me in today and for . . . OK, I'm going to cry, so time to go.'

'Lucy,' he said, as she started for the door.

She turned back, and seeing the tenderness in his eyes, she almost couldn't bear it. 'I'm sorry, I have to go,' she said shakily. 'I'll call later to set up a time for tomorrow. I'll fit in with you.' Before he could stop her again she escaped through his secretary's office, wishing she was able to be more polite. Unfortunately, though, her emotions had got the better of her again.

Philippa was sitting at the kitchen table when John came in, looking, she remarked fondly to herself, quite dapper with his new haircut and spruced-up complexion. It was in Rose's honour, of course, which was touching, she thought, in a man his age.

And no doubt he was secretly counting the hours till her plane landed on Wednesday. In spite of the turmoil they were facing, Philippa was unable to be anything but happy for him, but would she ever forgive him for the decisions he'd taken all those years ago? Well, she guessed she must have at some point along the way, or they'd never have survived it.

'Everything all right?' he asked, looking both concerned and wary as he tried to read her expression.

Glancing down at the small object on the table in front of her, she waited for him to register it too, and tried not to smile as he grimaced awkwardly.

'Och, woman, you've been going through my desk,' he protested, pretending to be angry.

'I was looking for a pen,' she admitted, 'and what should I find instead but this little chap here, bless his Tibetan cotton socks – and now comes the story of how he found his way to our house when I was sure he'd gone by courier to Lincoln.'

With a sigh, he pulled out a chair to sit down. 'He did go,' he told her, 'but then he got sent back again.'

She waited.

'OK, I did it for Sarah,' he confessed. 'And for Douglas, I suppose, but mainly for Sarah, so I could help her to do what she wants to the house. That place meant a lot to her father, and after everything he did for my children, I thought this was the least I could do for his.'

Having already guessed this would be the answer, Philippa's watchful eye was showing as much affection as exasperation as she said, 'What am I going to do with you, John Mckenzie?'

'You'd have done the same, if you'd thought of it,' he informed her.

She blinked rapidly. 'Fifty thousand pounds for a piece of junk? I think not,' she argued.

With a smile he said, 'We've got more than enough, and I couldn't offer it as a gift, she'd think I'd lost my mind, so I decided this was the best way.'

Shaking her head as she continued to look at him, she said, 'Well, you certainly had me fooled. How on earth did you come up with the idea, and who was I speaking to on the phone?'

Fetching himself a glass of water, he said, 'The idea came from the same chap who told me about the Ring. He was someone I shared a cell with for a couple of years, and he was always full of stories about the antiques trade. One of them concerned an Arabic chess piece that someone he knew had picked up at a provincial auction for ten thousand quid and managed to sell on for a quarter of a million.'

Philippa's jaw dropped. 'Well, I suppose I have to feel relieved that we got off so lightly. Now, who was on the phone – and who is Mr Everett?'

John's eyes twinkled roguishly as he said, 'Craig Duncan was on the phone, who you might remember from . . .'

'. . . our Glasgow factory, indeed I do. The best managing director we ever had. Just wait till the next time I see him. And Mr Everett?'

'Is Craig's brother-in-law who happens to be in the antiques business. I had a chat with him, he told us how to go about it, and, well, a flurry of bids and couple of bank transfers later, Bob's your uncle – or Charlie's your chess piece.'

With a delighted chuckle, she tucked the worthless chunk of wood into her pocket. 'If Douglas isn't looking down on you now saying what a flipping idiot you are, then I'll say it for him. You're an idiot, John Mckenzie.'

Coming to give her a kiss, he said, 'I just dropped in to make sure you're all right, so if you are I'd better be on my way. I've a van full of deliveries outside that need to be in their rightful homes by the end of the day.'

'Before you go,' she said, as he turned to the door, 'the antiques chappie you shared a cell with? What was he in for?'

He shrugged. 'No idea. Not something you ever asked.'

After he'd gone, Philippa went to stand at the window to watch him backing carefully down the drive and wondered, as she had many times over the years, how bad it had been for him in prison. He'd never discussed it, wouldn't even allow her to ask when she came to visit, but she knew what sort of treatment a prisoner who had harmed children could expect. The fact that he'd never harmed anyone in his life, much less his own precious daughter, would have meant nothing to the other inmates. They'd have meted out their own form of justice, with only the odd officer who didn't turn a blind eye to stop them.

How unspeakably cruel life was to have put such a worthy and decent man through the ordeals her dear brother had suffered. A lesser man would never have survived them, she was in no doubt about that, and would never have managed to keep intact his generosity and tenderness.

* * *

Lucy was gazing out of the car window, watching the wind whipping the moor as Michael drove them along the winding road that led to the small hamlet where she'd spent so many lonely holidays as a child. Thinking now of what her parents' reasons might have been for always staying so remote from other people and communities, she felt a burning tightness inside that wouldn't go away.

Over the last forty-eight hours she'd found herself wondering if there really had been an insurance company who could only rely on Brian Fisher, their 'top man', as he occasionally boasted, to set up their new offices. Perhaps the crystal decanter marking twenty-five years of service was something her parents had had engraved in order to perpetuate the myth. Except they had never seemed short of money, so her father must have worked somewhere for all those years. Perhaps the insurance company had been real.

So much doubt, so many suspicions, lies and a depth of deceit she couldn't even begin to comprehend, if it were true.

'Is that it?' Michael asked as they drove over the crest of a hill to see a small sprawl of cottages in a shallow valley below.

Lucy's heart churned with nerves. What was going to happen when they got there? How would her parents – her parents? – react to the questions she was almost too afraid to ask? Realising that by the time she came away the very core of her life, her belief in who she was, along with her trust in the people she loved, could have been shattered, she had to force herself not to tell Michael to turn back. 'It's the last house on the right,' she said, 'the one that's set slightly apart.'

Glancing over at her, he gave her a reassuring smile before easing the car carefully over the potholes that littered the road, down to where the ruins of an old farm sat forlornly in the rain, and threads of a low-lying mist clung to the hillsides. A few metres further on they passed a set of smart black gates that fronted the drive to the hamlet's largest property. It belonged to a Devonshire businessman and was, like the rest of the dozen or so houses, only used for weekends and holidays, so it wasn't particularly surprising that there were no signs of life anywhere. Nevertheless it was unnerving Lucy to find everything so silent and still, particularly as the last time she'd received any sort of communication from her mother was almost a week ago.

'Are you OK?' Michael asked.

'Yes, I'm fine,' she assured him. Then, 'I'm glad you came. Thank you.'

Bringing the car to a stop outside the quaint, double-fronted cottage surrounded by a rambling garden that was part vegetables, part shrubs and part wilderness, Michael followed the direction of Lucy's eyes as she took it in. There was a wheelbarrow next to the garage with a rake leaning against it and a pair of old gloves draped over a handle, giving the impression that someone had just popped indoors for a drink or to answer the phone.

'They can't have heard us pull up,' Lucy said. 'Why don't you sound the horn, let them know we're here.'

As the double beep rolled around the low-lying hills it roused a few linnets from the gorse, but provoked no further sign of life.

'Perhaps they're taking a nap,' Michael suggested, and pushing his door open he got out of the car. 'Come on, let's go and find out.'

Following him along the randomly paved path, Lucy kept hold of her mobile as though it were some sort of lifeline. Why had no one come out yet? They must surely be in there.

Finding the front door locked, Michael rapped the knocker and stood back to look up at the first-floor windows. 'Hello?' he shouted. 'Daphne! Brian! Are you at home?'

When there was no response Lucy went to peer in through the kitchen window. There was no one inside, but a couple of cups were on the table, along with a notepad and pen that gave the sense of having recently been left. 'Mum!' she called out. 'Are you in there? It's me, Lucy.'

The silence that followed seemed to be full of echoes. She turned to Michael, and finding him no longer there she had a fleeting panic. He'd vanished to wherever her parents were and she was left here, abandoned. She thought of the woman who shouted in her dream with her arms outstretched . . . She could hear the screams . . .

Returning from around the back, Michael said, 'Maybe they've gone into town for some . . . Are you OK?'

'I'm fine,' she lied. 'It's just that I really thought they'd be here. I'm sorry to bring you all this way for nothing.'

'Try calling,' he said, 'because if they have gone into the local town they might get reception there.'

Looking down at her own phone, Lucy shook her head. 'There's no signal up here for my phone either.'

After checking his own and finding the same problem, he started towards the garage. 'If the car's not there then we'll know they've gone out,' he said.

Lucy watched as he hauled open one of the doors,

and seeing the old Rover sitting there alone she felt an uncontrollable surge of frustration. 'This is crazy,' she cried. 'If they're not here then surely they must be somewhere they can call me – except I'm bloody well here now, so they can't get through.'

'I have an idea,' Michael said. 'Why don't you take my car to wherever they go shopping, and I'll wait here in case they come back.'

'I can't let you do that. If we could get into the house, maybe, but . . .'

'I expect we'll manage it somehow,' he said, and sure enough a few minutes later he'd managed to force open the back door without causing any damage.

'There,' he said, holding up his car keys. 'I'll make myself a nice cup of tea while you go off in pursuit.'

'Are you sure? This isn't what I expected . . .'

'I know, and I'm sure, unless you'd rather stay and I'll go.'

Not too keen on that idea, Lucy took the keys and after telling him to make himself at home, she went to get into the kind of car she'd never even travelled in before today, much less driven.

An hour later she was back, and seeing the Rover still alone in the garage she gave a growl of despair.

'No sign of them, and no reply from the mobile,' she announced, finding Michael seated comfortably next to the hearth with his feet on the fender, reading a book.

'No, there wouldn't be,' he said, nodding towards the phone he'd left on the table. 'I found that next to the kettle, so wherever they've gone they've forgotten to take it with them.'

Lucy's eyes closed in dismay. 'They're both so forgetful these days it's a wonder they can remember who they are, never mind that they even have a phone. Whatever happens when we finally catch up with them, I'm going to insist that they move out of here. I shouldn't have allowed it in the first place, but they bought it especially for their retirement . . .'

'Well, it does have a lot of charm,' he pointed out, 'and if you like being this remote . . .' Understanding from the look on her face that she didn't, he glanced at his watch as he rose to his feet. 'I'm afraid there's a meeting I have to get back for.'

'Yes, of course. I'll leave a note to let them know we came and tell them they have to get in touch.' She thought of the envelope in her bag and said, 'Do you think I should leave the cuttings too?'

He frowned. 'No, it's probably best to hang on to them for now,' he decided, and leaving her to her task he went to rinse the cup he'd used, then checked the back door was secure before they returned to the car.

A little over two hours later Lucy was driving her old Peugeot out of Chipping Sodbury, trying to contain the anger towards Joe she'd built up during the journey. If he'd done as she'd asked at the weekend and gone down to Exmoor, she might not have had a wasted trip today at a time when she could least afford it.

'Oh great, so everything's my fault again,' he cried when she connected to him. 'Like I told them not to be in when you got there, and maybe I even got them to leave their phone behind, because that's the kind of thing I'd do.'

'Why do you have to be like this?' she snapped angrily. 'You always used to be there for me, and my parents . . .'

'Oh, so they're your parents again now, are they?

I thought you'd managed to slough them off like a bad skin, the same way you're trying with me.'

Not bothering to consider how much truth there might be in that where he was concerned, she said, 'If anything's happened to them, Joe, I want you to know that I shall hold you responsible,' and without caring how unreasonable she was being, she cut the line dead.

Sarah was in the office, going over the paperwork John had brought back from his deliveries half an hour ago. As always, with him, everything was in perfect order, making it a simple job for her to enter the information into the computer before the notes themselves were filed away. Since she'd known he was coming she'd had time to work out what to say to him without, she hoped, making either of them feel awkward about the fact that her mother was due to arrive tomorrow. If she kept everything on a friendly but professional level, that should do it, she'd told herself. So she'd been all prepared to show him the email that had arrived from Maureen Crumpton earlier, until he'd walked in the door with his new haircut and a merry twinkle in his eye, when all she could think about was her father and how little he seemed to mean to everyone now.

'Oh darling, of course I loved him,' her mother had assured her when she'd called to ask. 'You know as well as I do that it was impossible not to.'

Yes, Sarah did know that, but it didn't change the fact that her mother had once been married to John, and had also had three children with him, before apparently divorcing him, and marrying again. So, was losing Alexandra the cause of the split? It must have been, not only because it had happened around the same time, but because no sane woman would ever stay married to someone who'd killed her child.

Except her mother was insisting that he hadn't, while John himself had told Simon that he'd pleaded guilty to the crime. Why on earth would he do that if he was innocent? No one would. It made no sense at all.

Feeling suddenly desperate to speak to her father, she began doing so in her mind. 'Should I go back online to find out what I can about Alexandra?' she asked him. 'Did you know her? Were you a part of their lives then?'

Though she'd opened up a search several times, so far she hadn't summoned the courage to go through with any of them. Maybe, if Simon or Becky were with her, or even Lucy, she wouldn't be so afraid of having to deal with yet more tragedy in her family. But they weren't, and though she sorely wished she was stronger, she was still too fragile after all the losses of the past few years to feel ready to cope with any more whilst sitting there alone.

Hearing footsteps coming across the courtyard, she quickly closed down the Google screen and returned to the Excel sheets she'd been working on until a few minutes ago.

'You're still here,' Lucy said, coming in through the door. 'Have you seen Hanna?'

'Yes, she came back about an hour ago,' Sarah replied. 'I think she went into the house. Isn't she there now?'

'I don't know, I haven't checked.'

'Are you OK?' Sarah asked, peering at her curiously as Lucy started to sift through her mail. 'How were your parents?'

Shaking her head, Lucy said, 'I've no idea. They

weren't there and God only knows when they're intending to come back. Plus, they managed to leave their damned phone behind.'

'Oh dear,' Sarah murmured. 'So a wasted mission?'

'Tell me about it. Michael suggested going again tomorrow, but I can't afford the time.'

'Michael?'

Remembering that Sarah didn't know her real reason for going to Exmoor, Lucy said, 'Yes, he has some . . . papers for them to sign so he offered to drive. I should go to find Hanna. Is everything all right here?'

'More or less, provided you discount a nasty little email from Maureen Crumpton demanding two years' salary as severance pay or she'll be suing for wrongful dismissal.'

Lucy's eyes flashed. 'Doesn't the woman realise we've got far more important issues to be dealing with than her petty claims?' she snapped.

'Or veiled blackmail,' Sarah pointed out.

'Well, they know where they can go with that. You'd better forward it to Michael,' she said, grabbing the phone as it rang. 'Hello, Cromstone Auc . . .'

'It's me,' Joe told her tightly. 'I don't appreciate the way you hung up on me just now, and frankly, if anyone's to blame for what's going on with you it's your bloody parents themselves, not me. OK?'

Since Sarah was right there, Lucy said, 'OK.'

He waited. 'Is that it? Don't I get an apology?'

'In your dreams,' she retorted, and hanging up on him again she said to Sarah, 'Is John still around?'

'I don't think so,' Sarah replied. 'I've just forwarded the email to Michael, so now, if it's all right with you, I'd better go and get some shopping in before my mother arrives tomorrow.'

Lucy blinked. 'Your mother's coming?' she said. 'Did I know that? Oh God, don't tell me I've been so preoccupied . . .'

'Don't worry, I didn't mention it, but yes, she is. Her plane arrives at midday and she's asked John to pick her up.'

Realising how difficult that might be for Sarah, Lucy tried to think of something suitable to say.

'Which means,' Sarah continued, 'that we won't have him tomorrow, so I've booked Sadwells to come and help with the house clearance over at Nailsworth.'

'Are you supervising that?' Lucy asked. 'I thought it was on my schedule.'

'It was, but I hope you don't mind, I need to lose myself in something for the day so I changed it.'

'That's fine,' Lucy assured her, coming to give her a hug. She needed some time in the office after being gone all day, and with no one else around she'd be able to have another look in the barn to see if her mother had left anything else behind. Maybe, by some miracle, there was another box that might offer some sort of rational explanation for what she'd already found.

'I'll be off then,' Sarah said.

Lucy was about to wish her goodnight when, realising how vulnerable she must be feeling, she said, 'I'm sure Hanna's already got plans for the evening, so if you'd like to eat here, with me, I'd love the company. I mean, when you get back from the supermarket.'

Sarah smiled. 'That would be great,' she replied. 'I can pick something up for us while I'm there, like . . .'

'Wine?'

Sarah laughed. 'Definitely that, and something wicked like pizza or fish and chips.'

'I'm sold, and I think that's your mobile ringing . . .'

Checking to see who it was, Sarah grimaced. 'My sister, Becky. This could be a tricky one, because she'll want to know why Mummy's summoned her to Cromstone this weekend.'

'Do you know why your mother's summoned her?' Lucy asked.

Feeling herself starting to colour, Sarah said, 'I've an idea, but I'm not the one to put it into words. I'd rather leave that to those who know the answers, namely my mother and John, that way I won't make any mistakes in the telling.'

Chapter Twenty-One

It was hard for John to believe that this day had finally come. He knew, without counting, how long he'd been waiting, hoping, even praying to a God he no longer believed in, that he would see her again. Thirty-four endless years – and four months, to be absolutely precise. And now, here she was, coming into the arrivals hall, making his heart trip and sing with her beauty that age seemed only to have enhanced. Seeing her appear a little anxious as she looked around for him, he started forward, then she saw him and he knew without any doubt that she'd been longing for this day too.

Not sparing a thought for the crowds around them, he pushed through to her, and drawing her into his arms he held her with a determination never to let go.

'John,' she laughed breathlessly, still clinging to him, 'we're blocking the way.'

Pulling back to gaze into the eyes that he had never forgotten, and that, to his joy, hadn't changed at all, he started to smile in a way that was impossible to stop. To say that everything he'd ever done was for her would be a claim that some men might find shaming, but for him it was a truth he knew with pride.

'You're still the same,' she told him, cupping a hand around his cheek.

His eyes twinkled. 'This is the silver-top version,' he joked, as a brutal-looking female with a psyche-delic roller bag crashed into them.

With the throaty chuckle he remembered so well, she said, 'I really think we need to move.'

Taking her hand and her bag, he walked her outside, hardly able to stop looking at her.

Laughing, and even blushing, she said, 'You're reminding me of when we first met.'

He laughed too, and watched her draw a hood up around her lustrous ebony hair that had acquired some glints of silver now, and lost much of its length. He remembered how she used to plait it, and the way he'd shake it loose and inhale the scent of her as though it were a drug that could make him high. How afraid he'd been that he would never do that again.

Leaving her under shelter he went to pay for the parking, and was aware of her watching the rain sweeping the landscape in soft, feathery waves. He wondered if she remembered how they'd never allowed the weather to get in the way of a family day out. Their children weren't going to be faint-hearts who cowered from storms, they were going to embrace everything life had to offer, good or bad, because they had parents who adored them and would always keep them safe, no matter what.

How right they were – and then how tragically, devastatingly wrong.

'There are some good pubs not far from here,' he said, as he drove them out of the car park. 'I was hoping you'd let me take you for lunch.'

Smiling, she said, 'I'd like that.'

Wanting to laugh and cheer in his happiness, he

somehow managed to hold on to his dignity as he said, 'So tell me about France. Are you enjoying it there?'

Her tone was droll as she said, 'It has its moments.'

Loving her understatement, he reached for her hand, and as he wound his fingers around hers he realised she was wearing the narrow band of sapphires he'd given her when the twins were born. 'You kept it,' he said.

Surprised, she turned to him. 'Of course. I have everything you gave me, including the boxes and the cards.'

Swallowing a rise of emotion, he said, 'Did Douglas know that?'

'Yes, but I didn't flaunt it. It wouldn't have been fair.'

Thinking of how deeply he had envied Douglas over the years for living the life that should have been his, he said, 'He was a very special man.'

Looking down at their hands, she said, 'I know he stayed in touch with you.'

He indicated to turn right into the Chew valley. 'I used to live for his letters. With his gift for writing he could bring you all to life for me in a way that went far beyond mere news. He'd send me photographs too, from time to time, mostly of the children, but occasionally of you.'

'I didn't know that,' she whispered, 'but I do know that you never wrote back.'

'Because he asked me not to, and I understood that. Once he'd adopted the children they had to be his, and I had to let go.'

'Oh John,' she murmured softly, her eyes welling with tears. 'Did we do the right thing? Maybe it was wrong to keep the truth from them.'

'Maybe, but it seemed the only way at the time, and if I had to do it over again I don't think I'd change my decision.'

Her hand tightened around his, and she caught a tear from her lashes. 'I used to think about you all alone, cut off from us . . .'

'Ssh, it's over now. It ended a long time ago.'

'But it still haunts me.'

Glancing at her, he brought her hand to his lips and kissed it. 'One of the officers said something to me once that has always stayed with me. He said, "As each hour passes it's like a door has closed. You will never be able to revisit that hour to undo something you regret, or to do something you should have, so it's important to make the hour you are in the one that counts."'

Gratefully, she said, 'I'm glad to think you knew someone like that while you were in that place.'

'Not everyone was bad,' he assured her, 'and after a while you learn how to stay away from those that are. But all those doors are closed now, thank God, and I'd rather think about the one we've just opened.'

With a playful ring in her voice she said, 'So what are we going to do to make this hour special?'

'It already is, with you being here.' Reaching a red light at roadworks, he turned to brush his fingers over her cheek. 'I'm starting to feel as though all the years have melted away and we're young again.'

She smiled. 'I think I am too,' she admitted. 'In fact, it's like we've never been apart.'

'Maybe that's because in our hearts we haven't.'

Bringing his hand to her lips, she said, 'That's true.'

Hearing someone beep behind he drove on along

the country road until they reached the pub he'd found earlier, before going to pick her up.

'This is lovely,' she murmured, as they came to a stop facing the view of meandering hills and a rain-spattered lake. 'Very fitting for our reunion, since our first date was spent rowing on the Serpentine in Hyde Park.'

Delighted that she'd made the connection, he said, 'I'd take you again today if the weather allowed, but I imagine you'd prefer something dry and a little less windswept.'

'You're right,' and after he'd come round and opened her door, she raised her hood again and ran with him across the car park into the bar.

Settling her at a table next to the window, he went to order their drinks while she sent a text to Sarah letting her know she'd arrived, but that she wouldn't be home right away. When John returned, she told him what she'd said.

'Do you think she'll mind?' he asked, setting down her glass of wine and his pint of beer.

'I'm not sure. She's confused about everything, understandably, and feeling very protective of her father since she found out you and I used to be married.'

'I didn't know you'd told her that,' he said, surprised. 'Do the others know yet?'

'No, but they're coming at the weekend. I thought we should tell them together.'

Thinking of how Simon might react, he said, 'Of course I'll be there if you want me to be, but it might be easier on them if they have a little time to themselves, once they know, before they have to face me.'

Realising he could be right, she paused. 'Shall we

discuss it with Pippa? She was always the wise one and I don't expect that's changed.'

His eyes were merry as he replied, 'I'd be more inclined to call her bossy myself, and no, she hasn't changed.'

Looking down at her glass, Rose said, 'She's devoted her whole life to you and now . . .' Her eyes came to his. 'How long has she been in remission?'

'Over a year, and you know her, she won't let it beat her until she's ready, which we hope won't be any time soon.'

Rose was gazing deeply into his eyes. 'I thought, after Douglas was killed, that you might get in touch . . . I wasn't sure where you were . . .'

'I wanted to come, but it wasn't the right time. I knew how hard his death must have hit you, and losing your grandson too . . . You didn't need me around to make life more complicated, or to bring back memories . . .'

She put her fingers to his lips, stopping him. 'Do you ever think about her?' she asked in a whisper.

Understanding who she meant, he found it hard to breathe for a moment. 'Not a day goes by when I don't.' He tried to smile, but couldn't. 'Tell me about Becky,' he said, having to change the subject. 'From the photos Douglas sent she's the image of her beautiful mother.'

Biting her lip, Rose said, 'Becky's cut her hair very short and she dresses in quite a mannish way, but you're right, she is like me. I can see you in her though, around her mouth – she has your smile and the shape of your face. So does Simon, but being fair everyone thought he was like Douglas.'

'He's like my father,' John said. 'Pippa notices it too.'

Rose's eyes drifted as she said, 'I think about her too, all the time wishing I could turn back the clock so I could do things differently. I'll never stop blaming myself . . .'

'Ssh,' he said gently. 'It wasn't your fault, you know that.'

'But it was. I've ruined your life . . .'

'Rose, my love, we mustn't allow ourselves to go back to that time.'

'It's not a question of going back, we've never escaped it, and we never will.'

'Maybe not, but there's nothing we can do to change it now, so we mustn't allow it to spoil what lies ahead,' John told her.

Her eyes were full of grief and tenderness as she gazed into his. 'Do you think fate will be kind to us this time?' she asked. 'Would it allow that, after what I did?'

'I have no doubt of it,' he murmured, taking her hand. Then, with a mischievous light in his eyes, 'To be frank, it's not fate that I'm afraid of now, it's my own children.'

Sarah was reading her mother's text as she walked into the office with a stack of mail she'd collected from the box in the gatepost.

'So you're going to deal with it?' Lucy was saying into the phone as she gave Sarah a wave, followed by a curious look as she remembered Sarah was supposed to be overseeing the house clearance at Nailsworth. 'OK, great. I'll be here all afternoon,' and ringing off she said, 'Everything all right?'

'More or less,' Sarah replied. 'The house turned out to be more of a shed, so we're all done and the van's on its way back. Which,' she continued, 'is more than I can say for my mother and John. Apparently they've gone for lunch.'

Lucy's eyebrows rose.

'The next thing you know they'll be getting married,' Sarah said snappishly.

Lucy blinked at the sudden leap from table to altar, but before she could respond the phone rang again and by the time she'd finished Sarah was on the line taking down the details of a toyshop on its way into receivership.

'I'm sure I've got an email somewhere,' Sarah said, going on to her computer as she rang off, 'from someone who's interested in old toys.'

'We've actually got a couple of collectors listed,' Lucy told her, 'and a dealer, if memory serves me correctly. Aaagh! The mail, I'd forgotten about it today. Anyway, that was Michael I was talking to just now. He's going to pop in later, but apparently he's received the Maureen email and he's happy to handle it. Plus, he hasn't heard anything back yet from the letters he sent out, but it's still early days, so he thinks we should only be quietly optimistic about the Ring business going away.'

'It would be a great relief if it did,' Sarah commented. 'The last thing we need is to start sinking all our profit into legal fees.'

'Too right,' Lucy agreed. 'Cromstone Auctions,' she said into the phone.

It continued that way for the next couple of hours, with no time to exchange more than necessary information between or during calls, until eventually Sarah had to leave for a viewing over in the next village.

'Could you please get that before you go?' Lucy said, hanging on the line as another started to ring.

Scooping up the phone, Sarah was about to announce Cromstone Auctions when a female voice said, 'Your mother would never have employed a child-killer, and none of us can believe that you're letting your daughter mix with him.'

It took a moment for Sarah to realise that the woman thought she was speaking to Lucy. When she did, she felt herself turning cold. 'Who is this?' she asked.

'It doesn't matter. It's just a few of us thought you should know that until you get the child-killer off your staff no one around here is going to want to work for you,' and with that the line went dead.

Replacing the receiver, Sarah busied herself with loading her bag as she tried to decide what to do. Since she hadn't yet told Lucy about John it didn't feel like the right time simply to blurt it out; however, if the locals were starting to make phone calls like that then maybe she didn't have a choice. Looking at her watch and seeing that she was already running late, she decided it was unlikely anyone would make such a call again in the next couple of hours, so it could wait till she got back. In fact, maybe she should consult her mother about it and even ask her to talk to Lucy, since Rose must surely know the truth of this mystery surrounding John.

It was early evening by the time Michael pulled into the farmhouse driveway, to be met by Hanna who was so busy texting as she came towards the car that she walked straight into it. Since it was no longer moving he knew she wasn't hurt, but he leapt out anyway, just in case.

'Sorry,' she said, as he reached her, 'I was miles away. I suppose you're looking for Mum.'

'Yes, I am. Is she here?'

'In the office, as usual.' She was about to go on her way, then thought better of it. 'You're a lawyer, aren't you?' she said, regarding him closely.

'That's right. Why, do you need some advice?'

Her expression remained sober as she said, 'Actually, yes I do. I want to know if it's possible to sue someone for telling lies about people.'

Giving the matter some thought, he said, 'Well, I guess that depends what's being said and who's saying it.'

Her young face was pinched with resentment. 'I don't want to repeat it,' she said, 'but if I hear anyone say it again I'll let you know. How much will it cost?'

'I'll give you your first consultation for free,' he promised.

'Cool. Actually, I might get my dad to have a word with them, because he knows how to shut people up when they're sounding off too much.'

Watching her walking on towards the gates, he was about to continue inside when she turned back, saying, 'If anyone says anything to you, tell them you're going to sue them for libel.'

'Slander,' he corrected, 'and I'll be sure to.'

Presuming she was involved in some teenage wrangle, he pocketed his keys and walked on under the arch into the courtyard, where some topiary sculptures had recently taken up residence around a fountain full of nymphs.

'Hi, am I interrupting?' he said, finding Lucy sitting at her desk with her head bent over a letter.

When she looked up he was taken aback by the terrible pallor of her face.

'You might want to read this,' she said, passing

him the letter. 'It would seem my parents have gone away for a while.'

'Do they say where?'

She shook her head, and pushed her hands through her hair as she felt herself starting to shake.

Tearing his eyes from her, Michael looked down at the letter.

My Dearest Lucy,

Dad and I have gone on a little trip for a while. Please don't worry about us, we are both fine. (I know, because of the very loving person you are, that you will care, in spite of everything. Can we take some credit for your kind and generous nature – I'd like to think so, but maybe you would rather we didn't.)

We always knew that what we did was wrong, but when God brought you to us it was like a miracle, so we allowed Him in His wisdom to be the judge. If He hadn't meant you for us, He would take you away, we told ourselves, but He never did and for that we have thanked Him every day of our lives. No one could be blessed with a more wonderful daughter. You always seemed more than we deserved, and we did everything we could to make ourselves worthy of you.

When we came to Cromstone we had no way of knowing what awaited us there. Now we are able to see how God was starting to bring together the people He had separated in His mysterious way, but at the time all we saw was a friendly little backwater and the opportunity to own a small auction room. We remember with many smiles how delighted you were when we found it. It has been a challenge, but a joy getting it to where it is now, and we know that

*you'll make an even bigger success of it, with Sarah's
help, and of course with John's.*

*You can perhaps imagine our great shock when
John first arrived in Cromstone. We hadn't heard
about him, or read about him or his wife, for many
years. We knew nothing of Sarah's family either,
apart from the fact that her father was the wonderful
writer Douglas Bancroft. How curious God is in the
way He moves.*

*It seems now that He has revoked his blessing on
us, which is why we have gone away for a while.
We shan't be gone long, and when we return we
will be very happy to see you, presuming, of course,
that you will want to see us. If you don't, we will
understand and won't blame you at all.*

*Until then we will sign off in the way we will
always think of ourselves,*

Your loving Mum and Dad. XXX

When he'd finished his eyes went straight to Lucy.
By now her face was so strained he could almost
see the veins beneath her skin. 'Is there a postmark
on the envelope?' he asked.

'Yes, it was sent yesterday from Maidstone, which
doesn't tell us anything apart from the fact that
they're the other side of the country without a
phone.'

And it's not so far from Hastings, he was thinking,
*where eighteen-month-old Lucy Fisher lost her life in a
fire.*

Her eyes were heavy as she looked at him. 'I know
it's not there in so many words,' she said, 'but you
can't read it any other way, can you? They're not
my parents.'

Unable to disagree, he simply held her gaze.

Feeling as though a wrecking ball had crept in quietly to finish shattering her world, she reached for the letter and took a tremulous breath. She couldn't make herself accept this. Throughout everything she'd experienced in her life, the loneliness and isolation, the rejection of other children, the feelings of never quite fitting in, she had always been able to hold on to her parents. They'd made everything right and safe, they'd never let her down, but now they were telling her it was all an illusion. The safety net had gone and she was falling, falling, disappearing into a void that was black and endless, and she was so afraid.

As though sensing her need, Michael stooped down in front of her and took her hands. 'It'll be all right,' he whispered gently.

She wanted to ask how, but what she said was, 'They're assuming I know more than I do.'

He nodded.

'So what do I do?' she asked. Her voice sounded hollow and distant, as if it, too, had stopped being hers.

'I think they're telling you in the letter what you should do,' he replied.

As her heart turned over she looked away.

'You need to talk to John.'

John! What did all this mean? 'He'll think I'm crazy.'

'Not if you show him the letter.'

Taking a breath, she closed her eyes as she tried to contain her emotions.

'Would you like me to come with you?' he offered.

Looking at him, and realising how alone she would feel right now if he weren't there, she almost sobbed as she nodded.

'Would you like to go this evening, or would you prefer to wait until you've had some time to think?'

'I can't this evening,' she answered. 'There's a pre-term meet and greet at Hanna's school. I have to go.'

'Of course.' Still holding her hands, he drew her up with him as he stood. 'It'll be fine,' he assured her, pulling her into a comforting embrace.

Not knowing what else to do, she held on to him and allowed herself to feel his quiet strength flowing through to her. 'Thank you,' she whispered.

Pulling back to look at her again, he put a hand gently to her face.

She tried to smile, but found she couldn't.

'If you like,' he said, 'I could show John the letter for you.'

Swallowing hard, she turned her head to one side as she thought. Then, realising how much easier it might be if he did, she looked at him again and nodded.

Half an hour later Michael was sitting on a sofa in John and Philippa's drawing room, watching John as he read the letter. Though his face had turned white he'd said nothing yet, and when he finished reading his head remained down. Then Michael realised he was sobbing, so hard that he could barely breathe.

'Oh my goodness, what is it?' Philippa gasped, going to him.

John pushed the letter into her hand and tried to speak, but it still wasn't possible. Michael had never seen a man so overcome, and felt a surge of sympathy.

'She's alive,' John finally managed. 'After all this time . . .' His voice gave out again, and he wrapped an arm round Philippa as she tried to take in what she was reading. Then she was crying too, and turning to John she whispered, 'Can it be true? Are you reading this the same way as I am? Yes, of course you are.'

John's reddened eyes went to Michael.

Realising he was seeking some sort of reassurance, Michael said, 'Obviously, I don't know the history, but it seems this letter is giving you some news that you've . . . Well, that you . . .'

'I'm too afraid to believe it,' John told him roughly. 'And yet . . . Oh my God, this is . . . We'd given up hope. I kept telling myself . . . We never thought to see her again . . .' He couldn't go any further, it was simply too much.

'John had a little girl,' Philippa explained in a voice that shook with feeling. 'A precious wee girl who . . .' She gasped for more breath. 'She was stolen from us when she was almost three, and we've never been able to find out what happened to her.' She used her fingers to dry her cheek. 'It devastated our lives,' she whispered raggedly. 'Everything changed from that day . . . We've none of us ever been the same again. You see, we thought she was . . . We thought so many things . . .'

Being a parent himself, it wasn't hard for Michael to imagine what they'd put themselves through, and he felt his heart churn with pity.

'She was so sweet and lovely,' Philippa told him. 'We adored her . . .'

'I have to speak to Rose,' John said suddenly. He was trying to collect his thoughts, but it wasn't possible. 'No, I must see Lucy.' He turned to his sister. 'I don't know what to do,' he said helplessly.

Thrown by the mention of Rose, Michael said, 'Lucy's gone to the school.' Did he mean Rose Bancroft, Simon's mother? Surely not, and yet some instinct

431

was telling him that it was Rose Bancroft. The implications started to make his head spin. Did Simon and Becky know they had a sister? Was Sarah aware of how she and Lucy were related? What was this going to mean to Lucy? How would she take it if he turned out to be right and Rose actually was her mother?

Silenced by the enormity of what was happening, Philippa was holding tightly to John's hand as she tried to cope with it all. She was thinking about the day Daphne Fisher had come to see them, just after they'd arrived. What a shock it must have been for the woman when they'd first arrived and confided in her why they were there. Yet the way she'd fled the baker's shop at their first meeting suggested she'd already guessed who they were. So why had she come that day? To be sure, Philippa supposed. Or to find out if they already knew who Lucy was. What a turmoil it must have thrown her into when she'd discovered who Sarah's mother was. To think that all these years Daphne and Brian Fisher had had their precious Alexandra, bringing her up as their own, apparently treating her well, but nevertheless depriving her of the life and family that should have been hers. What they'd done to John and Rose, to her too, and Alex, was monstrous and unforgivable, yet never in a hundred lifetimes would she have imagined them capable of such a terrible crime. They should be made to pay, but even if they were, nothing could ever make up for what they'd done. The years, the lifetimes, the dreams that had been stolen could never be returned.

When he sensed they were ready for him to speak again, Michael said, 'I think, before we go any further, that we must be certain we're not misunderstanding anything.'

432

Though Philippa nodded agreement, Michael couldn't be sure how much she was taking in.

'From the letter and its allusions to John,' he continued, 'it seems fairly certain that Lucy is . . .'

'Alexandra,' John broke in hoarsely. 'Her name was Alexandra.'

Unable even to imagine what he must be feeling, Michael tried to set aside his own emotions, but it was hard. He liked this man and respected him immensely. He'd also developed a very real fondness for Philippa, so it was impossible not to be affected by their reactions. More than that, though, was what he felt for Lucy, who meant far more to him than Carlotta ever had. What was all this going to mean for her? Right now it wasn't possible to say, but what he could be certain of was that they all, John, Philippa and Lucy, were going to need his professional guidance. So, keeping his voice gentle and clear, he said, 'The most sensible next step is to organise a DNA match.' He waited for one or other of them to respond, but as their shock apparently deepened they remained silent. 'I'll need to make some calls,' he continued, 'but I'm pretty sure if we do it privately there's a chance we could have the results within a day or two. I'm not sure of the cost . . .'

'It doesn't matter,' Philippa told him. 'Please, let's just do it.' Then, seeming only now to think of Lucy's situation, she cried, 'Oh my goodness, the poor girl. It must have been such a shock for her to receive this letter. Does she understand its implications? Do you think we should talk to her?'

Touched by her concern, and feeling sure Lucy would be too, Michael said, 'Why not let me speak to her again, and then we can decide what . . .'

'I'm sorry, I can't keep this from Rose,' John interrupted, getting to his feet. 'As Alexandra's mother, she has a right to know what's happening.'

'You mean Rose Bancroft?' Michael said, needing to hear it confirmed.

'Yes, yes of course,' John replied. 'She's up at the manor.'

Finding himself suddenly overwhelmed again as he thought of his childhood friends and of Lucy, Michael could only look at Philippa as she said, 'I'll call and ask her to come.'

When Rose arrived she was looking anxious and hesitant, but after receiving a reassuring look from John, she greeted Michael warmly before turning to Philippa.

'Hello,' she whispered cautiously.

'Hello,' Philippa responded, holding her gaze.

Rose swallowed. This was the first time the two women had come face to face in over thirty years, yet neither was assessing how the other might have aged, they were thinking only of the man they both loved and the dear little girl they'd lost.

Knowing how unlikely it was that Philippa had ever forgiven her, Rose tried to speak, but three decades of guilt were choking her.

'It's all right,' John said softly, coming to put a hand on her shoulder.

Rose glanced at him, then back to Pippa. 'I . . . Are you . . . ?' she stumbled. 'John told me . . .'

'I'm fine,' Philippa assured her.

Rose nodded. 'That's good. I was . . . I wish I knew what to say to you. After what I did . . .'

'Ssh,' Philippa said, opening her arms. 'Don't say anything, just come here.'

With a tortured sob of relief and despair Rose sank into Pippa's embrace and held her close. 'I thought . . . I was afraid you'd still hate me . . .'

'Och, such nonsense,' Philippa chided. 'I never hated you, but I was angry, it's true, and for a long time I wished that foolish brother of mine had developed more sense than he was born with.'

Rose stood back to look at her. 'I shouldn't have let it happen,' she said earnestly. 'You must know I tried to stop him . . .'

'Yes, I do, and I often wished you'd succeeded, but it's all behind us now. We're a lot older and hopefully a little wiser.'

'Rose, my love,' John said softly, reaching for her hand, 'we have some news that we need to share with you. It's about . . .' He glanced at Michael. 'It's about . . .'

Rose's eyes darted between them.

'Alexandra,' John said.

As the blood drained from Rose's face, she sank down on the edge of a chair. Her voice was no more than a whisper as she said, 'News?'

'We think . . . Well, it seems we might have found her.'

As Rose let out a cry of anguish she looked to Pippa, then Michael, before returning her bewildered, frightened eyes to John.

'It's true,' he said gently. 'We'll show you the letter, but if it means what we think it does, then she's here, in Cromstone.' Since hearing this amazing news, having had a little time to register it, he was able to laugh incredulously. 'Can you believe that? She's actually here and I know her.'

Rose's eyes were wide with confusion as she looked at them all again.

'Her name's Lucy,' Pippa told her. 'I'm sure you'll have heard Sarah speak about her.'

Rose's eyes returned to John, and as they filled with tears he gathered her tightly to him. 'Did you know this when you picked me up today?' she asked.

'No, my love, I didn't. I only found out a few minutes ago. Now you need to read the letter Michael brought with him.'

As he went to fetch it Rose got to her feet, looking as though she might flee, but then she was holding the letter and reading words that began to turn her heart, her entire life, inside out.

By the time she'd finished she was barely able to stand. 'John, John,' she cried, sinking to her knees. 'It can't be true. Someone's playing a trick.'

'Ssh, my darling, it'll be all right,' he said, going down with her.

Rose turned imploring eyes to Philippa. 'Is it true?' she asked. 'No, it can't be.'

'You read the letter,' Philippa answered. 'I don't think there can be much doubt.'

To John, Rose said, 'I have to see her.'

'Of course,' he replied.

'Let me call to find out if she's back,' Michael said, taking out his phone. Then realising why it wouldn't be a good idea to see Lucy tonight, he put it away again. 'She'll have her daughter with her,' he explained.

'Her daughter,' Rose broke in raggedly. 'Oh John . . .'

'She has a son as well,' he told her, 'who's travelling around the world.'

'Oh my goodness.' Her hand went to her mouth. 'So grown up.' Then, to Michael, 'You must tell us about them.'

436

With a smile, Michael said, 'John knows as much as I do – in fact, he and Philippa know Hanna a lot better.'

'Hanna is your granddaughter,' Philippa said fondly, 'and you're going to be very proud of her, Rose, typical teenager that she is. I know this because John and I love her to bits already.'

Rose still seemed dazed, until suddenly her expression changed completely. 'Oh my goodness,' she gasped, turning to John. 'How could I have forgotten about Sarah? We must call her straight away and tell her to come. We can't wait till the weekend for the others. She has to be told now.'

As Philippa went for the phone, Michael said, 'I'll leave you to that, but before I go I should probably take some DNA samples from the two of you. A few strands of hair will do, then, provided Lucy's in agreement, I'll arrange for it to be sent to the labs first thing tomorrow.'

Much later that evening, after Hanna had gone up to her room, Lucy was sitting with Michael in the kitchen, listening quietly as his words not only tore apart the fabric of her life, but the very essence of who she was. Her parents were strangers, and more strangers had taken their place. She had a brother and two sisters. She'd grown up in the wrong family. *The wrong family.* Everything was clattering around her like stones, hitting her, but then falling away.

She tried to picture John and Rose, but reeled from it. She thought of her parents, and felt herself falling apart. The shock, the horror of it all, was too hard to grasp.

'They wanted to come straight away,' Michael was saying, 'but I was concerned about Hanna . . .'

'She doesn't know anything yet,' Lucy broke in, realising how little she knew herself. Yet it was enough to make her fearful of how she was going to go forward from here, and of how she would tell Hanna and Ben when, if, the time came. What was it going to be like for them finding out that their mother wasn't who they thought she was, and that their grandparents . . . *Oh dear God, how could they have deceived everyone like this? They couldn't. It wasn't in them. Yet apparently it was.*

Suddenly she didn't want it to go on. She wanted life to return to the way she'd always known it.

'It seems your real name is Alexandra,' Michael told her softly.

Though her initial instinct was to pull away, the tone of his voice was calming and as her eyes came up the name seemed to float through her like petals. *Alexandra Mckenzie.* She wondered what she'd have been like if she'd grown up with it. Would she have felt any differently about herself from the way she did now? Then she realised that of course she'd have been different, because she'd have been raised by parents who were wholly unlike those she'd known, in a family she . . . *She had a family.* Wasn't it what she'd always wanted?

No, a voice inside her was crying. She didn't want a sister, or a brother. She wanted the parents she'd always known and loved.

Yet how did she feel about them now?

She swallowed hard and looked helplessly around the room. It felt as though someone might be watching from the shadows. The ghost of the real Lucy Fisher? Who was Alexandra? Did she even exist any more? 'How much do you know already?' she heard herself asking Michael.

'Some, but not all.'

'Do I need to be afraid? Did something terrible happen that I've blotted from . . .'

'You have nothing to be afraid of,' he assured her.

'So what happened? How have I ended up here? Why didn't I know any of this?'

'I don't know the whole story,' he replied, 'so it's probably best for Rose and John to tell you rather than let me mislead you or get anything wrong.'

Rose and John. Her parents. Inside she was still reeling. 'Why aren't they married?' she asked. 'Who's Douglas? Sarah thinks he's her father . . .'

'He is,' Michael broke in gently, 'but I'm afraid I don't know why Rose and John broke up. I only know that Rose married Douglas after she and John divorced.'

'But why did they divorce?'

Michael shook his head. 'I'm sure they'll tell you themselves,' he replied.

Lucy looked down at the drink he'd poured her, which she hadn't yet touched. She was seeing John's face in her mind, the way he frowned when he was thinking, and threw back his head when he laughed. Instead of resisting it this time she waited for something to happen inside, like a spark of recognition, or even a rejection, but nothing came. 'He's a lovely man,' she said, feeling as though she should, and anyway it was true. 'It never occurred to me that he . . . Oh my God, Michael,' she suddenly sobbed, 'how can I make this stop?'

'Hey, hey,' he said softly, reaching for her hands. 'It's bound to feel overwhelming, because it is.'

Wiping away her tears, she picked up her drink and took a sip. The taste was bitter, metallic, nothing like the wine she was used to. She put the glass down again. 'What's going to happen about my parents?' she asked. Then, remembering, 'Can I still call them that?'

'One step at a time,' he advised. 'We need to get the test results first, and . . .'

'How long will it take?'

'I'll have to check, but hopefully not more than a day or two.' Then, after a pause, 'John and Rose would like to come and talk to you tomorrow.'

Her eyes shot to his.

'I think they feel that to wait would put you all through unnecessary strain, especially when there doesn't seem much room for doubt.'

'Isn't there?' she asked, wanting to push herself through the small, remaining chink that was closing so fast.

He only looked at her.

She tried again to make herself accept what was happening, but she couldn't. 'Hanna can't be here when they come,' she told him. 'I can't expect her to . . .'

'Philippa's already thought of that. She's going to ask for some more guidance with the Wii Fit.'

Lucy felt oddly disoriented as the new connection between Hanna and Philippa became apparent. 'Philippa's her great-aunt,' she said, as though testing the words. Then, imagining how Hanna might take it, she said, 'I think she'll like that. She's very fond of Philippa.' *But what about Brian and Daphne, the grandparents Hanna had grown up with?* She put a hand to her head as it started to hurt. 'What am I going to tell her?' she said. 'She loves them. So does Ben.'

Michael frowned, unsure what she meant.

'Brian and Daphne,' she explained. 'Oh God, how has this happened? It's a nightmare. It can't be real.

440

They'd never do something like this.' Except they clearly had, because her mother's letter was more or less admitting it. 'What's going to happen to them?' she cried. They deserved to be punished for this, to be made to rot in hell, yet how could she wish that on people she loved?

'It'll take a while to work out the right way to go forward,' Michael said gently. 'For now, I think you should try to get some sleep. You look exhausted, and you've got a pretty big day ahead of you tomorrow.'

A day, Lucy was thinking, as he left, that she wanted never to dawn, because it was going to start tearing her away from everything she knew and believed in, when all she wanted was to hold on as tightly as she could. Except if everything he'd told her was true, there was nothing to hold on to any more.

It wasn't long after Hanna left to go to Philippa's the next morning that Lucy saw Michael pulling up in his car. She'd asked him to come since she wasn't sure she could face meeting Rose and John on her own. It wasn't that she was viewing them as the enemy, exactly, but Rose was a stranger to her, and John was more than she'd realised, and it seemed they had a history together that she was a part of, but knew nothing about. It was making her feel vulnerable, at a disadvantage, even afraid she might disappoint them in some way. In truth, it was hard to know how she was feeling when her mind was flitting about like a bird too skittish to land.

'Are you OK?' Michael asked, his concern showing as he came into the kitchen.

She gave a shaky sort of laugh. 'I'm not sure,' she said honestly.

Coming to give her a hug, he said, 'It'll be fine. The samples have gone to the labs. Someone there will call my mobile as soon as they have the results.'

Shuddering with the kind of nerves she'd never known existed until now, Lucy said, 'You make it sound as though it might be today.'

'That's probably a little too soon, but don't let's rule it out, because the labs are always looking for funding and John wrote a cheque that should get you to the front of the queue.'

Wondering how anxious John must be now, and Rose, Lucy found herself wanting to back away from it all again. 'Wouldn't it be better for us to get together once we know the results?' she said. 'I mean, if there is a mistake, if we're reading this the wrong way, it could be a waste of their time.'

'Do you think there has been a mistake?' he asked gently.

There has to have been, she wanted to shout. *I can't be one person one day and somebody else the next, and the parents I've always known are mine.* 'I'm not Alexandra Mckenzie,' she told him. 'The name doesn't mean anything to me.'

'You were very young when you were taken,' he told her, 'so it probably wouldn't.'

Taken? As in stolen? Feeling the madness of it bearing down on her again, she wanted only to escape it. 'What about Simon?' she heard herself ask. 'If John's his father why isn't his name Mckenzie?'

'They're going to tell you everything when they get here.'

As the words registered, her head started to spin. 'Who – who's coming? Both of them?'

'I believe so.'

Feeling a cruel bolt of nerves tearing through her,

442

she tensed hard to try and make herself stronger. 'I don't know why I'm so afraid,' she said irritably. 'It's not as though they're going to hurt me. Is it?'

'No, they're not going to do that.'

Thinking of the woman Sarah had talked about, so loved and revered, and yet so fragile, it panicked Lucy again to realise that Alexandra was very probably the cause of the depressions and withdrawals that had blighted the childhoods of Sarah and her siblings. Would they blame her? Had this happened because of something she'd done?

'Does Sarah know?' she asked.

'I believe they told her last night.'

Lucy felt suddenly fearful of how she might have taken it. Had it been as devastating for her to find out that her father wasn't her mother's first husband, as it was proving for her, Lucy, to realise that her parents weren't her own?

'Do you think Sarah will come?' she asked, not sure what she wanted the answer to be.

'I think Rose is keen not to overwhelm you, so I expect it'll be just her and John.'

Was she pleased about that? She didn't know. It showed a sensitivity that she could appreciate, because maybe having Sarah there would have made it harder, though she couldn't say why. Maybe she needed to see Sarah on her own.

'Remember you already know John,' Michael said.

She couldn't deny that, but as a friend and neighbour, not as her father. *Oh dear God, where were Brian and Daphne, what had happened to them?* She turned around, wringing her hands, then turned back again. 'I used to dream about this as a child,' she said. 'When I was angry with my parents – with . . . I used to long for someone else to come along and claim

443

me as theirs. All children go through that, don't they?'

He appeared amused. 'I was always convinced my real father played cricket for England.'

Lucy laughed and to her surprise it seemed to release some of her tension. Then, hearing footsteps on the gravel, she turned towards the window and her insides dissolved into chaos. They were here. John was coming down the drive with a very elegant-looking lady dressed in a flowing black coat, with the hood up to protect her from the rain. The image made Lucy think fleetingly of the French Lieutenant's Woman before she found herself wanting to run to her children and gather them up, because they were her family, her reality, and no one, nothing, could ever change that.

Looking at Michael, she said, 'I'm a basket case.'

'You're fine,' he whispered, and turning as Rose and John appeared in the open doorway, he went to greet them before standing aside for them to come in.

At first Lucy felt frozen, too afraid to move or speak or even attempt a smile. She was transfixed by the woman who was lowering her hood, like an actress at the denouement of a play in which her face had remained hidden throughout. Then her heart tripped to see how beautiful Rose was.

John was the first to speak. 'Lucy,' he said, his voice shaking slightly, 'this is Rose.'

Lucy could hardly breathe as Rose's eyes came to hers. This woman, this vision of elegance and gentility, was her mother? It couldn't be true. It was like a dream. She thought of the portrait Sarah had sold at auction that did Rose no justice at all, and wondered where it was now.

'Alex?' Rose whispered shakily. 'Oh, my darling, you're so lovely.'

As tears flooded her eyes, Lucy felt her heart stretching across her chest. What had this woman been through? How had she survived it?

'I've thought about this moment,' Rose told her. 'I used to . . . Oh God, I'm so sorry . . . What I said that day . . .'

'Ssh,' John came in gently. 'It's all right.'

Though Rose glanced at him, her eyes quickly returned to Lucy. 'I don't mean to embarrass you,' she said. 'It's just . . .'

'It's OK,' Lucy heard herself saying. Was it? She had no idea. She was waiting for a bond that had lain dormant for years to start tightening. For a brief moment it had seemed to, but nothing was happening now. Yet maybe she was understanding why she was so tall and slender, with eyes that slanted at the corners and one eyebrow that arched higher than the other.

'I'll make some coffee,' Michael said.

Remembering her manners, Lucy said, 'Please come and sit down. Maybe we should go through to the sitting room.' She looked at John, as though he might have the answer.

'Wherever you feel most comfortable,' Rose told her, and the throatiness of her voice, though neither strange nor familiar, seemed to curl around Lucy's heart.

Lucy tried to smile. Maybe she should tell her she was lovely too, because she was. So lovely, in fact, that the word could have been created for her. Then, seeing how hard Rose was struggling to hold on to her emotions, she felt her own courage staging a return. 'Perhaps we should stay here,' she said, only realising now how wrong it seemed to be doing this in Daphne and Brian's house. Or was it wrong? How much respect or consideration did they deserve? Shouldn't they be here now, explaining themselves? Of course they should, but they'd be afraid and who could blame them? Where the heck were they? 'I'll help Michael with the coffee,' she said. 'How do you like yours?'

'We both take it black with no sugar,' John answered, pulling out a chair for Rose to sit down.

Of course she knew that about him, but there was so much else to learn, a whole lifetime of experiences and dreams that had gone towards making him who he was now. The biggest question of all, of course, was why he and Rose were no longer married, when the tenderness between them was so evident it was almost palpable. Had her disappearance been the reason for their break-up? What could have happened to tear them apart, when even after all these years they still seemed so connected to each other?

Watching them sit together and John's hand covering Rose's, Lucy found herself thinking of Sarah and how deeply attached she'd been to her father. How hard was she finding it to witness her mother's closeness to the man who'd fathered her other children, Lucy wondered.

After bringing the coffees to the table, Michael silenced his phone as it started to ring and sat beside Lucy. There was a moment's awkwardness until Rose said, 'I know it's selfish of us to want to see you today, but I . . . If you . . .' Collecting herself, she said, 'If you'd rather wait until we have official confirmation, please say so and we'll leave.'

Hearing the desperation behind her words, Lucy

felt her heart going out to her. 'You're welcome to stay,' she said. 'I just . . . I . . .' What more did she want to say?

There was another stilted pause before John said, 'The letter you received . . . We want to thank you for letting us see it, but if you're regretting it now . . .'

'I'm not,' Lucy told him, 'at least I don't think I am. To be honest, it's hard to know what I'm thinking.'

His eyes were full of understanding. 'Which is why we thought it might help if you heard the whole story,' he explained. 'Of course, as Rose said, we can wait, but unless you say you want to, I . . .' he glanced at Rose, Michael, then, '. . . don't think there's a need to.'

As Lucy looked from one to the other she was wondering how they could be so ready to accept her when they hardly even knew her. Maybe this was what happened to people who lost a child, they were ready to claim anyone just to fill the gap. Yet that was an unkind, unjustifiable way to think when she'd read the letter too, so how could she not understand what it must have meant to them?

'I'd like to hear what happened,' she said, realising that even if the results proved she wasn't who they thought she was, they needed to go through with this now. And maybe she did too, because it might give her something to hold on to, some small shred of truth, or hope, that would help take her beyond the lie her life had become.

With a small smile of gratitude, Rose reached into her bag and drew out a large white envelope. 'I brought these for John,' she said, laying the envelope on the table. 'I wasn't sure . . . I thought they

447

might help to get us started. They're photographs that . . . Well, I'm sure you won't remember them, but perhaps you'd like to see them.'

Feeling her heart turn over as John pushed the envelope towards her, Lucy was aware of her fingers shaking as she tipped the photographs out on to the table. She looked at the top one, and felt dizzied by the vision of a little girl with her arms around a young John's neck, squeezing so tight that all her tiny teeth were bared.

Swallowing, she picked it up and looked more closely. The girl was as cute and lively as any healthy young child could be. Her eyes moved to John's face in the photo and she found herself responding to his grimace at being held so tight, and to the glimpse of his large hand holding the tiny little back. A proud and happy father with the greatest joy of his life.

The next photograph was of the same little girl, this time wearing a red swimsuit and a yellow rubber ring while standing on the edge of a pool ready to jump. John was in the water with his arms held out waiting to catch her. In the next picture she was flying into his chest with a giant splash. Then she was asleep on the floor next to a Christmas tree, dressed as an elf. The image was so touching that Lucy felt her lips tremble as she smiled. Then came one with Rose, and they were laughing so uproariously that it made Lucy's heart turn over. How happy they looked. How close and secure. The last shot was of a small baby in a bath, with Rose holding her steady to stop her from slipping under.

Lucy was thinking of Hanna now, and the 'guess the baby' competition that had been abandoned because of the weather. If it was reinstated, would anyone guess that this little girl was her? She looked at John and wondered, had things been different, if she would have shared the same closeness with him that Hanna did with Joe. Then, realising how deeply this was affecting him, she said, 'When was the last time you saw these?'

'Before last night,' he answered gruffly, 'it would have been over thirty years ago.'

Seeing Rose's hand tighten on his, Lucy tried to put herself in their shoes and imagine how she'd be feeling if she was showing something like this to Hanna or Ben.

It was inconceivable.

'You can keep them if you like,' Rose told her. 'We can always get more copies made.'

'Thank you,' Lucy said. Then, 'I wish I could tell you . . . I'm afraid they're not jogging any memories for me.'

Rose's mouth trembled slightly and she looked at John as he said with a chuckle, 'I often think the same about photographs of myself at that age. Who's that pudgy little chap, I ask. Nothing to do with me. Our parents could show us photos of any old baby and say it was us and how would we know?' Not until the words were out did he seem to realise that Daphne and Brian might have done that to Lucy, and he immediately started to colour. 'I'm sorry,' he said, 'I could have put that . . .'

'It's OK,' Lucy assured him, 'because you're right, of course. Most of us don't bear much resemblance to the funny little creatures we were when we first came into the world. I know my two don't.'

John appeared grateful, and glanced at Rose as she squeezed his hand again.

'We need to explain now,' Rose said, 'why these early pictures of our daughter, Alexandra, are the only ones we have.' She took a breath. 'I should begin by telling you that what happened was my fault . . .'

'Rose . . .'

'No, John, please. You promised to let me do the talking and it's the truth, it was my fault. Alexandra was with me that day. I was the one who failed to get her off the train in time.'

At the mention of a train Lucy's heart skipped a beat. She glanced at Michael who gave her a smile of reassurance.

Returning her soft, melting gaze to Lucy, Rose said, 'We'd been to see my mother. She was feeling under the weather, so I went because it always cheered her up to have the children around. We were living close to Wimbledon then and she was in Hammersmith, so the journey wasn't too far, but it wasn't direct, and getting on and off Tubes with a twin pushchair and a lively two-year-old was never easy, even at the best of times.

'We got there without too much fuss, but on the way back you – *Alexandra* – decided she wanted to run up and down the carriage. Then Becky wanted to join her . . . She was a year and a half but she'd been walking since she was eleven months, and it was always a struggle to keep her reined in.' She attempted a smile that was part pride and part grief for where this early skill had taken them. 'Since there was only one other person on the train who told me not to mind him I decided to let them have their way for a few minutes and off they went, toddling along at their fastest pace, so pleased with themselves, arms waving and shrieking so loudly I felt sure they must be annoying the other passenger. Except he didn't seem to be taking too much notice . . . Then we were

450

close to our station so I called the girls back and . . .' She swallowed hard as her voice started to falter. 'Becky won the race to reach me so Alex pushed her over and I was angry, because Becky hit her mouth . . . There was blood all over the place and I told Alex she was in big trouble . . .' Her head went down and John slipped an arm around her.

'Those were the last words I spoke to her,' she said brokenly. 'I told her she was in big trouble and it frightened her, so she didn't get off the train.'

As she started to break down Lucy felt so wretched for her that she wished she could make this stop. She shouldn't have to go through it again, no mother should, and yet if she didn't nothing would be explained.

'I only realised when we were on the platform,' Rose finally managed, 'that you weren't with me, and then I saw you standing where I'd left you, like you were frozen to the spot.'

Did she realise, Lucy wondered, that she'd changed from the third person to the second?

'I shouted at you to come, but you wouldn't move. I dropped Becky and rushed to the doors, but they were already closing. I shouted for someone to open them, but no one heard. The man ran over from his seat, but the train was starting to move. I screamed out for it to stop but it didn't. I banged on the doors, and ran with the train, screaming for help, but the only person who seemed to realise what was happening was the man who was with you. He – he pointed down the carriage and said, "Next station."'

Realising that the woman who shouted in her dreams must be Rose, Lucy felt as though she was being borne away into that tunnel again, dragged from the world she knew into another that seemed dark and terrifying, with no way out.

'I – I rushed back to Becky and Simon,' Rose was saying with a stammer, 'and I waited what felt like an eternity for the next train. If I'd been in my right mind I'd have gone straight to the station manager, but all I could think about was your face as the train pulled away, and getting to the next station.'

Almost feeling her horror as she stood on the platform with two children who might be crying, or mute with fear, Lucy glanced at John. His face was pale and strained, and his eyes showed how deeply he'd suffered.

'I can hardly remember getting on the next train,' Rose said. 'I think Simon and Becky were still crying, but all that mattered was getting to Southfields where the man would have you safe and everything would be fine.' She swallowed hard. 'But it wasn't, because when I got there he was nowhere to be seen, and nor were you. I'm sure I started to scream, because a woman came running. I told her what had happened and she ran off to find someone, but I didn't wait for her to come back. I raced out of the station with the pushchair and began running up and down the street, calling your name. Then it occurred to me that he might have bumped into someone who knew you and they'd told him where you lived. So instead of going back to the station I ran all the way home. I realised later, of course, that I'd done everything wrong, but I was in such a state I hardly knew what I was doing.'

Knowing how distraught she'd have been in the same circumstances, Lucy completely understood the confusion.

'When I got home and you weren't there,' Rose

continued, 'I called John to tell him what had happened. I'm sure you're wondering why I hadn't contacted the police yet, and I did try, but there was someone in the only phone box I passed and she wouldn't come out. She even hit me as I tried to grab the phone. I kept trying to tell her why I needed to use it, but it turned out she wasn't English so she didn't understand.'

She put her head down and inhaled shakily.

After a moment John said, 'Maybe I should take it from here?'

Rose looked at Lucy, and Lucy could see from the determination in her eyes that she needed to go through with this herself. 'After I rang John,' she continued, 'I rang the police. I know it was the wrong order . . .'

'By then it wouldn't have made a difference,' John reminded her. 'They still got there before I did.'

'But it added to the mistakes I made that day, and when I think of how we've paid for them since . . .'

'It's OK,' John said softly as her voice gave out.

'You were the one who paid the most,' she whispered, gazing at him with eyes so full of pain that Lucy could hardly bear to look.

'We all did,' he said. And turning to Lucy, 'The worst part of it was knowing that it was a man who'd taken you. You were a very engaging little girl, so we could only think the worst. Being a mother yourself, I'm sure you can imagine the kind of hell we went through.'

In no doubt of where their minds had taken them, and knowing she'd probably rather kill herself than go through the same torment, Lucy said, 'I know it's too late now, but nothing like that happened to me.'

Rose's eyes came back to hers. 'If we'd known that then,' she said, 'we might have been able to cope with it better, but we didn't. All I could see or hear in my mind was you crying for us, or screaming, or thinking I'd left you on purpose because I'd said you were in trouble.' Her hand went to her mouth as a sob took her words. 'Sometimes I used to pray you were dead,' she admitted. 'I could stand that more easily than I could the thought of someone hurting you.'

Though Lucy understood that too, the question that kept repeating in her mind now was *why didn't you find me?*

'Those weeks, months, were the worst we've ever lived through,' Rose told her. 'It seemed as though the whole country was involved in the search. John made an appeal on TV for the man on the train to come forward, or anyone who might know who he was, but none of the responses we got ever came to anything. The police interviewed hundreds of people, all our friends, our families, total strangers, but as time rolled on there was still no sign of you. Then, just as we thought it couldn't get any worse, the police turned up one day to start digging up our garden.'

Lucy stopped breathing.

'It went on for days, and the way the press turned on us was terrible. They accused me of making up the train abduction in order to cover up my crime; they even found experts to say that a mother's first instinct in such a situation would be to call the police. So why had it taken me so long? They found the woman who'd gone for help at the station, and she said she'd thought at the time that I might be putting on an act. No one ever found the woman in the phone box, so I was accused of lying about that too. Then the police started to view us as abusive parents, their evidence being the cut on Becky's lip when they'd first come to the house. There was even talk of taking her and Simon into care. Thank God that didn't happen, but the nightmare was still far from over, because then they arrested me for murder.'

Lucy's head started to spin. All this injustice and terror because Daphne and Brian had decided to make her theirs.

'The interrogation they put me through wasn't only relentless, it was often cruel and vindictive,' Rose continued. 'They kept on and on trying to make me tell them where I'd hidden the body. They even dug up my mother's garden, and part of a woodland in a nearby park. Then they tried to make me say that John had done it and I was covering up for him. They told me it would go easier for me if I admitted it had been an accident. They even described various scenarios that could have happened. No one wanted to believe the truth.

'In the end, after I'd been formally charged and remanded in custody our lawyer warned us that though there wasn't any actual evidence to prove I'd done anything, it wouldn't be the first time someone had been found guilty without it, and the signs for us weren't good. That was when . . .' She turned to John, and her eyes were only on his as she said, 'That was when John went to the police and offered a full confession if they'd let me go.'

Stunned, Lucy looked at John too, but he only had eyes for Rose.

'He'd decided, along with his best friend, Douglas,' Rose told her, 'that the only way to end the ordeal was for him to give the police what they wanted so that I could go home to the twins. They could manage without him, he said, but they couldn't without a mother and of the two of us he would be more able to cope with prison. I argued with him, and begged him to change his mind, but he wouldn't listen, and nor would the police. They had a signed confession, which was all they needed to get the case cleared up and off their books. It didn't even seem to make a difference that there was still no body, or that John, in the early stages, had provided an alibi for where he'd been that day. According to them the crime could have been committed at any time, so the fact that he'd been at work while I was causing a scene at the station was no proof of anything.'

As the unimaginable horror of what they'd been through folded its terrible weight around her heart, Lucy could only wonder what Daphne and Brian had been doing while this was going on. With so much media attention they must have known they were devastating the lives of innocent people. How could they have let that happen? The people she'd known as her parents surely never would have behaved like this.

'So the police went ahead with the prosecution,' Rose continued, 'and John was given a life sentence. I was allowed to see him before they took him away, and that was when he told me about the pact he'd made with Douglas. Douglas had always had a strong affection for me, and because John didn't want Simon and Becky growing up with a convicted murderer as a father, the best thing I could do for everyone was divorce him and marry Douglas. He even wanted Douglas to adopt the twins so they wouldn't be Mckenzies any more.'

Her eyes went down to where her hands were bunched around John's on the table. 'The only reason I went through with it was because I wasn't in my right mind, and of course for the children. If it hadn't been for them I know I'd never have agreed to the divorce, no matter how long John was forced to serve.' She looked at Lucy again. 'Over the years Douglas never stopped trying to find you, in spite of knowing he'd lose me and the children if he did. I lost count of how many private investigators he hired, but none of their leads ever came to anything. He wrote to John, quite often I believe, but John didn't write back, nor would he allow either Douglas or me to go to see him. His only visitor was Pippa.'

John nodded. 'It wasn't easy cutting myself off like that,' he admitted, 'but I was convinced it was the right thing to do, unless you were found. Obviously everything would change then, but it never happened, and by the time I was released it would have been wrong of me to try to disrupt Douglas's family then. Simon and Becky believed he was their father and because I knew what an honourable man he was, I was in no doubt that they loved him too. I knew Rose would too, in her way, so the best thing for me to do then was to go north with Pippa, back to our roots and the small electronics company she had bought with her inheritance from our father.

'And that is where we stayed, building the business together until we had several factories, and plenty of offers to buy us out. We eventually sold just after Philippa's cancer was diagnosed. Her health had to come first, and I knew if I continued to work then so would she. As you know, she's in remission now, thank God, but it was her brush with mortality that made her determined to see me reunited with my family before it was too late. Ironically, it was while she was sitting in a doctor's waiting room, in fact on the very day he gave her the good news, that she came across a newspaper advertisement for a house to rent in Cromstone Edge. It seemed like fate, and I couldn't disagree, and so we came.'

As the journey reached a place she was familiar with, Lucy sat back in her chair knowing that later she'd probably have a hundred questions to ask, but right now all she could think of was the extraordinary, almost breathtaking way in which life had contrived to bring them to where they were now. The manor house, Douglas, Daphne's ambition, Philippa's illness, even her own failing marriage, had been used, even exploited, by a wayward and uncaring fate to map their lives and break their hearts. How shocking and terrifying it must have been for her mother when she'd found out who the Bancrofts and Mckenzies really were. It was no wonder she'd turned to God, but hadn't He already forsaken her by bringing her here? Wasn't He treating her with the same sort of indifference that He'd once shown towards John and Rose?

As her eyes went to Rose she saw the woman who'd screamed in her nightmares, and she felt such pity for her that her heart could barely contain it. How could her mother – Daphne – have comforted her during those troubled nights and pretended there was nothing to be afraid of, when all the time she knew what she'd done? How heavy had her conscience been at the time? How heavy was it now?

'Of course Becky and Simon don't know any of this yet,' Rose told her.

'When they come on Saturday,' John said, 'we're intending to tell them everything, of course, and at last we can introduce them to the sister they . . .'

'Actually,' Lucy said, getting to her feet, 'would you mind excusing me for a moment?' and before anyone could even express surprise she ran upstairs to her room.

Chapter Twenty-Two

A while later Lucy was still curled in the window seat of her room gazing down at the lawns below, trying to work out why she'd rushed off like that – apart from suddenly feeling that she couldn't take any more, at least for a while. Were they thinking her rude now, or sick? A coward, or someone who was unfeeling? Were they still as certain she was theirs – as certain as she now was?

Letting her head fall back against the window, she closed her eyes in bewildered despair. All these years she'd been living a life that wasn't hers, with people she didn't belong to, in places she should never have been, so was it any wonder that nothing had ever felt right? She wondered how she could have forgotten the Underground train, and yet she hadn't, because a dislike of travelling that way had obviously been born that day, along with the morbid dread of letting go of anyone she loved. And how was she supposed to feel about it all now? Angry? Cheated? Betrayed? Joyful that something was making sense at last? Vengeful towards two people who loved her so much? Happy for the parents who'd lost her? How could she even begin to know what to do?

Hearing a knock on the door, she looked up as it

opened. Her heart contracted when she saw it was Rose.

'May I come in?' Rose asked.

Inhaling deeply as she pushed back her hair, Lucy nodded and lowered her feet to the floor.

'Sarah's just arrived to start work,' Rose told her, coming to sit on the edge of the bed. 'She hopes you don't mind, but she knows there's a lot to do so she thought she ought to carry on.'

'No, it's fine. I'm glad she's here. How did she . . .? Is she all right?'

'I think so. She was shocked, of course, when we told her, and upset about her own father, but pleased about you.'

Lucy swallowed dryly. Sarah was her half-sister. How was it going to be when she next saw her? Or when Simon came? Knowing Lucy as a friend was one thing, finding out she was a member of their family was another altogether. Would she seem like an intruder, an impostor even? Someone who was trying to break into their exclusive world? It was how she felt. 'I'm sorry I ran out so abruptly,' she said.

'You don't have to apologise. It was a lot to take in, and expecting you to share our joy this soon . . . Well, it's asking too much.'

Appreciating her understanding, Lucy looked down at the floor as she tried to think what to say. 'I keep wondering if there's been a mistake,' she said. 'Do you think there has? We haven't had the results yet.'

Rose's eyes were gentle as she looked back at her.

Lucy's head went down again, and as she thought of her parents she felt another unsteadying rush of emotion. 'I keep remembering how nervous my

461

mother was before she left,' she whispered. 'I thought it was to do with the business, but now I realise it was because of John.' She took a tremulous breath. 'She kept going to church to pray. She must have been so afraid.' She paused again as she tried to cope with her mother's fear. 'They're very simple people, my parents . . .' She stopped suddenly, as though the word were a block. Keeping her eyes down, she said, 'I don't suppose I should call them that any more, should I? Their names are Daphne and Brian.'

Rose said nothing, and Lucy didn't even want to try to imagine what she might be thinking.

'What they did,' Lucy continued. 'I know it was awful, unforgivable, but if you knew them . . . Of course you wouldn't want to, but you'd never imagine them hurting anyone . . .' She felt a catch in her heart as she thought of how deeply they'd hurt Rose and John. 'Knowing what they put you through, what they must have *known* you were going through when they'd lost a daughter themselves . . .'

'What's important,' Rose said gently, 'is that they were good to you and gave you the best life they could.'

Thinking of all the loneliness and never seeming to fit in, Lucy gave a humourless laugh. 'What they gave me . . .' She stopped, realising she was about to sound resentful, which she was, in a way, when she imagined the kind of life she should have had. They'd never been cruel, or neglectful, though. In fact, they'd done everything in their power to make her feel happy and safe. 'They never did anything but love me,' she said softly.

'Then given where we are today, that's the best we can hope for to help us go forward.'

'But it still doesn't make it right.'

'Of course not. Nothing will ever do that.'

Not blaming her for the note of bitterness in her voice, Lucy heard a note of contempt in her own as she said, 'You read the letter they sent. They saw me as a gift from God. It was how they tried to justify what they did.'

'I'm sure it worked for them,' Rose responded, her tone as flat as the light in her eyes.

Lucy looked at her and wasn't sure whether to apologise, or defend them, or swear some sort of awful retribution.

'From the little I've heard about them,' Rose continued, 'I'm sure they'll be judging themselves very harshly now.'

Not doubting that for a moment, Lucy felt her heart tearing in two. 'We don't even know where they are,' she said hoarsely.

There was a small irony in Rose's tone as she said, 'Well, it's sad but true to say that they have something of a skill for disappearing.' Then, 'I'm presuming it was Brian who was on the train.'

Lucy said, 'I presume so too.'

'All I really remember about him was how sad he seemed. After that he turned into a monster in my eyes.'

'I'm sure, but he wasn't, at least not in that sense.' She took a breath. 'I guess he was sad because they'd lost their little girl. I found some newspaper cuttings . . . She died in a fire.'

It was several moments before Rose spoke again, and Lucy wondered if she was asking herself how someone who knew what it was to lose a child could have inflicted such pain on somebody else.

'Do you remember anything about that day?' Rose eventually asked.

Lucy shook her head. 'No, nothing. Maybe I've blocked it from my mind, or . . .' She shrugged. 'I don't know.'

'So you have no idea where they might have been hiding you when the search was going on?'

Lucy shrugged. 'We lived on Lundy Island until I was four and needed to go to school, but whether or not we went straight there . . . My dad – *Brian* – worked for the Landmark Trust back then.'

'And no one recognised you from all the publicity.' It wasn't so much a question as a sad statement of fact.

'I don't remember much about being there,' Lucy said, 'but I don't think there are many people on the island, and for all I know there was no TV at that time. Maybe no one saw me. Perhaps I was kept shut up in the house, except I've seen photographs of myself on the beach.' Thinking of how forlorn she looked in them, playing with stones on her own and trailing after Brian on a fishing trip, made her want to weep when she recalled the vibrant little soul hugging John with all her might.

It was a while before Rose said, 'What would you like to do now?'

Lucy's head came up and she felt suddenly afraid as she said, 'You mean about tracking them down?'

Rose met her eyes. 'We will need to at some point, of course, but what I was meaning was would you like some more time to yourself, or is it OK for me to stay and chat for a while?'

After giving it some thought, Lucy said, 'There's so much to try and get used to. I know I'll have a lot of questions once I've taken it all in and I'm sure you will too, but for now . . .'

'Say no more,' Rose said, getting to her feet.

Lucy looked up at her. 'I hope I haven't offended you.'

Coming to cup a hand gently round her cheek, Rose gazed incredulously into her eyes as she said, 'Not at all. I think we all need some time to assimilate and decide where we go from here.'

Remembering that she'd only arrived yesterday – to see John for the first time in so many years, and then to have this thrust upon her – Lucy could only wonder how she was seeming to cope so well. She didn't look like the frail depressive Sarah talked about, but maybe finding her missing daughter was all the cure she had needed.

As Rose reached the door, Lucy said, 'I can't imagine what you and John must be feeling towards Daphne and Brian at the moment, but can I ask you . . . Would you mind not going to the police yet?'

Turning back, Rose said, 'At the moment, Lucy, you and I are strangers, and the people who've called themselves your parents have made us that way, so in my heart I have little compassion for them. However, I do understand that you've had a very long, and apparently loving, relationship with them, so it's only natural that you want to protect them. Fortunately for them, John and I have been through too much to start wasting time now on vengeance. All we want is to go forward together, hopefully with you too, so we will let you decide what has to be done about the Fishers.'

The Fishers. No longer her parents, just the Fishers.

By the time Lucy went back downstairs, an hour or so later, only Hanna was in the kitchen, making herself some lunch.

'Hey Mum,' she said, glancing over her shoulder as Lucy came in. 'I thought you were in the office.'

'I'm just on my way there,' Lucy told her, presuming it was where she'd find Michael, since his car was still outside. 'Are you OK? What are you doing this afternoon?'

'Juju and I are getting the bus into Bath, if that's all right. They've got some really cool shops there apparently. Where's the ketchup?'

Taking it from the fridge, Lucy said, 'You need to keep an eye on that cheese, it's starting to burn.'

Leaping to the rescue Hanna yanked it from under the grill, and slid both pieces of toast on to a plate before coating them in sauce. 'So, that was OK at the school last night, do you think?' she said, starting to eat.

'They all seemed very nice,' Lucy agreed, feeling as though the meet and greet had happened in another lifetime. In a way it had. 'I particularly liked your form tutor.'

'Yeah, me too. She reminds me a bit of Granny, but younger.'

With an unbearable heaviness in her heart, Lucy attempted a smile as she said, 'So how was Philippa this morning?'

'Oh, you'll never guess what,' Hanna chirped excitedly. 'She's only gone and ordered a Wii dance thing. It's so cool. You should see it. We were watching it online. She says we can use it whenever we like, and if we can get John boogieing on down, that's what she said, boogieing on down, it was hilarious . . . Anyway, if we can get John to do it we have to let her know so she can secretly video him and put it on YouTube. She is so out there, that woman. John always says she's a real handful and

I can see what he means. Do you want some of this?'

Having nothing even resembling an appetite, Lucy dropped a kiss on Hanna's forehead as she said, 'All yours. Have you heard from Ben today?'

'Not yet, but he said he was going on some elephant ride in the jungle so he might not be in touch till he gets back.'

Trying not to imagine drug lords and guerrillas leaping out from behind every bush, or deadly snakes dropping from trees, Lucy went to pour herself a coffee to take to the office with her. 'I don't suppose you've heard from Granny and Grandpa either,' she said lightly.

Biting into her toast, Hanna shook her head. 'Have you?'

'I had a letter yesterday letting me know they'd gone on a little trip. They didn't say to where, but I guess they could be back in Exmoor by now.'

Hanna shrugged. 'Do you know when Dad's coming, Friday or Saturday?' she asked.

Already dreading the prospect, Lucy said, 'I think Saturday, but I expect he'll let us know.'

'So have you two made up yet?'

'I'm not sure, we haven't spoken much since last weekend.'

Looking almost parental, while sounding very sure of herself, Hanna said, 'I honestly don't think it's serious between him and Annie, you know. She's not really his type, for a start, not when you compare her to you, and I think he only did it because he was mad at you for ignoring him so much, and you can't really blame him for that.'

Thinking with a tinge of irony how little time it had taken for the issue to become her fault, and even accepting that in part it probably was, Lucy said, 'How would you feel if it *was* serious between him and Annie?'

Hanna shook her head confidently. 'It's just not,' she told her.

Though Lucy wanted to say something like *you can never be too sure about people*, or *you only know the side of your father he wants you to know*, she reined it in and said instead, 'I need to get going. Do you have some money to spend in Bath?'

'Yeah, but if you want to give me more . . .' She waggled her eyebrows mischievously.

Treating her to a menacing look, Lucy dug into her purse and handed over a twenty-pound note before heading towards the door.

'Mum?' Hanna said, drawing out the word.

Lucy turned back.

Hanna shrugged. 'Is something wrong? I mean, I know you're upset about Dad, and everything, but you're like . . . I don't know . . . Different from the way you usually are.'

'Am I?' Lucy said, wondering if it was possible for a difference to be any greater.

'Yeah, you're like kind of sad, or not sad exactly . . . I don't know, but I just wanted to say that if you're worried about stuff, especially, you know, with what's going on with Dad, you can always talk to me. My friends all say what a good listener I am, and they're always coming to me for advice.'

Loving her so much she wanted to squeeze her, Lucy said, 'Thank you, I appreciate that.'

'So?' Hanna prompted.

'I'm fine,' Lucy told her, 'but we will have a chat soon, because there are a few things going on that I need to tell you about.'

Hanna scoffed the last of her toast. 'Cool,' she said. 'I'm kind of busy today, but any time after that. Hey, Sarah.'

Feeling a jolt in her heart as she turned around, Lucy was aware of the heat in her cheeks as she said to Sarah, 'Hi, I was just on my way over. Is everything OK?'

'It seems to be,' Sarah replied, her own awkwardness showing in the way she didn't come right into the room. 'Michael's helping Maeve to man the phones at the moment. I have to go over to Cirencester to look at one of the antique shops. Apparently the owner wants rid of everything so he can turn it into a wine bar.'

'Sounds like a plan,' Hanna commented chirpily. 'Is Cirencester anywhere near Bath? If so, could Juju and I catch a lift?'

'Opposite direction, I'm afraid,' Sarah answered, 'but Michael might be going that way.'

'Which way would that be?' Michael asked as he came to join them.

'Bath,' Hanna told him.

'I can take you as far as Chipping Sodbury, if you're not in too much of a rush. I need to have a chat with your mum before I leave.'

'Cool,' Hanna assured him. 'I'll call Juju to let her know.'

As she went outside to use her mobile Lucy looked at Sarah.

'Are you OK?' they said in unison, then laughing and crying they walked into each other's arms.

'Does it sound corny if I say I've always felt there was something special about you?' Sarah asked.

'And I've often thought the same about you.'

'But it's not just me, is it?' Sarah said, pulling back

to look at her. 'It's so huge for you. I can't begin to imagine how you must feel.'

'I'm not sure I can either at the moment,' Lucy confessed. Then to Michael, 'I'm sorry I left like that.'

'Perfectly understandable,' he assured her.

'She's on her way,' Hanna shouted.

'I'll come and find you,' Michael shouted back.

'I should leave you two to talk,' Sarah told them. 'Simon's flying in later, so I'm not sure what'll happen tonight.'

Feeling a strange unsteadiness at the thought of seeing Simon, Lucy managed a faint smile, before taking Michael's arm and walking with him over to the barn. 'I don't think anyone's in there at the moment,' she said, 'so we shouldn't be interrupted.'

'I just wanted to make sure you were all right before I left,' he told her.

'I guess as all right as I can be under the circumstances.' She gave a shaky sigh. 'It's a bit like finding out you've been locked away all your life, and now I'm being let out I don't know what to do next.'

'I don't think you need to worry about that – with Simon and Becky arriving events will take care of themselves, at least for the next few days.'

Shrinking from the thought of it, she said, 'I take it there's no news from the labs?'

'Not yet. And none from your parents today?'

She shook her head. 'I keep thinking of how afraid they must have felt when they realised who John was. It explains the way they've been these last few weeks, and all the time I was thinking it was about Maureen and this blasted ring.' The disgust she felt towards Maureen now was such that it had to be left for another time.

Michael's voice was gentle as he said, 'I think we need to make another trip to Exmoor, don't you?'

Though Lucy could feel herself shrinking from it, she knew very well that it couldn't be avoided.

'Unless you'd rather go alone,' he added.

'Oh, no, no,' she assured him. 'Please come with me, I mean, if you can spare the time.'

'Of course I can.' Then, 'I know it won't be easy, but at least it'll give you an opportunity to talk to them before the authorities become involved.'

Unable even to begin facing that yet, Lucy said, 'John must be feeling quite anxious about seeing Simon, considering how hostile Simon's been towards him.'

'Mm, I'm sure he is, but I've known Simon for many years, and his bark is far worse than his bite. What did you think of Rose?'

With a gentle sigh Lucy said, 'She's very beautiful and . . . I don't know . . . She feels a bit like a dream.'

'That's funny, because she said much the same about you. I guess it's all going to seem unreal for a while, but I don't have any problem seeing you start to bond, given time. My concern, for the moment, is John and what's happening in the village.'

Frowning, Lucy asked, 'What do you mean?'

'Sarah just told me about a phone call she took yesterday. She's pretty certain whoever it was thought they were speaking to you, and they wanted you to know that you're going to lose your temporary workforce unless you let John go.'

Stunned, Lucy said, 'But why? He's so wonderful with everyone.'

'I'm afraid it's got out that he was in prison for killing a child. I'm pretty sure Hanna's heard about it from something she said to me yesterday, and she was most indignant, wanting to know if it was possible to sue.'

Thinking of Hanna's relationship to John, and then to Brian, Lucy felt so many mixed emotions that it was a moment before she could say, 'She's very fond of John.'

'And so are you, which is why I have to ask you to start thinking about how and when you're going to go public with things, because I know you won't want to see him hurt and humiliated for something he didn't do.'

Which brought them right back to the dreaded prospect of dealing with Brian and Daphne.

Staring absently at the objects around them, each with their own hidden story and unpredictable future, she said, 'Suddenly, seeing Simon and meeting Becky isn't feeling in the least bit daunting when compared to the thought of watching my parents fall apart.'

Lucy was in the office alone when Daphne rang, just after six.

'I'm such a daft thing, not taking my phone.' Daphne tried to laugh while managing to sound as anxious as she obviously was. 'I expect you've been thinking all sorts of things . . .'

'I got your letter,' Lucy told her.

'Yes, yes, I thought you must have by now. Dad and I are heading back to Exmoor the day after tomorrow. I wanted to let you know that, in case you were worried.'

'Of course I am, after everything you said . . .'

'There's a lot to explain, I know, and I will. I promise. I'll ring again when we're home.'

'Please don't hang up yet.'

'I have to, there's someone waiting outside.'

'No!' Lucy shouted, but the line had already gone dead. Slamming the receiver down, she snatched it up angrily as it rang again.

'You sound stressed,' Michael told her.

'My mother just called, and before you ask, I mean Daphne.'

'I see,' he responded carefully. 'What did she say?'

'Absolutely nothing, apart from the fact that she was on her way back to Exmoor. She didn't even give me a chance to ask how she was.'

'How did she sound?'

'Worried, nervous, everything you'd expect.' She closed her eyes as she tried to quell her temper. 'I guess the important thing is that she's been in touch,' she said. She wouldn't admit that she'd started to fear the worst, because she didn't want him to say that he had too.

'I was hoping to get over to see you this evening,' he told her, 'but I'm afraid there's a meeting of the Law Society in Bristol that I have to be at.'

'It's OK, I've taken up so much of your time lately. I hope you're remembering to bill me.'

'I've been there as a friend,' he assured her, 'and I wish I could be now, because I've just heard back from the labs.'

Feeling strangely as though she was being moved to another dimension, Lucy braced herself, too tense now even to breathe.

'You are Alexandra Mckenzie,' he told her softly.

Though she knew she shouldn't have felt shocked, or upset, or angry, she did, and afraid again and panicked. It was as though something awful were thundering towards her, roaring, gushing, coming so fast it was unstoppable . . . She took a gasp of air, and then oddly it was gone, leaving her to drift in a silence that seemed endless and shapeless, as though she'd somehow become suspended in time, or perhaps somewhere inside her own mind.

'Are you OK?' he asked.

Putting a hand to her head as though to stop it from throbbing, she said, 'I think so. Have you told John and Rose yet?'

'No, I wanted to call you first.'

She was listening to the birds now, and the sound of footsteps that seemed a long way away. 'Thank you,' she whispered.

'It's going to be all right,' he said gently. 'I'll ring again in the morning, but if you need to talk before that, leave a message for me to pick up when the meeting's over.'

'Thank you,' she said again, 'but I'm sure I'll be fine.'

Was she sure, she asked herself after he'd rung off. It was hard to say, when she still had no idea how to feel about anything. She was part of a family with whom she shared no history, and with so little, apart from blood, to tie them together. What was it going to be like starting from the beginning, when they were already so far into the future? And what about the parents she knew and loved, what on earth was going to happen to them?

Sarah was watching Simon as he sat in the window seat of the front parlour staring down over the village as he listened to what their mother and John were telling him. His apparent determination not to engage was upsetting her and making her feel sorry for John, who was clearly not finding this easy, even though her mother had done most of the talking so far.

Turning her thoughts to Lucy and the dreadful turmoil she must be going through now, Sarah tried to imagine how she might feel in her position, but it was hardly possible. Since Brian and Daphne were the only parents Lucy had ever really known, it was quite possible that she didn't want to belong to another family. Yet once the truth was out, what choice would Lucy have? For her part Sarah was more than ready to accept her, and she felt sure Simon would be too. She suspected, however, that their new relationship was a long way from the front of Lucy's mind right now. What must be causing her unimaginable distress was the thought of what might happen to her parents when the authorities became involved, since stealing a child was a wicked and unforgivable crime, no matter the motive, and no matter how well cared for the child had been.

Sarah was in no doubt that losing Jack in an accident, knowing that he was dead, could almost be considered a blessing when compared to what her mother had been through. At least she knew where he was and what had happened to him. Not knowing who had taken her baby girl, what they might be doing to her, or if she would ever see her again, was clearly the reason why her mother had been so tormented all these years. It was a miracle she'd come through it, particularly when it was added to the sacrifice John had made so that his wife and children could stay together. To think of his terrible existence behind bars for a crime he hadn't committed, a crime for which other prisoners would have made him suffer . . . It was so heartrending and unjust that, speaking for herself, Sarah could only hope that Brian and Daphne Fisher were ready to pay for what they'd done.

On the other hand, if it weren't for them she, Sarah, wouldn't exist, because her mother would never have married Douglas.

'Simon?' she heard her mother say.

Sarah watched him continue to stare out of the window, as though no one else was in the room and he'd taken in nothing of what had been said. Then, getting to his feet, he turned around and her heart ached to see how stricken he looked. He'd loved her father so much, and though she'd have never admitted it to her mother, it pleased her to see his loyalty to the man who'd loved him as his own. Yet it hurt her for John, who had done nothing to deserve Simon's antagonism, and whose only desire now was to be reunited with his son.

'I guess you're looking for an apology,' Simon said gruffly to John.

'No,' John replied. 'You didn't know who I was when we first met, and you understandably felt protective of Douglas.'

'He's still my father,' Simon stated curtly. 'I can't think of him any other way.'

Sarah looked at her mother as John said, 'I wouldn't expect you to, and I wouldn't want it either. He's done everything a loving father could to help make you who you are today. I know he was very proud of you, because he often wrote about you. If you'd like to read the letters I'll be happy to show you.'

It was only when Simon turned away that Sarah saw how close he was to tears. 'Mum,' she said softly.

Rose held up a hand for her to wait.

Sarah looked at Simon again, realising that for

him this was like losing Douglas for a second time and he could hardly bear it.

In the end, unable to bear it either, Sarah went to put her arms around him. 'He really loved you and that's never going to change,' she whispered brokenly.

Simon tried to speak, but his voice was too strangled, then he buried his head in Sarah's shoulder as he started to break down.

Coming to them, Rose wrapped them in her arms and held them close as they tried to absorb this shattering change to their world. 'I'm sorry, I'm so, so sorry,' she whispered raggedly. 'Maybe I should have told you a long time ago, but we did what we thought was best.'

'You lied,' Simon told her angrily. 'All our lives you've been lying to us, making us afraid that we were to blame for the way you were. Why couldn't you see how much easier it would have been if you'd just told us the truth?'

The instant Joe emerged from the station with an arm wrapped around the shoulder of a man Lucy had never seen before, she felt her heart sink like a stone. Since it was clear he'd been drinking, she was tempted to turn the car around and drive off without him. However, knowing it would only cause more wrangling and bitterness later, she remained where she was, watching him saying goodbye to his new best friend.

'Hey, it's great that you made it,' he said happily as he got into the car.

Trying not to wince at the stench of whisky, she started the engine and reversed out of the space.

'I was afraid, after the way we left things last week,' he went on, 'that I might not be welcome.'

'Hanna's looking forward to seeing you,' she informed him.

Apparently choosing to ignore the fact that she'd left herself out, he said cheerily, 'That's my girl.' Then, with no preamble at all, and even less sensitivity, 'So how have things been this week? Found out who you are yet?'

Flinching as though he'd struck her, she said, 'Actually, quite a lot's happened since we last spoke.'

Flipping open his mobile as it rang he said, 'Hey Mac. How's tricks? Did you get my message?'

Waiting as he spoke to his fitness instructor, Lucy felt herself becoming ludicrously emotional. She'd always known she couldn't lean on him, so to start letting it upset her now was pathetic and untimely. She must get herself back in control.

'Good. Can't wait to hear,' Joe said into the phone. 'Call me as soon as you know,' and ringing off he said, 'So where were we? That's right, a lot's been happening.' He turned to look at her and smiled. 'God, it's good to see you. You're looking pretty damned gorgeous, you know.'

Tensing, and not in the least inclined to tell him anything at all now, she was about to try and make a start when he said, 'Why don't I give you my good news first? It's going to blow you away. I've only got a part in *EastEnders*. OK, it's not huge, at least not yet, but the producers are saying that the character's going to be coming and going quite a bit over the next few months, and there's a chance he might turn into a regular. I am so chuffed, I can't tell you. It's right up my street, and if it does work out, well, best not to get too carried away, I guess, but it's pretty damned amazing, right?'

'Right,' Lucy agreed, wishing she could feel pleased

for him, but finding herself unable to feel anything at all. In fact, it was as though he'd stumbled into the wrong play, bringing a mood and dialogue with him that had no relevance to her world, and she just wanted him to go.

'Can't wait to tell Hanna-Banana,' he went on chirpily. 'It's going to be such a trip for her, having her daddy on the telly every week.'

Knowing that it would be, Lucy managed a smile.

'So what news on your parents?' he demanded. 'Have you got any answers out of them yet?'

'Actually, not out of them,' she replied, 'but I do know a lot more now than I did last week.'

He turned to look at her, all interest and smiles.

However, by the time they walked into the kitchen, twenty minutes later, his temper was starting to boil over. 'It's all bullshit, that's what it is,' he was shouting as he followed her in through the door. 'Total effing bullshit.'

'Hey Dad,' Hanna sang, skipping in from the hall.

'Hey you,' he responded, drawing her into a less bearish hug than usual.

'So what's bullshit?' she wanted to know as he let her go.

'All this crap your mother's spouting,' he retorted, waving a hand at Lucy.

'Joe, no!' Lucy cautioned.

'No what?' he demanded. 'Oh Christ, you're not seriously expecting to pull this off without telling her, are you? You're losing it, Lucy, do you know that? You're . . .'

'Tell me what?' Hanna broke in, starting to look worried. 'What's going on?'

Glaring at Lucy, Joe said, 'Well, it seems your mother . . .'

479

'Joe, this isn't the way to do it.'

Hanna looked suddenly afraid. 'Oh my God, she's going to divorce you,' she cried. 'Tell her you didn't mean it, Dad . . .'

'It's not about his affair,' Lucy cut in angrily.

'Oh, no, nothing so simple,' Joe told her savagely. 'No, she's got some delusional thing going on . . .'

'Hanna, go to your room,' Lucy commanded.

'I'm not going anywhere until you tell me what this is about.'

Lucy's eyes blazed into Joe's. 'I swear, if you do this now it'll be the end for you and me.'

'Don't say things like that,' Hanna cried, punching Lucy's arm. 'You know you don't mean it. Dad, make her take it back.'

'I don't think I can make her do anything,' he snarled, meeting Lucy's glare, 'because according to her she's not even my wife. I think that's what you're saying, isn't it?'

'For God's sake,' Lucy muttered, turning away before she slapped him.

'What do you mean?' Hanna demanded. 'Mum, what's he talking about? Of course you're his wife.'

'Yes, I am,' Lucy confirmed, without actually knowing if it was true.

'Well, the way I'm reading it,' Joe pronounced, 'is that she's found a very convenient way of getting around a divorce.'

Before she could stop herself Lucy shouted, 'Well, wouldn't I be the lucky one if I could? And if you had any idea of how big this is for me you'd keep your damned stupidity to yourself.'

'Mum! Stop! He's . . .'

'I told you to go to your room.'

'Don't speak to me like that. I'm not a child.'

'That's exactly what you are, and until I'm ready to speak to you I'll thank you to do as you're told.'

'No way!'

'That's right, you stay put, sweetie,' Joe encouraged, 'because I just can't wait to hear how your mother's going to tell you what she's just told me. Hang on, for the record, are you still Hanna's mother? I'm just trying to keep up with the plot, you understand.'

'You don't have to do this,' Lucy said through her teeth. 'She's your daughter, you should have more respect.'

'Oh, here we go again. This is how we turn it all around to make it Joe's fault. OK, I can take it . . .'

'You're drunk and completely out of order,' Lucy raged.

Joe's eyebrows went up as he looked at Hanna. 'She's off her trolley,' he told her.

'Dad, you shouldn't be saying these things,' Hanna cried. 'Mum's upset, you can see that . . .'

'You're too easily taken in,' Joe retorted. 'The performance Mum's giving now . . .' He gasped as Lucy threw a drink in his face. 'What the . . .'

'You need to sober up,' she shouted, 'and until you do I don't want you coming anywhere near Hanna or me,' and grabbing Hanna's arm she started to frogmarch her out of the room.

'Just a minute,' Joe hissed furiously. 'It might suit you to think I'm drunk, but what the hell do you think our daughter's going to make of *you* when you tell her that in order to try and slough off her grandparents and her father, you're claiming that you were abducted as a child – not by aliens, I'll give you that – but by Brian and Daphne . . . Are you getting this, Hanna? You're supposed to believe that your simple, adoring and honest grandparents didn't give birth to your mother, but stole her from the bosom of another family, and guess which family it is?'

As Lucy buried her face in her hands, starting to sob, Hanna quickly put her arms around her.

'Dad, stop. *Stop!*' she yelled. 'You can see you're upsetting her.'

'And what do you reckon she's doing to me?'

'Hanna, come with me, please,' Lucy said softly. 'I promise I'll tell you everything, just not like this.'

A while later Hanna was sitting cross-legged at the foot of her own bed, looking worriedly at her mother, as Lucy finished telling her what she'd found out over the last few days. 'So there you have it,' Lucy said. 'Obviously I'm still trying to get used to it myself, but if there's anything you want to ask . . . Well, I'm sure there is.'

Hanna continued to look at her, saying nothing, until finally she whispered, 'Wow, that is totally awesome.'

Lucy couldn't help but smile.

'When you said earlier that we should have a chat,' Hanna continued, 'I must admit I wasn't expecting anything like this. You are so amazing.'

Laughing as tears flooded her eyes, Lucy said, 'Do you know how much I love you, Hanna Winters?'

Hanna shrugged. 'Yeah, I guess so,' she replied. Then, 'What Granny and Grandpa did . . . I mean, depriving you of your family . . . Actually, I get it now, why you've always been so posh. You were born that way. So what does that make me? Posh or not? Oh God, I so hate Posh's clothes.'

482

'Hanna . . .'

'I know, I know, it's not about that, but they really are crap. Anyway, Granny and Grandpa should *not* be allowed to get away with what they did, because no one should get away with something like that.'

'You're right,' Lucy agreed, realising that Hanna still hadn't quite thought it all through yet. 'But remember how much you love them.'

'Yeah, but . . .'

'Listen, instead of thinking how wrong they were to keep a child that wasn't theirs, let's try to think of John and Rose and how proud they're going to be of you. John already is, obviously, and when you meet Rose . . .'

'Oh my God, John's my grandfather,' Hanna cried, finally starting to catch up. 'Which makes Pippa my . . . ?'

'Great-aunt,' Lucy supplied.

Hanna's eyes widened. 'Cool,' she decided. 'Seriously cool.' Then she began to frown. 'The thing is though . . . Oh my God, Mum, this might sound terrible but I really love Granny and Grandpa. I mean, I know that's probably the wrong thing to say after what they did . . .'

'No, sweetheart, it's the right thing to say because they've always loved you, and never given you any reason not to love them.'

'And you feel the same way, don't you?' Hanna urged, clearly wanting her to. 'I mean, I know they shouldn't have done what they did, but if they lost their real daughter . . .' She trailed off as she tried again to assimilate it all.

Deciding not to get into the rights and wrongs of it for the moment, Lucy sat quietly watching her. Finally Hanna's eyes lit with a different intensity as she said, 'It must have been so weird for you when you found those cuttings saying you were dead. That is soooo spooky. I know if it was me it would have totally freaked me out.'

'I admit, I've made better discoveries,' Lucy replied drily.

The humour seemed to pass Hanna by as she said, 'So anyway, what's going to happen about Granny and Grandpa now? Are people going to say they're nuts and lock them up in an asylum or something? Oh God, I don't think we should let that happen.'

'To be honest, I'm not sure where we go from here,' Lucy told her. 'Obviously I need to talk to them, but I don't know if they're back from their trip yet, so it's difficult to say when I'll be able to. I'm planning to go down there sometime in the next few days.'

Hanna's eyes were imbued with empathy as she said, 'Do you want me to come with you? I think it might be hard to try and do it on your own.'

Feeling another overwhelming surge of love for her, Lucy said, 'Let me think about it, because it might be hard for you too.'

Hanna didn't argue, merely seemed to drift off into how amazing it was all over again. 'So Sarah's my auntie and Simon's my uncle?' she said, evidently still testing it out.

'It would seem so,' Lucy answered. 'They've got another sister, Becky, who's Simon's twin. She's arriving tomorrow.'

Hanna immediately looked cautious. 'What's she like?'

'I don't know, I've never met her.'

'Apart from when you were like, two?'

'True, but I expect she's changed since then.'

It took a moment for Hanna to laugh, and when she did she scooped up her old teddy and hugged him to her chest. 'I can't wait to tell Ben all of this,' she declared. 'I'll send him a text, shall I? Mum abducted from train age two and three-quarters . . .'

'Don't you dare.'

'Just joking, but it will totally blow him away when he finds out.'

'I'm sure it will, but you must keep it to yourself for now. You can't even tell Juliette or any of your other friends.'

Hanna pulled a face.

'I'm sorry, I know you're probably dying to, but we have to talk to Granny and Grandpa first.'

Hanna nodded. 'I get it, and don't worry, I'm really good at keeping secrets. Everyone says so.'

Reaching for her hand, Lucy pulled her across the bed so they were sitting together.

'Why do you think Dad got so mad about it?' Hanna asked after a while.

'I suppose because he wants things to stay the same, and now they're changing it's making him feel a bit . . . Well, insecure, I suppose.'

'You are married to him though, right?'

'To be honest, I'm not sure. I'll have to talk to a lawyer.'

Lifting Lucy's hand to look at her wedding band, Hanna said, 'Do you think we ought to go down and see where he is?'

'Probably.'

As they got up from the bed Lucy said, 'Are you OK with all of this? Is it making you feel insecure too?'

Hanna thought about it. 'Not really,' she replied, 'because you're still my mum and Dad's still my dad, so what's to worry about?'

Feeling thankful that her age only allowed her to see it from her own point of view, Lucy gave her a hug. 'Nothing,' she told her.

When they returned to the kitchen they found a note from Joe letting them know that he'd gone to the pub. Lucy's eyes closed in dismay as she realised he was probably down there regaling anyone who'd listen with his wife's 'bullshit' story.

'Are we going to join him?' Hanna asked tentatively.

Lucy shook her head.

'What about if I go and get him?'

'I don't expect he'll come.' With any luck he'd stay out all night again, except what good would that do, apart from allowing her to sleep alone?

Putting her arms around her, Hanna said, 'I know he still loves you, so you don't have to worry.'

Smiling, Lucy kissed her head. 'I'll try not to,' she said, and screwing Joe's note into a tight little ball she tossed it into the bin.

It was a little after midnight when he came home as intoxicated as she'd expected, but fortunately too tired, it seemed, to start railing at her again, or, even worse, to attempt to have sex.

For a long time they lay side by side in the darkness, neither of them speaking, until in the end she felt his hand moving to hers as he said, 'I'm sorry about earlier. I was well out of order.'

'So how many people have you told?' she asked.

'Actually, I didn't tell anyone.'

'Is that the truth?'

'And nothing but.'

She turned to look at him. 'Why didn't you?'

'Because I knew you wouldn't want me to.'

Would it be foolish to believe him? Probably, but there was nothing to be gained from arguing.

'I don't want to lose you,' he whispered. 'Tell me what I have to do to stop that from happening.'

Knowing it was already too late, she turned to stare at the ceiling again.

'I guess I owe Simon an apology,' he offered, clearly hoping it might help his case. 'And about Annie . . .'

'Please don't let's go there,' she interrupted.

After a while he said, 'Don't shut me out. I'm doing my best here. I want to be there for you, I swear I do.'

Though she didn't disbelieve him, she could only wish that he knew how to fulfil his promise, but he didn't, so all she said was, 'I'm tired and we both need to get some sleep.'

Lucy knew when Becky arrived in Cromstone because Hanna came running in to tell her that a taxi had just pulled up outside the manor and a 'really tall woman with short dark hair and great big sunglasses' had got out.

'You should have seen her, Mum,' she gushed. 'I swear she's a bloke really, except she's not, because she was carrying a really cool bag and wearing seriously high boots. I reckon they were Jimmy Choo, but it was hard to tell without being up close.'

'Did she see you?' Lucy asked. 'Where were you?'

'I was feeding the ducks like you told me to.'

Lucy's eyes widened with astonishment.

'Joke!' Hanna grinned.

Flipping her, Lucy said, 'Well, I guess we'll get to meet her later, presuming she wants to meet us, that is.'

'Who could not want to meet us?' Hanna cried. Then, 'You know, I'd be really excited if I was you. I mean, that's if we don't think about Granny and Grandpa, because that's definitely not good.'

Though she was unable to think about much else, Lucy said, 'I suppose I am a little excited, but anxious too.'

'Yeah, I guess I can understand that, because it must be totally weird going from being an only child one day to someone who has one and a half sisters and a brother the next. So, have you heard yet how Simon took it?'

Feeling a wave of nerves catching her breath, Lucy said, 'No. I thought Sarah might be over this morning, but there's no sign of her so far. I'm not sure whether that's good or bad.'

Apparently deciding she wasn't sure either, Hanna said, 'Shall I go and wake up Dad, or should we let him lie in a bit longer?'

'I think we'll leave him. Hello,' she said into the phone, 'Cromstone Auctions.'

'Lucy, it's Rose. I hope I'm not disturbing you.'

As her heartbeat slowed Lucy looked at Hanna. 'No, of course not,' she replied. 'What can I do for you?'

'I was just wanting to find out how you are today, and to let you know that any time you want to talk I'll be here.'

'Thank you, that's very thoughtful of you.' Then, after a pause, Lucy said, 'I believe Becky's arrived.'

'Yes, she's upstairs unpacking.'

She wanted to ask about Simon, but wasn't sure how to frame the words.

'I was wondering,' Rose said, 'if you might have spoken to Hanna yet.'

Experiencing another catch in her heart, Lucy's eyes returned to Hanna as she said, 'Yes, I have. She's taken it very well, but obviously she's worried about the grand— About Brian and Daphne.'

'Of course. I'd like to meet her, when she's ready.'

'I'm sure she'd like that. We – uh, I'll have a chat with her and work something out.'

'Lovely. Can I give you my mobile number?'

Reaching for a pen, Lucy wrote it down and said, 'Thank you. I guess we'll speak later.'

After ringing off she said to Hanna, 'That was Rose. She'd like to meet you.'

Hanna's eyes lit up. 'When?'

Starting to feel slightly overwhelmed, Lucy said, 'Actually, can we do it later? It's just . . . Well, what are your plans for the rest of the morning? I don't suppose you feel like getting out of here for a while and going shopping with me?'

Hanna pulled a face. 'Juliette and I were planning to go and see if Lucas is back . . . But hey, no probs, I'm here for you, so I'll text Juju now and tell her I can't make it.'

'Are you sure you don't mind?' Lucy asked. 'I don't want to be stuck here waiting for something to happen with Becky, or Simon, and it's making me feel better having you around.'

Glowing with self-importance, Hanna said, 'I told you before, I'm a really good listener, and you're my mother, for God's sake, so I'm definitely going to be there for you.'

After arranging to meet ten minutes later, back in the kitchen, Lucy left Hanna sending her text while she ran upstairs to change into a smarter pair of jeans and one of her better tops. With any luck she'd come back from their shopping trip with something that made her look, if not as chic as Becky sounded, then at least a little better groomed than she was right now. She'd like to think she could achieve something of Rose's elegance, but that was probably far too tall an order for a mere morning's shop.

After pulling a brush through her hair, she was on her way out of the room when Joe started to come to.

'Hey,' he said croakily from the bed. 'Where you off to?'

'Shopping with Hanna.'

'No kidding? You're going to take some time off. Well, that's good news.'

Deciding she had to invite him, even though she didn't want to, Lucy said, 'Would you like to come with us?'

Yawning and stretching, he said, 'Yeah, I might. You'll have to give me time to shower and shave.'

Eager to be gone now, Lucy said, 'On second thoughts, you know you don't like shopping, so why don't you come on later and meet us for lunch? We'll probably go to Chipping Sodbury, or Cirencester. I'll call to let you know and leave you some cash for a taxi.'

Nodding agreement, he yawned again and threw back the duvet. 'Actually,' he said, planting his feet on the floor, 'I think I'll come now, because with the way things are going there might be a lot more of us around the place later, so I ought to make the most of my girls while I can.'

Biting down on her disappointment, Lucy said, 'OK, I'll wait downstairs.'

'Hang on, before you go, I was wondering what you want me to call you now. I mean, if your real name's Alexandra, is that what you want . . .'

'Lucy's fine,' she interrupted.

'Up to you, but I have to say I kind of like Alexandra, and the more I think about it the more it seems to suit you.'

Resisting the urge to ask if he felt the same about Mckenzie, as opposed to Winters, she picked up her bag and left the room.

An hour later she and Hanna were in the office catching up with emails while continuing to wait for Joe. Inwardly Lucy was seething that he was taking so long, since being in the same vicinity as the entire contingent of Bancrofts was wreaking increasing havoc on her nerves as the minutes ticked by. She knew so little about Becky that she couldn't even begin to guess how she might be reacting, but her instincts seemed to be telling her that Becky wouldn't be taking it well.

'I'm going to find out where he is,' Hanna suddenly announced. 'He's worse than us, the amount of time he takes to get ready.'

As she ran off to the farmhouse Lucy's heart somersaulted at the sound of her mobile phone starting to ring, and when she saw it was someone from the manor her nerve almost failed her altogether.

'Cromstone Auctions,' she said, hiding behind her professional persona.

'Hello dear,' Rose said. 'Simon would like to come and see you, so I'm calling to find out if it's convenient.'

Lucy's throat turned dry. 'Uh, yes, of course,' she said. 'And what – how about Becky? Is she . . . ?'

'Just a moment. Becky, Lucy's asking if you're going too?'

Lucy's heart turned over as a voice in the background said, 'Not right now.'

'It's OK, I heard,' Lucy said as Rose came back on the line. 'Please tell her . . . Well, it's fine. I don't want to force myself . . .'

'I know,' Rose said gently. 'Nor do we, so we must all take it at our own pace.'

After ringing off Lucy tried, and mostly failed, to stop smarting at Becky's summary dismissal. *Not right now!* It had been hard to gauge her tone from the end of a phone line, but the words were enough to warn her that Becky was less than thrilled by the news her mother had imparted. Finding herself on the brink of rejection suddenly made Lucy realise how much she wanted to be accepted, which was both annoying and upsetting. It made her seem pathetic and needy when she was actually neither. She simply wanted the chance to get to know Becky, and find out if she felt the same sort of bond with her as she did with Sarah. Was that asking too much? She didn't think so, but she guessed what mattered right now was what Becky was thinking, and since Becky had barely had time to start assimilating the changes to her life, Lucy decided she must be more understanding of why Becky wasn't ready to meet her new sister just yet.

Simon, on the other hand, was on his way over, and torn between nerves and relief that he was at least coming, Lucy started back to the farmhouse. Since they'd got along well from the start she was going to take heart from that, and do her best to stop feeling so fearful all the time. What will be, will be, she muttered to herself as she entered the kitchen, and if they ended up not wanting her as part of their family she would simply remind herself that she'd managed this long without them, so she could do so again.

Finding no sign of Hanna or Joe in the kitchen, she went to the bottom of the stairs. Hearing Hanna chatting to someone on her mobile and Joe singing along to the radio in the bathroom, she decided to leave them to it for now. Joe and Simon in the same room was a ticking bomb she didn't feel much like dealing with today, so she was going to remain hopeful that Joe stayed right where he was for at least the next half an hour.

Knowing the chances of that were about nil, she quickly went to make fresh coffee, then rummaged in her bag for some make-up. She'd just finished touching it up when she heard footsteps coming along the drive. Bracing herself with a stern reminder that she could deal with this, she began taking down cups ready to play the welcoming hostess.

'Lucy, we're here,' Sarah said from the door.

Turning, with her heart in her mouth, Lucy met Simon's eyes. Seeing a mix of amazement, amusement and tenderness there, she let her breath go in a gusty laugh.

'Who'd have thought it?' he said, coming to wrap her in his arms. 'The answer to everything.'

With a mangled sob she said, 'Can you believe it?'

'I'm doing my best,' he replied, continuing to hold her as though worried she might slip away, or simply evaporate. Then, tilting her face up so he could look into her eyes, his own lit with more irony as he said, 'Another sister, just what I always wanted.'

Laughing, she said, 'You know what they say about being careful of what you wish for.'

Clearly delighted, he hugged her to him again, while holding out an arm for Sarah to come and join the embrace.

'Are you OK?' Lucy asked her.

Sarah smiled. 'Still getting used to my demotion to half-sister,' she tried to joke.

'That's not how it is,' Simon said firmly. 'You're still every bit as special as you always were, possibly even more so now that you have exclusive rights on Douglas.'

His joke didn't quite make it either.

'You heard what John said,' Sarah told him, 'he'll always accept that Dad has been more of a father to you than he has. He doesn't want to force himself into your life, he just hopes you can be friends, for Mum's sake as much as anyone's.'

Sighing, Simon said, 'I know. I guess it would just be easier if Dad were here. He always had a way of making things seem clearer when the rest of us were flailing about in the dark.'

'I think,' Lucy said tentatively, 'that John has his qualities too. Doing what he did so that you could stay with your mother . . . There aren't many men with that sort of integrity, or courage.'

'Or foolishness,' Simon added, but there was no rancour in his tone, only a lingering residue of bewilderment and perhaps, Lucy thought, a last belligerent soldier of male pride still refusing to lie down.

'Shall we have some coffee?' she suggested. If it weren't for Becky she might have offered champagne, but with that ominous cloud still hovering on a close horizon, along with those formed by her parents, any kind of celebration would have been completely out of place.

'I'd love one,' Joe announced, coming into the kitchen.

Lucy immediately tensed, but to her relief, with

494

no hesitation at all Joe turned the charm to full flow as he went to shake Simon by the hand.

'Seems I got it wrong about you,' he said with no small irony, 'and for that, as well as the right hook, I owe you an apology.'

'Accepted,' Simon told him, though his tone wasn't quite as warm as Joe's.

Telling herself this was the best she could hope for right now, Lucy watched Joe overdoing his fondness for Sarah with a giant bear hug, and was just starting to pour the coffee when someone else appeared in the doorway.

Knowing instantly who it was, Lucy felt her insides dissolve into turmoil. She might be a taller, less radiant version of Rose but the similarity was striking, as was the directness of her gaze, which was scything through the room straight at Lucy.

'Becks,' Sarah said, glancing nervously between her and Lucy. 'You came, that's great.'

Becky's eyes didn't leave Lucy. 'Well, your colouring's similar,' she stated matter-of-factly, 'and I suppose, at a stretch, we could say you resemble John . . .'

'Becky,' Simon cut in darkly.

Aware of Joe bristling, Lucy said, 'We're about to have coffee, if you'd . . .'

'The family has no money, I hope you're aware of that,' Becky told her. 'Oh, but of course, John does, so I guess that's . . .'

'Who the hell do you think you are?' Joe snarled, starting forward.

'It's all right, Joe,' Lucy said, catching his arm. To Becky she said, 'I didn't ask for this.'

Becky's brows formed a supercilious arch.

'You haven't even given her a chance,' Sarah told her.

'I'm not as gullible as you,' Becky retorted. 'Or as taken in by a pretty face as my brother seems to be.'

'Becky, why did you come?' Simon demanded.

'I wanted to see her for myself, and I'm telling you, Simon, she's no sister of ours,' and giving no one the opportunity to respond she turned on her heel and left.

Chapter Twenty-Three

After settling Brian comfortably in his chair, Daphne passed him a cup of tea and went to check her phone to make sure it was charging. She hadn't meant to leave it behind when they'd set off, but by the time she'd discovered she'd forgotten it they were already too far into their journey to turn back.

The trip to Hastings had really taken it out of Brian. He was worryingly pale now, and could hardly keep his head up, he was so tired. It was alarming her to see how rapidly he was fading. Even taking a week to make the journey, stopping often and doing none of the driving himself, had been too much for him, but she knew he wasn't sorry they'd gone. They went every year to put flowers beneath the tree they'd planted themselves, at the edge of a playground close to where they'd lived before the tragedy of the fire.

After making sure he was still comfortable in his chair, she wrote a note to remind him where she'd gone when he woke up, then put it on his lap along with the note Lucy had left when she'd come with Michael. Daphne could only feel relieved that she and Brian had already set out on their journey by then, because they'd needed to make one more visit to the tree before they faced the consequences that were swarming in over the horizon.

The drive to the lay-by was mostly downhill, winding and dipping as she cut through the swathes of mist like a lonely apparition. Beside her on the seat her mobile was starting to come to life, letting her know that there were voicemails and texts all needing attention.

As she pulled into the lay-by tears were blurring her vision, and she could hardly see where she was going by now. After turning off the engine she sat for a while with her eyes closed, her heart so full that it was a struggle for it to beat. In the end she picked up the phone and without listening to her messages or reading the texts, she scrolled to Lucy's number and pressed to connect.

'Mum!' Lucy cried after the second ring. 'At last. Where are you?'

Mum. She was still calling her Mum, and Daphne was so moved that she almost couldn't speak. 'We're home now,' she told her croakily. 'We got back about an hour ago.'

'Where did you go? I've been so worried.'

Daphne took a breath to answer, but found she couldn't.

'Mum, are you OK?'

'We had to see someone,' she finally managed. 'It turned into a longer trip than I expected and . . . I'm sorry. How are you, dear? Is everything on track for the next auction? Is there anything I can help you with?'

'Mum, we need to talk. You said the last time you rang . . .'

'Yes, I remember.'

'You have to tell me . . .'

'I will, dear. It's why I'm ringing.' Her eyes closed as words and images swam like a jumbled puzzle in her mind.

'I'm coming down there,' Lucy told her.

'You don't need to do that.'

'You know I do.'

'Yes, of course.' Daphne was thinking of Brian now at home on his own, perhaps reading the notes she'd left, or more likely still asleep. 'When will you come?'

'Hanna starts her new school tomorrow, so I'll be there on Wednesday. OK?'

'Lovely,' Daphne murmured. 'I'll get a panettone to have with some tea. You and Hanna always like panettone.'

At her end, as she rang off, Lucy was torn between relief and frustration. 'Well, at least we know where they are now,' she said to Sarah, who was sitting at her own desk.

'Did she say where they've been?' Sarah asked.

Lucy shook her head. 'Just that they had to see someone, but who that might be or where it was . . . your guess is as good as mine.'

Glancing at the phone as it started to ring again, Sarah let the machine pick it up as she said, 'So you're going down there?'

Though she was baulking inside, Lucy nodded, and took out her mobile. 'I should call Michael to find out when works for him.' She could go alone, and maybe she should, but she truly didn't feel capable of making the journey on her own. Besides, they were going to need Michael not only as a friend, but as their lawyer – and moreover, he'd help to keep things calm and rational in a way she knew

499

was simply beyond her, given the terrible conflict of emotions that assailed her every time she as much as thought about Daphne and Brian.

After leaving a message for him to get back to her, she looked at Sarah as she put the phone down again. Sarah, her half-sister, who was still so damaged and vulnerable after all she'd been through, and surely in need of some sort of reassurance, with all that was going on. 'We have a lot to talk about,' she said gently.

'It can wait,' Sarah told her. 'For now this is more important.'

Since she was probably right, Lucy let it go for the moment and with a shuddering sigh she pulled her hands over her face. 'Do you think I should let Rose and John know they're back? They might want to come with me, but I'm not sure that's the right thing to do.'

'If you're asking me,' Sarah said bluntly, 'then I think Brian and Daphne should be made to face the people whose lives they wrecked.'

As Lucy's heart contracted she found herself unable to disagree.

'OK, I wouldn't be here if it weren't for them,' Sarah continued, 'but it hardly excuses anything, does it?'

Lucy shook her head. 'I keep thinking of the kind of life I should have had,' she admitted. 'They stole that from me, and forced me to lead an existence that was . . . Well, a lot lonelier than the one I would have had, that's for sure, and the more I go over it the more bitter and angry I'm starting to feel.'

'Which is hardly surprising, when they stole you – an innocent child – from your own mother and kept you as though they had some sort of God-given right to you. It was unforgivable.'

'I know, I know, and believe me I'm not about to start defending them, but then I see their faces in my mind's eye and remember how much I've always meant to them . . . And they've always meant the world to me too. In a way it still hardly seems real. I mean, you read about this sort of thing in the papers, but you never imagine it'll happen to you.' She looked at Sarah again, and felt another wave of despair come over her. 'When I wake up in the morning everything seems fine, and then I remember what's happening and it's like I'm losing control of who I am and where I'm supposed to be going.'

Clearly starting to connect with the terrible dilemma she was in, Sarah's tone was much softer as she said, 'For what it's worth, I think you're handling it really well. Most of us would go to pieces . . .'

'And you think I'm not?' Lucy came in with a smile.

'You're much tougher than you're giving yourself credit for.'

Lucy arched a cynical eyebrow. 'Not tough enough to go and face them alone,' she confessed.

'But I think it's right that Michael comes with you.'

Lucy nodded and took another unsteady breath. 'If we had more time on our side I might be able to figure out how best to approach them, but with the way the locals are turning against John . . . He's suffered enough, and I know I can't let it go on. The trouble is, telling the truth is starting to feel like throwing my parents to the wolves. Except they're not my parents, are they?'

'Oh Lucy,' Sarah murmured, her voice imbued with feeling.

'In spite of everything, it's how they still feel,'

Lucy told her, 'and I can't pretend . . .' Trying to swallow her emotions, she said, 'I want to punish them and walk out of their lives for ever, but then I want to protect them and stop anyone doing anything to hurt them.'

Reaching for her hands, Sarah said, 'I know it's too early to remind you that you have another family who's ready to stand by you, it might not even be what you want to hear at the moment, but nevertheless we're here for you, Lucy.'

Lucy's eyes were tender as they came to hers. 'Are you speaking for Becky too?' she asked wryly.

Embarrassed, Sarah said, 'I know when she came here on Saturday she wasn't exactly . . .'

Turning away Lucy said, 'I'm sorry, I shouldn't have mentioned her. She's not my main concern right now.'

'For what it's worth, Simon gave her a serious dressing-down . . .'

'Please don't tell me that,' Lucy protested. 'I don't want to be responsible for causing a rift between them. How did she react to John?'

'Actually, she's taking to him in a very Becky sort of way, which means she's either quizzing him about the business he and Pippa had in Scotland, or she's testing his views on everything from climate change to animal rights to healthy options for breakfast. Rozzie and Pippa, I'm relieved to say, are already great hits.'

'And Simon and John? Has there been any breakthrough there?'

'Si's definitely thawing, but his pride won't let it happen too fast. They're both, him and Becky, still really angry with Mum for not telling them the truth long before now. Becky's even admitted to being in therapy to try to deal with her feelings of inadequacy and abandonment.'

'Oh God,' Lucy groaned. 'How's Rose taken that?'

'Actually, better than I might have expected, but she seems a lot stronger already with you back in her life, and John, of course. And she's spending a lot of time talking to Becky.'

'What about Simon?'

'He's being a typical male, saying he doesn't need to keep going over it, but I know he's had several long conversations with Giselle about it all. It's good that they're so close, because he definitely needs someone. We all do, and I know he won't talk to me about this because he thinks he has to protect me.'

'Does he have to?'

'Not really, I can cope. He keeps saying he wishes Daddy was here, which John seems to take very well, considering, but I'm sure it's hurtful. I don't know if they can ever be the father and son John must hope for, but over time I'm sure they'll start to bond. They're both too caring and sensible not to at least give it a try. Anyway, Simon can't wish for Daddy more than I do, because I'd give anything to be able to talk to him right now. I feel as though he and I are a bit like outsiders in all this . . . Well, I suppose we are really, because obviously Mummy wouldn't have married him if . . . Well, if things had turned out the way they should have.'

Feeling as though her own heart was wrapping around Sarah's, Lucy pulled her into an embrace as she said, 'Maybe that creates something special for us, because in a way I'm on the outside too.'

Sarah's evident relief was so touching that Lucy could only feel thankful that she was able to provide some of the reassurance she so clearly needed.

'Sorry if I'm interrupting,' John said from the doorway.

Turning around, Lucy felt her loyalties being torn apart as she realised, from the dockets he was holding, that he was there in his capacity as driver-cum-storekeeper, apparently not wanting to let her down in spite of what was being said about him in the village – not to mention everything else that had changed between them. Some semblance of normality, as well as moral support, was what he was clearly trying to convey, and as he threw out his hands in an ironically helpless sort of way, she found herself wishing they could simply go back to the way things had been before. Or perhaps to the very beginning.

'I've got a vanload outside,' he said, 'and I was hoping Joe might help me unload.'

Realising that Carl must have decided to join the others who were boycotting the company because of John, Lucy's heart ached with guilt as she said, 'He went back to London this morning. Shall I ring around to see if we can find someone else?'

'Tell you what, I'll go and get Simon,' Sarah declared, and allowing no time for an objection she was gone.

Left alone, Lucy looked at John again and hardly knew what to say. Only a few days ago he'd been someone she'd grown very fond of, now she had no idea at all how to feel about him.

'She could have rung him,' John said, 'but I don't think he'll come anyway.'

'We'll see,' Lucy responded, 'but I suspect she didn't use the phone because she wanted to give us a chance to talk.'

As his eyes searched her face she could sense the

oceans of kindness inside him and knew, instinctively, that had she been allowed to be his daughter all her life she'd love him now every bit as much as Sarah had loved Douglas – and as much as she used to love Brian. Did she still? With so much doubt and confusion smothering her feelings, it was impossible to know anything for certain. 'My parents . . .' She broke off awkwardly. 'They're back,' she finished lamely.

'Here?' he asked in surprise.

'No, they're at the cottage on Exmoor.'

He nodded, as though that made more sense.

'I'm going down there,' she continued. 'I think Michael will probably come with me, but if you want to see them . . . Obviously you have that right, I'd just rather . . . I know they don't deserve . . . I can't expect you to . . .' She stopped as his hand went up.

'I don't know what you think they do or don't deserve,' he told her, 'but I do know that you don't deserve what you're going through now. None of us do, but if I've learned anything in my life it's that we have to play the hand we've been dealt, and we have to play it with as much integrity as we can. That's not to say I can find it in my heart to forgive them, because I'm sure I never will. They've taken too much from me for that, and I'm only human, so I'm afraid I would like to see them pay for what they've done. However, Rose and I are aware that we have to consider the fact that you've had a relationship with them for most of your life, and it would be foolish of us to expect your attachment to them to be any less than it is.'

He paused as though expecting Lucy to speak, but there was nothing she could say in Brian and Daphne's defence that he would have wanted to hear. She wasn't even sure she wanted to defend them.

'From my own brief experience of knowing them,' he continued, 'I don't find it hard to believe that they are fundamentally decent people, but that doesn't take away the harm that they did. In truth I'd like never to see or hear of them again, but obviously that can't be possible, and perhaps Rose and I do need to meet them. I'll talk it over with her, but for now, I can see that it's important for you to see them first, so that you can ask all the questions you need to without feeling distracted or crowded by too many people with questions of their own.'

As Lucy struggled for something to say, he reached for her hand and held it gently between both of his. 'I appreciate that we still have a long way to go before you can think of me as your father,' he said, 'but it's who I am and who I'm proud to be.'

As her heart overflowed with emotion, there was nothing Lucy could do to stop herself breaking down.

'Sssh, sssh, it's all right,' he soothed, pulling her into his arms. 'We'll work this out, I promise.'

'I'm sorry,' she sobbed, 'it's just that I honestly don't know what to do . . . I mean of course I want to get to know you – and Pippa and Rose, even Becky if she'd allow it.'

'Don't you worry about her,' he said confidently, as though he'd known Becky all her life, 'she's a pushover, she just doesn't know it yet.'

Lucy found a smile. 'I hope you're right,' she told him, feeling pleased for him that he was starting to forge a connection with his younger daughter. However, Becky was the least of her problems right now, and they both knew it.

* * *

On Wednesday morning Lucy was up at six, unable to sleep in any longer since she'd been awake half the night, tearing herself apart with how she was going to confront her parents when she saw them later in the day. Hanna, God bless her, having sensed what a difficult time she was having, had come to offer some words of wisdom in the night, though Lucy could barely remember them now. Something about keeping cool and remembering that Granny and Grandpa had made her who she was today, and given her the business and a lovely home, so she mustn't be unkind to them. Not that Lucy had any intention of being unkind – she only wished, caught as she was between outrage and despair, she knew what she *was* intending.

Leaving Hanna still snoring softly on Joe's side of the bed, she went to shower and dress before going downstairs to immerse herself in work until it was time for Hanna to get up. At least, with her head in some accounts, she might stop talking herself round in so many circles that she had no idea where one began or the other ended. Just thank goodness Hanna's first day at her new school yesterday had gone as well as it had, because were she to be facing problems on that front too at the moment, she had no idea how she'd manage them.

'Ben,' she whispered into her phone as she crossed the courtyard to the office, 'it's me.'

'Who's me?' he whispered back.

Laughing, she said, 'Who do you think?'

'Would it be Alexandra Mckenzie by any chance?'

Lucy came to a dead stop.

'Mum, I reckon you're doing a double take now, and it's costing a fortune.'

'How much has Hanna told you?'

'Just look at her next phone bill.'

Still stunned, yet loving the fact that they were so close, Lucy said, 'So what do you think?'

'What do I think? Well, apart from knowing that I have the world's best mum and nothing's ever going to change that, the big question is, what do you think?'

She swallowed as she smiled. 'What I think is that I have the world's most disloyal children and I wouldn't swap them for all the riches in Christendom.'

'I'll remind you of that next time you're mad at us. Seriously though, are you OK?'

She looked around the courtyard. 'I think so,' she decided.

'So what are you going to say to Granny and Grandpa today?'

With a shudder of nerves, she said, 'I haven't really worked that out yet, but actually, I'm hoping they're going to do all the talking.'

'Of course. Boy, have they got a lot of explaining to do. Is Dad going to be there?'

'No. Didn't Hanna tell you, he starts rehearsals today for *EastEnders*?'

'Actually, she did. So you're going on your own? I should be there.'

Wishing with all her heart that he was, she said, 'Michael, the lawyer, is coming with me.'

'OK. That's good.'

'What's Hanna told you about everyone?'

'As far as she's concerned they're all really cool, especially Pippa who's apparently a female Johnny Depp. You might understand that better than I do.'

Choking on a laugh as she got the reference to *Pirates of the Caribbean*, Lucy said, 'Probably, but we'll wait till you meet Pippa so you can see for yourself.

Where are you now? Please don't tell me in the middle of a poppy field, or being held hostage by desperate guerrillas?'

'How did you guess? The ransom's going to be huge.'

'Just tell me it's not true.'

'It's not true. I'm actually in Josie's parents' villa in Bali, which is major to die for.'

'Josie?' she repeated. 'Oh, you mean the Australian girl you met up with in . . .'

'Cambodia. That's her. Ali's due to arrive tomorrow, then we're going on to Oz, but not for another couple of weeks.'

Suddenly terrified that he might fall in love with an Aussie girl and never come back, she had to quickly remind herself that it wasn't happening at this moment – or she presumed it wasn't – so she must stay focused on the present. Except that was almost equally alarming. 'Will you do me a favour?' she said. 'Text Granny and Grandpa that you love them. It'll be important for them to know that, with all that's going on.'

'I'll do it as soon as we ring off. But tell me this, do you actually want to be a part of this new family of yours?'

Realising she hadn't even asked herself the question, Lucy had to think for a moment before she said, 'I have to admit it's feeling a bit overwhelming, but I guess I'll get used to it. I just don't want anyone to be hurt.'

'That's so you, but you'll get through this, and you know, if you want me to come back, you just have to say the word.'

'No, no, it's fine,' she assured him, though she wanted it more than anything. 'It's important for you to do this trip, and for me to carry on learning to let go. Just keep in touch and stay safe, that's all I ask.'

'You got it. Love you, Mum.'

'Love you too,' and as she heard the line go dead she was already crying as she prayed desperately that he wouldn't really end up emigrating to Australia, because if there was one person in the world she could never live without, it was him.

And Hanna too, of course.

It was just after eight when she returned to the kitchen, to find Hanna looking so smart and fresh in her grey and lavender uniform that she'd have reached for the camera again, had she not used up the entire memory card taking the very same shots yesterday. She wondered if she should take them to show Daphne and Brian. They'd be thrilled to see how sophisticated Hanna looked, but with a terrible heaviness in her heart she couldn't work out how on earth she could fit such a simple action into the complications that lay ahead.

How was she going to bear to cut them out of Ben and Hanna's lives, never mind her own? She couldn't do it, she just couldn't, because without the family they'd created there would be nothing left for them.

'I'm making porridge,' Hanna told her. 'Good for you?'

'Great, thanks.' Then, scowling as she turned Hanna's face up to the light, 'Are you allowed to wear all that make-up?'

'Oh, Mum, this is nothing compared with everyone else, and it's typical of you to make a fuss when . . .'

'All right, all right,' Lucy cut in, not wanting to

get into an argument this morning, and letting her go she went to start laying the table. 'I just spoke to Ben,' she said, feeling another wave of dread coming over her as she tried to imagine the Australian girl.

'Cool,' Hanna retorted. 'How is he?'

'Enjoying Bali, by the sound of it – and apparently up to speed on everything that's happening here.'

'Ah, yes.' Hanna cast her a sheepish look. 'You had to know I was going to tell him.'

Lucy smiled. 'I suppose so,' she conceded. 'I just hope you didn't do it by text.'

'Partly, and email, but the first one was a call if that helps.'

'It does.' She allowed a few moments to pass while taking some bowls from a cupboard, then, trying to sound casual, she said, 'So do you think it's serious with this Josie?'

Hanna merely shrugged. 'Who knows? Can I have honey with mine instead of jam? Oh, this is my fave,' she cried as a Lady Gaga number swooped out of the radio.

Putting a jar of Gales on the table, Lucy started to make some tea while Hanna managed to sing, dance and share out the porridge in some impressively seamless moves.

'So, how are you feeling about today?' Hanna remembered to ask when they were sitting down. 'Are you nervous? I know I would be if I was you. What are you going to say to them?'

As Lucy's butterflies juddered into flight she said, 'I'm still thinking about it, but I don't imagine I'll be doing much of the talking.'

Hanna's expression was all sympathy as she said,

'No, I guess not. Actually, the more I think about it, the more I can't help feeling sorry for them. I mean, I know what they did was terrible and everything, but they're not like murderers or paedophiles or anything, are they? And like I said in the night . . . Oh, who's that?' she cried, grabbing her mobile as a text dropped in. As she read it Lucy watched the colour flow into her cheeks and guessed immediately who it was from.

'Oh my God, Mum,' Hanna murmured ecstatically, 'it's only Lucas asking what I'm doing after school.' Her eyes were so bright and her smile so wide that Lucy could only wish that she was a teenager again.

'Wouldn't homework be the answer?' she suggested, deadpan.

Hanna's eyebrows went skywards. 'Yeah, like I'm really going to say that,' she retorted, and starting to tap in a reply she continued to glow until she suddenly put the phone down again. 'I don't want to look too eager,' she explained, 'so I'll wait till I'm on my way to school to text back. So, what time are you going?'

Unable to eat any more, Lucy carried her bowl to the sink and rinsed it. 'I'm meeting Michael at ten thirty,' she said, 'so we should be there around one.'

Hanna was starting to look worried. 'You know, I reckon I should come with you,' she said. 'At least I'm family, and I'll be able to stop you if you start going off on one.'

'That's not going to happen,' Lucy assured her, even though she knew very well that it might, 'and this is only your second day of school, so no way are you taking any time off. In fact, you need to start getting yourself together or you'll be late. Don't forget, you've got gym today so I've put your sports bag at the bottom . . .'

'. . . of the stairs. Yeah, I saw it. Thanks,' and after wolfing down the rest of her porridge she abandoned the bowl and thundered up to her bedroom to collect her blazer, books and laptop.

'Text to let me know how it goes,' she said, as she rushed back through the kitchen. 'And don't forget to send them my love.' She came to a sudden stop at the door. 'Do you think that's the right thing to do?' she said, clearly confused.

In spite of not really knowing the answer, Lucy nodded. 'They've never done anything to hurt you,' she reminded her, 'so yes, I think it is.'

'Cool,' Hanna declared, and coming back to give Lucy a hug she added, 'love to you too.'

Lucy's mouth trembled as she smiled. 'And to you,' she whispered.

After Hanna had gone, leaving a bruising imprint of good luck on her mother's cheek, Lucy watched her run along the drive. She felt baffled about how seriously – or not – Hanna was taking this. Then, reminding herself that instead of worrying she should be relieved that it wasn't having a negative effect on Hanna's first week at school, she began trying to psych herself up for what lay ahead.

Ten minutes later she was sitting at the table with her head in her hands, feeling utterly desperate as she pictured the police escorting her parents from their home, driving them into town and charging them with a crime normally associated with monsters, or the mentally deficient. It might be what they deserved, but she couldn't even convince herself of that now. What would happen to them after they were charged, she wondered. Would they be released on bail, or left to moulder in prison cells? Surely to God they wouldn't be locked up straight away? It wasn't as though they were a threat to the community, and she didn't see them as a flight risk either, or not one that would get very far. She even started to wonder if it might be possible for them not to be locked up at all, because they really didn't belong with the likes of Rose West or Ian Huntley, or anyone who wilfully broke the law. They were totally unlike such criminals. They were honest and decent and they belonged together more than any other couple she'd ever known. It was the thought of them being separated, perhaps never to see one another again, that was breaking her heart in two.

How could she let them go through this?

What could she do to stop it?

Thinking of John and what it would cost him if the truth was never revealed, she felt her conscience flaring up with the realisation that she couldn't back away from this. He'd already suffered too much. It would be cruel beyond measure to expect him to go through any more when, of them all, he was the one who'd suffered the most. So his name had to be cleared and his life properly returned to him. More than anything this was what she wanted to achieve, until she thought of Brian and Daphne and what the future held for them when what they had done became known.

For a while she cried so hard she could barely breathe. Never in her life had she faced such a harrowing dilemma, nor had she felt so lost for where to turn. It was as though everything in her world had changed shape, moved away from her, turned into something she could barely understand. Nothing was the same, nor would it ever be again, and right now she wasn't even sure if she wanted it to be. She imagined all the objects around her witnessing her despair and storing it away to take down the years. How she longed to be as impervious, as detached and unfeeling, but right now she was anything but.

Seeing John driving by on his way to the barn, she toyed with the idea of going to speak to him, but what did she expect him to say? He'd already told her that he and Rose were willing to let her decide how they went forward with this. She knew very well, however, that neither of them was prepared for her to request that Brian and Daphne should get away with their crime. And she wouldn't ask that, because she knew it was madness even to think it.

Realising John was heading her way, she quickly dried her eyes and felt relieved that he had no way of knowing what was going through her mind. She wondered how he was feeling this morning – thankful that his ordeal was finally coming to as good an end as he could ever have hoped for? Of course. Excited to have Rose and his children back in his life? How could he not be? Glad that the people who'd ruined his life were about to start paying for the terrible crime they'd committed?

'Good morning,' she said, trying to sound bright as he came into the kitchen. 'Coffee's under way.'

'Just what I need,' he responded, rubbing his hands together, and taking a carton of milk from the fridge he went in search of some mugs.

As she passed them to him their eyes met, and seeming to sense her inner turmoil he put the mugs down and took her hand.

'I know today's not going to be easy for you,' he

told her, 'that's why I'm here early, in case you'd like to talk.'

Feeling her heart swell with emotion, she tried hard not to break down again as she said, 'It's OK, I know what I have to do, and I promise, I'm going to do it . . .'

'Ssh,' he said gently, and easing her into a chair he sat down too and kept her hand loosely in his. There was so much tenderness and understanding in his eyes that she had to look away. 'If life had done us the favour of making the Fishers ogres,' he said, 'then today would be far less difficult, but on the other hand it would mean that you'd grown up with people who'd hurt and abused you, which is something we thankfully don't even have to think about any more.'

This was why, Lucy reminded herself, Brian and Daphne should pay for what they'd done, because no parent should ever have to suffer the torment of not knowing what was happening to their child.

'I wish,' he continued, 'that I could take this burden from you, and believe me if I could, I would, but even if we do nothing today or next week, or next month, we both know that eventually the truth will out. There are probably already more people aware of it than we realise, and the longer we leave it the less chance you will have to be able to speak to Brian and Daphne before the police become involved. And I don't think you want to miss that chance, do you?'

Lucy looked down as she shook her head. 'I just can't make myself see what good it's going to do anyone for them to be locked away in the kind of place that's going to scare them half to death.'

'Lucy, listen to me,' he said with gentle forcefulness.

'What they did can never be condoned, you know that . . .'

'Of course I do, but . . .' *They're the only parents I've ever known,* she wanted to cry, but she couldn't because she knew it would hurt him. And it was hardly his fault that she was in the position she was now, it was solely due to Brian and Daphne, and she mustn't let herself forget that. 'Michael's driving me down there later,' she said, 'then we'll let him decide what needs to be done after I've spoken to them.'

John's eyes remained steadily on hers as he said, 'That sounds the wisest course.'

Swallowing hard, she stood up to find out whose car had just pulled into the drive. Frowning, she glanced at the clock. 'It's Michael,' she said. 'I thought we were meeting at his office.'

John shrugged as she turned to him. 'Maybe he has some business to discuss,' he suggested. 'I should probably go and look at the day's schedule. Simon's offered to come and lend a hand again, but he has some calls and things he needs to sort out first.'

Pleased to think that a friendship, at least, might be developing between them, Lucy only had time to say, 'Thanks for the chat,' before Michael appeared at the door. He looked so grave that her heart immediately turned inside out. 'Is everything all right?' she asked hoarsely.

'I have some news,' he told her. 'I think you'd better sit down. You too, John.'

Fighting back a surge of panic, Lucy glanced at John and sank stiffly into a chair.

'This arrived at my office this morning,' Michael went on, holding up an A4-sized envelope. 'Inside there's a letter for me, and another for you, Lucy.'

Lucy's mind started to race.

'After I received it I immediately contacted the police, but I'm . . . I'm afraid it was already too late.'

She suddenly couldn't breathe.

'I'm very sorry, Lucy,' he continued quietly, 'but your parents . . . Brian and Daphne . . . have taken their own lives.'

'Oh my God, no,' Lucy cried, clasping her hands to her mouth. 'They can't. Please. No, no.'

Stunned, John could only look on as Michael stepped forward to take her in his arms.

'I should have gone straight there,' she sobbed. 'As soon as I knew they were back . . . Oh my God, this is my fault . . . I should have known . . .'

'Ssh,' Michael soothed, holding her tight.

'I'm such a coward. I was afraid to face them, and now . . . Oh Mum, Dad,' she gasped, falling to her knees as the devastation of their end hit her with all its terrible force. 'I'm sorry, I'm so so sorry. I should have been there for you.'

A while later Lucy was lying on the bed staring at nothing, as her heart seemed to shatter over and over again. She didn't yet know how, or where they'd ended it, she only knew that it was as if a part of her was still caught up with them, following them over the moors as they departed, enmeshed in their kindness, absorbed by their love. She was holding on as tightly as she could as though to keep them with her, needing to let them know that in spite of everything her feelings hadn't changed, they were still the dearest, kindest people she'd ever known. It would be the same for Ben and Hanna when they found out, and she hoped with all her heart that Brian and Daphne realised what wonderful grandparents they'd been. They surely must have known as the children had so often been in touch with them to say goodnight, or hi, thinking of you, or simply how are you? Knowing it was Rose and John who should have been receiving those messages wasn't making this loss any easier to bear, if anything it seemed to be taking something special from Brian and Daphne, who'd already lost so much.

Lucy tried to comfort herself by thinking of the disgrace and humiliation they'd been spared, and though she couldn't help but feel glad of it, she was overcome with shame and anger with herself for not having gone to see them sooner. She'd known how terrified they would have been of facing the law, of prison and most of all of being separated. She should have found a way to protect them, to redirect the course of fate so that they could at least have stayed together, but she hadn't, so they'd done it for themselves. No one could tear them apart now, or force them to pay for their crime, or even ask them to say they were sorry. Perhaps they weren't, because without her their lives would have been childless, empty – perhaps, to them, even worthless?

Remembering the letters Michael had brought with him was what, in the end, took her back downstairs. She guessed that the police would arrive soon, or perhaps they'd send for her, or speak to her on the phone. She had no idea what the procedure for something like this might be. She only knew that in the days ahead she would have to start making plans for a funeral, and the mere thought of it made her stop on the stairs as the shock of their loss hit her once more. They'd gone and she would never see them again. She pushed a hand to her mouth to stifle a scream. She was now in a world where the two people who'd been at the centre of it for as long as she could remember were no longer there. Two people who'd given her everything of themselves, while depriving her of so much. Some might ask how it was possible to go on loving them after what they'd done; all she knew was that it was impossible not to.

And now it was too late to tell them that.

'Are you OK?' Michael asked, putting away his phone as she walked into the kitchen.

Aware of how she must look, she gave a lopsided sort of smile. 'Where's John?' she asked.

'In the office talking to Sarah. He'll break the news to Rose and the others after.'

Nodding, Lucy pulled out a chair to sit down. The envelope was in the middle of the table.

As gently as he could, he said, 'The police have been in touch. They need someone to go down there to identify the bodies.'

Lucy flinched at the word, and felt herself starting to panic again. *Bodies? They couldn't be bodies, they were her parents.*

'I can go if you'd rather not,' he offered.

She shook her head. No matter how difficult it might be, she wasn't going to let them down again. 'Where are they?' she asked quietly.

'They might already have been moved, but if you're asking where it happened, it was in the garage.'

She looked up, knowing, even before he told her, that they'd been found in the old Rover – the car they'd kept because *she* couldn't bear to let it go. How was she going to live with herself after this? How could they have lived with what they were facing?

'It wouldn't have been possible in a newer car,' he explained, not realising how painfully his words were chafing her guilt. 'They aren't made the same way these days.'

Realising they must have known that, Lucy covered her face with her hands. She wanted desperately to block out the image of them walking to the garage, setting everything up and then, perhaps, saying goodbye to one another before her mother put her head on her father's shoulder. *She couldn't bear it. She just couldn't.*

'The police need to see the letters,' Michael told her softly.

She looked at the envelope and knew that once she started to read she'd be plunged into the most difficult goodbye of her life, and it really wasn't where she wanted to go. However, there was no avoiding it. She had to make herself pick up the envelope and then face the fact that whatever they'd written, this would be the last time she'd ever hear from them.

Mum! Dad! Come back, please, please come back!

Picking up the envelope, she said, 'If you don't mind I'm going to take it into the sitting room.'

'Of course,' he replied. 'I'll wait here and if you need me . . .'

Swallowing hard, she nodded and got to her feet. 'Thank you,' she whispered. 'I'm not sure what I'd do . . .'

'You don't have to think about it,' he came in gently.

As she walked away Lucy wondered if she should call Joe, but then the thought was gone and moments later she was curling into a corner of the sofa with a letter, written in Daphne's familiar hand, trembling slightly in her own.

Dearest Lucy

This is a letter Dad and I have long feared we might one day have to write, but now that day has come we find ourselves approaching our task with more relief than we might have expected.

Having you in our lives, my dearest girl, has brought us more joy than any parent could ever wish for, and coming to us, as you did, at a time of such darkness we hadn't imagined ourselves ever knowing joy again. After God called our own little Lucy to His side He left us with too much emptiness to fill, too much despair to overcome. There could be no more children for us, we knew that, and it might have been easier to bear had we not had the brief and beautiful experience of our dear little girl. When she went our hearts, our hopes and dreams went with her. We had lost our sense of purpose; there was no longer a reason to continue, nothing to keep us here. God had forsaken us, and the world was a place we no longer wanted to be in. So it wasn't a hard decision for us to take, to escape the pain and cruelty of our existence.

Lucy had been gone for a little over three months by the time we started to act on our plans. Acquiring enough sleeping pills to ensure our departure was going to take time, and it was during this period that we were offered a position with the Landmark Trust. Though we had no intention of taking it up, and had even written a letter to thank them for considering us, before we could send it God intervened in the most unexpected and magnificent way. This was when He brought us the most beautiful little girl in the world. Since losing our own dear child we had prayed with all our hearts for a miracle that would bring her back to us, and that day, God in His infinite wisdom and mercy decided to answer our prayers.

That morning I had been to see a doctor in Wimbledon to obtain more pills, and Brian was on his way to meet me so we could journey back into London together. On his conscience, as it had been for some time, was the fact that we had still not registered our Lucy's death. I'm sure if we'd been prompted we would have forced ourselves to do it, but we never received a communication from the authorities, and because we so dreaded that awful final act of letting go we were still struggling to make ourselves face it. Then, out of the blue, you were brought to us in the simplest and most gloriously unexpected way.

At first, when you were left on the train, Brian had every intention of getting off with you at the next stop, but then it occurred to him that if he did he could be refusing a gift from God. So he kept you with him to the end of the line where I was waiting, and when I saw you looking so tiny and afraid and Brian explained what had happened, I understood too that God had decided to smile on us again. Your mother had three children and we had none. She couldn't cope and we could. She didn't need you and we did. So we decided that unless we saw your mother waiting at Southfields station on our return we would continue into London with you curled up on my lap, perfectly safe and already loved. This is what happened, because there was no sign of your mother as our train passed through, and when we got you home I continued to hold and comfort you while Brian went out to buy you clothes and delicious things to eat.

From that day on we deliberately stopped

watching the news or buying papers in order to avoid the furore, and nor did we take you out. We knew your picture would be everywhere and we didn't want to run the risk of you being taken away from us when we felt in our hearts that you were where you belonged. Then we left for Lundy where nobody knew us and so accepted us as the proud and happy parents we were again.

It wasn't until long after John Mckenzie – your father – was sent to prison that we learned of his fate. I read about it one morning in an old magazine I found in an antiques shop. It came as a terrible shock, but by then you were seven years old and we loved you so much that we couldn't even think about giving you up. We reminded ourselves that God was in charge of all our destinies, and that He had brought you to us in a way that had made it abundantly clear He meant you for us. Whatever life journey your birth parents were on was between them and God, and nothing to do with us. We had no idea then what had happened to your mother, the article didn't mention her, so as far as we knew your parents were still married and she was bringing up her other children while waiting for their father to come home.

Of course we know the truth now, that your parents had divorced and your mother remarried, but it was many years before we were to learn that. It never even occurred to us when we moved to Cromstone that Douglas Bancroft's wife had once been the Rose who was married to John Mckenzie. Maybe, if we'd met her, we'd have recognised her, but I think it is doubtful as we had always been so careful to steer clear of the publicity surrounding our blessing.

It would appear now that God, in His divine wisdom, has finally chosen to remove you from our safe keeping and reunite you with the family He took you from at the beginning. It isn't our right to question why, or to try to defy Him. We must accept that our time with you has reached an end and we must thank Him with all our hearts for the years of happiness you have brought us.

I hope, Lucy my dearest, that you will not judge us too harshly and that you will try to understand why we believed it was God's will for you to stay with us. We have loved you and cared for you as if you were our own, and this is how we have always thought of you. Your happiness has always meant everything to us. I hope you know that – I think you do. Over the years we have never allowed ourselves to talk about or even think of your natural parents, but now they are constantly on our minds, and of course on our conscience. We will not try to ask for their forgiveness, because we feel sure it's not something they'd want to consider. We will simply ask you to extend our sympathy for all they have suffered, and it is our sincere hope that from now on God will smile on them the way He has on us for so many years.

You are a beautiful woman, Lucy, in every way, and you have been the most wonderful daughter any parent could ever wish for. Ben and Hanna have brought even more joy to our lives than we ever dared dream of, and whatever the future might hold for you and Joe we want him to know that he's been a very kind and considerate son-in-law to us.

As you know the business and the farmhouse already belong to you, but in the name of Lucy Winters. Just in case this causes a problem, we have sent a letter to Michael that we hope will make our wishes perfectly legal and clear. Should you decide to sell everything in order to draw a line under Lucy

*Fisher and start again as Alexandra Mckenzie, then
you will be free to do so. There are no strings attached
to your inheritance, everything we have is now yours
and is given with love.*

*We are deeply sorry, my dear, to be putting you
to the trouble of dealing with the police and funeral
arrangements, but we have given Michael the details
of where we would like our ashes to be scattered so
hopefully that will be of some help. In order not to
cause any further inconvenience we have chosen the
moor near our home. I hope you will not think us
selfish or inconsiderate for leaving your life this way;
we believe it's for the best all round as we wouldn't
want you to feel bound to us in any way after the
truth is out, and we are, I'm afraid, not courageous
enough to bear being parted from each other by
justice and prison.*

*God bless you, dearest, dearest daughter of our
hearts. Be happy in your new life, surrounded by
those who love you.*

*With our love and eternal devotion
Daphne and Brian*

*   *   *

It was a very long time before Lucy could see through
her tears and raise her head. Their kindness and
humility was almost as hard to bear as their delusion
and loss. She kept picturing them at the end, her
mother driving to the postbox to send the letters; her
father waiting patiently at home. She wondered what
their last words had been to one another, and if they
really were together now. She had to believe they were,
or there would be no point to anything. Yes, what
they'd done was wrong, in many ways indefensible,

and there would be those who'd scorn and revile them for trying to hide behind God. But who were they to say that God, destiny, karma hadn't played a deliberate hand in the way it had woven the fates of her two families together? It was perhaps the only way they would ever make any sense of it all and be able to go forward without bitterness and recriminations.

Though her eyes were swollen and sore, she unfolded the letter to Michael and started to read.

Dear Michael,

First and foremost we wish to thank you for your friendship and advice over the time we have known you, but most of all for how supportive you have been to Lucy since she took over at Cromstone Auctions. We had hoped that Maureen and Godfrey would remain with the company, and had increased their salaries as an incentive, but it would appear that things have not worked out. We are confident that you will help Lucy to resolve this problem, and have enclosed a cheque made out to the Crumptons which we hope will demonstrate our gratitude for their assistance during our time with the company. (We have only recently become aware, through Lucy, of a certain malpractice on the part of the Crumptons, but we feel this matter is best kept out of the courts, so please do your best to persuade the Crumptons to accept our cheque with goodwill.)

Lucy turned the letter over and searched the large envelope, but it seemed Michael had already removed the cheque, so she had no idea yet how much the Crumptons were being paid to go away. Whatever it was, in her opinion it would be too much.

Going back to the letter, she read,

Because we have no wish to be deterred from taking the course we have chosen, we have decided it would be unwise to go to a lawyer at this time. So we are hopeful that this letter and its contents, addressed to you, will serve as a final codicil to our joint will.

We, Daphne May Fisher and Brian Edmond Fisher, do hereby bequeath all our worldly goods, as indicated in our last will and testament, to include all properties, businesses and bank accounts, to Lucy Winters, née Alexandra Mckenzie.

Lucy's heart skipped a beat as she read her name. This was the whole point of the letter, she realised, to make sure that no one could contest their wishes or take away what they wanted to be hers.

Beneath this small paragraph they had both signed and printed their names, together with the date and an imprint of their thumbs that came close to breaking her heart.

The second page of the letter said,

I am sure, dear Michael, that you will find a way to make this legal and binding. Please know that we wish to impose no restrictions on whatever Lucy (Alexandra) might choose to do with her inheritance, and we have no final demands of her. However, we do have two small favours to ask of you: should Lucy not wish to scatter our ashes on Exmoor herself, we would be most grateful if you would do this for us (please find enclosed a cheque for one thousand pounds which we hope will be adequate compensation for your time, together with a token of our appreciation). And secondly, we have enclosed a small map that shows a playground near Hastings. For this we enclose a cheque for twenty thousand pounds which we would like to donate to the local council with the proviso that they keep the playground safe and clean and a happy place for the local children to be.

May God bless you, dear Michael, for your kindness and generous indulgence of our wishes. It has been a great pleasure working with you and it affords us enormous comfort to know that you are there to help Lucy through this difficult time.

Until we meet again we remain,
Yours most sincerely
Brian and Daphne Fisher

Chapter Twenty-Four

Snow was falling in big fat flakes, turning Cromstone into a Christmas card and the duck pond into a skating rink. All the shopfronts were lit by colourful lights, and the sound of seasonal music spilled into the freezing afternoon as doors were opened and quickly closed again. A comical assortment of snowmen had taken up residence on the green, along with a gaily decorated Christmas tree, while several glittering reindeer appeared to be grazing the rooftops of the valley below.

Outside the farmhouse, where abundant holly wreaths were hanging from the door and gate, Sarah and Hanna were easing a bulky parcel from the back seat of Sarah's new Clio. 'You go on ahead and see if she's there,' Sarah whispered as they carried it towards the arch. 'If she is tell her to keep her eyes closed and no peeping.'

Thrilled by the subterfuge, Hanna kicked her snowy boots off in the porch and skipped into the kitchen to find her mother attaching a huge silver bow to a very smartly wrapped Christmas present. 'Wow, is that for me?' she demanded, her eyes turning bright with hope.

'No,' Lucy replied airily.

Hanna came closer. 'What is it?'

'A bird-feeder for Pippa.'

Though not what she'd expected, Hanna looked impressed. 'Cool,' she declared approvingly. 'She'll like that.'

'I certainly hope so.'

'OK,' Hanna said, moving on, 'we've got to bring something in now and you're not allowed to look, so can you please go and shut yourself in the pantry?'

'Oh yes, I'm sure I'm going to do that,' Lucy replied smoothly. 'I'll keep my back turned and promise not to look.'

'If you do, you'll ruin everything, and then Santa will pass straight over us tonight.'

Smiling at the echo of her own words, Lucy went to the sink and put her hands over her eyes.

'OK, you can come in now,' Hanna shouted to Sarah.

'Make sure she doesn't cheat,' Sarah instructed, as she bundled the parcel in through the door, 'or she'll guess from the bag what's inside.'

'Don't worry,' Hanna replied, holding up a towel like a curtain, 'I've got her covered.'

Laughing as Sarah edged her way round the table and into the hall, all the time cautioning Hanna to hold her position, while Hanna told her to take care in case something broke, Lucy waited until the towel had dropped and Hanna was following Sarah upstairs to her bedroom before turning around again. There were so many surprises in the works this Christmas that they'd had to draw up a schedule determining when and where each one was to be delivered.

Picking up the gaily wrapped bird-feeder, Lucy was about to carry it through to the sitting room when she became aware of a wave of sadness trying to steal her smile. Though it made her heart ache with grief and guilt to think of Daphne and Brian and how desperately she still wished she'd gone to them sooner, not to think of them at all would have been wrong and disloyal. So she almost never pushed them from her mind.

In many ways it was hard to believe that nearly four months had passed since they'd taken their own way out, yet in other ways it felt like a lifetime. Much of what had happened over that time was lost in a haze of self-recrimination and longing now, but there were certain things she remembered, such as how kind the police had been when Michael had taken her to identify them, and how peaceful they'd looked. She often read the last letter they'd written, and was able to find some comfort in how unafraid her mother had seemed of going to join the God she so fervently believed in. In a way she'd almost sounded relieved, and though it racked Lucy with sadness to think of it she could imagine that perhaps Daphne *was* relieved, after so many years of wondering when God's blessing, as she saw it, might be revoked. And if the truth were told, Lucy felt relieved too that they were not having to endure the unimaginable loneliness of separation, each in a prison cell knowing that they might never see one another in this world again.

The cremation had been the small, unfussy affair they'd requested, with just her, Michael and Hanna in attendance – and Ben, who'd interrupted his gap year in order to come and say his goodbyes. How deeply it would have pleased them to know that he'd made such a long journey just for them – it would probably have worried them too, given how bad they always felt about putting people out of their way. John had paid for Ben's flight, which Lucy had only found out about later when Ben himself had told her. He'd stayed for ten days, which seemed like ten minutes now, but having him there had meant the world to her. Though Joe had wanted to come too his shooting schedule had prevented it, and given how emotionally fragile she'd been at the time Lucy had felt secretly relieved.

So it was John and Michael who'd driven her and the children down to Exmoor in order to scatter the ashes, waiting in the car while they walked to a hilltop to carry out her parents' final wishes. It had been the saddest, and for Lucy, the hardest part of the process, watching the soft clouds of ash mingling together like ghosts as they blew out gently over the moor. She'd wanted desperately to make it stop, to somehow make them come back, but the wind had carried them away, while Hanna and Ben had taken her hands, holding her still until the panic subsided and she was finally able to let go.

The following day Ben had returned to his travels and Hanna to school, while Lucy had sat down with Michael, Rose and John to decide how best to proceed from there. Knowing there was likely to be a media circus once the truth was made public, they'd all agreed that they'd prefer to keep it to a minimum if they could, so Michael had set up an exclusive interview with one newspaper and one TV programme. When the time came only John and Lucy were interviewed, since Rose didn't feel able to cope with all the questions, and in spite of how discreetly and sensitively their chosen reporters handled the exclusive, the story was inevitably taken up by the world's press and making every headline and bulletin by the end of the same day. Matters weren't helped by Joe's decision to sell his version of events to a tabloid, but rather than take him to task about it Lucy had decided instead to inform him that this time he'd gone too far, and there would be no going back.

Though their story remained in the news for weeks after it had broken, being constantly analysed, criticised, sensationalised and occasionally even doubted, fortunately it was mostly hailed for giving hope to families whose loved ones had disappeared without trace. Since then Rose and John had become actively involved in an organisation that helped those people, while Lucy, Sarah, Pippa and Hanna were doing their best to reply to the thousands of letters and emails that came flooding in from around the world. Though Simon and Giselle helped with that too, Becky had declined to become involved on the grounds that she was already helping people as a life coach and was too busy to take on any more.

It was soon after the interview that Michael had delivered a fifteen-thousand-pound cheque to the Crumptons, only handing it over on the signed proviso that they would not seek any further compensation from Cromstone Auctions, nor attend any future sales. Since the Peter Kinley painting had been authenticated, this would mean that the Crumptons – presuming they were aware the piece was an original – were going to miss out on as much as twenty, even thirty thousand pounds when it went under the hammer in the spring. A small triumph in itself, as far as Lucy was concerned, and she could hardly wait to start publicising the sale. As for the solicitors' letters requesting explanations or investigations on behalf of the clients who'd very probably been cheated by the Ring, since Michael had directed them to the company's terms and conditions, there had been no further communications.

Then came some news that Lucy hadn't been expecting at all: with most of his immediate duties on behalf of the estate and company discharged, Michael was leaving for Italy in order to try and repair his marriage. He was worried about his children, he'd explained. Their mother wasn't providing the kind of stability they needed so it was his duty, as their father, to try to work things out.

'I know this is terrible timing for you,' he'd continued apologetically, 'with everything still in the process of being changed into your legal name ... Incidentally, I take it you're sticking with your decision to be known as Lucy, even though officially you're now Alexandra?'

'Yes,' she'd replied, still reeling from the shock of his news. 'It would be too confusing to ask everyone to change.'

Nodding his agreement, he made an attempt at irony as he said, 'How are you feeling now about being closer to forty than you thought?'

She hardly knew how to answer that, when it felt as unreal as the fact that her birthday was in July, not January.

Going on awkwardly, he said, 'You can decide on which surname to use once we've received a decision on the validity of your marriage, but in the meantime I think, for the sake of ease, it's best to continue with Winters.'

She nodded agreement.

'You already know my partner, Teresa. She'll be taking care of everything while I'm away, but if there's anything you're unsure about, or feel you need to discuss with me, I'll be at the end of a phone.'

His departure had been a horrible blow for Lucy, not only because of how much she'd come to rely on him as her lawyer, but because her feelings for him had gone way beyond mere friendship. She'd even dared to hope he might share them, in fact she'd felt sure he did. Once he'd told her about his plans for his marriage, however, she could only thank God that she'd never embarrassed them both by admitting to her hopes for their relationship.

The struggle to get over him had seemed to become harder as each day passed. Its one benefit had been that she and Sarah were now even closer. Her half-sister had been so supportive and understanding, not to mention discreet, in never telling anyone about her mental state that Lucy still wondered how she'd have got through that time without her.

A decision was expected any day now on the validity of her marriage, but whatever the outcome she'd made it quite clear to Joe that as far as she was concerned it was over. Though she hadn't expected him to take it well, the violence of his re-action had actually scared her. Had Sarah and Hanna not come running when they'd heard him raging about like a bull, smashing things up and threatening to 'take her down', she felt sure he'd have ended up hitting her. Luckily, their timely rescue had sent him storming out of the house, all the way back to London, but he'd rung later that night with a warning that he was going to sue her for every last penny she had.

'I don't think you get what kind of damage you've done to my career,' he'd yelled. 'You made me a fucking laughing stock when you told that reporter I had no idea what was happening in your life. I looked like some snivelling little nobody shut out of the party, so you're going to pay for that, Lucy, and you're going to pay big.'

'Your career hasn't suffered one bit,' she shot back. 'In fact you're doing better now than you have in years. But do you know what? I'm not having this conversation. It's over between us, Joe, so for once in your life try to be dignified and live with it.'

When a letter turned up from his solicitor the following week, informing her that he considered himself entitled to fifty per cent of the business, farmhouse, cottage and any capital she'd inherited, she flew into a rage of her own.

Tempers had cooled a little by now, but Joe's bitterness remained ugly and abusive, and there were still no guarantees that Ben and Hanna, who'd taken it upon themselves to try to make him see reason, were going to have any success in persuading him to accept the cottage on Exmoor and fifty thousand pounds in settlement. If he didn't there was a very good chance they'd end up in court, which would create another media circus that made Lucy cower inside even to think of it. The fact that John had already informed her that under no circumstances would he allow that to happen was certainly a comfort, but she'd told him quite firmly that she'd only accept his help as a loan. Just thank goodness Joe didn't know anything about that, because being as angry as he was, he might just try to take John's money and still not let go.

Lately, however, Joe's character in *EastEnders* had, as promised, started to make more regular appearances, and given how much being on the screen meant to him, Lucy was daring to hope that the long-awaited breakthrough in his career would help to boost his self-esteem. If that were to happen there was a chance they might go forward in a slightly more amicable fashion, which mattered most to the children, but also to her too, since the last thing she wanted was Ben and Hanna feeling torn between them.

'Oh, is that right?' Joe had retorted sarcastically when she'd told him that only last week. 'So you're having Christmas down there with your *new* family, and to hell with mine who Hanna's known all her life, and who happen to want to see her.'

'She spent the whole of last week with you all,' Lucy reminded him heatedly, 'and where were you? Working.'

'She's still got aunts, uncles, cousins *and a grand-father* . . .'

'Who's never been interested in anyone but himself.'

'He's still family. We all are, and you don't get exclusive rights . . .'

'Joe, let it go. You're only going to make this more difficult for her than it already is, because obviously she'd rather we were all together, but since that can't happen anyway, with Ben in New Zealand . . .'

'Just tell me this,' he broke in savagely, 'how come you get to have everything your way, while I seem to get sweet FA?'

Exasperated by his self-pity, she said, 'I'm sorry if that's how you're seeing it.'

'Yeah, it's exactly how I see it. She's my daughter, I want to spend Christmas with her and I'm damned well going to.'

'Stop putting yourself first all the time. She's already made plans for the next few days . . .'

'Then I'll come there.'

'Don't be ridiculous. You know very well that won't work . . .'

'So that's it then? No Christmas, no kids, and no effing marriage, because *you've* decided you don't want it any more. And no Hollywood movie, because *you* don't want that either, even though you know what a fantastic break it would be for me.'

Since she'd had that argument with him too many times already, she hadn't bothered to remind him that neither John nor Rose was interested in selling the film rights of their story either. Nor was there any guarantee anyone would want to cast him if they did – in fact she couldn't imagine that they would. However, what the interested producers might or might not do hardly mattered, since the film wasn't going to happen, so all she'd done was end the call as agreeably as she could and send a text later to tell him he'd be welcome if he wanted to come on Boxing Day. It was when Rose's sister Sheila was coming over from France with her daughter and son-in-law, so still not ideal, but at least he wouldn't get a chance to spoil the wonderful Christmas Day they had planned. The text she'd received back had told her to go to hell. Later, however, he'd sent another to Hanna saying he was thinking about it.

Hearing Sarah and Hanna coming back down the stairs, whispering and laughing together, Lucy smiled fondly to herself as she reflected on how close they'd become, more like sisters in some ways than niece and aunt.

'Do we know if Mum and John are back from the mall yet?' Sarah asked, as she followed Hanna into the kitchen.

'I haven't seen any sign of them,' Lucy replied, 'but Simon rang to say the flight's been delayed by an hour, so they'll be here around seven instead of six.'

Glowing with pleasure, Sarah treated her to an impulsive hug, then grabbing Hanna's arm she said, 'We're baking this afternoon, remember?'

'We are?' Hanna said, mystified. Then, 'Oh yeah, we are. See you, Mum – and no going upstairs peeking, OK?'

'OK,' Lucy promised, realising that more plotting was probably about to get under way.

After they'd taken themselves off across the courtyard to the small barn which had been beautifully renovated over the past few months for Sarah, Lucy returned to her present-wrapping, and soon found herself thinking of Ben and how wonderful it would be if he were able to join them tomorrow. Though it was awful to imagine the empty space at the table, what mattered, she kept reminding herself, was that he was having a fabulous time where he was – with a different girl now. This one was from Connecticut, her name was Alicia and her parents ran a school for children with special needs. Whenever she spoke to him, which was about once a week, she invariably ended the call with a few tears, in spite of being thrilled to know that he was safe and enjoying himself. It was the way he was becoming so independent that was always difficult to handle.

What was very much easier was watching Sarah blooming over there in her new home, so excited to be in before Christmas that it was as though her spirits were doing even more to light up the place than the decorations she and Lucy had strung up along the drive and around the courtyard. The idea of giving Sarah the small barn had come to Lucy within hours of Rose and John's announcement that they were going to restore the manor and its gardens to their former glory. With so much needing to be done, they'd decided it would make more sense for Rose and Sarah to move in with John and Pippa until work was complete. While Sarah was happy enough about that, she'd been absolutely delirious when Lucy had put forward her suggestion.

'I've got the windfall from the auction,' she'd cried excitedly, 'and I expect I'll be able to borrow whatever else I need to make sure it's done to the highest spec. Oh Lucy, this is so fantastic. We'll both be right there, on top of the business, but not under each other's feet.'

'Why don't we get you some help from an interior designer?' Pippa suggested. 'That way you'll have an expert overseeing the work, making sure it runs to schedule and that it ends up looking an absolute treat.'

Sarah grimaced. 'I don't think my budget will run to that,' she admitted, 'but it is a good idea while Lucy and I are working so hard.'

'It's an excellent idea,' Pippa informed her, 'and since it's mine I shall be very happy to pay for it.'

Sarah's eyes widened in amazement and protest. 'I couldn't possibly . . . I mean, it's really lovely of you . . .'

'My mind's made up,' Pippa interrupted bossily. 'Now I have nieces to spoil it's what I intend to do. Nephews too, of course, and we shan't forget the younger generation – as if Hanna would ever let us.'

True to her word, Pippa had written a cheque large enough to make heads spin and builders keep to deadlines in order to achieve their bonuses. The designer came down from London and proved such a hit that John and Rose promptly hired her to help out with the manor. Though that was still some way from completion, there was a good chance the kitchen, front parlour and two new en suite bedrooms would be ready by the time the Mercers returned to the Lodge in February. Sarah had spent her first night in the luxurious master bedroom of the small barn exactly two weeks before Christmas, with her old friend and new lover, Jean-Marc, to keep her company. He'd also been responsible, with John, for transporting and installing the giant Christmas tree which they'd cut themselves at a local forest, and with his artist's flair for colour and style, Jean-Marc had created a small sensation around the village, after everyone had dropped in for a glass of mulled wine and a viewing.

Lucy knew he was the reason Sarah had glowed so winningly just now, since he was flying in later with Simon and Giselle to come and spend the festivities with them. Though it was still early days in the relationship it was clear to everyone, including Sarah, how besotted Jean-Marc was with her, so it was highly possible that the barn's mezzanine floor with its wide skylights and ample space might soon find itself transformed into the kind of studio where an artist of great passion and wicked humour could feel happy committing his inspiration to posterity. Meanwhile, the large, open-plan living space, with a state-of-the-art kitchen at one end, and huge open fireplace at the other, would accommodate them all for Christmas lunch tomorrow, since no one else had the room for such a big table.

Realising she ought to start thinking about what to prepare for dinner tonight, Lucy began counting up how many they would be, until noticing how much heavier the snowfall had become she stopped to watch for a while. Since the ground was already covered in several inches they probably didn't need any more, but it would be wonderful if they really did have a white Christmas. Pippa was looking forward to it so much that she might have been even more excited than Hanna, and everyone suspected that Rose and John would be making a special announcement at some point during the festivities. Though Lucy still had difficulties in thinking of them as her parents, she was certainly developing an attachment to them, and luckily they were being patient and sensitive enough not to try and hurry or force it. She had to admit she loved seeing them together, and the way Hanna had taken to them was encouraging too, though she still had tears over Daphne and Brian, and probably would for a long time to come. Apart from the fact that she'd loved them and naturally missed them, it was as though she shared some of Lucy's guilt about feeling happy to be part of another family. It seemed disloyal and uncaring to be getting on with their lives as if Brian and Daphne had never been a part of them, yet in her heart Lucy felt sure it would have been what Brian and Daphne wanted.

Hearing her phone bleep with a text, she hiked it out of her pocket and smiled to see it was from Simon and had probably been sent to them all. *About to board plane. Please have wine at ready and fires lit. S&Gx PS Sarah, told JM that you adore Chanel 5, hope I got it right xx.* Knowing that he had, Lucy sent a quick text back wishing them bon voyage, then another reminding Ben she was going to call him at midnight her time. By then he'd be in the middle of the beach barbie for which he and Alicia had flown over to Sydney, and very possibly already quite merry. She wondered if he felt any pangs of homesickness, given the time of year, then decided it was unlikely. He was in the middle of a fiercely hot summer, so for him it probably didn't feel like Christmas at all. She thought fleetingly of Becky then, the other person who'd be missing tomorrow. Though Lucy certainly didn't wish her ill she couldn't help feeling thankful that she'd decided to stay away, since Sarah was so thrilled about hosting the day that she really didn't need Becky doing anything to cast a pall over it all. On the other hand, it would have meant a great deal to Rose and John if she had decided to come, so if only for their sakes Lucy felt sorry that she hadn't been persuaded to change her mind.

Hearing a car pulling into the drive, she looked up from the packets of fresh pasta she was starting to open, and seeing it was Michael she felt her heart lighten with happiness. Almost equally wonderful to see was the tangle of small limbs, bobble hats and scarves as his boys tumbled out of the back seat, breaking instantly free of each other to come charging into the house. She knew it wasn't honourable to feel such relief that his attempted reconciliation with Carlotta hadn't worked out, but if it had they'd never have got together, and though it had barely been a month since he'd walked, unannounced, into her office to let her know he was back, she already couldn't imagine life without him.

'I'm not going to lie to you,' he'd told her that day, not even bothering with hello, 'the main reason I couldn't make a go of it is because of how I feel about you. I think about you all the time, I want to be with you, laugh with you, hold you . . . Am I embarrassing you? Should I stop now, or can I dare to hope you might feel the same?'

Dazed and euphoric, she'd gone straight into his arms, saying softly, 'I think you know I do, so please don't stop.'

'Unless for this?' he'd murmured, and as he covered her mouth with his own she'd sunk against him in a way that had released all the pent-up desires and emotions they'd tried to hide from themselves, as well as each other.

'Hey Lucy, happy Christmas,' Charlie the eldest boy cried with a beaming grin as he bounced into the kitchen.

'Happy Christmas,' Luke and Harry echoed, looking so flushed and similar in their excitement and colouring they could almost have been twins. In fact there was a year between them, with Harry being the older of the two at eight, while Charlie had just turned ten so was proudly into double figures now.

'Hey boys,' she responded, going to take a bag of chocolate pennies from the dresser. 'Did you remember to bring carrots and milk for the reindeer?'

'Yes, Dad's got it all.'

'And sherry for Santa?'

'And presents for everyone.'

'I'm having a Wii Sports.'

'I'm having one too.'

'No you're not.'

'Yes I am.'

'We've brought our pyjamas and our stockings. Dad said we can hang them by your fire. Is that OK?'

'Of course it is. We need to be sure Santa finds them, don't we?'

'Can we go and play snowballs on the green?'

'Hey, you lot,' Hanna greeted them, coming in behind them. 'I thought I heard you. Do you want to come and see what we're giving Mum for Christmas?'

'Yes, yes, yes,' they cheered at once.

'It's a surprise, so you mustn't tell her afterwards, OK?'

Their eyes grew round as Charlie crossed his heart and the others followed suit.

'Come on then, it's down the road at Auntie Pippa's.'

'I thought Pippa was over at Sarah's,' Lucy said.

'She is, but John and Rose just called to let us know they're back. Oh my God, Michael, who are all those presents for?'

'They're for us!' Harry and Luke shouted. 'Mummy sent them from Italy, and Granny Givens has brought loads with her too. Granny, we're going to see what Hanna's got for Lucy for Christmas. Do you want to come with us?'

Michael's eyes were twinkling as his mother, snuggled up warmly in a downy coat and trendy Ugg boots, pretended to think it over, then made them all cheer when she said, 'Shall I give you a race to see who gets there first?'

'We'll win,' Charlie told her, as his brothers dashed out the door.

Laughing, Evelyn Givens turned to give Lucy a quick peck hello, then helping herself to a chocolate penny she started gingerly through the snow after Hanna and her grandsons.

'Ho ho ho,' Michael said, lowering the enormous sack of gifts from his shoulder.

Laughing, Lucy went to put her arms around him.

'Everything OK?' he murmured, touching his mouth to hers. 'You're sure you don't mind us all landing on you like this?'

'Of course not. You're the most special guests of all. Anyway, Sarah and Pippa are doing all the cooking. All we have to do is turn up on time and eat it.'

'And what about this evening? Maybe I should take us all out for pizza?'

'Don't worry, everything's under control, and there are only seven of us here. The others are eating much later, down at John and Pippa's.'

His eyes were teasing as he regarded her more closely. 'You know, you're looking a little flushed, my love, and I can't help wondering if it might have something to do with me – or maybe you've already been at the Christmas grog?'

Raising her mouth for another kiss, she said, 'Absolutely, and not yet.'

As he kissed her more deeply the soft swell of desire coasted magically between them, holding them together until a pained voice in the doorway said, 'Sorry to interrupt, but we're desperate for more oven trays.'

Still looking at Michael, Lucy said to Sarah, 'Help yourself. You know where everything is.'

'I'll be really quick,' Sarah assured them, 'and I'll get that for you too, if you like,' she added as the phone started to ring. Without waiting for a reply she snatched it up saying, 'Cromstone Farmhouse, can I help you?' Hearing the voice at the other end, she grimaced as she turned to Lucy. 'Oh, hi Joe,' she said. 'Merry Christmas to you too. How are you?'

As he answered Lucy shook her head. 'I'll call back,' she mouthed.

Nodding, Sarah said, 'Yes, I'm fine too, thanks. I'm sorry, but Lucy's just popped out. Can I take a message? Actually, no, her mobile's right here so . . . OK, I don't think she'll be long. Yes, thanks, you too.'

As Sarah rang off Lucy said, 'He probably wants to talk about Boxing Day.' She sighed. 'I'm afraid I made the grand mistake of inviting him, but don't worry, I'm sure he won't come. Anyway, it's best I speak to him when Hanna's here, unless you happen to know what my daughter has planned for the day after tomorrow?'

'Not off the top of my head,' Sarah replied, scooping a pile of oven trays out of a cupboard. 'By the way, Michael, did you pick up Pippa's surprise for tomorrow?'

'Absolutely,' he assured her, 'and it looks a treat.'

Sarah beamed. 'Excellent. Now, this is me loving you and leaving you,' and hugging the trays to her chest she took off to half skate, half run back across the courtyard.

'Actually, Joe's call was quite timely,' Michael commented, peeling off his overcoat while Lucy sneaked a quick peek inside his Santa sack. 'I have some news, but I'm not sure if now is the right time to tell you.'

Immediately guessing what it was about, Lucy felt her heart catch on a spasm of unease. 'If it's good,' she said, 'why wait? If it's bad, let it keep for a year or two.'

Tilting his head to one side, he replied, 'Let me see, good or bad? I guess you'll have to be the judge.'

Bracing herself, she kept her eyes on his as he said, 'They've decided your marriage isn't valid as it stands, but they are inviting you to contact them when their offices open again in the new year to discuss their findings. They've also provided details of the three closest registry offices so you can rectify matters by booking a wedding – should you so wish.'

More thrown by the decision than she'd expected,

Lucy felt a strangeness unsettling her as she took a moment to try and absorb the news. 'So, I'm not married,' she said quietly. It wasn't that she wanted to be, but how much more of her life was going to turn out to be false?

Going to take some wine from the fridge, Michael poured two glasses and handed one to her.

'This isn't going to make Joe very happy,' she muttered, already shrinking from the thought of his reaction.

Lifting her chin so he could look into her eyes, Michael said, 'More to the point is how it makes you feel.'

She shook her head slowly, then managed a shaky sort of smile as she told him, 'One thing's for certain, it's a great relief to know that I don't have to go through a divorce, especially when I see what's happening to you.'

Grimacing as he sipped his wine, Michael said, 'As Simon puts it, Carlotta's never been someone to pass up the chance of making a crisis out of a drama, but we'll get something worked out, eventually. And I'm ever hopeful that I'll be able to have custody of the boys more often than she's allowing now.'

Knowing that he'd only had them for Christmas because Carlotta had been invited to stay with friends who preferred not to have children around, Lucy said, 'How many times have I met them now? Four? Five? But it's obvious they love being with you.'

He smiled. 'You've made them very welcome,' he said softly, 'and that's helped a lot.' Then he sighed wearily. 'I hate to admit it, but I think they're a little afraid of their mother with her fiery temper and random impulses. Charlie's definitely more nervous

549

than a boy his age ought to be, and I get the impression that the other two look more to him for guidance than they do to their mother. That's a hell of a responsibility for a ten-year-old, and it has to stop before it gets any worse.'

'Have you spoken to her about it?'

'Not since I was last there. To be frank, I'm afraid she'll take it out on them if we end up rowing on the phone. At least when we're face to face I can protect them from the worst of it. Anyway, today isn't about my family, it's about yours, and how you're going to handle telling the children that you're not married to their father.'

As Lucy's heart jolted, she drank some wine. 'Actually, there's a chance they might not have too much of a problem with it, because they really didn't want to think of us trying to slug things out in court. And since half their friends' parents aren't married to one another, it's hardly unusual these days. No, I'm afraid it's Joe who's most likely to have a hard time with it.'

'In spite of already knowing that you want it to be over? Incidentally, if he does come on Boxing Day . . .'

'I'm sure he won't – apart from anything else, he'll be too hung-over to make the journey.' Not wanting to give that any more room than it had already taken up, she returned to her own feelings about the news. 'So Lucy Winters really doesn't exist any more,' she said, finding the fact as impossible to grasp as the words themselves. It was as though the substance of her self was as ephemeral as the snowflakes drifting outside, there one minute, gone the next. 'It seems so strange to think that I'm not the person I thought I was. It's as

550

though I've been living someone else's life, which I suppose I have.'

'It's only a name,' he reminded her, 'you're still you inside, the person we all know and love, whether we call you Lucy, Alexandra or Titania Buttercup.'

With a choke of laughter she said, 'Where on earth did that one come from?'

'Absolutely no idea.'

'Oh Come All Ye Faithful,' Pippa sang from the door. 'On my way home,' she announced. 'I believe Hanna's taken the boys for a viewing of your big surprise for tomorrow, so will I be sending them back for their tea, or keeping them a while longer?'

'Time they came to unpack their bags,' Michael told her. 'And I'm sure my mother's ready for a glass of wine.'

'Och, if you think my brother hasn't already taken care of that then you don't know him at all,' she informed him, and with a jaunty wave of her hand she went on her way.

'Please God let me be like her when I'm that age,' Lucy commented as she watched her through the window, trudging down the path and apparently carolling away again. 'Actually, I wouldn't mind being like her now,' she corrected herself. 'She's amazing, isn't she? Always so up, and ready to give anything a go.'

'She is very special,' he agreed.

Lucy's heart swelled with affection as she smiled. 'I think she's going to like the surprise we have for her tomorrow,' she decided happily.

He was in no doubt of it. 'Hopefully as much as you like yours,' he murmured.

Turning to him with playful eyes, she said, 'Are we

talking about the puppy Hanna thinks she's got for me, but that is actually for her, or do you happen to have something else in mind?'

Pulling her to him, he said, 'I'm afraid you'll have to wait till tomorrow to find out.'

Much later that evening, after leaving Pippa dozing in front of her TV with both puppies curled up at the foot of the bed, John tiptoed across the landing to close one of the guest-room doors. With at least one of the big surprises hidden in there, and a few others in with Pippa, he was starting to lose track of what was for whom, never mind who was supposed to be giving it. He was even half afraid of blurting out the wrong thing to the wrong person, which was why he was doing his level best to leave all the subterfuge and chicanery to Rose and Hanna. Of course, they didn't know what was in store for them either, and right at that moment he wasn't sure he could remember anyway.

Satisfied that all was in order upstairs, he took himself down to the kitchen where Sarah and Rose were peeling, scraping and dicing ready for tomorrow, while Giselle and Jean-Marc rustled up a gourmet supper for tonight. Since it was usual for them, being French, to celebrate with a big meal on Christmas Eve, it was lucky they'd agreed to limit themselves to four courses instead of the seven Giselle had suggested, or twelve – *twelve* – that Jean-Marc had been ready to dish up.

As John met Rose's eyes he felt an almost overwhelming urge to kiss her, or waltz her around the kitchen, or simply laugh out loud. She was here, they were together, and if it were possible to feel any happier then he was damned if he knew how.

'Here, you be the judge,' Jean-Marc commanded, passing him a spoonful of soup that, when tasted, floated John straight to heaven.

'I think it needs a little more saffron,' Giselle stated. 'Do you agree, John?'

Clocking Jean-Marc's scowl, John tried not to panic.

Coming ungallantly to the rescue, Rose said, 'He doesn't know what saffron is, do you, my darling? Personally, I think it's divine as it is, but if you add a little more we'll love that too.'

'Absolutely,' John agreed. 'Now, how's everyone doing for drinks?'

'Not for me, thank you,' Giselle responded, her hypnotic doe eyes going to Simon as he carried a basket of wood in from outside. Though John, personally, would never have described her as beautiful, he'd have been the first to agree that there was a magnetism about her Latin looks and voluptuous physique that made it hard to look away. That she was completely mad about Simon was evident in almost every glance she gave him, though John was finding it highly amusing to discover that, in spite of how smitten Giselle appeared, Simon was as easily bossed around by a female as he was.

However, both father and son could make a stand when necessary, he reminded himself, which the womenfolk would do well to remember.

Relieved that neither Pippa nor Rose was able to read his mind – though perhaps the jury was still out on that – he turned to Jean-Marc who, still stirring his soup, was already holding out his glass.

'This is a very fine aperitif wine,' he informed John. 'I bring him in case you not know that he exist. He is from my region, which is Bourgogne ... *Oh là là*, Giselle, you have created a miracle,' he swooned, as she opened the oven. 'It is always great sadness to me that I cannot paint the smell of something beautiful,' he explained to John, 'because it is, sometimes, the most important part of the beauty.'

Finding himself in surprised agreement with that, John poured even more wine into Jean-Marc's glass, then looked all innocence as he caught Rose laughing. Though it might be difficult for Jean-Marc to measure up to a movie star in looks, there was no doubt in John's mind that next to the Frenchman's fiercely aquiline features and riotous cap of inky black corkscrews most male idols would appear downright bland. Douglas, John felt sure, would have been thoroughly approving of his prospective son-in-law, because who could possibly have wanted more for Sarah than the fact that she was clearly so loved, and in love (or at least getting that way), and that the man, even though he was an artist, was successful.

Following Simon's brave lead in sampling a slimy-looking something stuffed in a vol au vent, he found it so much to his liking that he readily accepted another when Simon secretly slipped him one. Then, realising he might be about to overflow with happiness as much because of the connection he was starting to feel with his son as for everything else, he took himself off to the dining room to try and calm down before he ended up making a fool of himself. With the table already laid and glistening with seasonal colour, he sat at the head of it and let his thoughts float like stars around him. How was it possible to feel so much joy and love in one moment? Was he really here, in the bosom of his family, after dreaming about it for so many years?

Though the desolate and desperate Christmases he'd spent in prison, when he'd try to picture what Rose and his children might have been doing, were a long way behind him, he knew that in spite of how he was feeling now, they would always be with him. Far worse, though, was the unending torment he'd experienced of never knowing where Alexandra might be. Was Christmas a special day for her, with gifts and laughter and people who loved her? Or was she, like him, locked away from the world, deprived of her freedom, her childhood, her innocence, lonely and terrified, perhaps even starving – or, God forbid, the object of savage abuse, or dead? It was, perversely, what had made his own ordeal more endurable, to be able to tell himself that she wasn't suffering alone, and that maybe his torment was a sacrifice that would persuade life to let her be. To know now that she had been loved and treated well was, for him, as great a gift as having her returned to them. Nothing that happened tomorrow, or at any other time, could ever mean more than having his little angel, who was now a beautiful and healthy young woman, safely back in his world. Though he and Rose understood that she might never call them Mummy and Daddy again, or perhaps even fully accept them as her parents, it was enough to be close to her and know what was happening in her life, and occasionally be able to play a role.

Rose, Alexandra, Simon and Pippa. Feeling his heart swell with far too much happiness, he imagined them all under the same roof tomorrow for Christmas, and had to blink back a tear. Maybe it was asking too much to wish that Becky could be there too, when life was already being so kind, but he wasn't going to give up hope, because there was always next year. If this past one had taught him anything at all, it was that absolutely anything was possible. And meanwhile there was his extended family of Sarah, whom he already thought of as his own, Michael, Jean-Marc and Giselle to fill up the table with their banter and laughter – and of course the children, without whom Christmas could never be complete. Thinking of the surprises in store for them all he smiled mistily to himself, because even if he couldn't remember exactly what was meant for whom, he knew without a shadow of a doubt that no one could possibly have been happier than he was with what this magical, wonderful Christmas had already brought.

Tiptoeing past the bedroom where Michael was reading the boys a story in a so far vain attempt to get them off to sleep, Lucy went quietly down the stairs to find Hanna and Evelyn in the sitting room, snuggled up in chairs either side of the fire. With the Christmas-tree lights casting a rich ruby glow over the gifts below, and the TV rerunning an old black and white film, they looked so cosy and settled that Lucy didn't have the heart to disturb them. It wouldn't be fair to make them go out at this hour on a wintry night just because she wanted to. So, closing the door again, she took herself off to the kitchen where an assortment of cereal boxes, pots of jam, plates and bowls were already laid out for the morning. With the boys around there was a good chance they'd be up at four, though she doubted any of them would be interested in breakfast then.

Since Midnight Mass wasn't due to begin until ten thirty she had a few minutes to spare before it was time to set off, so, bracing herself, she took out her mobile to call Joe.

Though he clicked on straight away, all she could hear was the sound of throbbing music and loud voices, telling her he was either at the pub or a party, which meant he was likely to be drunk, or certainly on his way there.

'At last,' he finally shouted down the line. 'I left a message hours ago.'

'I'm sorry, but it's been quite hectic here.'

'You'll have to speak up, I can't hear you. Or hang on, I'll go in the conservatory.'

Knowing now that he was at Charlie's, where the party would probably throb on through the night, possibly even to Boxing Day, she could hardly have felt more relieved not to be there. Not that she'd spent many Christmases in London with his family, but whenever she had done so, she had sworn that they'd go to her parents again next year.

'So, you finally deigned to call back,' he stated, over the sound of a door closing. 'You know I've already spoken to Hanna?'

'Yes, she told me, and it's lovely that you're going to take her and Lucas to see a show the day after Boxing Day. They'll enjoy that, and if they decide to stay the night with you we can always bring them back with us on Thursday.'

'You're coming to London?'

'Yes, we're taking the boys to a matinee and we'll have two cars, because Rose and John have decided to come with us.'

'Oh, is that right?' he commented nastily. 'Sounds like a right happy little family outing.'

Since it was pointless going any further with that,

she breezed on past it, saying, 'I read in the paper that you're seeing Imogen Fields.'

'So, do you have a problem with it?'

'Not at all. She's very beautiful.' She wouldn't add 'in a tarty sort of way', because it wouldn't have been kind, and anyway she'd never met the girl, so for all she knew she could look more natural in the flesh.

'Yeah, and young, I guess that's what you're thinking,' he challenged.

'Actually, I wasn't, but no matter how old she is, if you think she's the right one then I'm happy for you.'

'Sweet.'

Realising her attempts at friendliness were going to carry on hitting a brick wall, she decided to stop wasting time and come to the point. 'There's been a ruling on the status of our marriage,' she told him. 'Apparently it isn't valid.'

There was a moment's silence, during which she became so tense she almost put the phone down. Then he gave a shout of laughter. 'And you think,' he said sneeringly, 'that lets you off the hook, I suppose. Well, I'm sorry to disappoint you, darlin', but you're dead wrong about that.'

'Joe, I don't want to argue about this . . .'

'I bet you don't when you're the one with all the dosh, but I'm afraid it doesn't work like that, Lucy whoever-the-fuck-you-are-now. Married or not, we were together for nineteen years, so no way do you get to walk away with everything. I want half, which is my legal entitlement . . .'

'You put nothing whatsoever into our marriage,' she cried angrily, 'so how the hell you think you can justify demanding anything at all, never mind half, beggars belief.'

'Well, you'd better start getting your head round it, because it's going to happen, and when it does . . .'

'Joe, listen,' she cut in harshly, 'I can tell you're drunk now, and I understand that you're upset, so why don't we leave this conversation until you've had some time to think things through?'

'I don't need it. I know my rights.'

'You might think you do, but what if a judge doesn't agree? You're a household name again now, and, unfortunately, I am too, so do you really want it splashed all over the press how you've never contributed to anything, yet you still seem to feel it's OK to try and destroy what's mine?'

'That's your way of telling it. Guess what, mine doesn't go anything like that.'

'But I can only give you what you're asking if I sell, and you know how much the business means to me. All right, it's why you're doing it, I understand that, to try and punish me for leaving you, because you don't need the money these days.'

'But I could in the future, so . . .'

'Look, I know the children have talked to you about the cottage. There's no mortgage on it, so you could easily end up with something worth two hundred and fifty thousand, possibly more. And I'm offering a cash settlement too, which'll wipe me out financially, but if I've still got the business I can recover.'

'And I should care about that because?'

'Because I'm the mother of your children, for God's sake. Do you really want to alienate them over this, because that's very likely what it'll come to? This business belonged to their grandparents, which happens to mean something to them . . .'

'Except they're not their grandparents, are they?'

'You know what I mean, and to try using that as some sort of justification to tear it all apart is beneath contempt.'

'And you think trying to slough us all off like we're yesterday's crap is any better?'

'For heaven's sake, you know very well it was over between us long before any of this happened . . . Anyway, I'm not arguing any more tonight. It's Christmas, and I won't allow you to spoil it, so you do whatever you feel you have to, and if you decide not to be reasonable we can both instruct our solicitors in the new year.'

'Except yours is already in your bed?'

Abruptly ending the call, she took a deep, unsteady breath, and was just turning the phone off altogether when she realised Hanna was standing in the doorway. 'Oh God, how much did you hear?' she groaned, holding out her arms.

'Enough, I guess,' Hanna replied, going to her. 'It'll be all right though, Mum, honest. He'll come round in the end, I just know it.'

Wishing she felt even half as confident, Lucy pressed a kiss to her head and thought how naive she had been to hope that Joe would let his bitterness go just because he had a new partner, and because it was Christmas.

'So, do you want to come to Midnight Mass with me?' she asked Hanna, smoothing her hair.

Looking up at her, Hanna said, 'You're only going because it's what Granny and Grandpa used to do, aren't you?'

Lucy nodded, and smiled past the heavy emotions in her heart. 'I feel I'd like to be close to them tonight,' she admitted, 'and I think going to church might do it.'

'Mm, me too,' Hanna agreed. 'I'll go and get my coat.'

The working clocks over in the sale barn were starting to chime midnight when Lucy, yawning and toasty warm again after freezing for an hour in church, picked up the phone to call Ben. At first she had a problem getting through, hearing his voice then being cut off, until eventually he was there crying cheerily down the line, 'Can you hear me now?'

'Yes, I can,' she replied, registering the sound of surf and music in the background. 'Happy Christmas.'

'And to you.'

'It sounds like you're on the beach.'

'Yeah, we are. The others are getting a barbie going. It's so cool having Christmas in the middle of summer. Like really way out. What's the weather doing over there?'

'We've had snow, so everything's looking very seasonal. Did you receive all your presents before you left New Zealand?'

'Yeah, and I brought them with me. It was really great of you to send them. I'll be opening them later, when everyone else opens theirs. How's Hanna-Banana, is she in bed yet?'

'No, she's here waiting to wish you a happy Christmas. Have you spoken to Dad?'

'No, but I will. I guess he's at Uncle Charlie's.'

'I think so. Who's at the party?'

'You mean here? Oh, just the usual gang, but we met up with a couple of South Africans last night, so they've joined us. We're thinking about making Cape Town our next stop, but we won't decide till the new year, because . . . Oh hey, I didn't tell you, did I? I've had the offer of a job for the next couple

561

of months, crewing on a yacht. How cool does that sound? If it comes off I'll stay here in Aus, because I so need to earn some money.'

Feeling as much pride as longing as she pictured him surrounded by friends and no doubt knocking back a beer or two, she said, 'I'd definitely rather think of you in Australia than somewhere as dangerous as South Africa, but OK, that's my last word on it. We really miss you, darling. Tomorrow's not going to be the same without you, but it's lovely to know you're having a good time.'

'I am, and sorry I didn't send any presents. I'll try to make up for it when I get back, but you know what it's like, I need every penny.'

'Don't even think about it. Now here, I'll pass you to Hanna. I'm sure she'll tell you how she managed to drop the collection tray during Midnight Mass.'

'Oh don't,' Hanna protested. 'That was so embarrassing.'

Leaving her to talk to Ben, Lucy went quietly upstairs to find Michael still in the boys' room, but fast asleep now, sitting up in a chair with a book on his lap. Shaking him gently awake, she put a finger over her lips and signalled for him to come with her. Once they were alone in her bedroom, she put her arms around him and snuggled in close.

'How was church?' he asked sleepily.

'Cold, but the carols were nice and I think the vicar was pleased to see us.'

'Surprised, more like,' he teased. 'So, did you get what you wanted out of it?'

'I think so. Or let's put it this way, I'm glad I went because I know it would mean a lot to them, and I didn't want them to think they'd been forgotten.'

Tightening his embrace, he said, 'That's never going to happen.'

Loving how understanding he was, she inhaled the wonderfully warm, male scent of him, and kept her eyes closed as she fought back a surge of longing for Ben.

'Time to start sorting out the stockings?' he whispered.

Treating him to a saucy smile, she said, 'I have some special ones for you.'

His eyes darkened with pleasure. 'As long as I'm not the one who has to wear them,' he murmured, 'I can hardly wait.'

Chapter Twenty-Five

It was just after five in the morning when Charlie, hair on end and pyjamas skewed, peeped round the bedroom door with Harry and Luke pressed in close behind.

'Is he awake?' Harry whispered.

'I don't know,' Charlie whispered back.

'We have to tell him Father Christmas has been,' Luke insisted.

'Ow, don't push.'

'You pushed me first.'

'Did not.'

'Did.'

'Did not.'

'Shut up or I'll smash you.'

'Come on then.'

Unable to stop herself laughing as Michael groaned, Lucy barely had a chance to disentangle herself before she was being buried under a pile of small boys raring for Christmas to begin.

By seven o'clock three stockings were open and breakfasts demolished, and they'd even been allowed a small present each from under the tree. Impatient now for their grandmother and Hanna to wake up, they began thundering up and down the stairs and singing carols at the tops of their voices.

Eventually Evelyn emerged from her room wearing a red fleecy dressing gown and a Santa hat – and carrying three more stockings.

'Not so fast,' she cried, as she was set upon. 'Father Christmas left these in my room by mistake, but they're for Lucy, Hanna and Daddy.'

'Can I take them down?' Harry urged.

'No, me.'

'Me.'

'One each,' she agreed, and after handing them out she followed them down to the kitchen, where Lucy and Michael were locked in a lingeringly romantic embrace.

'Ugh! They're kissing,' Harry protested.

'That's rude,' Luke told them.

'Mind your own business,' Michael retorted, 'and please don't tell me you've got more presents to open.'

'They're for you,' Charlie explained, and after dumping his on the table, the others followed suit with theirs and charged after him into the sitting room to wait impatiently in front of the tree.

Shaking his head in despair, Michael gave his mother a hug while Lucy poured her a coffee and put on some toast. 'You know, I think I'm ready to open a present myself,' she decided with a twinkle.

Michael's eyebrows rose. 'In which case, I shall go to fetch something from under the tree.'

Feeling certain he'd be back with the boys all eager for her to open a present from them first, she was surprised when he returned alone with a gift that was surely a book, and whose tag told her it was from him, with love.

Trying to remember which books she'd expressed an interest in, she carefully untied the ribbon before removing the wrapping paper, and when she realised what she was holding she experienced such a surge of emotion that her eyes instantly filled with tears.

'Oh my God,' she whispered shakily. 'I don't believe it. How did you . . . ? Is it a real book?'

Smiling, he said, 'Open it up and see.'

For the moment, though, she couldn't stop gazing at the title: *Secret Stories*, by Daphne Fisher. 'How did you get them?' she asked, finally opening the cover. Then, seeing the stories listed, she felt herself tumbling straight back through the years. *The Scuffed Saucepan Lid Called Mike; Sue the Empty Salt Cellar; Bossy Boots and her Broken Zip; Two Leaves, a Twig and a Tortoise; Who's Coming to Betty Table's Party?; Three Wooden Penguins; Dolly Daydream and her New Record Player; The Princess's Slippers*. There had been many more, but these were the only ones Daphne had found the time to write down, and now here they were in this wonderfully unique little book. 'I think this is the most special present I've ever had,' she said huskily.

'That would be apart from me,' croaked a bleary-eyed Hanna as she came through the door. 'Hey, everyone. Happy Christmas.'

'Same to you,' Lucy said, still gazing at her book. 'Have you seen this?' she asked.

Coming to inspect it, Hanna said, 'I was the one who photocopied the stories so Michael could get them put on disc. It's really cool, isn't it? I never expected it to look as good as this.'

'May I?' Evelyn asked, holding out a hand.

Though she didn't really want to let it go, Lucy made herself pass it over and turned to Michael again. 'Thank you,' she said softly. 'I'm sure it goes without saying that I'll treasure it, but I'm saying it anyway. I can't imagine anything meaning more than this.'

'Just you wait,' Hanna told her. 'I mean, OK, that is pretty fantastic, I have to admit, but there's other stuff coming that I think you're going to like.'

'I'm sure she is,' Michael agreed, watching Lucy going to look over his mother's shoulder. 'By the way, Hanna, I hope Santa didn't wake you in the night.'

Hanna's eyes narrowed as she glared at her mother. 'Well, seeing as a certain person *fell* on me while she was delivering my stocking, I guess it's pretty certain that *Santa* did wake me up.'

'It was an accident,' Lucy protested, 'and your own fault for leaving whatever it was in the middle of the room.'

Laughing, Michael said, 'Then let's hope the presents you found in the stocking this morning made up for your broken night.'

'Like ye-es,' Hanna assured him. 'I mean once I got past all the fruit and nuts and make-up and stuff . . . You know, I only nearly missed it,' she informed her mother.

'What was it?' Evelyn wanted to know.

Hanna beamed at Lucy. 'An iPhone,' she answered ecstatically. 'Thanks, Mum. It's exactly what I wanted.'

'Really?' Lucy said in mock amazement. 'How lucky I got it right.'

Flipping her arm, Hanna went to pour herself some juice, while Lucy carefully rewrapped her book and put it high up on the dresser.

'You know, I'm never too sure whether this thing's in a bad mood, or if it's feeling abundantly generous,' she commented, as the toaster flung out two slices of crisply golden bread.

'You're so weird,' Hanna informed her.

Chuckling, Evelyn said, 'What time is everyone coming this morning? I am right in thinking that the first official present-opening session is happening here, am I?'

'You are,' Lucy confirmed, glancing at the clock, 'and it's due to begin at ten thirty, so we've still got time to shower and dress.'

Looking a little anxious, Evelyn said, 'I'm not sure the boys will be able to hold out till ten thirty.'

'They'll have to,' Michael said strictly.

'Oh no,' Lucy disagreed. 'There's no reason why they shouldn't open at least a couple more each before everyone arrives.'

'Hear, hear,' Hanna cheered. 'They're so cute and I love it when they get excited.'

Looking at her as though she must have already OD'd on Christmas spirit, Michael said, 'Then I'll go and break the good news. Just don't forget that I haven't had a present yet – not that I'm complaining, you understand, I simply thought I ought to point it out in case someone had forgotten.'

Laughing as Evelyn played an air violin, Lucy said, 'You've done very well for stockings, I believe, and there's another there from your mother that should fit nicely.'

Trying not to laugh as he scooped it up, he carried it off to the sitting room, where they found him a few minutes later buffing his nails with one of the simpler-to-identify items from his stocking, while the boys waited with bated breath for something magic to fly off his fingers.

* * *

With the turkey now tastily strapped, stuffed, seasoned and basking in the glow of a medium hot oven, Sarah tucked the tea towel back on the rail and went to make yet another inspection of the immaculately set refectory table that ran almost the entire length of her exquisite barn conversion. The minute the table had been brought in for auction last month she'd snapped it up, knowing they were going to need every inch of it for today since there were so many of them, but in the new year it would return to the saleroom ready to continue its journey.

It gave her such a thrill to see how beautifully matched everything was on the table, from the cloth, to the crackers, to the napkins, to the chargers, even the wine glass stems and cutlery handles blended perfectly. What a fabulous time she'd had in Paris with Jean-Marc choosing it all, sailing about the most expensive stores, unable to believe how easy it was to be there when she'd dreaded it so much. Though she hadn't actually run into Kelvin and Margot, she had, amazingly, spotted them in Printemps, and the fact that they'd seemed to be bickering had afforded her a certain satisfaction. Better still was the fact that Margot, oddly, hadn't appeared as stunning as she remembered, and Kelvin had definitely put on weight. Heaven only knew where the baby was, because there had been no sign of him, and for that, she had to admit, she was grateful.

Perhaps the best part of being in Paris, however, apart from the way Jean-Marc had made her feel so cherished, was spending time with Simon and Giselle, who, she happened to know, had their own special surprise for everyone today. It had also been wonderfully gratifying to discover how much she'd looked forward to returning to Cromstone when the weekend was over. It was where she belonged again, she'd realised happily, the way she always had while growing up – and since her mother and John had decided to make the manor their home the relief she'd felt at having the burden of its restoration lifted from her shoulders could almost have made her float.

And now, here she was, in her very own home with a part share in a business she'd quickly grown to love – and even to show a little knack for – and with a man she was actually daring to trust. It was amazing to think of how her life had turned around, and to realise how much more courageous she was feeling now. She had Lucy to thank for so much, including how much easier she was finding it to talk about Jack. Lucy wanted to know all about him, and loved looking at his photos. She even cried with her when the grief and longing became too hard to bear. By now he'd have been the same age as Michael's middle son, and though Sarah wouldn't have dreamed of spoiling the day by mentioning it, knowing that Lucy understood and had even checked to ensure she didn't mind about the boys coming today was making her feel particularly welcoming towards them.

'Aha, here I am,' Jean-Marc announced from the mezzanine. 'I think you are looking for me, *non*?'

Laughing, because she had just started to wonder where he was, Sarah said, 'We need to go over to the farmhouse now. It's surprise time.'

His expression turned grave as he said, 'Me, I am not always sure that surprises are good, but today, with what I know . . .' He stopped as he reflected some more. 'There are other things that I still do not know,' he said, 'so maybe I remain worried.'

'With the wonderful paintings you're giving to the girls, I really don't think you have anything to worry about.'

'*Ah, non, c'est vrai,*' he agreed. 'They are going to love their paintings, this is for certain. But they are for later. What I am asking myself, *ma belle,* is whether you are going to love what I have for you?'

By the time everyone started pouring into the farmhouse there was so much noise coming from so many quarters that it took John some time to track it all down to an iPod blaring through new speakers, a computer game turned up to full volume, several TVs being ignored, and a xylophone and a new set of drums helping to form the next boy band.

However, he soon had everyone congregated in the sitting room ready to begin the surprises, and because Simon and Giselle had asked to go first, he handed the floor straight to them.

'We have some things for you all to unwrap later,' Giselle told them, as Simon came to put an arm around her, 'but now we are very 'appy to tell you that we are expecting a baby.'

As everyone whooped and cheered and a delighted John swooped in to embrace them, Rose's eyes went straight to Sarah. When she realised that this wasn't news to her youngest daughter, she went to her son and thanked him for his sensitivity in not springing this on his sister in public. Then Michael, having been tipped off by Simon, was popping open a bottle of Moët while Lucy fetched the glasses – plus some orange juice for the mother-to-be.

'It is perhaps my turn now,' Jean-Marc declared, as the excitement started to die down. 'I must do this quickly,' he went on, almost collapsing on to one knee, 'because I am very nervous. Sarah, *ma belle*, please do not leave me on the floor like a piece of lettuce, say you will accept to be my muse from this time on.'

Laughing, and adoring him, Sarah fell to her knees in front of him and didn't even notice the diamond he'd almost forgotten to fumble from his pocket, until Giselle tapped her shoulder and pointed it out. 'Oh my God!' Sarah gasped, pressing her hands to her cheeks. 'Is that for me?'

'I hope she is welcome,' he replied, taking the sparkling solitaire out of the box. 'She is symbol of my feelings for you, and you can accept her on the finger you choose.'

Blushing furiously, Sarah glanced at her mother, then Lucy, who were smiling all over their faces.

'Left,' Lucy mouthed.

Sarah laughed, and tentatively offered her left hand.

Beaming with relief, Jean-Marc slipped the ring on to her third finger and swept her into his arms as everyone cheered ecstatically and more champagne was poured.

Deciding it was time for the boys to open another present each now, Lucy clapped for attention, and everyone watched and oohed as Charlie shyly opened a new pair of Nike trainers, while Harry and Luke wasted no time in tearing apart the wrapping to get to new baseball bats and mitts.

'Mum next, Mum next,' Hanna insisted with a hiccup.

'Actually, you next,' John told her after getting the nod from Rose.

Hanna's eyes rounded. 'There's one for me?' she said, with such touching amazement that Lucy could be in no doubt that she and Sarah had pulled off the surprise spectacularly.

'Yes, you,' John assured her, and turning towards the door he gave a little whistle.

'Are you playing my tune?' Pippa asked, popping her head round the door.

'Yes, that was your cue,' John confirmed.

Pippa's one eye seemed to cross, then turning to look behind her she said, 'Oh, all right, all right. Yes, it's time for your big entrance,' and after a moment or two of nothing at all an adorably timid Labradoodle puppy poked its fluffy head briefly round the door.

Hanna couldn't have looked more shocked if she'd tried. 'Oh my God, oh my God,' she cried. 'Is he mine? Oh Mum, I bet this is you. I know it's you.'

'You chose her,' Lucy reminded her.

'No I didn't . . . I mean, oh look, she's so cute, come on little sweetie, come here.'

'Dad, can we have one too?' Luke pleaded as Hanna scooped the puppy into her arms.

'What's his name?' Harry wanted to know.

'It's a she,' Lucy told him.

'I know, I'll call her . . . Lily, after Lily Allen,' Hanna declared with a speed that assured Lucy she'd change her mind by the end of the day.

'That's a cool name,' Charlie said approvingly.

'Very cool,' Pippa agreed.

'That's a lovely top you're wearing,' Sarah told Pippa. 'Turquoise suits you so well.'

Pippa looked thrilled. 'I think you probably know it's my favourite colour,' she responded, 'and actually this is what your mother treated me to for Christmas. It's a lovely fit. I'm very pleased with it indeed.'

Giving Lucy and Sarah a wink as Pippa gazed admiringly down at herself, Rose said, 'So who's next for a surprise?'

'I think it should be Pippa,' Lucy suggested.

'Och, no, no, it should be you,' Pippa insisted. 'I don't think it would be fair to make you wait any longer.'

'Actually, yes, it should be Lucy,' Sarah decided. 'Yours is somewhere under the tree,' she told her, 'you just have to find it.'

Baffled and intrigued, Lucy looked at Michael who was clearly pretending to know nothing, then at John who was grinning mischievously, and said, 'There are a lot of presents there, so what exactly am I looking for?'

'You'll know when you find it,' Sarah told her.

With a glance at Hanna, who was struggling not to squeal with excitement, Lucy went to kneel in front of the tree and began sifting through the presents, only stopping when a voice behind her said, 'Hey Mum, happy Christmas.'

Lucy's heart leapt so hard it hurt. It couldn't be, it simply wasn't possible. She spun round, and when she saw her tall, suntanned and shamelessly handsome son leaning in the doorway, all she could do was break into tears.

'Oh Mum,' he laughed, coming to seize her in his arms. 'This was supposed to make you happy.'

'But you were on the beach last night,' she protested, pulling back to look at him. 'I heard the waves and the party . . .'

'Sound effects,' he told her. 'We had it all set up at John's ready for when you rang.'

'It's where Rose and I were yesterday,' John told her, 'collecting him from the airport.'

Laughing with amazement and too much joy, Lucy hugged Ben again, and again, and still not able to stop crying, she said to Hanna, 'You knew about this?'

Hanna fluttered her eyes. 'Yeah, like you knew about my dog,' she replied, ruffling the puppy's ears.

'We double-bluffed you,' John explained, not entirely sure he followed it himself. Still, it all seemed to be working out well, so he wasn't going to start trying to sort it out any more.

'Hey boys,' Ben said, going to high-five them. 'You did great, keeping the secret.'

Lucy watched them in astonishment. 'So when you took them to see my surprise present, which you were pretending was a puppy, last night . . .' she said to Hanna.

'I was taking them to meet Ben, because he'd just arrived and I couldn't wait to see him.'

'And we had to hide the puppy fast,' Rose informed her, 'because she was already with us.'

'So the bed and collar and everything that I've been hiding in my room,' Hanna said to Sarah, 'so Mum would find them and think we were getting her a dog, were actually for me?'

'Well, for the dog,' Sarah reminded her, making everyone laugh.

Putting her arms round Ben again, Lucy said, 'I can't believe you've done this. Do you have any idea how happy you've made me? How long are you here for?'

'Till the second, then I'm flying back to Sydney. I just wish I'd registered for air miles, with all this jet-setting I'm doing. Hey, cool,' he said as Michael passed him a glass of champagne.

'It's good to see you again,' Michael said, wincing as Luke trod on his toe.

'Dad, *please* can we have a dog?' Luke begged.

'How about we discuss it later?' Michael suggested.

'OK, it's time for Pippa's surprise,' Sarah announced.

'Och, you haven't gone to any trouble or expense, I hope,' Pippa retorted, 'but if you haven't I shall want to know why.'

As everyone laughed Sarah took the box Michael was passing her, and said, 'I think we've probably met all your requirements, at least I hope so. It's from all of us, and it's given with more love than you can ever imagine.'

'Och, now listen to you and your nonsense,' Pippa protested, in a voice that wasn't quite steady. 'So what do we have here? From all of you, you say.' As the lid came off the box she looked perplexed for a moment, then realising what it was she gave a whoop of laughter.

'You rascals,' she told them, picking up the turquoise leather eyepatch with a sparkly motif in one corner.

'Just in case you don't realise,' Sarah said, 'the diamonds are real and the colour of the leather matches your top and, more importantly, your wonderful eye, perfectly.'

'Och, look at me,' Pippa laughed as a tear dropped on to her cheek. 'You've spoiled me rotten, so you have. All of you *and* diamonds . . .' Suddenly it was too much for her, and as she started to sob with joy John came to wrap her in his arms. 'I'll have to wear it today,' she told them, 'so if you'll excuse me, I'll pop out to the kitchen to do a quick change.'

While she was gone more champagne was poured,

and the boys got another turn at opening presents. Then everyone was toasting the most beautiful woman in the room, with her turquoise top and very special jewels.

'OK, I think Mum and John must be next,' Simon declared.

From the way Rose and John exchanged glances Lucy knew they were hoping to see Becky walking in through the door, and she felt angry with Becky all over again for hurting her parents when it would have cost her no more than an air fare to make this gesture for them. However, she hadn't obliged, so it was lucky, Lucy decided, that she, Simon, Sarah and Pippa had managed to come up with something that she felt sure would please Rose and John very much indeed.

'Are you ready?' Sarah asked, as Rose slipped her hand into John's.

'We're ready,' he assured her, clearly still hoping for the self-appointed prodigal.

'Do you want to do this, Pippa, or shall I?' Sarah asked.

'You go ahead,' Pippa told her.

Sarah returned her eyes to her mother and John, and said, 'We've decided to throw a party on Valentine's Day to celebrate what would have been your ruby wedding anniversary.'

Rose's eyes started to shine with amazement, but before she could respond, Pippa was saying, 'We're telling you now to give you time to turn it into a wedding, which I expect you'd like to.'

As Rose gasped, John threw out his hands in despair. 'Isn't that just like my sister to go and do the proposing for me? And you didn't even go down on one knee,' he complained.

Pippa regarded him archly. 'Did you the first time?' she demanded.

'No, but . . .'

'So how can you expect me to get down there now, at my age, if you couldn't even manage it at twenty-four?'

'Three,' Rose corrected, 'and whoever's asking, standing, sitting, lying down or kneeling, the answer is yes.'

'Yay!' everyone cheered, clapping their hands.

'Yay!' the boys echoed, jumping up and down.

'Oh my God, she's peed,' Hanna cried, leaping up.

'I did not,' Pippa protested.

Laughing, Ben said to Hanna, 'It's your champagne, stupid. You've knocked it over.'

Spotting the glass lying on its side, Hanna heaved a sigh of relief and gathered her puppy back in her arms.

'Right, now,' Pippa said, 'I do believe we have something wonderful here for Michael and Evelyn.'

Apparently astonished to be included, Michael started to object, until Lucy put a finger over his lips and passed him a present from under the tree. 'No surprise visits or proposals, I'm afraid, but I hope you're going to like it. And here's one for you too, Evelyn,' she added, handing her a similar-shaped gift.

Their faces glowed with pleasure when they each discovered a solid silver photograph frame, showing a winning picture of the boys.

'There is more,' Lucy whispered as Michael came to kiss her, 'but I thought this was a good one to start with.'

'It's perfect,' he told her.

'And thank you for giving me the book earlier,' she added.

He only winked. Neither of them needed to spell out that giving it now wouldn't have been entirely appropriate.

Digging into her bag, Rose said, 'I have something for Lucy that I'd like to give her now.'

Feeling both thrilled and a little apprehensive, Lucy watched her take out a small bundle of tissue paper which was worn and torn, showing that it must have been protecting whatever was inside for a very long time. She unwrapped something so exquisitely lovely that it took her breath away.

'It was your great-great-grandmother's,' Rose said softly, as Lucy lifted the diamond and amethyst necklace from its humble bed. 'The box has been mislaid down the years, but I'm sure there was one once. It was given to her by the Maharaja of Jaipur as a token of his high esteem, for which we could possibly read love.'

Lucy's eyes were sparkling with excitement.

'I believe they were a little bit of a scandal at the time,' Rose continued in a whisper.

Adoring the mere thought of it, Lucy lifted the necklace and pressed it to her cheek.

'This is my mother in total heaven,' Ben informed them all.

'It's so romantic,' Lucy sighed. 'Just think of what might have happened between them. Clandestine meetings full of passion . . .'

'Mum, there are children present,' Hanna reminded her.

Lucy laughed, then suddenly remembering Becky and Sarah she immediately felt anxious.

'Don't worry,' Sarah said, clearly reading her mind, 'he didn't only give her a necklace, there were quite a few other pieces and Mum has been sharing them out over the years.'

Relieved to hear it, Lucy went back to the necklace. 'How amazing to have a real heirloom,' she murmured. 'And one day it'll go to you,' she told Hanna.

Hanna glanced up from her puppy. 'Awesome,' she responded. Then, apparently deciding it actually was, 'You know, it'll go really well with the top you bought me last week, and I'm wearing it to London on . . .'

'Don't even think about it,' Lucy replied, pulling the necklace away. 'This is going in the safe tomorrow and only coming out again for very special occasions . . . Such as,' she informed Simon and Giselle, 'a christening. Or,' she said to Sarah and Jean-Marc, 'an engagement.' Her eyes went to Rose and John, and feeling a flutter in her heart she said, 'Or perhaps my parents' wedding?'

Flushing with pleasure, Rose pulled her into a warm embrace. 'Thank you,' she whispered, as, wrapping his arms around them both, John pressed a kiss gently to Lucy's head.

Melting into the moment Pippa gave a contented sigh, then started as her own forgotten puppy let out a yowl from the kitchen. 'Och, heavens,' she cried, going to fetch her, 'what a dreadful mother I am.'

As she disappeared from the room, Sarah said, 'I think we should be moving over to my place now. The vicar and all sorts are due for drinks at twelve thirty, besides which we need to check on the turkey.'

* * *

A couple of hours later, with the vicar and several more neighbours merrily on their way home again, Sarah began trying to boss everyone into place according to her seating plan until she realised it didn't really matter where everyone was, just as long as they were all there. For a while, though, they thought they'd lost Luke, until they found him curled up under the table with both puppies, at which point Michael conceded that a dog might be joining the family sooner than he'd thought.

'OK, smoked salmon starter,' Sarah announced, indicating the platters set out down the middle of the table. 'Help yourselves, everyone. There's plenty of lemon, lime, dill, horseradish, brown bread, but don't fill up too much because there's tons to come. Whose phone is that?'

'Yours, *chérie*,' Jean-Marc told her, passing it over.

Since she was still in the kitchen, she had to lean across the countertop to take it from him, and without checking to see who it was she clicked on saying, 'Hello, merry Christmas.'

'Hello. Merry Christmas to you too.'

The voice was so familiar that Sarah felt her knees go weak.

From where she was sitting Lucy could see that something wasn't going quite to plan, and was quickly trying to work out how to get to Sarah without anyone suspecting something was wrong when Sarah put the phone down again.

'OK,' Sarah said, turning around. 'Let's eat.'

Realising who it must have been, Lucy tried to think what to do. As she was at the other end of the table, for the moment there was nothing.

'What is it?' Michael asked, seeming to sense her concern.

'I think it was Kelvin who just rang,' she said. 'Don't ask me why he'd call today, unless his marriage has broken up, and if that is the reason then believe me, I'll break something over his head.'

'Mum, what's going on?' Ben whispered from the other side of her.

Before she could answer Simon said from across the table, 'More champagne, or would you rather go on to wine?'

Aware that he was concerned too, Lucy fixed her eyes on his, and what she received in return was either an unspoken caution to wait, or a signal to leave it to him. Though she felt more inclined to go and take Sarah to one side, she reminded herself of how much longer he'd known their half-sister, and having never been in any doubt of how protective he felt towards her, she decided to let him take control.

By the time everyone had helped themselves to smoked salmon and yet more wine or champagne, Lucy was starting to wonder if she'd misread everything, because Sarah was as joyful as she'd been all morning and Simon was in earnest conversation with the boys. Clearly it was going to take some time to get the hang of this sibling business, she reflected, and picking up her glass she was in the process of resisting a second helping of salmon when someone opened the door and a cold draught blew in.

Half afraid it was Sarah leaving, Lucy turned around so quickly that it took her a moment to realise that no one had left at all – however, someone had come in, and when she saw who it was she immediately felt herself tensing.

'Is there room for one more?' Becky asked, with a lovely smile in her mother's direction.

As Rose sobbed a laugh and went to embrace her, Lucy watched John getting to his feet too, and Simon and Sarah, all of them as thrilled to see her as she was to see them. When Michael went to greet her too Lucy was reminded of how close they'd once been, like brother and sister, but also for a while as boyfriend and girlfriend. Pippa too was on her feet, and Giselle and Evelyn, eager to make Becky as welcome as they could.

'Who is it?' Ben murmured, as Hanna moved into the seat Michael had left.

'The demon sister,' Hanna whispered across her mother. 'She was a right bitch to Mum the last time she was here.'

Sensing Ben's hackles rising, Lucy continued to watch the welcome, not sure whether to try and join in, or simply to stay where she was. She felt Hanna's hand sliding into hers and Ben moving in a little closer. They were her real family, she reminded herself defensively, her children, the two people who mattered most in her world and always would. It didn't matter that she was feeling like an outsider, and put there by her own sister, because she was sitting where she really belonged.

Then the small crowd at the door parted, and as Becky's eyes came to hers Lucy felt her heartbeat starting to slow. Though Becky's expression was unreadable, the smiles she'd come in with were gone, leaving the same fierce intensity Lucy remembered from before. Aware of everyone watching her, Lucy met Becky's stare unflinchingly, knowing that if Becky went on the attack again and ruined this day for Sarah she would never forgive her.

As Becky started towards them Hanna's hand tightened on her mother's, while Ben's arm slid along the back of her chair. The tension in the room was palpable. Annoyed by how much she was shaking, Lucy forced herself to her feet and waited until Becky was in front of her.

'Hello Becky,' she said, coolly.

'Hello Alexandra,' Becky replied.

Lucy's heart turned over, stealing her next words.

Becky said, 'The last time I was here . . .' She stopped and started again. 'If you'll give me a second chance, I'll try to do better this time.'

It took a moment for Lucy to register the olive branch. When she did, with a sob of laughter just like her mother's, she pulled her sister into a crushing embrace.

While the others clapped and heaved a few heart-felt sighs of relief, Hanna leaned into Ben behind their mother's back and said, 'Wonder what all the antiques in the room are making of this?'

Acknowledgements

A huge thank you to David Rolfe for so generously sharing his expert knowledge of provincial auction rooms, and for explaining how a 'ring' might operate within the context of my story.

Also a very big thank you to Lesley Wood for allowing me to 'use' her boutique, Lesanne, and its very stylish champagne bar. A must for anyone visiting the quaint old market town of Chipping Sodbury.

And once again an enormous thank you to my hero, Carl Gadd, for such invaluable information regarding the handling of suicide.

Getting to know

Susan Lewis

Read on for exclusive content including an insight into
Stolen, all about Susan and an extract from
No Turning Back

Thank you for choosing *Stolen* and I hope you found the story of Lucy and both her families as engrossing and moving as I did while writing it.

I am often asked what inspires me and perhaps more than anything it's the way people deal with the challenges life throws their way. It's so easy to say how we'd react in a certain situation, but time over time I find that no one ever really knows until they're in it.

There can't be many things worse than having a child stolen from the heart of a family and never to know what might have happened to him, or her. Everyone's life is altered from that day on – no one, nothing, will ever be the same again. The only hope we can have is that the child is being loved and cared for and that they might one day be returned. Until that time comes the struggle to move forward and somehow resume a normal life doesn't always become easier because loss, fear and guilt form a presence that's virtually impossible to escape.

In this book I have tried to paint a picture of how fate might go about trying to right its wrongs, even soothe its cruelty, though for Rose and John nothing will ever make up for what they lost. Nor will Lucy ever be the person she should have been, living the life she'd been born into. On the other hand Sarah would never have been born.

How a family moves on from this kind of tragedy is perhaps a subject for another book; for now I guess all we can do is offer as much kindness and understanding as we can to those who are suffering this terrible loss, and do our bit to help organisations such as Missing People who offer a vital and specialised lifeline of support.

Again, thank you for choosing this book and if you would like to be in touch with me about it I'd love to hear from you. You can write to me through the Contact link on my website www.susanlewis.com, or if you prefer, you can share your thoughts through Facebook.

Susan

About Susan

I was born in 1956 to a happy, normal family living in a brand new
council house on the outskirts of Bristol. My mother, at the age of
twenty, and one of thirteen children, persuaded my father to spend his
bonus on a ring rather than a motorbike and they never looked back. She
was an ambitious woman determined to see her children on the right
path: I was signed up for ballet, elocution and piano lessons and my little
brother was to succeed in all he set his mind to.

Tragically, at the age of thirty-three, my mother lost the battle against
cancer and died. I was nine, my brother was five.

My father was left with two children to bring up on his own. Sending
me to boarding school was thought to be 'for the best' but I disagreed.
No one listened to my pleas for freedom, so after a while I took it upon
myself to get expelled. By the time I was thirteen, I was back in our little
council house with my father and brother. The teenage years passed and
before I knew it I was eighteen…an adult.

I got a job at HTV in Bristol for a few years before moving to London at
the age of twenty-two to work for Thames. I moved up the ranks, from
secretary in news and current affairs, to a production assistant in light
entertainment and drama. My mother's ambition and a love of drama
gave me the courage to knock on the Controller's door to ask what it
takes to be a success. I received the reply of 'Oh, go away and write
something'. So I did!

Three years into my writing career I left TV and moved to France. At
first it was bliss. I was living the dream and even found myself involved
in a love affair with one of the FBI's most wanted! Reality soon dawned,
however, and I realised that a full time life in France was very different
to a two week holiday frolicking around on the sunny Riviera.

So I made the move to California with my beloved dogs Casanova and
Floozie. With the rich and famous as my neighbours I was enthralled and
inspired by Tinsel Town. The reality, however, was an obstacle course of
cowboy agents, big-talking producers and wannabe directors. Hollywood
was not waiting for me, but it was a great place to have fun! Romances
flourished and faded, dreams were crushed but others came true.

After seven happy years of taking the best of Hollywood and avoiding the rest, I decided it was time for a change. My dogs and I spent a short while in Wiltshire before then settling once again in France. Perched high above the Riviera with glorious views of the sea. It was wonderful to be back amongst old friends, and to make so many new ones. Casanova and Floozie both passed away during our first few years there, but Coco and Lulabelle are doing a valiant job of taking over their places – and my life!

Everything changed again three months after my fiftieth birthday when I met James, my partner, who lives and works in Bristol. For a couple of years we had a very romantic and enjoyable time of flying back and forth to see one another at the weekends, but at the end of 2010 I finally sold my house on the Riviera and am now living in Gloucestershire in a delightful old barn with Coco and Lulabelle. My writing is flourishing and twenty-six books down the line I couldn't be happier. James is still in Bristol, with his boys, Michael and Luke – a great musician and a champion footballer! – so I believe James and I are what's called very happy LATTES (Living Apart Together – don't quite see how that acronym works but I'm told that's what we are!)

It's been exhilarating and educational having two teenage boys in my life! Needless to say they know everything, which is very useful (saves me looking things up) and they're incredibly inspiring in ways they probably have no idea about.

Should you be interested to know a little more about my early life, why not try *Just One More Day*, a memoir about me and my mother? In November, the story continues in *One Day at a Time*, a memoir about me and my father and how we coped with my mother's loss.

1. What made you want to become a writer?

It's something I instinctively felt would happen one day, though I didn't do much about it until I began working in TV drama. Editing scripts, pulling together storylines, dreaming up characters and their backgrounds was something I enjoyed so much that when an agent suggested I turn one of my projects into a book I decided to give it a go. That book was never published, but the bug had bitten and the rest, I guess, is history.

2. Describe your routine for writing and where you like to write, including whether you have any little quirks or funny habits when you are writing.

I have a study at home that overlooks a beautiful spread of lower Cotswold countryside where I aim to be by ten each morning, through until six or seven in the evening. For a long time I wrote seven days a week taking a break only when I was so exhausted I couldn't do any more. Now, I pace myself a little better by doing only five or six days, but even that is pretty gruelling. I don't have any quirks particularly, but I do have a very bad but thoroughly enjoyable habit of drinking a glass or two of wine when I read back over what I've written during the day.

3. What themes are you interested in when you're writing?

I'm always interested in the strange or terrible things fate inflicts on innocent people and how courageously (or not) they strive to overcome it.

4. Where do you get your inspiration from?

The most obvious source of inspiration is life itself. Added to that there are certain authors I find very inspirational in the way they write, such as Lionel Shriver; Jodi Picoult; Anita Shreve; Susan Howatch and Irène Némirovsky whose book, *Suite Française*, played a very big part in my own book, *A French Affair*.

5. How do you manage to get inside the heads of your characters in order to portray them truthfully?

It's all done through imagination, I guess – I can't think that there would be any other way.

6. Do you base your characters on real people? And if not, where does the inspiration come from?

Very occasionally they're based on people I meet, but as a real character is so highly complex it would only ever be one or two aspects of them. I guess you could say that personality traits are perhaps more inspiring than actual characters.

7. What's the most extreme thing you've ever done to research your book?

I once allowed myself to be locked up in a Filipino jail when researching *Last Resort* – that was pretty scary, and it didn't smell too good either!

8. What aspect of writing do you enjoy most?

I enjoy it all, especially when exciting and pivotal things happen that I hadn't seen coming!

9. What's the best thing about being an author?

For me it would definitely be doing the second draft when all the really hard work is done, and the smoothing out is underway. After that comes a lovely freeing time when I hold onto the book before giving it to my editor – this is a period when there is no pressure at all, or anxiety about whether or not she is going to like it. That begins the moment I send it from my computer to hers.

10. What advice would you give aspiring writers?

Probably that you have to be serious about writing to make it work, not simply think 'I'm going to write a bestseller' or 'I'd write a book if I only had time.' It takes a huge amount of dedication and belief in yourself; if you have that then I think the best advice I could give is pay great attention to your characters and who they are, and don't forget to listen to them. It's uncanny how often they'll help out when you find yourself stuck.

11. What is your favourite book of all time and why?

There are many books I could list here, but I'm going to settle for *Suite Française*, because it's the only book I've ever finished reading and then gone straight back to the beginning to read it again.

12. If you could be a character in a book, or live in the world of a book who or where would you be?

I wouldn't mind being one of Georgette Heyer's heroines back in Georgian times, but as they didn't have much in the way of anaesthetic then, perhaps I'd rather be Claudine in my own book, *Darkest Longings*.

I lost my mother Eddress, to breast cancer when she was thirty-three and I was nine. This was back at a time when women, even doctors, spoke in hushed tones about the dreaded Big C. Nothing was discussed, no counselling offered: there was even a kind of shame attached to having fallen victim to this terrible disease. Luckily all that has changed. These days almost two out of every three women diagnosed survive beyond twenty years. Today someone is always there to offer advice and support to those who need it, or simply to lend an ear if all that's required is to talk. Many of these people are doctors, nurses or members of the health-care professions; but just as many are women who selflessly give up their time to be there for those in need. Losing my mother left an irreparable hole in my life, which is why I'm a supporter of Breast Cancer Care and a fantastic Bristol based charity, the Breast Cancer Unit Support Trust. The amazing women behind BUST have raised almost a million pounds in the last twenty years to help provide care and support for the local community, as well as the latest in medical technology for the Bristol based Breast Cancer Unit.

It also means a great deal to me to be a supporter of Winston's Wish, the charity for bereaved children. How I wish this marvellous charity had been around at the time of my family's loss. It's my aim to raise awareness of the vital role Winston's Wish plays in the lives of children who are unfortunate enough to lose a parent.

If you feel you need support, wish to raise money or are interested in learning more about any of these charities you can find them at the following addresses:

www.winstonswish.org.uk Tel 01242 515157 Helpline 08452 03 04 05.

www.bustbristol.co.uk email bust@bristol.co.uk Tel 07971 968244

Breast Cancer Care www.breastcancercare.org.uk
Helpline 0808 800 600

One mistake can last a lifetime...

Eva Montgomery is at the peak of her career when she is viciously attacked by a stalker. While still traumatised by the event she makes the biggest mistake of her life – one she can never turn back from.

Sixteen years later, Eva has managed to rebuild her life in a way that seemed impossible after the attack. Her home in Dorset, high on the cliffs overlooking the sea, is as elegant as Eva herself, but bears none of the scars. The love she shares with her husband, Don, has become the very mainstay of her existence. Her beloved sister, Patty, lives nearby. To an outsider, Eva's world seems perfect in every way. However, behind the facade there is more tragedy and deceit than even she is aware of.

It is when the past starts to invade the present that the greatest betrayal of all shatters Eva's world, over and over. Hurt, frightened and confused, she struggles desperately to put right the terrible mistake she made sixteen years ago and finally break free from a past that nearly destroyed her.

Read on for an extract from *No Turning Back*
OUT NOW!

'Go away.'

Eva turned her face into the pillow, wincing at the pain that seared and crackled all over her, splintering her flesh, as though her entire self was trying to burn and bleed out through the wounds. There were so many of them, cruel, jagged gashes torn into the flawless fabric of her skin, grinning, grimacing, like silent, gruesome mouths. From her eye to her jaw, across her lips, slicing her ear, down into her neck and shoulders, gouging lethally into her chest and lungs. Each wound was held together by stitches now, or clamps, or grafts of gossamer-fine flesh that had been carefully harvested from tender places untouched by the maniac's blade. Somebody else's blood now ran through her veins, and perhaps it was someone else's heart beating dully in her chest, and a stranger's mind that had taken control of her senses.

Everything hurt.

There was nothing, not a single part of her that didn't ache, throb or blaze with the kind of pain that was as relentless and cruel as the memories of that terrible night. She had no idea where he'd come from, how he'd got into her flat, or why he'd chosen her. She still didn't know his name, nor did she want to. All she wanted was Nick.

Nick. Nick.

The screaming had stopped now; long shrill echoes of human torment that had filled the labour room for the past six hours, rushing out into the corridors, fleeing through open windows into the night. They stretched all the way into the past, contracting time, bringing the attack to now, taking her back to the horrific, unstoppable slashing of the blade.

She couldn't breathe. Panic was overwhelming her.

'It's all right,' someone whispered. 'Everything's fine.'

It was Patty, her sister. Patty was there, next to her, keeping her safe.

How could Patty say everything was fine when she knew that nothing ever could be again?

We have to put what happened behind us and move on.

Nick's voice. The coldness and betrayal cut through her more cruelly than the knife.

Anger, fear, desperation surged out of nowhere. He knew what had happened; he'd been there. If it weren't for him she wouldn't even be alive now; she wished she wasn't. What had been the point in saving her only to leave her like this?

'Why don't you hold him?' Patty whispered gently.

She was talking about the baby.

I can't. I can't. Take him away.

'He's so sweet,' Patty murmured softly. 'He needs you to feed him.'

Eva's breasts were full and disfigured as though someone had tried to slice them open for milk, and a careful hand had tried to stitch them together again.

The baby started to cry.

Eva turned her face more deeply into the pillow.

Patty looked at the nurse who was holding the infant, her eyes pleading and helpless. 'She needs more time,' she said, as though apologising. The nurse would understand. No one was surprised. 'Perhaps later, or tomorrow,' she added.

'No! Never!' Eva's fury was muffled by the pillow. 'Get out of here! Go away . . .'

'Ssh,' Patty tried to soothe.

'I said go away.'

Afraid of the mounting hysteria, knowing what it would do to her sister's wounds, as well as her mind, Patty obediently backed away.

Outside in the corridor she took the baby from the nurse and held him close to her face, inhaling the intoxicating scent of him. 'I'm sorry,' she whispered brokenly, to him, not the nurse, 'I wish there was something I could do, but there isn't.'

2

'It'll change,' the nurse assured her.

With all her heart Patty yearned to believe that, because she never wanted to let go of this tender little soul, not ever. He was her nephew, a living, breathing part of her, and she could already feel him burying himself deeply in her heart.

His mother would love him too, she reminded herself, given time. She hadn't meant what she'd said, that she didn't want him and never would, because Eva wasn't cold-hearted and selfish, much less cruel or vindictive. This was only a temporary change in her character, brought on by shock and post-traumatic stress. Four months wasn't nearly long enough to get over what she'd been through, so Patty must be patient and try to make the right decisions for her – for them all, especially this dear little boy.

Knowing what they were facing, how could she possibly fathom what the right decisions should be?

'Patty?' a voice said behind her.

She turned to find the detective in charge of Eva's case coming towards her. He'd visited often during these past few months, had actually come to feel like a friend, even a saviour in some ways.

As he drew closer she felt embarrassment warming her cheeks. The last time she'd seen him she'd broken down, spilling out her emotions as though they had no right to exist, and he'd been so kind, so sensitive. He hadn't even backed away when she'd confessed her biggest fear.

Lowering his eyes from hers he looked at the sleeping baby, and put a finger to its cheek. 'Are you all right?' he asked quietly.

Knowing what he was referring to, what he was waiting for her to tell him, Patty tried to summon a smile of reassurance, but it wouldn't come. She should never have told him. He wasn't a relative, he shouldn't be made to feel responsible or as though he had to carry any more burdens for her family.

He looked up at her, and held on to her gaze in a way that made her almost fearful of letting go. 'Have you heard?' he asked.

She nodded, and felt herself starting to fall apart.

Waving to a nurse, he waited until she'd taken the baby,

then easing an arm through Patty's he led her to a chair.

Patty didn't want to talk; she didn't have the courage to repeat what she'd been told that morning. So she simply watched the nurse walking away, listening to the soles of her shoes squealing quietly, following the rhythmic sway of her hips, while trying not think of herself, or anyone else, just that dear little baby and the fear that she might not live to see him again.